THE CONVICT'S SWORD

I. J. PARKER, winner of a Shamus Award for the short story "Akitada's First Case," is the author of *The Dragon Scroll*, *Rashomon Gate*, *Black Arrow*, *The Hell Screen*, and *Island of Exiles*. She lives in Virginia Beach, Virginia.

THE
CONVICT'S SWORD

A MYSTERY OF ELEVENTH-CENTURY JAPAN

I. J. PARKER

PENGUIN BOOKS

PENGUIN BOOKS
Published by the Penguin Group
Penguin Group (USA) Inc.,
375 Hudson Street, New York, New York 10014, U.S.A.
Penguin Group (Canada), 90 Eglinton Avenue East, Suite 700, Toronto,
Ontario, Canada M4P 2Y3 (a division of Pearson Penguin Canada Inc.)
Penguin Books Ltd, 80 Strand, London WC2R 0RL, England
Penguin Ireland, 25 St Stephen's Green, Dublin 2,
Ireland (a division of Penguin Books Ltd)
Penguin Group (Australia), 250 Camberwell Road, Camberwell,
Victoria 3124, Australia (a division of Pearson Australia Group Pty Ltd)
Penguin Books India Pvt Ltd, 11 Community Centre,
Panchsheel Park, New Delhi – 110 017, India
Penguin Group (NZ), 67 Apollo Drive, Rosedale, North Shore 0632,
New Zealand (a division of Pearson New Zealand Ltd)
Penguin Books (South Africa) (Pty) Ltd, 24 Sturdee Avenue,
Rosebank, Johannesburg 2196, South Africa

Penguin Books Ltd, Registered Offices:
80 Strand, London WC2R 0RL, England

First published in Penguin Books 2009

3 5 7 9 10 8 6 4 2

PUBLISHER'S NOTE
This is a work of fiction. Names, characters, places, and incidents
either are the product of the author's imagination or are used
fictitiously, and any resemblance to actual persons, living or dead,
business establishments, events, or locales is entirely coincidental.

LIBRARY OF CONGRESS CATALOGING IN PUBLICATION DATA
Parker, I, J. (Ingrid J.)
The convict's sword : a mystery of eleventh-century Japan / I.J. Parker.—1st ed.
p.   cm.—(The Akitada series)
"A Penguin Mystery."
ISBN 978-0-14-311579-3
1. Sugawara Akitada (Fictitious character)—Fiction.   2. Murder—Investigation—
Fiction.   3. Exiles—Fiction.   4. Smallpox—Fiction.   5. Japan—History—Heian
period, 794–1185—Fiction.   I. Title.
PS3616.A745C66 2009
813'.6—dc22   2008043475

Printed in the United States of America

ACKNOWLEDGMENTS

I am indebted to a number of friends and fellow writers who were kind enough to read and make comments on this novel, among them especially John Rosenman and Jacqueline Falkenhan.

To my great delight, I also worked with a new editor, Rebecca Hunt—an association that was not only a pleasure but helped make this the best of my novels so far.

My debt to my agents, Jean Naggar, Jennifer Weltz, and Jessica Regel, increases with every book and every contract. They are simply the best in the world.

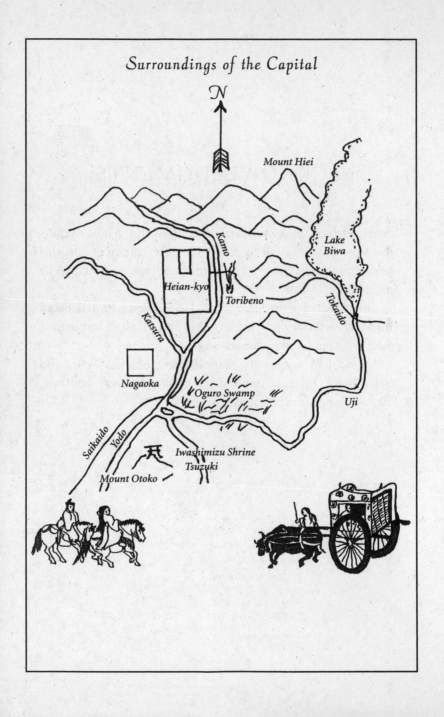

Surroundings of the Capital

N

Mount Hiei

Kamo

Lake Biwa

Heian-kyo

Toribeno

Tokaido

Katsura

Nagaoka

Oguro Swamp

Uji

Saikaido

Yodo

Iwashimizu Shrine

Tsuzuki

Mount Otoko

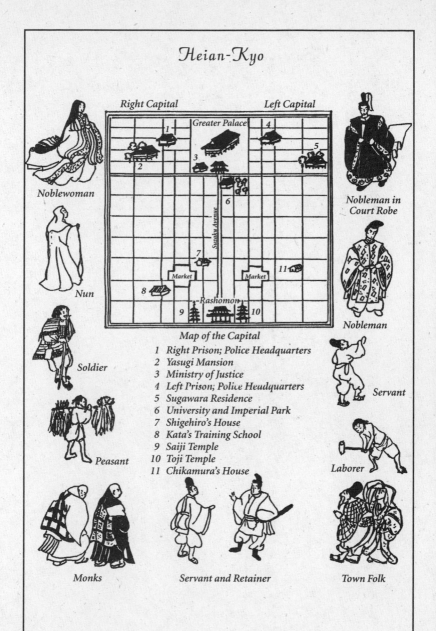

Heian-Kyo

Right Capital — Left Capital

Greater Palace

Suzaku Avenue

Market — Market

Rashomon

Noblewoman

Nun

Soldier

Peasant

Monks

Servant and Retainer

Nobleman in Court Robe

Nobleman

Servant

Laborer

Town Folk

Map of the Capital

1 Right Prison; Police Headquarters
2 Yasugi Mansion
3 Ministry of Justice
4 Left Prison; Police Headquarters
5 Sugawara Residence
6 University and Imperial Park
7 Shigehiro's House
8 Kata's Training School
9 Saiji Temple
10 Toji Temple
11 Chikamura's House

CHARACTERS

Japanese family names precede given names.

Main Characters

Sugawara Akitada	Senior secretary in the Ministry of Justice
Tamako	His wife
Yori	His small son
Seimei	Elderly family retainer of the Sugawaras
Tora	A former deserter, Akitada's retainer
Genba	A former wrestler, also Akitada's retainer

Characters Connected with the Cases

Haseo	A dead convict
Lord Yasugi	Wealthy overlord of the Tsuzuki district
Lady Yasugi	One of his wives; a woman of great beauty and mystery
Sukenari	A famous swordsmith
Kata	An infamous owner of a martial arts school

Kinjiro	Kata's young recruit
Matsue	A swordsman of ill repute
Tomoe	A blind street singer
Shigehiro	A stonemason, the timid husband of a shrew
Chikamura	An elderly man whose house has been taken by thugs

OTHERS

Soga	Minister of Justice, Akitada's curse
Nakatoshi	Soga's clerk, bright and proper
Sakae	Akitada's clerk, inept and sly
Fujiwara Kosehira	Akitada's friend, wealthy and influential courtier
Kobe	Superintendent of police
Ihara	Police lieutenant, Tora's curse
Kunyoshi	An elderly archivist with a bad memory
Masakane	An aged judge with a sour disposition

ALSO: Assorted noblemen, thugs, merchants, soothsayers, beggars, peasants, servants, and children.

PRONUNCIATION
OF JAPANESE WORDS

Unlike English, Japanese is pronounced phonetically. Therefore vowel sounds are approximately as follows:

"a" as in "father"
"e" as in "let"
"i" as in "kin"
"o" as in "more"
"u" as in "would"

Double consonants ("ai" or "ei") are pronounced separately, and ō or ū are doubled or lengthened. As for the consonants:

"g" as in "game"
"j" as in "join"
"ch" as in "chat"

This fleeting world is
A star at dawn,
A bubble in a stream,
A flash of lightning
In a summer cloud,
A flickering light,
A phantom,
And a dream.

—THE DIAMOND SUTRA

THE
CONVICT'S SWORD

TEMPLE BELLS

The fifteenth day of the Fifth Month was the day Tomoe died. It was also the day of her birth, but otherwise unremarkable. She knew her way, had walked it daily now for two years, always before dark, because then she could dimly make out shapes.

She passed the restaurant, caught the rich smell of fish soup, and felt a fierce craving for it and for a cup of wine to celebrate. But there would be no wine, not even the cheapest, and no fish soup either, though there was a silver coin among the coppers she had earned today. She clutched her lute to her chest to feel the pressure of the coins inside her robe.

As she passed under the market gate, she was jostled by someone. Suddenly, a hand came from behind and felt her breast. She swung around with an angry cry and pulled the scarf from her face. The man who had touched her so familiarly cursed. He had not fondled a pretty young harlot, but an ogress. Tomoe was tempted to hiss and bare her teeth at the unseen tormentor, but she resisted.

People hated to look at her face, and she did not blame them. She had seen smallpox victims before the disease struck and blinded her. Their faces were deeply pitted with scars, their noses and mouths distorted and twisted, and their skin grotesquely stained in hues of fiery red and purple—horrid demon masks. The trouble was, she still had a young and slender body and filthy men lusted for it.

When she emerged from the gate into the street, she calmed her fury and listened for horsemen and carriage wheels. Runners, too, were a danger. More than once she had been knocked down and trampled.

But she had other fears than those inherent in her blindness. Among the desperately poor, beggars and whores could expect a friendly hand, but a woman of her class would be left to die in the gutter. Until recently she had believed herself safe in her chosen life.

The sun was gone already, and Tomoe hurried. With her free hand, she felt for the bamboo fencing at the corner of the next street and, having found it, walked alongside until it made way for the wall of a house. She recognized her world by touch and smell. And as always she listened. When she smelled food cooking, her empty stomach contracted painfully. There was nothing at home except some millet, part of an old cabbage, and a tiny sliver of dried fish. Never mind. She could manage for a little while longer.

Then, as she passed the long tenement where the day laborers rented cheap rooms, she heard the footsteps again, and her blood froze. Step, shuffle. Step, shuffle. The first time he had followed her, she had thought he was just some old man on his way home. When she heard him again another day, she had gathered her courage and stopped to see if he would speak. But the steps had stopped too, and suddenly she had been afraid.

That was the worst part of being blind: what you cannot see takes on bizarre and menacing proportions.

She walked faster, clutching the lute and her money, passing her free hand along walls, gates, fences, and shrubbery. Another turn and she would be home. She paused to make sure she had lost her pursuer, but at that moment the evening bells began their booming call to prayer, their deep clamor swallowing all other sounds. Seized by sudden panic, she ran.

She reached the rickety gate to the stonemason's yard, slipped the latch with clumsy, trembling fingers, ran through, and slammed it behind her. In her panic, she bruised her shin on one of the stone markers her landlord stored here, but she gained her backdoor, unlocked it, plunged inside, and dropped the latch in place.

Outside the bells stopped ringing.

Leaning against the door, she caught a deep, shuddering breath and willed her hammering heart to calm. Then she set down her lute, and took the money from her gown. It was not enough, but she could not wait any longer. By early morning light she would leave the city. She felt her way to the trunk, lifted out her bedding, spread it on the floor, and was about to put away the money when she heard someone try the latch.

Her landlord? The small room had two doors. The other led to the quarters of the stonemason who rented her this room. The Shigehiros were not kind people; he often spied on her through the cracks in the backdoor, and his wife knew it and hated her.

She pushed the money back inside her robe, slammed down the lid of the trunk, and called out, "Go away, you dirty animal!"

No answer, just some hard breathing.

Seized by sudden anger, she went to the door, pulled the latch back, and threw it open. She knew him instantly, but he pushed hard against her chest and the door slammed shut as she stumbled backward, falling across the bedding with him on top of her.

She had been raped before, at night on the streets when the

men could not see her face. She tried to lie still, tried to turn her face away, but a violent revulsion seized her; she gagged and struck out at him.

He cursed, and she felt her face sting, then felt the hot blood pouring from a wound, and knew he had a knife. Screaming, she fought him, fought to get away, scratching, clawing, and hitting, felt the knife as it cut her hand, then felt it sink deep into her upper arm. She twisted away, crawling through her own blood and feeling along the wall for the door to the house, to the Shigehiros and help. He cursed. The knife slashed across her back and, deflected by a shoulder blade, sliced into her buttocks. Pain racked her body. Through her own screams, she heard his rage and realized with almost detached surprise that he meant to kill her. She had feared torture but never murder. Oh, dear heaven, what would become of the children?

Crying, slipping in her blood, she managed to reach the door and rise to her feet, but he barred her way. The knife struck again, into her chest, and then into her belly. There was a roaring in her ears. She choked on blood. Touching the door, she slipped and fell into blinding light.

CHAPTER ONE

THE TWO CLERKS

The strange "thwack, thwack" noise coming from outside penetrated the warm, scented tangle of silk robes under which Akitada dozed, his face burrowed in his wife's warm neck. The curious noise warred for a time with some rather pleasant stirrings of desire for Tamako until Akitada opened his eyes and saw the lines of gold made by sunshine falling through the closed shutters.

Tamako turned to him with a soft rustle of silk, her bare feet seeking his. Her pretty face was flushed with sleep, her eyes heavy, perhaps with desire.

But he decided it was too late for lovemaking. With a smile for Tamako, he rose, pushed back the shutters, and walked out onto the veranda.

It was one of those perfect mornings: blue skies, bird song, the wisteria heavy with purple blooms scenting the warm air. Then, from beyond the garden wall, came a ferocious, "Take that, you son of a mangy rat!" Thwack! "And that, you foul piece of dung!" Thwack! "And that, you empty gourd not good enough to hold dog's piss!" Thwack!

Akitada smiled, his heart filled with almost perfect contentment.

"Yori!" murmured Tamako, stepping out behind him and covering her ears.

Akitada laughed softly. "Ssh! He is practicing with his new sword. Tora must have built a straw man for him. I think Yori may grow up to be a famous swordsman. We have never had anything but dry poets and clerks in the Sugawara family."

His wife shuddered. "I hope not and I wish you would not encourage him. His language is abominable. That was also Tora's teaching, I suppose?"

Akitada thought how very pretty she was, standing there in her thin white under-robe, the silken hair rippling down her back and shimmering where the sun touched it. He reached for her and pulled her into his arms, whispering in her ear, "Yori is almost five and I have a great desire for more children. Let us go back inside."

To his delight he could feel the warmth of her flush against his cheek, and through the thin silk his palms sensed the merest shudder of desire. For a moment she relaxed against him, but then she pulled away gently. "The sun is high already. Aren't you going to the *Daidairi* today?"

The *Daidairi,* or Greater Palace, was the walled and gated government complex occupying the northernmost center of the capital. It encompassed the imperial residence and all the ministries and bureaus. Akitada worked in the Ministry of Justice.

With his wife's question, memory returned and drowned his joy. He released Tamako. "You're right. It's late." He clapped his hands sharply.

From the other side of the wall a child's voice called out, "Good morning, honorable father and mother. Shall I bring your morning rice?"

Akitada shouted back, "Good morning, Yori. Thank you, but Seimei will do it. Ah, here he comes now. Keep up your practice."

Seimei had served Akitada's father before him. He was well past seventy now and his thin back was bent from years of service. He moved slowly, but carried himself with the natural dignity of a respected family elder. There was no need for him to perform such humble services for his master, but the old man insisted, and his presence was a comfort to Akitada.

Seimei bowed as he entered the room and set down the tray with two bowls of rice gruel. "Will you be wearing your ordinary robe today?"

"Yes." Akitada eyed his food with distaste. The thought of his problems at the ministry had taken his appetite.

Seimei departed with another bow, and husband and wife sat on the veranda, sipping their gruel to the accompaniment of more thwacks and ferocious language. From time to time, Tamako glanced uneasily at her husband's thin features. She was too well-bred to pry into her husband's affairs, but after a long silence, she said cautiously, "I suppose your new position entails many difficult cases?"

"What? Oh. Not at all. Just dull routine. Though there is enough of it." He fell back into his black mood and stared into his half-filled bowl. When she reached across to touch his forehead, he raised his eyes, surprised.

"You're not eating. I wondered if you might be feverish. There has been talk about smallpox."

"I'm perfectly well." He took a small sip from the bowl to prove it. "There are always rumors about some disease. We've had twenty years without a major outbreak of smallpox in the capital. You must not pay attention to such tales."

"They say if the illness has stayed away for many years, it returns with much greater virulence," she said defensively.

"Nonsense."

Tamako bit her lip. She was becoming impatient with her husband's mood. "Then what is the matter?" she demanded bluntly, adding for form's sake, "Please forgive my rude curiosity."

Akitada looked at her and set aside the half-eaten gruel. "I ran into an old acquaintance yesterday. Do you recall the very important guest we entertained in Echigo?"

"Oh." Her eyes widened. "His Majesty's private secretary?"

Her husband nodded. "He has retired and become a monk. They all seem to do that nowadays. Afraid of death, I suppose. He asked about you and Yori."

She bowed slightly. "I am honored, but I have not forgiven him for putting you in such danger on that terrible island."

"We owe him our present comfortable life. But he reminded me . . ." Akitada stopped himself. He had never told her—partly to spare her the details of the horror he had lived through, and partly because Haseo's story was still unfinished, the solemn promise made to a dying friend still unkept. Only Tora knew, because he had been there with them after that final, terrible battle. Since then, nearly five years had passed, five years during which Akitada had been chained to his duties in Echigo and after his return had dealt with a series of family catastrophes. And now there were new duties in the ministry: a promotion to first secretary, all the meetings and attendance at official affairs that entailed, piles of paperwork, and a bitter enemy for his superior.

Some days he felt the shame of that half-forgotten promise almost like a physical blow, or a sword thrust into his belly, like the agonizing wound that had taken Haseo's life.

Tamako still waited for an explanation, and he forced himself to smile. "I suppose it brought back some bad memories."

"Oh." She smiled also, relieved. "Yes, it's a wonder you don't have nightmares. But you're home now and must not let the past trouble you. We are all healthy and happy, and you finally got your promotion this year. All will be well. It will be a fine year for you, you'll see." Slowly a faint pink crept up her slender neck and into her smiling face. "And perhaps there will soon be another child, too."

◆

Though Akitada forced himself to show her a happy face, depression returned when he left for his office.

The fact was, the previous day had been a disaster. A small quarrel between the two young ministry clerks had led to an unpleasant confrontation between himself and the minister. Nakatoshi, an intense young man who wrote a very elegant hand and was therefore Soga's clerk, had lost his temper with Akitada's clerk, Sakae. Sakae's characters resembled chicken scratches, though he insisted that his speed produced a cursive script much admired among the younger courtiers. The two were jealous of each other.

Yesterday Nakatoshi had followed Akitada to his office, a large room furnished with a low desk and many shelves holding document boxes and rolls of book scrolls. Akitada had moved up in the world since his promotion, much against the will of Minister Soga, to be sure, who had done his utmost to banish Akitada from his sight permanently. He had failed because Akitada had a few friends who interceded for him, and now Soga relieved his frustration by heaping as much work as possible on his detested senior secretary. The large desk had been covered with papers.

Akitada had stopped in astonishment. "What happened? We worked late last night and finished all the pending cases. There was nothing left. What is all this?"

"I am very sorry, sir, but the minister sent a messenger. You are to have these ready for him when he arrives."

"Where is Sakae?"

"He stepped out for a breath of fresh air." Nakatoshi bit his lip. "Could I help, sir?"

Akitada had considered the offer. Nakatoshi was by far the brightest young law clerk to pass across the ministry's threshold for some time, and he was eager for work. Therein lay the problem. Soga had instantly chosen Nakatoshi as his personal amanuensis, and Soga hardly ever did any work. That meant that Nakatoshi spent most of his time sitting outside the minister's room, waiting to write a letter from Soga to a friend, or to copy a memorial or proposal with which Soga hoped to curry some favor or justify his position. All the real legal work was done by Akitada, with some minimal assistance from Sakae.

"It's not as if I ever do anything important," Nakatoshi had grumbled, eyeing the documents almost hungrily. "Soon I will have forgotten all I ever learned. I would be so grateful, sir, if you would allow me to help you and Sakae sometimes."

But it would not do. If nothing else, Soga knew Nakatoshi's brush too well. And so Akitada had said, "I'm afraid that anything which passes His Excellency's desk is out of the question, but if you just want to keep your hand in and have spare time, you might check on an old case in the archives," and he had told him about Haseo, condemned to exile for a crime he had not committed.

"It sounds like a fascinating project," Nakatoshi had cried. "I shall need the family name and the date and nature of his crime."

Haseo had revealed his former name reluctantly, and only at the brink of death. For serious crimes, a man's name was taken from him as part of his sentence. This had hampered Akitada's own searches. "I believe the family name was Utsunomiya, but since it was confiscated along with his property, it won't do you much good. Most references have been expunged."

"Ah," Nakatoshi had cried, "that must have been a very significant case, sir. What are the details of the crime?"

"I don't know. He died before he could tell me anything else."

"You don't know? But how am I to . . . ?"

"You may not find anything. I didn't. But I had too little time for a thorough search. Whatever happened, happened over five years ago. When I reached Sadoshima, Haseo had already been there several months, perhaps as much as a year. Longer he would not have survived." Nakatoshi had stared at this and Akitada had explained. "Conditions for prisoners on the island were very bad then. I believe they are more humane now. There is a chance that some reference to the Utsunomiya name escaped the attention of the clerk who was charged with removing it. Also, it is highly unlikely from what I know of the man that his crime was political. That leaves a possible domestic offense. His punishment suggests that the crime was particularly vicious. Or, alternatively, he may have become involved in a private dispute with a high-ranking noble and killed him. The latter seems the most likely scenario to me. If you were to look at cases that happened five to seven years ago and would justify his particular sentence, you might come across something."

"Did it happen here in the capital, do you think?"

"Not necessarily. From what he said, he was raised in the country."

"Oh."

"Yes, I know. Like looking for a particular pebble in a very long stream. You don't have to do it."

"Oh, no, sir. I'll get started as soon as His Excellency is finished with me."

And at that moment, Sakae had walked in.

"Start what?" he had asked, his short, round-faced figure slipping in silently through the open doorway.

Akitada did not like his clerk, who was uncooperative, lazy, and insolent. He had greeted him with a frown. "I've been wondering what has become of you. There seems to be quite a bit of work here."

Sakae had looked at the pile of documents and instantly protested, "I really don't feel up to it today, sir. Why can't Nakatoshi do it? I don't understand why I always get all the work, while Nakatoshi has the time to stand around and chat."

Nakatoshi cried, "You can have my job, Sakae. Take it. Right now! Go and wait for the minister to run his errands and take care of his social correspondence. You should find it most interesting, as it presents little challenge to your pitiful mind. And I'll gladly do your work, which is at least related to legal matters, something that does not seem to hold much interest for you."

Sakae did not take this well, and Akitada had intervened in the squabble of raised voices, when a sharp voice from the corridor demanded, "What is going on here?"

Instant silence followed.

The minister, portly and with his usual air of impatient superiority, typically focused his irritation on Akitada. "If you must reprimand the clerks, Sugawara, there is surely a more seemly way than shouting at the top of your voice. And what are you doing with Nakatoshi anyway?"

"It is my fault, Excellency," Nakatoshi had said quickly. "I was arguing with Sakae. It was very wrong of me, and Lord Sugawara was quite right to correct me. I apologize, sir."

But Soga was undeterred. "You should not permit arguments between the clerks, Sugawara. It shows a lack of proper authority. But I suppose your present position is perhaps, how shall I say, a bit too much for you?"

Akitada had bitten his lip. "Not at all, Excellency. May I be of some assistance to you?"

"Ah, yes. I came for your report."

"I am afraid I'm not quite ready, Excellency. Perhaps in an hour?" More like four hours, but Soga might get busy with other things and forget.

"Not ready? What do you mean? You have had all morning. Surely you are not that incompetent? What is taking so long?"

At that moment, Sakae had murmured, "Lord Sugawara just arrived and has not really had time to read the documents, Excellency. I'm certain he will prepare a brilliant report as soon as he puts his mind to them."

Soga had stared from Sakae to Akitada. "Just arrived? Not had time to read? How so, Sugawara? I sent a messenger at dawn and it is almost midday now."

"I worked late last night clearing up the other cases and overslept, Excellency."

"Hah!" Snapping his mouth shut after the single outraged syllable, Soga had stalked from the room, slamming the door behind him.

Bad as that scene had been, it had not ended there, and that was why Akitada dreaded the coming day. He approached Suzaku Gate along with a stream of government officials, clerks, scribes, and servants. Beyond rose the many green-tiled roofs of government buildings and palaces, some two hundred halls, great and small, in their own walled and gated compounds, their red-lacquered columns bright in the morning sun. Because of his stiff silk robe and the black hat with the colors of his rank, the guards saluted him. He nodded and turned left in front of the Grand Administration Hall, walking briskly along the wide avenue past the Festivals Hall, then turned left again and entered the courtyard of the Ministry of Justice.

He grew hot with anger when he recalled walking into Soga's office after finishing the report. The minister had been seated at his desk, drumming his fingers impatiently on the glossy expanse. No piles of documents there. "Finally!" he had grunted, extending his hand. Akitada bowed and offered the stack of documents he was returning. "Not those, you fool," snapped Soga. "The report only."

Nakatoshi had rushed up to relieve Akitada of the documents. Akitada was too shocked to speak. For a moment, he considered a challenge, but killing Soga, while it would be a satisfying gesture, would also earn him exile. On the other hand, if word got out that he had allowed Soga to call him a fool, his reputation and career would be in shreds. In the end he had demanded, "What did you say just now?"

Soga had flushed and looked away. "What? Oh, I was speaking to Nakatoshi. Youngsters always have their minds on foolish things when they should be alert. Alertness is all, Nakatoshi. Remember that and be quicker next time. Er, you do have your report, Sugawara?"

"Yes, but I had hoped to give it orally. I had to send my clerk home. He was not well."

Soga's eyes had sharpened. "Sakae? Was it serious, do you think? A fever? There's talk of smallpox in the city. Is he the sort of fellow to seek out bad company?"

"I don't think so, sir. More likely he was at some poetry party and drank too much wine."

"Ah, yes, I forgot. That boy has good connections. But you should have been done with the report when I arrived. I have already missed an important meeting because of your inattention to your duties. I hope you will not allow this to happen again."

"No, sir. What about my report? Don't you want to hear it now?"

"Certainly not. Write it out and leave it on my desk." And without another glance at Akitada, Soga had left his office.

◆

Today he found Nakatoshi waiting for him again. He looked tired and disappointed. His robe was creased and dusty, and a smell of stale candle wax hung about him.

"I found nothing, sir, even though I looked all night. I had all the document boxes down, every year from the beginning of Jian to the end of Chogen. You did say that it must have happened about five or six years ago, or perhaps a little more? I must have read all the major civil cases in the country in a ten-year period. Either there's some mistake or another name has been substituted. Nobody by the name Utsunomiya was accused of anything during those years, and only one Haseo occurs and he was some peasant who killed both his parents. I'm sorry, sir. Did I overlook something?"

"Heavens, man," cried Akitada, aghast, "I didn't mean for you to stay up all night. No, I don't think you missed anything. As I suspected, the name was expunged, and apparently rather thoroughly. I shall go to the Ministry of Popular Affairs later and have a look at the tax rolls." Hearing a movement behind him, he swung around. He had left the door open. Steps padded away softly in the corridor outside.

"I think that was Sakae, sir," offered Nakatoshi. "He's punctual for once."

The footsteps returned and Sakae made his official appearance with a bow and "Good morning, sir." Then he turned with an accusing look to Nakatoshi. "Did *you* burn all those candles in the archives? The night watchman said you were here all night, and there are fifteen stubs lying beside the candleholder."

"What business is it of yours? I had some work to finish."

Sakae flushed with anger. "Not for the minister, surely? Have you taken on private consulting work? It's about time you spent some money on a new robe. You look filthy."

"Sakae," snapped Akitada, "you will never again have the ill manners to insult a colleague in my presence. What Nakatoshi was doing is, as he said, none of your business, but it was not private work, which is, as we all know, forbidden. He was looking up some information for me. If you recall, you were too ill to do much of anything yesterday."

Sakae bit his lip and muttered an apology. Akitada was rather pleased with himself for having disarmed Sakae so easily.

The next few hours passed with the usual routine. Sakae

was quiet and cooperative for once. Akitada closed the last file
he had been working on and told Sakae, "I have some business
in the Popular Affairs Ministry. If you will put away the documents, you may leave early for your midday rice."

Glad to have escaped another unpleasant meeting with
Soga, Akitada walked quickly across the government compound. The senior archivist in the stuffy and dusty tax office
greeted him as an old acquaintance. Akitada had paid prior visits when he was investigating a case against an official who had
been appropriating the rice tax for his private use.

"I know I'm a bother, Kunyoshi," Akitada said loudly, for
Kunyoshi was rather deaf, "but I mislaid a document and must
finish a report tonight. It concerns allotment land, a rather large
parcel as I recall. Until about five years ago it belonged to a family called Utsunomiya, but the name was officially removed due
to some crime. I need to know the location of the land. Both
province and district."

Kunyoshi pursed his lips and studied the cobwebs on the
ceiling. "Not much to go on. I see so many names every day.
Still, Utsunomiya? It's an unusual name. Why do I think Izumo
Province?"

Akitada's heart sank. Izumo was far from the capital. But at
least Kunyoshi recognized the name. He said encouragingly, "It
might be. What do you remember?"

"Oh, there was some reference just the other day. Now why
does that name remind me of Izumo?" He scratched his head,
dislodging a small shower of dust particles, and turned to study
the long rows of shelving that held the nation's tax records, records of land rent, lists of public lands, stipendiary lands, and
possessory fields. "I think I may be getting it confused with another allotment case. The claimant was very unpleasant but
definitely not called Utsunomiya." He made a sudden dash along
a wall of documents, pushed a short ladder up to one section,
climbed it nimbly, and began to shuffle boxes around. Clouds

of dust rose. "Not this one. Perhaps this?" He sneezed. "Ah! An interesting case. A temple, cultivating public land, wants to claim tax exemption. No doubt it will come your way soon. Would you like to take a peek?"

"Is it Utsunomiya land?" Akitada shouted.

"Oh, no. Another case altogether. You don't want it? All right. It must be here somewhere. I recall when I was putting it back I was so angry I almost dropped the box . . . there! I put it in the wrong place." Kunyoshi clambered down and brought over a large box. Brushing more dust off the top with his sleeve, he undid the silk clasp and lifted the lid. Inside was a small pile of papers, rolls of documents, and some maps. Akitada's fingers itched to go through them, but he waited patiently as Kunyoshi slowly and lovingly inspected the contents. "Hmm, yes. It was in Izumo. I see it also involves abandoned fields in Hoki Province. But no reference to anyone by the name you mentioned. No. Sorry. My mind must have been playing tricks on me. Perhaps it was some other matter." He replaced everything and closed the box again.

"Wait. What other matter?" Kunyoshi shook his head and dashed back to his ladder. Akitada called after him, "Can you not recall anything at all? It's important. Think, man!"

The archivist peered down from the top of his ladder. "I wonder," he asked, "would you care to consult the main register? An awful lot of entries, but maybe the right place will pop out. Just a moment." He scrambled back down and disappeared into the depths of the archival hall.

Discouraged, Akitada stepped out onto the veranda for some fresh air. To his surprise, he almost fell over Sakae, who yelped and jumped out of his way.

"What are you doing here?" Akitada demanded. "I thought I sent you home quite a while ago."

Sakae's look of having been caught out at something forbidden changed to smug satisfaction. "Yes, sir, but the minister wants you. I am so glad I remembered that you would be here. When I saw how angry he was about Nakatoshi doing all that work for you, I rushed over here. Now you can explain the matter to His Excellency yourself."

◆

"What's this I hear, Sugawara?" the minister demanded. "You have had the audacity to ask my clerk to do your personal work for you?"

Akitada glanced at Nakatoshi, who stood behind the seated Soga, pale to the roots of his hair and very angry. Nakatoshi grimaced and inclined his head slightly toward Sakae.

So the malicious little toad had made trouble for Akitada and Nakatoshi both, no doubt out of resentment for having been asked to do some work for a change. But Akitada was even angrier with Soga for using this tone with him in front of two juniors.

"It was a private matter, Excellency," he said through stiff lips, "and Nakatoshi did the research after working hours." Akitada was afraid that Soga was about to overstep the line again, and this time he would not let it pass.

"What private matter?" demanded Soga.

"Surely Your Excellency understands the meaning of 'private'?"

Soga turned a deep red and sputtered, "What? How dare you? Nothing that takes place on these premises and involves one of my clerks is private. I demand an answer."

Akitada glanced at the two clerks. Nakatoshi looked at him beseechingly; Sakae's face, caught in a little smirk, became wooden. "Perhaps," Akitada told Soga icily, "we can discuss this between ourselves."

He was desperately trying to avoid what would happen if this ridiculous scene continued. Soga was much too angry to keep a rein on his tongue, and Akitada could not swallow another open insult.

Soga seemed to realize it, too. In a much calmer voice, he said, "My clerk told me that you are looking into a case involving someone called Utsunomiya. Is that correct?"

No point in denying it. "Yes. It concerns a promise I made to a friend who died five years ago. Neither I nor our clerks have used working hours on this matter. That is what I meant by it being 'private.'"

"You know very well that I frown on any of my people dabbling in criminal investigations. I trust this is not a police matter?"

"No, it is not." At least not yet.

Soga smoothed the ruffled feathers of his anger, obviously reluctant to lose such a tasty example of his hated assistant's insubordination. He rose abruptly. "You have been warned, Sugawara. Do not let me catch you again."

Akitada flushed and bowed.

"I must go home," Soga said. "I have decided to move my household to the country and shall be absent for a few days. See to it that things run smoothly in my absence."

Akitada bowed again. He was still too angry to trust himself to speak. When Soga had left the room, he took a deep breath and asked Nakatoshi if the minister had received any special duties or new cases.

"No, sir. Just the usual calendar. I'm really sorry . . ."

"Never mind," interrupted Akitada. "It was not your fault." During Soga's tirade, he had come to a decision. Turning to his own clerk, he said, "Since there is no urgent business at the moment, I have some other work for you, Sakae. Report to me in my office."

Back in his office, he tried to control his temper. He wanted to strangle the malicious little beast but decided instead to keep him busy with a long overdue reorganization of the filing system in the archives. As for Soga—well, the next few days would tell.

When Sakae arrived with his writing utensils, Akitada began by dictating a report to Soga that laid out the details and advantages of a new filing system, while watching with satisfaction the dismay on Sakae's face when the clerk began to suspect that this project would involve him. As soon as the report was written, Akitada signed it and had Sakae take it to Nakatoshi. "Then come back so that I can show you where to start," he said. "I hope to present the minister with the finished product when he returns. It is very important that you pay attention and follow instructions precisely, as I shall not be able to be here myself."

Sakae stared at him. "You are leaving me to do all this alone?"

Akitada smiled. "Yes, Sakae. I have other duties. It will be your chance to impress the minister. I have the utmost confidence in you and shall make it a point to tell him that you did the job all by yourself. Of course, if you don't feel up to it . . . ?"

"Oh, I'm definitely up to it, sir," cried Sakae, flushing. "But shouldn't you be here? What if I have a question?"

"Well, I rely on your judgment. If you cannot handle it, consult Nakatoshi." He watched the conflicting emotions on Sakae's round face and knew that ambition and malice would win out over his indolence. Sakae planned to impress the minister with his industry while proving Akitada unfit for his post.

"I can handle it, sir," said Sakae.

After leaving Sakae to his chore, Akitada went to see Nakatoshi. "I'm leaving you in charge. If there is any unforeseen business, send a message to my house. My secretary Seimei will find me. I expect to be back tomorrow or the day after."

Nakatoshi looked extremely uneasy but did not argue.

As Akitada walked homeward, he wondered if, by this unprecedented act of rebellion and dereliction of duty, he had just taken an irreversible step toward a permanent break with Soga and ended his career in the government. Was his desire to honor his promise to Haseo merely a pretext to shed a burden which had become intolerable? He did not know the answer, only that he had to get away from Soga, from his office, and from this life, even if only for a day or two. Fate would decide. If his defiance of Soga's orders went unnoticed, and if that little weasel Sakae kept his mouth shut, he would continue his drudgery. If not, he would find other work. If worse came to worst, he could become a farmer on the little piece of land his family owned in the country. But his steps slowed as he approached his residence. He did not know how to tell Tamako.

CHAPTER TWO

TEMPTING SOGA'S WRATH

*W*hen he turned the corner of his street, he saw Tora coming toward him. Tora sauntered along whistling, his hands tucked into his sash, his eyes directed at the cloudless sky, and a look of contentment on his handsome face. Not for the first time, Akitada was struck by the contrast between them. Tora never worried. He took each day as it came and found endless pleasure in the surprises that fate, or his master, had planned for him. Today Akitada was envious.

"Where to, Tora?" he asked.

Typically, Tora saw no need to make up some official errand to account for his strolling off in the middle of the afternoon. "There you are, sir," he cried, "home early. I was going to the market. You want to come along? I know this blind girl who has the voice of a fairy and yet sings tales that make a seasoned warrior shiver with fear."

Akitada was tempted. The gods knew he felt terrible. Glancing at the gate to his home, he decided he need not face questions about his early return. Besides, Tora was just the person to discuss Haseo with. "Lead on," he said. "Knowing you, I trust she is as pretty as she is entertaining."

Tora chuckled. "Tomoe? Not really. She's just the best street singer in the city." He shot his master a sidelong glance.

"Very well," said Akitada. "We'll have a cup of good wine somewhere, listen to your street singer, and come home." By that time, he reasoned, nobody would wonder what had happened at the ministry. He would postpone unpleasant explanations until tomorrow.

They headed southward along busy Suzaku Avenue, where porters trotted with their loads slung on their backs, and a few messengers, at a full run, dodged horsemen and the occasional ox-drawn carriage. These tall two-wheeled vehicles were reserved for the good people and moved along sedately as their drivers walked beside the oxen and a retinue of servants followed behind. Their noble occupants sat inside, hidden behind bamboo blinds, protected from the dirty and ramshackle world of the common people. But most people were pedestrians like themselves, on their way to the business center of the city.

It was still early in the year, but the weather was getting warm already. There had been no rain for days, and a thin cloud of dust, stirred up by wheels, hooves, and feet, covered everything. The willow trees lining the avenue drooped motionless in the still air.

"Tora," said Akitada, "do you remember Sadoshima? Did Haseo speak to you at all before he died?"

"What made you think of that again?"

"Guilt. That day I promised to clear his name. It's been on my conscience, and today I decided to do something about it. The trouble is, I know next to nothing about his background."

Tora clapped his hands. "Good! A new case. Just what we need. But I can't help you much. He wasn't up to talking, remember? Muttered a bit, though. His mind was wandering. I thought maybe he was praying."

Praying? That did not sound like Haseo. "Try to remember his words."

"I don't know that I can, sir. It's been five years." Tora scrunched up his face in thought. "Well, he said something about a sword. But he'd been talking about swords before the battle. A good swordsman would, you know."

"Yes." Akitada thought about it and had an idea. If Haseo had been an expert sword fighter, perhaps his name would be known to other swordsmen. "Yes," he said again with a nod. "That's very helpful. We can make inquiries here in the capital. The training schools for young noblemen may know something or point us to someone who does." Akitada's mood lifted. "What did he say about this sword?"

"It's been so long, sir. All I remember is some muttering about 'my sword' or 'where's my sword,' or 'my fine sword.' Sorry, sir."

"Never mind. I should have asked him before he got fatally wounded, but my mind was on other matters then. Do you remember anything else? About this praying, for example?"

Tora, though visibly concentrating, shook his head.

They were passing the walled and gated compound of the administration of the Left Capital. Akitada stopped. "I wonder if Haseo spent any time studying swordsmanship. Perhaps the city administration has a record of him."

"Ah," said Tora. "Very good! Wish I'd thought of that. But what about Tomoe?"

"Later. Where does this street singer of yours perform?"

"On the tower platform of the Left Market."

Akitada suppressed a shudder. What had he been thinking of to agree to go to such a public place and listen to a common trollop? "You have low-bred girlfriends," he said.

"She's not low-bred and she's not my girlfriend," Tora said, a little stiffly. "Can't a fellow have women friends without sleeping with them?"

"In your case it's doubtful." Akitada chuckled as he turned into the offices of the Left Capital. Tora's romantic pursuits were legion. He felt a great deal better. Tora always had that effect on him because he approached all obstacles with energetic zeal, unlike Akitada, who was invariably torn by conflicting duties and agonized over every decision. Even now, he was guiltily aware that he should be in his office.

The city administration, like other official buildings in the capital, existed in two separate halves, one on each side of Suzaku Avenue, each responsible for its half of the capital. The Right Capital had, soon after its inception, fallen into ruin and ill repute and was now mainly occupied by the poor, the gangs, and a few holdouts. Akitada assumed that Haseo, as a member of the provincial gentry, would have resided in the Left Capital.

Since he was still wearing his official silk robe and stiff gauze hat and was accompanied by a servant, Akitada was greeted by the head clerk, who listened to his question and shook his head. "Utsunomiya? A single gentleman taking lodgings? And this was more than five years ago? Maybe as many as ten? Impossible, my dear sir. There is considerable coming and going in the city. Unless his family maintains property here, we won't find anything."

The man was not trying very hard, but he had a point. Akitada sighed and glanced around at the shelves of ledgers and registers of city wards. "Perhaps he resided in the area where the training schools in martial arts are located."

The clerk was beginning to fidget. Only Akitada's rank kept him from throwing up his hands and sending this bothersome person away. "Such schools exist in three different wards."

"Ah," said Akitada encouragingly. "That should help. Can we look through the residential registers of those wards for the years I mentioned?"

"But," protested the clerk, "we don't keep records of the students attending every training academy in the capital. Besides, there is no certainty that he even registered. He may simply have been someone's houseguest. How long was he here?"

Akitada did not know and decided that he had to use different tactics. He raised his brows. "What possible difference does it make? Don't you have your wardens report the names of everyone in their ward for every month of each year? Surely that is what the law requires."

The clerk capitulated. "Of course," he muttered. "Just a moment." He went to consult with an assistant, who went to consult with several more, who dispersed and returned carrying enormous stacks of documents. "There you are," said the clerk with a smirk. "The registers for the twelfth, thirteenth, and fifteenth wards for the past fifteen years. They are the wards which have or had training schools for martial arts."

The stacks were enormous. Akitada saw no point in sifting through tens of thousands of entries. Instead, he informed himself about the location of the wards, the names of the schools, and the identity of the local wardens, and they left.

The first training school belonged to a master called Takizawa. They found him and his disciples already hard at work. The students, two agile youngsters in their mid-teens, were facing each other barefoot on the gleaming wood floor, while their teacher moved around them, calling out instructions. They were using wooden swords, but even a wooden sword could do considerable damage. As Akitada and Tora watched, one of the youngsters did not parry properly and had his wrist injured by his opponent. He bore the pain manfully, only asking the master's assistant, who was putting on a splint and a bandage, if he would ever fight again.

The accident created an opportunity for Akitada to speak to Master Takizawa. But the name Utsunomiya meant nothing to the man.

"I never had a student by that name," he said. "A colleague of mine once had quite a good pupil called Haseo. But his family name was different."

They walked to the next school, where they met with nearly the same answer, although the master in this instance—they had to wait through two instruction sessions before he was at liberty to speak to them—suggested that a serious student of swordsmanship was likely to invest in a good sword made by a master swordsmith. Such an order was expensive and not many really fine swords were sold. The swordsmith would remember his customer. He provided them with the name of the best smith.

As they approached the Left Market, Tora said, "We could stop for a bowl of noodles or a cup of wine now, sir."

"Later. We have hours until the evening rice."

Tora drew in his breath. "I was hoping to introduce you to Tomoe, sir. She leaves early."

Akitada glowered at him. "Surely even you can see that this is more important than your affairs. And please spare me the particulars."

Tora, who had opened his mouth in protest, snapped it shut and looked offended instead.

They walked in silence through a quarter where all sorts of artisans lived and worked. Signs at gates or on door curtains advertised lacquer work, wood carving, paper making, weaving, and dyeing. Each craft had its own street, and each craftsman belonged to his own guild. The swordsmiths shared their section with the attendant trades of the polishers, as well as of makers of scabbards, pommels, sword guards, and sword stands. Most of the houses here backed on the Arizu River, a small branch of the Kamo. Good, pure water was essential to their craft. Iron sand and carbon could be brought in from Bizen Province, but not water, and all three were ingredients in the forging of steel blades that were both hard and flexible.

The name they sought was inscribed beside the gate of a small villa: Sukenari Munechika. The size of the property and the fact that the owner had two names meant that he was descended from a family that had once been noble, and that he was held in high esteem, well above the rest of the craftsmen and merchants.

A servant received them with a bow and took their shoes. The house was quiet, but from a distance they could hear the steady rhythm of hammers striking steel. They stepped up into a large beautiful room, softly lit through paper screens. It was nearly empty, except for a few silk cushions on thick grass mats and an alcove with a calligraphy scroll and a single sword displayed on a stand.

"The master is at work, but I shall announce the gentlemen," said the servant with another bow and disappeared on silent feet.

They sat down and looked at the sword in its scabbard covered with intricate silver overlay. The calligraphy on the scroll was also quite beautiful.

Tora asked, "What does it say, sir?"

Akitada read, "Using the sword when there is no other choice is also Heaven's Way."

Tora nodded. "Very good. We soldiers know that sometimes you have to kill to save lives. Right?"

"Yes. The master is also a philosopher, it seems."

"I've watched a swordsmith. Before he starts, he prays to the gods to favor his work. It's very inspiring."

"Yes." Akitada's mind went back to Haseo, who had wanted a sword in his hand more than anything else in the world. Akitada, not knowing this, had kept the only sword for himself. In the subsequent battle against overwhelming odds, Haseo had fought first with a pole, and then, after unseating and killing a horseman, with his victim's sword. It was from that moment on, when his hand had at last gripped a sword, that Haseo's face had been filled with pure happiness. He had fought and killed, and by doing so he had saved their lives, though he had lost his own.

The hammering in the distance had stopped, and now they heard the soft footfall of the master swordsmith Sukenari. He was a middle-aged man, not tall, but with the broad shoulders and muscular upper arms of his trade. Dressed in a dark silk robe, his graying hair tied smoothly on top of his head, he looked more like a nobleman than someone who had just hammered red-hot steel into a deadly blade.

Sukenari's manners and speech were as impeccable as his appearance. Introductions out of the way, he presented his visitors with wine and made polite small talk about the season, the recent Kamo festival, and the deep honor of their presence in his humble house. Akitada responded with compliments on the wine, comments on the unseasonably hot weather, and an anecdote about an incident during another Kamo celebration. Tora was silent, shifting in his seat. His eyes kept moving to the sword on its stand until he could not restrain himself any longer. "Did you make that?" he asked.

Sukenari smiled and shook his head. "You flatter me, young man. That sword was made by my namesake, Sanjo Munechika. I strive to learn from its perfection."

"Could I see it?"

The smith rose immediately and took the sword from its stand. He presented it to Tora with both hands and a small bow. "Your interest honors me."

Tora grunted and slid the blade from the scabbard. "Moves as easily as floating on air," he commented. The blade gleamed blue in the soft light coming through the shoji screens. Its slender shape was incredibly graceful, thirty inches of narrow, curved steel so finely honed that it could split a man in half as smoothly as if he were a melon. "Sharp," muttered Tora, touching the edge, "and straight," extending it and looking down its

length. Then, before Akitada could stop him, he had jumped
up, taking the swordfighter's stance. The air hissed as he performed a series of slashes with the weapon. When he sat back
down, his eyes shone. "A man would be unbeatable with such a
sword."

"Tora!"

"Oh. Sorry, sir. Here you are." Tora passed the sword to
Akitada. "Just look at that blade! I believe it's lighter than yours."

Akitada received the sword and turned to Sukenari. "Please
forgive my friend. He's very enthusiastic and forgets his manners when his heart is moved."

"I understand. Mine is moved in the same way. The gods
dwell in that blade."

Akitada noted the beauty of the temper lines that ran along
the sharp edge like waves. Tora asked, "Do you think Haseo's
sword would have been as fine as that?"

To their surprise, Sukenari leaned forward, his face intent.
"Haseo?"

Akitada reinserted the blade in its scabbard and, holding
the sword in both hands, returned it with a bow of thanks. "I
had a friend who loved swords and was a fine fighter. His family
name was Utsunomiya. We came to ask if you had heard of
him, thinking that perhaps he had once, years ago, had a sword
made for him."

Sukenari's face fell. "No," he said regretfully. "No, that is not
the same man. I did make a sword once for a young man named
Haseo, a very common name to be sure, but his family name
was Tomonari. I don't suppose you can describe this sword?"

"I've never seen it. In fact, there may not be such a sword at
all. It was a foolish idea."

"Not at all. Sometimes a fine sword will become known in
the trade." The smith made a face. "Sometimes, sadly, our best
work ends up in the wrong hands. I had hoped to locate a particular sword and purchase it back."

Akitada said, "Please accept my apologies for taking up your valuable time. Perhaps you may hear something about a young swordsman called Utsunomiya, while we may hear of the sword you seek. Can you tell us about it?"

Sukenari nodded. "Thank you. That is very kind of you, Lord Sugawara." He picked up the Sanjo sword. "Mine was the same length as this. I follow the great master in most details. But the scabbard of mine was made from magnolia wood and covered in white sharkskin. Very plain. The sword guard was of iron and showed a gilded pine tree and a shrine on the upper side, and flying geese on the bottom. The hilt was wrapped in green silk in a diamond pattern, and the pommel was gold. The blade," Sukenari removed the Sanjo blade from its scabbard and pointed, "had an inscription inside the hilt. My name and the year it was made. The third year of Kannin." He sighed and slipped the sword back into its scabbard. "It is not as perfect as this, but flawed as it is, I was particularly fond of that sword . . . and of the young man I made it for." He rose to return the Sanjo sword to its stand. Akitada and Tora got to their feet.

"A very fine man," reflected Akitada as they walked away. "Have you ever thought that some men are a greater gift to humanity than others? This one is not only a pleasant, courteous person, but one who has perfected an art that will make our soldiers invincible."

"I don't see how a common soldier will be able to afford a sword like that. The ones we had in Sadoshima were poor stuff. My sword broke right away, remember? It's still going to be the rich guy killing the poor fellow. And besides, what good was Haseo's fine blade to him in the end? They took it away from him, and sent him to a place where he was tortured and killed."

This was so unlike Tora that Akitada stopped and looked at his companion. "You haven't talked like this since we first met. What's wrong?"

Tora glowered and said, "Forget it. I'm just in a bad mood all of a sudden. Where to next?"

Akitada sighed. "I am the one who should be discouraged. We're no closer to the solution of the mystery." They'd reached the corner of Suzaku Avenue and Rokujo, and glanced up at the afternoon sun. "I'm absent from the ministry without permission."

"I figured it was either that or you'd been dismissed."

Akitada raised his brows. "Don't you care?"

Tora shook his head. "No. You're not happy there. Maybe you'll be happier not working."

"And how am I to feed all of you?"

Tora's good humor returned. Slapping his master's shoulder, he cried, "Don't you worry about that. I can get work anytime and earn enough for our rice. Genba can do the cooking and keep the roof mended. And Seimei will take care of the light housework. Your lady, being a great gardener, will grow vegetables, and as you won't have anything to do, you can teach Yori how to be a gentleman." He laughed out loud and a passing official, whose retinue of servants kept a proper distance behind him, shot disapproving glances their way.

Tora still forgot his manners all too often in public, but how was one to discipline a servant who had just expressed his willingness to support his master and his master's family? In private their relationship was, in any case, much closer than that of some brothers. But human bonds also brought responsibilities. Akitada suppressed a sigh and said, "Thank you. It is good to know that I can count on you. Let's stop by the market for something to eat and to hear your street singer before going to that last training school."

CHAPTER THREE

GHOSTS

𝕿he market thronged with people. Maidservants and house-wives shopped and chattered as they filled their baskets with fish and vegetables for the evening rice. Young gallants strolled about, ogling pretty prostitutes who tripped by in their colorful finery and peered at them over their painted fans. Solicitation was illegal here, but the law turned a blind eye unless quarrels broke out.

Akitada liked markets. They were noisy, smelly, and full of excitement. Vendors cried their wares, and porters passed through the crowd with their heavy baskets suspended from the ends of long poles, shouting, "Watch out! Watch out!" Musicians played, jugglers juggled, live birds in cages sang, cooks fried, boiled, and stewed snacks on small portable stoves, singing out their specialties, and stray dogs searched the garbage that lay about in corners.

Each of the city's two gated markets covered several city blocks with its shops and stands. The market office provided constables, controlled the many shopkeepers and vendors, and maintained the drum tower, which rose four stories into the air and overlooked the market and part of the city. On its top floor was a large drum that gave warning of fires, while the middle levels allowed constables to keep an eye out for pickpockets, quarrelsome drunks, and thieves in the crowds below. The lowest level was used by popular performers, and here was Tora's latest conquest.

A crowd had gathered to listen to her. She stood above them, small and very slender in her plain white cotton gown. Her long hair was twisted into a knot low on her neck. This very modest appearance, along with the fact that she was neither young nor pretty—her face was badly scarred—astonished Akitada profoundly. What could Tora possibly see in her?

Female street singers, as a rule, were vagrants who eked out their poor daytime earnings by selling their bodies at night. Akitada considered them a public nuisance because they kept stubbornly outside the law. But as this woman was blind, he was willing to make some concessions. Besides, she had a pleasant voice.

She looked detached from her surroundings as she sang, her sightless eyes turned into the distance and a fixed expression of unhappiness on her scarred face. Her remarkably elegant hands worked the strings of a lute. The instrument was a nice one, made of sandalwood. Street singers usually accompanied themselves on small hand drums that required little musical talent.

So Akitada granted her a modicum of respect. She played her lute well, her voice was full and warm, and she told a good story about two unhappy lovers who died in war. Akitada knew it. A young woman had followed her lover into battle disguised as a common soldier. When he found her fatally wounded on the battlefield, they bade each other a touching farewell, and he ended her suffering by striking off her head and then plunged the sword into his own belly. It was a story of love and death, designed to please a simple crowd and romantic enough to be performed by a woman.

There was a smattering of applause, the singer bowed, and a few small coins fell at her feet. Tora, a silly grin on his face, shouted into Akitada's ear, "Isn't she wonderful?" and made his way to the front. His master wished himself elsewhere, but the blind woman began another song and Tora stood rooted at her feet with a look of rapture on his face.

Something tugged at the skirt of Akitada's robe and he looked down. A half-naked beggar crouched there. He extended a filthy hand, keeping a firm hold on Akitada's silk robe with the other. "A copper from the rich lord?" he whined. "In Buddha's name? Only a copper?"

"Let go of my robe this instant," Akitada snapped, seeing the dirty streaks he was leaving on the fabric.

It was against the law for beggars to seize people's clothes or harass them in any way, but this fellow was not easily intimidated. He grinned, revealing nearly toothless gums, and released Akitada only after rubbing the material between his fingers and saying, "Such thick silk! It must be lovely to have that against your skin. I'd be grateful for a bit of food in my empty belly."

Frowning, Akitada dug a copper out of his sash and dropped it into the grimy hand with its long, curling yellow fingernails. "You should not grab people," he said severely. "The constables frown on that. Besides, next time you may get a kick instead of alms." He looked the man over. The beggar was middle-aged, bony, and utterly filthy, but he did not seem to be crippled. "What's wrong with you anyway? Why don't you work?"

The beggar tucked the coin into a small pouch he wore on the rope around his waist. "My health is poor," he whined. "Can't afford to buy medicine. It's a hard life." He coughed.

Akitada gave a snort and looked around for a good example of a working man. His eye fell on the street singer. "Look at her," he said. "She's blind, yet she works for her daily rice."

The beggar spat. "Her! She's a whore. You think she's living on the coppers she gets singing a few songs? She isn't pretty, but she's got a mouth and men have cocks. They give her silver and when she's done singing, she'll give them her personal attention."

A well-dressed man standing near them laughed. "When the sun sets, the pleasure women drop their silken sashes. It's easy to forget a face then."

The beggar was disgusting, and the stranger was not much better, but Akitada knew that they were probably right. This woman was not attractive enough for anything but the most basic of sexual services, though silver was hardly what she would earn for that.

Tora had climbed the steps and was talking to her, pleading even, and she touched his arm in a familiar manner. Akitada regretted his generous impulse. Trust Tora to set up an assignation while his master waited.

The beggar snickered. "See? She'll open her mouth and spread her legs for that one all right. You'd think a blind whore wouldn't care who she does it with, but that bitch thinks she's somebody special."

Akitada snapped, "Keep your dirty gossip to yourself!" and stalked to the steps of the tower. "Tora!"

Tora came down. "Sorry, sir, this is not a good time. She can't leave yet."

"Tora?" asked the woman on the platform, her hand searching the air. "Where are you?" A street urchin burst into laughter, and someone in the crowd joined in. Akitada saw that the pile of coppers at her feet was pitifully small and felt a twinge of guilt. The blind engaged in certain professions because it was the only work they could do. They did not need eyes to sing a few songs, to wash someone's hair, or to massage a body. And women needed no eyes to provide sexual services either.

"I'll tell her you'll see her later," Tora said.

"No."

Too late. Akitada glared after Tora as he ran back up the steps. He told the woman, "We'll come back and you'll tell him what you told me, won't you? He's very good at solving mysteries."

Akitada raised his voice. "Tora!"

The woman turned her head toward him and bowed a little from the waist. She said in her warm voice, "You are doing too much honor to this insignificant person, my lord."

Akitada said brusquely, "We were only passing." He had no intention of listening to a street singer's private affairs. Tossing a few coppers at her feet, he snapped, "Come, Tora. It's getting late."

Tora looked stricken. He said hurriedly to the woman, "I'll try to be back in time, but if I'm not, remember what I told you. And lock your door." Then he joined the fuming Akitada.

Akitada said, "Next time don't get me involved with your women."

"I'm sorry, sir. But something's really wrong. You can see that Tomoe's blind and can't help herself."

Akitada thought of what the beggar had said. A woman need not have eyes to earn a living by selling her body. "She's a prostitute," he said coldly. "They learn to handle themselves."

Tora gasped. "A prostitute? Tomoe? Never! She's afraid to death that some guy will rape her again."

"Hmmph, spare me. I have more important matters on my mind than street singers."

Tora's fixation on this woman irritated Akitada. To his knowledge, it was the first time in the many years they had been together that Tora had ever shown a romantic interest in a plain woman who was older than he. And in addition to being unattractive, this one was blind and had a bad reputation, regardless of what Tora thought of her. It was not normal, and something must be done before Tora ruined himself. The trouble was that ordering Tora to stop seeing the girl would only produce the opposite result.

Near the wine shop beside the market gate, Akitada remembered that he had promised to treat Tora. Perhaps it would make up for his refusal to speak to Tora's girlfriend. The waiter scraped and bowed before the tall official and his handsome servant and quickly led them past the customers filling the rooms at street level and up some narrow stairs to a pleasant private room overlooking the bustling market below.

Akitada ordered a flask of their best and two servings of noodles. Tora looked dejected and kept glancing through the thin bamboo railing toward the drum tower where the blind woman was singing another ballad. He muttered, "That girl will not listen, no matter how hard I try to talk sense into her stubborn head."

They seemed to be well matched in personality at least. Akitada asked, "Why not?" and regretted it immediately. He had no intention of becoming involved in the woman's alleged problems. In his opinion, she was just using her helplessness to attach Tora more firmly to herself.

Tora plunged into explanations. "It's like this, sir. Somebody's been following her home. She can hear his steps. Once she turned around and asked who was there, but he stopped and didn't answer. It scared her. She says she can smell him. He has a disgusting odor, and she's sure it's the same man each time."

"In her way of life, what does she expect? I imagine it's a customer who is a bit shy and loses his nerve."

"There you go again. I told you Tomoe is no whore. People make up bad tales about single women like her. When someone's as hard up as she is, people should try to help. The trouble is, Tomoe doesn't complain. She's too proud to ask for help, even if she's blind, and very poor, and all alone in the world." Tora glowered at Akitada. "And she's only a woman," he added, as if that made her case even more pathetic.

Akitada's heart sank. He saw the whole scenario now. This Tomoe, clearly in need of a protector and a meal ticket, had found the perfect fool in the softhearted Tora. Pity for her situation was just about the only thing that would make him forget her lack of physical charms. He controlled his anger at the cunning vixen, and said soothingly, "I am sorry, Tora. No doubt, she has a hard life. But she seems to manage very well and has survived so far."

Tora said bitterly, "That woman knows nothing about taking care of herself, but she's as proud as a lord."

Akitada flinched.

The waiter arrived with the wine and two steaming bowls of buckwheat noodles and vegetables in a savory broth. The food was excellent, and for a while they ate and drank in silence.

Finishing his noodles first, Tora picked up his tale again, "Take this business with the gangster, for example. It's funny, but some people seem to think a blind person is also deaf and dumb. They go right ahead talking about private business just as if she wasn't there at all. This character thinks she brings him luck. He asks her to sing a special song before he does a job. I asked her for his name, but she won't tell me. Doesn't think it's right to carry tales. Hah! I told her it's dangerous, but does she care? Why are women so stupid?" Tora scowled in frustration.

"Well," said Akitada, weakening, "perhaps I'll have a talk with her after we've made some progress tracing Haseo."

"Thank you, sir! You won't be disappointed. And you'll see that Tomoe's a very refined person."

Akitada suppressed a snort.

Tora's eyes went to the drum tower again. "It's getting late. We could go around to that last school tomorrow," he suggested.

"Why not today? I like to finish what I start."

"But you could take off from work again tomorrow."

"No."

"Why not? I thought you were ready to quit anyway."

The notion apparently did not trouble Tora at all. Akitada reflected bitterly that the people who depended on him for their livelihood seemed to place total trust in his ability to provide. "Don't be a fool," he snapped. "I just took off a few hours. The minister is only going to be away for a short time."

Tora looked at him. "Slacking off's not like you, if you don't mind my saying so."

"I am not slacking off. Sometimes more important matters take precedence."

"I guess you don't want his high and mighty lordship to find out, because that bastard's just waiting for you to make a mistake."

Akitada glared at Tora. "You must think me a coward."

"No, sir. I know better. But you'll do crazy things when you think it's your duty to do them. And I'm confused. You used to think being an official and working for the emperor was the most important thing in the world."

Akitada had no answer to this. He had walked away from his work because he could no longer bear Soga's insults and the dull routine of paperwork. Would he have put aside a more challenging and interesting assignment for Haseo's sake? Haseo had died five years ago on a distant island, and they had hardly known each other. It struck Akitada forcibly that he was trying to solve a criminal case without knowing what crime had been committed, who the victim was, or where it had happened. All he had was the name of the alleged culprit. It would have been so much easier if the government did not expunge the records every time someone made a case for doing so. To Akitada, records were inviolable.

But he said stubbornly, "A promise to a dying man cannot be broken."

Tora nodded and finished his wine. "Maybe we'll pick up something at the next school," he said with a sigh.

As they rose, Akitada glanced out at the market. Though the

sun had not quite set, a lantern lighter was already lighting the
big paper lanterns in front of the restaurant. The housewives
and maids with their baskets had disappeared, and the crowd
was mostly male now. Government clerks, artisans, laborers,
farmers on a city visit, soldiers, servants on their night off,
teachers, and a few young rakes of noble blood strolled about,
eyeing the wares of fan sellers and comb shops for a present to
give to some woman, peering at waitresses, and shouting rude
compliments at the pretty harlots. Tora's singer had left. The
tower platform was empty except for a tall man who was leaning against one of the pillars.

Akitada looked, then looked again. It could not be. He felt
the hairs on the back of his neck rise.

"What is it?" Tora asked, following his glance.

The man turned his head a little, and Akitada took a deep
breath.

"A ghost."

The stranger walked down the steps of the tower and disappeared in the crowd.

"A ghost?"

"That man at the tower. I swear it was Haseo."

"Ah." Tora nodded wisely. "It happens when you're thinking
too much about the dead. They take shape in someone's body.
Even animals sometimes. I had an aunt who . . ."

"Never mind your aunt. You're right. I must be seeing things.
Let's go." Akitada paid for their meal and they left the market
just as the temple bells began to ring.

Akitada still felt shaken. The image had been so vivid. It was
nothing but foolishness, of course, or an overwrought conscience,
not ghosts. The man had not really looked much like Haseo. He
had worn good clothes, and his hair and beard had been
trimmed neatly, while Akitada and poor Haseo had been in rags
and half-naked, their hair and beards grown long and tangled.

Kata's training hall was on the wrong side of the city and

surrounded by the huts and tenements of the poor. The building, a former warehouse, was open to the street. A small crowd
of ragged idlers had gathered there to watch the lesson. They
expressed their interest with raucous cries of, "Kill the filthy
bastard!," "Cut off his nose and ears!," "Split him down the middle!," and "Show us some blood!"

This was a far cry from the quiet, intense silence of concentration that had prevailed at the other two schools. Several students
watched two of their fellows circling each other, wooden swords
in hand. Two other men practiced stick fighting with long bamboo poles, and several more tumbled, kicked, and wrestled on
mats. They looked like unemployed soldiers or underweight wres-
tlers, and the fighting style had an aggressive edge to it which had
more to do with achieving a quick kill than matching skills in
single combat. Akitada doubted that Haseo would be known here,
and was about to turn and tell Tora so, when he caught sight of a
familiar figure in the shadows. There, on the far side of the hall,
just behind the master, stood the man from the drum tower.

Akitada blinked, but the shadowy figure remained, a silent
onlooker of the swordfighting bout. Again, Akitada was shaken
by the resemblance. It was in the way the man stood, wide-
shouldered and with an unconscious grace, and also in the way
he held his head.

"Tora," Akitada said in a low voice, "look at the man in the
shadows behind the master."

Tora leaned forward and peered. "So?"

"The man from the market. And he still looks like Haseo."

He must have felt their eyes on him, for he turned his head
their way, then leaned forward to say something to the master.
The master, a short middle-aged man with the wide-legged
stance of the professional soldier, shot a sharp glance toward
Akitada and Tora.

Tora muttered, "They've seen us. In this crowd we stand out
like a pair of hawks among crows."

It was true. Even Tora's plain blue cotton robe looked almost distinguished among the multihued assortment of rags, loose shirts, and short pants that covered those around them, and Akitada wore his official's silk robe and small black hat. He met hostile stares from the crowd but was not about to retreat. "Come," he said, touching Tora's arm, "we'll have a word with Master Kata and his friend. I want a closer look at the fellow." He moved past two burly loafers toward the training hall.

Inside, the man from the market spoke again, rapidly, to the master, then melted into the shadows as if he had never been.

"Quick," said Akitada. "Around the back. He's getting away."

They separated, each running for a corner of the long building. But suddenly Akitada's progress was impeded. People moved into his path, legs were extended, elbows protruded, and a basket of bamboo scraps fell over, scattering in the dirt before his feet. He heard shouts and curses, and finally the cry, "Stop, thief!" When he finally reached his corner, he had a shouting mob on his heels. A rock hit the back of his head, knocking off his small black hat and causing him to stumble. Someone laughed, and the next moment he was face down in the dirt with people on top of him. He struggled, then roared, "Stop! In the name of the emperor." Instantly more weight piled on, taking his breath away. He tried to cry out again, but there was dirt in his mouth and he had trouble breathing. Strangely, what he felt most at that moment was a sense of outrage that the rabble had dared attack an official.

Through the roaring in his ears, he heard Tora shouting. Then—blessed relief—the weight eased, lifted. He was rolled on his back, and Tora's anxious face peered down at him.

"Are you all right, sir?"

"Of course not, you idiot," gasped Akitada ungratefully and struggled to sit up. "What is the matter with these people? Are they mad?" He wiped the dirt from his face and looked around him. The ragged creatures had retreated; a few were nursing bloody noses and black eyes. Dull, hostile eyes.

"This is a bad neighborhood," said Tora, shaking a broken fence rail in their direction before giving him a hand to get up. "They don't like officials here."

"Outrageous!" Akitada glowered at his attackers. "Who threw that rock?" he demanded. There was no answer, but they retreated a little more. He raised his voice. "Where is the warden for this quarter?" They began to melt away, slinking along the wall of the building and disappearing down alleyways. "It seems they do have a little respect for authority," Akitada said sourly, feeling a tender lump on the back of his head. "I suppose the fellow got away."

"Afraid so. When I saw the crowd going after you, I turned around. I expect he's long gone by now."

Akitada scooped his hat from the dusty road, brushed it off, and tucked it into his robe. "I'm going to have a word with this Kata. You go take a look around the neighborhood. See what you can find out about Haseo's double."

Tora trotted off, and Akitada approached the training hall again. The master, surrounded by his pupils, was waiting. The pupils looked belligerent, their hands on their swords, but the master bowed deeply. He had the broad, flat face and squat build common among the peasants of the South, but his military stance and the scars on his face told Akitada that he had an army background.

"You are Kata?" he demanded.

"Yes, that is my name." The man bowed again. "I hope the gentleman has not suffered any ill effects from this stupid mistake?" The students eyed Akitada as if they hoped the opposite.

"Mistake? Someone threw a rock at me, and then a crowd attacked me. I might have been killed. Did you see who was involved?"

"I'm very sorry, but I was in the middle of a lesson. There

are many rude and stupid youngsters about." He turned to his students. "Did any of you see anything?" They shook their heads as one, and chorused, "No, Master."

A lie, of course. Kata had been looking at Akitada only a moment before the incident. Akitada narrowed his eyes. "I wish to speak to the man who stood behind you and left just before the incident. What is his name?"

Kata gestured. "These are all of my students for today. Please feel free to speak to the one you mean."

"No. There was another man. Back there." Akitada gestured to the back of the hall. "He spoke to you and then left."

"He spoke to me?" The master looked blank. "Impossible. Nobody interrupts me during a lesson." He turned to his students. "Isn't that so?"

They all nodded and said in unison, "That is so, Master."

Akitada let his eyes move from face to face. They gloated, each man locking away his knowledge firmly. For a moment he was tempted to force the issue, but they all clutched their wooden swords and poles, and his ragged attackers no doubt still hovered nearby.

"I shall report this incident to the authorities," he threatened. "They will get the information from you, or your business will be closed."

Kata bowed, but not soon enough. Akitada had caught the fear in his eyes.

He met Tora coming back from his own futile errand and told him about Kata's words. Tora said angrily, "He lied. And those students are cutthroats if ever I saw any."

"Probably. The man is nervous about being investigated. Whatever his background, and I suspect he's a former army officer, he's illegally training common roughnecks." In order to keep the peace, the carrying of arms was strictly regulated in the capital. Only men of good family and their retainers could carry swords, but few paid attention to such laws any longer.

Tora looked back over his shoulder. "I wouldn't be surprised if Kata was training them to be bandits."

"And the fellow who ran away was one of them. When he saw us looking at him, he got frightened."

Tora looked down at himself. "Amida," he muttered. "I think you've got it. I look like a thief-taker to them. Should've worn my sword."

Akitada suppressed a smile. Having once belonged to the class not permitted to wear or use a sword, Tora was inordinately proud of his present status as a retainer.

But life is a candle in the wind, and not all men can have what they wish for. Akitada had hoped for a modest career of legal scholarship, drafting codes and writing commentaries on the law, or perhaps a minor governorship administering those laws in some distant province. Instead he had been assigned to the Ministry of Justice, where a vengeful Soga had kept him at dull paperwork. And now he had even lost that position. And he had failed again to keep his promise to Haseo. As head of his family, for his people, and for his son's future, he must return to duty until Soga returned. And then he must suffer Soga's insults in order to avoid a negative evaluation that would make it impossible to get another appointment.

◆

But sacrifices are not without their rewards. Happy laughter greeted him at home. Genba was cavorting about the lantern-lit courtyard with Yori on his back as Seimei and Tamako watched from the veranda.

Genba had joined Akitada's household shortly before his master's marriage and had made himself indispensable without quite achieving the closeness that existed between Tora and his master. For one thing, Genba was too much in awe of his master. He was a huge man, taller than either Akitada or Tora, both of whom were above average, and he was quite fat these days.

He had developed a passion for food when he had prepared to become a wrestler.

Now his face was red from exertion, and sweat glistened on his bulging neck as he pranced and huffed around in a circle, his belly and buttocks bobbing, while Yori shouted and made passes with his sword at the straw man Tora had built.

Tora gave a sharp whistle, and Genba whinnied and stopped, letting the boy slip from his shoulders before he trotted to the house and collapsed on the veranda steps.

"Father, Father," cried Yori, catapulting himself into Akitada's arms. "I hit him six, no, seven times. It could have been more, but Genba is so slow and clumsy."

"Genba is no horse," said his father. The big man was wiping the sweat off his crimson face, and his huge chest rose and fell as he drew breath. "Perhaps we should get you a small horse instead. What do you think, Tora?"

Tora was dubious. "Not many around that are small enough. Maybe a donkey?"

"No," shouted Yori, outraged. "A horse. A proper horse. I shall not sit on a donkey."

Tamako called out anxiously, "You are too young for a horse, my son. Wait a few years first."

Akitada regretted his rash offer. Putting Yori down, he said, "I shall consider your request, Yori, when your writing improves."

He went to greet Tamako and Seimei and then sat down beside Genba to remove his shoes. He was very tired. They had walked far, and his old leg injury still ached occasionally.

Seimei said, "That nice young man from the ministry stopped by on his way home."

Akitada's heart stopped for a moment. He looked up at the old man. "Some problem at the ministry?"

"No, sir. He said to tell you that all was quiet *still*. His exact words. I wondered why he would bother to bring such a message."

But Akitada knew. Nakatoshi had warned him that, though Soga had not returned today, he might be back tomorrow. Well, it was settled. Akitada would return to work in the morning. The game was over—and he had lost.

He had little appetite for his evening rice that night and soon retreated to his own room. Taking a slim roll of brocade from the bookshelf, he went out onto the veranda. The air had cooled off and it was quite dark, but a few stars glimmered in the heavens. This was the time of night when trees and shrubs took on an impenetrable blackness and loomed against the lighter sky and the faint glow of the city beyond. He thought of the blind woman. Once he had been buried underground for many days and found his terror of the darkness had been greater than his fear of his captors. Tora was right: People should not turn their backs on those whose distress was manifest. He would at least listen to the woman's problem.

From the corner of the house, a cicada called, and another answered from the neighboring garden. Now and then there was a small splash, as one of the carp in the tiny fishpond jumped for an insect.

Akitada unrolled the brocade and took out his flute. He touched the familiar shape lovingly. As always, when he placed the flute to his lips and began to play, his sadness lifted, the tension in his muscles eased, and his mind emptied itself of worries. He felt as light as a moth on the night wind.

Much, much later he stopped. He was still tired, but his mind was calm now. Putting the flute back into its cover, he rose and went inside. Someone had spread his bedding. Tamako. He felt vaguely guilty but was too tired to go to her. Taking off his robe, he slipped under the quilt and closed his eyes.

In that last half-conscious moment before sleep, it occurred to him that the swordsmith had said something significant, but he was too tired to remember.

CHAPTER FOUR

THE BLIND STREET SINGER

Seimei shook him awake long before he was ready. Heavy with unfinished sleep, he struggled to a sitting position. It was pitch dark outside, but Akitada customarily arrived at the ministry before sunrise. "Is it time already?" he grumbled. "I feel as if I'd just lain down."

"No, sir. It's Tora."

"What?" Akitada rubbed his eyes and blinked against the light of the flickering candle. "What does he want in the middle of the night?"

"He's been arrested for murder. Someone from the Metropolitan Police is outside. Tora gave your name, and they sent an officer."

"It must be a ridiculous mistake. Tell them Tora is here. He came back with me." Akitada lay back down with a sigh of mingled irritation and relief.

"Tora is not here, sir. He left again after you retired."

Akitada sat up again, wide awake now. "He left again? Why? Where did he go?"

"I don't know, sir." Seimei held out Akitada's trousers and robe.

Pushing aside the bedding, Akitada got up, stepped into the wide silk trousers and tied them around his waist and ankles. Then he put his arms into the sleeves of the silk robe he had intended to wear to the ministry, and felt his topknot to make sure it was reasonably tidy.

"Where is the constable?" he asked.

"In the reception room. But he's a police lieutenant."

"Hmm." Barefoot, Akitada padded out of the room.

The lieutenant was young and excessively proper. Dressed in his uniform of white trousers, red coat, and black hat, he was still standing in the middle of the room and came to stiff attention when Akitada entered. His bow was snappy and precise. "Lieutenant Ihara, sir. Is it my honor to address First Secretary Sugawara?"

"Er, yes. Please be at ease, Lieutenant. What is all this about?"

"A female was murdered in the ninth ward. The man arrested at the scene of the crime claims to be your retainer, sir. Name of Tora?"

"I have a retainer by that name. Describe him!"

"Taller than I by a hand's width. About thirty years old. Small mustache. Pale features. Good teeth. Wearing a plain blue robe with black sash. No other identifying marks that I could see."

Akitada sighed. No doubt Tora had gone out after some female and got himself into trouble. "It sounds like him," he admitted. "What happened?"

"The warden of the ninth ward received word that a crime was being committed and sent some constables. They walked in on the murder scene and found this Tora bent over the victim with a knife in his hand. The knife was covered with blood. The constable placed the killer under arrest and sent for us. We were notified two hours ago, and I was dispatched to the crime scene to interview the killer. That was when he gave your name, sir."

"Did Tora confess to the murder?"

"No, sir. But then few killers will. At least not until they are questioned under torture."

Akitada shuddered. "In that case," he said, "you must not call him a killer yet. He is a suspect."

"Yes, sir. Sorry, sir. I meant the suspect."

He did not look as if he thought there was a difference but probably had not made too many arrests that did not produce a guilty plea in court. Akitada thought of Haseo. He must have pleaded guilty once. Had he been tortured, too? His back had been deeply scarred, but he had blamed that on the cruel guards in Sadoshima. A commoner like Tora would hardly be spared.

"Where is Tora now?"

"He has been taken to the Western Prison."

The Western Prison served the disreputable right half of the capital. It was more crowded than its counterpart, and the crimes punished there tended to be more sordid. Akitada asked, "Who is in charge of the case?"

"I am, sir."

"Ah. Very good. I want to see the crime scene. Can you take me there?"

The lieutenant looked shocked. "I am very sorry, sir, but that is not permitted. Besides, the body has been removed already."

"When do you expect the coroner to examine it?"

"Early this morning, I think. Doctor Okubo is very punctual."

There was an indrawn breath behind him and Akitada turned. Seimei hovered near the door, his face drawn with worry. "What time is it now, Seimei?"

"The hour of the ox is nearly over. We should hear the gong striking the hour of the tiger soon."

Two, perhaps three hours till dawn. Akitada would not be

able to see Tora or the coroner until daylight. He pulled his ear-lobe and considered.

"Perhaps Tora surprised the real killer," offered Seimei. "It isn't like him to do such a thing." He addressed the police offi-cer. "You see, Lieutenant, Tora would never kill a woman. It isn't in his nature."

The lieutenant looked embarrassed. "As you say, sir. In that case, there is nothing to worry about. The authorities will have the truth out of him soon." To Akitada he said, with another precise bow, "If there is nothing else, sir, I shall take my leave. I only needed verification of the suspect's identity and to find out if anyone here knows anything about the murder. I see that you had no knowledge of the incident."

"Wait a moment," Akitada said quickly. "I must insist on the details of the murder. Also, surely you should ask when Tora left here. For all you know, the crime happened at a time when he was with us."

The officer flushed. "Sorry. It being the middle of the night, I did not want to make a nuisance of myself. I thought I'd come back in the morning. But if it is no imposition . . ." Pulling a sheaf of paper from his sleeve, he glanced around helplessly for writing utensils.

Akitada took pity on him. "Come," he said, taking his arm, "we will go to my study."

His study was in some disarray, with his bedding and some of his clothes still on the floor. Seimei bustled about, muttering nervously under his breath. He lit more candles and brought paper and brushes, inkstones and water containers. For the lieutenant he supplied a small desk and settled him in front of it. Then he busied himself with the bedding and clothes.

"Never mind those, Seimei," Akitada said impatiently. "The servants can take care of them later."

Actually there were few servants in the Sugawara household.

Akitada customarily put away his own bedding every morning, but the lieutenant would not understand this and might be less respectful if he knew of Akitada's modest circumstances.

When they were alone, Akitada rubbed some ink and dipped his brush in it. The lieutenant was doing the same. He probably expected to conduct the interrogation himself. Akitada cleared his throat. "You may begin. Tell me about the victim."

The lieutenant had been darting curious glances about the room. It had once been Akitada's father's and was elegantly furnished as a gentleman's study. The tall shelves held document boxes, scrolls, and books accumulated by generations of Sugawara males. A handsome landscape scroll hung in the alcove, and the writing implements on the large old desk were fine antiques. He seemed impressed with the evidence of scholarly pursuits and did not balk at Akitada's brusque order.

"The victim is a poor woman who may have earned a living by occasional prostitution. She was found in the room she rented from a stonemason in the ninth ward. She had multiple stab wounds. It is thought that your retainer was her customer and that they had quarreled." He glanced about the room again and added apologetically, "Sorry to bring bad news in the middle of the night. Such women have very bad reputations. They have been known to steal from their customers. I am sure there will be extenuating circumstances."

"Tora attaches little importance to casual sexual encounters or to money. In fact, I have never known him to purchase his pleasures. He is very handsome and never short of female company."

The lieutenant shifted on his cushion. "Nevertheless, he was caught in the act."

"When did the woman die?"

"The constable from the warden's office claims she was still warm when he got there."

Akitada frowned. This was not good. Unless the real killer was found quickly, Tora was in for a most unpleasant time. He asked, "How was the crime discovered so quickly?"

"The woman's landlord and his family heard sounds of a struggle and screams. They sent their boy to the warden's office for help."

"Do I take it that they did not go to the woman's aid themselves?"

"No. They were afraid."

"Did they hear or see anyone arrive or leave prior to the crime?"

"No. All was quiet. They were preparing for bed. People go to bed rather early in poor households, to save on oil. The suspect entered by a back door."

"What is known about the woman's associates?"

"Not much. She worked in the market in the daytime and kept to herself. Being blind, she earned money by singing. She may have augmented that income by performing sexual services after dark."

Akitada sat up in surprise and stared at the officer. "What? The blind street singer?"

The lieutenant was instantly alert. "The woman's name was Tomoe. Was your honor, by chance, acquainted with her?" His tone and manner were rapidly changing back to suspicion.

Akitada came to a decision. There was little point in suppressing facts. Rather, if he hoped for cooperation, he would have to offer assistance. Besides, the little he knew was bound to come out in any case. "Yes," he admitted, "you surprised me. Your calling the woman a prostitute made me think this a matter unrelated to any of us, but Tora had taken an interest in this blind woman because she was afraid of someone. He spoke to me about her, asking me to investigate. I refused to become involved. Apparently I was wrong in thinking her problem trivial. But it means that Tora's presence can be explained by his being worried enough to check up on her. He must have arrived on the scene shortly after the murder." Akitada clapped his hands, and Seimei appeared so promptly that it was clear he had been eavesdropping outside the door. Akitada asked him, "Seimei, when did Tora leave here?"

"Right after his evening rice, sir. Just before the gong announced the hour of the boar."

"The alarm was given in the last quarter of the hour of the boar," said the lieutenant.

Akitada thought. "Probably less than an hour after Tora left here. He must have gone directly to her place. What does he say?"

"That he found her dead. But it is what the killer would say, isn't it?"

"Yes." Akitada sighed. "I should have listened to Tora. But this accusation against him is ridiculous and must be proven wrong. The dead woman's ghost will not be at peace until we find who did this." He got to his feet. "I would like you to show me the scene of the crime."

The lieutenant shook his head stubbornly. "I'm sorry, sir. Impossible."

Akitada stiffened. "What do you mean? Superintendent Kobe will vouch for me . . ." He stopped. His friend Kobe was superintendent of the police, but Akitada had no wish to cause him trouble unless Tora's life was in danger. Kobe had earned his position by diligence and hard work, but his job was sought by one of the Fujiwaras, a distant cousin of the Minister of the Left and a man who, though more familiar with courtly protocol than criminal investigation, was known for his ruthless pursuit of advancement. If he caught Kobe in the slightest bending of the rules, he would see him ousted. Akitada said instead, "But if we wait until the authorities give permission, valuable clues may be lost." On second thought, he decided that this young lieutenant would not take kindly to having police methods questioned and explained, "The local warden's people are often untrained in looking at a crime scene. They deal mostly with ruffians and thieves. I have some experience in criminal investigations. Under the circumstances, I would be glad to offer my assistance."

The lieutenant looked puzzled, then brightened suddenly. "Of course. How stupid of me! You are that Sugawara. I should have remembered. In that case, while it isn't precisely according to the rules, an exception might be made. And as it is too early to get official permission, we could just go and have a quick look. I would be grateful for any suggestions from someone with your reputation, sir."

"Thank you." Sometimes notoriety was a good thing. Akitada's interest in criminal cases, some of them involving the lowest type of criminal and crime, was so extraordinary in someone of his birth and position as an imperial official that it had caused him mostly trouble, especially with Soga.

The thought of Soga brought new worries. There was little chance now that Akitada would be safely behind his desk in his office when the minister arrived. But it could not be helped.

As they left his study, Akitada caught a glimpse of his wife at the end of the corridor. She stood in the dark, a pale, ghostlike presence in her white undergown. Her face was filled with anxiety. Akitada told his companion, "Please go ahead. I'll catch up with you," and turned back to Tamako.

Her eyes searched his face. "Something bad has happened," she said with a little catch in her soft voice. "I was afraid for you."

His heart filled with contrition. "It has nothing to do with me," he said, taking her clenched hands in his—they felt cold and clutched his warm ones eagerly. "Tora was mistakenly arrested. I must see what I can do. Don't worry. More than likely it will turn out to be nothing."

"Oh, I hope so." She bit her lip. "You will be careful? And Akitada, whatever you decide, it will be my wish also." She paused, anxiously waiting to see if he understood her meaning. When he looked at her doubtfully, she said, "I think that something else has been troubling you."

So she had guessed his problem with Soga. Ashamed, Akitada could not meet her eyes. He said, "I'm sorry that I've been so preoccupied." He touched her shoulder and said again, "Do not worry!" and hurried after the lieutenant.

Outside, the night air was oppressive. The smoke from thousands of cooking fires, oil lamps, and torches hung in the still air. They encountered few people. A young nobleman hurried home from a tryst, and a page boy ran toward the palace with a flowering branch; somewhere a lady or her lover had attached a poem to the branch, to commemorate their lovemaking. Among the good people, nighttime was for romance, not murder.

As they walked along Nijo Avenue, they heard the gong in the palace grounds striking the hour of the tiger, and then faintly the voice of the guard officer, giving his name and the time. Shortly after, the soft twanging of bowstrings came from the imperial residence. Eternal vigilance was required to keep evil spirits from entering His Majesty's chamber and wreaking havoc there.

Apparently evil did its dirty work unhampered in the great city beyond the palace walls. Akitada felt another twinge of guilt for having ignored Tora's pleas. He walked silently and glumly beside the lieutenant, who led the way with his lantern.

It was a long way to the ninth ward, and Akitada had walked a great distance the previous day. He had a hard time keeping up with the young lieutenant's long strides. Spending hours sitting or kneeling in his office bent over documents seemed to age a person beyond his years, and the old knee injury did not help. Eventually the lieutenant noticed and slowed down. Ashamed, Akitada forced himself to walk more briskly and evenly.

When they reached the street of shacks and dilapidated wooden houses where the stonemason lived, he was bathed in sweat and wished only to sit down. It was still dark, but there was enough light to see that the small yard was littered with samples of the mason's work. More stones leaned against the walls of the house, and a light flickered inside. There was no one about. The lieutenant gave a grunt and pushed aside the front door curtain. Ducking in, he barked, "What are you doing, you lazy oaf? I told you to stand guard."

Akitada followed. A family huddled in a corner of what must be the main room. They were curled up close together under quilts, their eyes startled and fearful. In the center of the room, a constable staggered to his feet and fell to his knees, beating his forehead against the dirt floor.

"I just came in for a moment," he babbled. "To make sure all was well." His sleep-puffed face gave away the truth.

"Outside!" snarled the lieutenant. The constable scrambled up and slunk past them to resume his guard duty. The lieutenant did not apologize for the negligent guard—Akitada rather liked that about the man. Instead Ihara told the family, "We're having another look at the room. Nothing to worry about. Go back to sleep." Taking up one of the small oil lamps in passing, he headed toward the back of the house. Akitada nodded a greeting and followed him.

In the back of the house, the lieutenant stopped in front of a door and ripped off a strip of paper that had been placed there to keep people from walking in on the crime scene. When the door was open, he directed the lantern light at the scene of the murder.

The street singer's room was small, windowless, and bare, a mere storage space for the main house. Once it might have been neat, but now it showed signs of a dreadful struggle.

A second door, old and badly warped but with a new wooden latch, probably led to a backyard. Someone had tried to cover the gaping cracks between the boards with strips of paper that would do little to keep out the icy blasts of the winter months.

The furnishings were meager. A single trunk for clothing stood askew in a corner, a broken shelf once held a bit of food and eating utensils, all of which now lay scattered about the floor. A small hibachi had fallen on its side, its coals and ashes spilled on the dirt floor. It must have served the blind woman as a stove. On top of a thin mat, some bedding had been spread. The bedding was also tumbled about.

They stepped across a pool of blood and closed the door.

The woman's body was gone, but her blood seemed to cover everything she had left behind. Thick, dark puddles marked the floor where she had died; streaks and spatters covered the walls, the mat, the bedding; and smears and bloody handprints defaced the walls and the door they had come through.

"Would you describe the body for me?" Akitada said to Ihara.

The young man pointed to the blood in front of the door. "She was just there, on her stomach, her head toward the door, and her feet toward us. She was wearing a white cotton robe, which was soaked in blood from many deep cuts on her back and front. Her hair had come loose, and she was cold to the touch when I arrived. Is that what you had in mind?"

"Yes. Did she have any money on her?"

"No."

Akitada began to move about cautiously, looking at everything. "She put up a terrible fight against her attacker," he muttered at one point.

The lieutenant gestured to the bedding. "After she accommodated him sexually."

Akitada bent to look at the blood-stained quilts more closely. "Really? How do you know?"

Ihara laughed. "Well, somebody's used the bedding and her sash was off when we found her. She was half naked."

"The coroner will tell us," Akitada said, straightening up. His eye fell on the back door with its many paper strips. "Was that door latched?" he asked.

"The suspect claims he found it open."

"Hmm." Akitada pursed his lips. "She did not try to escape that way," he said. "I wonder why not."

"I imagine she was trying to reach her landlord and his family."

"Yes, perhaps." Akitada studied the back door, then opened it. The flickering light from their lantern fell on a tiny veranda. Beyond lay a service yard containing a laundry tub, clothesline, some baskets, a small pile of faggots, a broom made of twigs, a rainwater barrel, and more stone tablets. A low wooden fence with a gate ran along a street that passed behind the houses.

"Bring the light closer." Akitada crouched down and looked at the weathered boards of the wooden stoop. Dusty shapes marked the print of boots and of dirty bare feet. It looked as though the boots went only one way, into the room, but the bare feet were both coming and going and had also shuffled about near the threshold. Akitada placed his own foot next to the prints. The boot print matched his closely, but the bare feet had belonged to someone much smaller.

"Was the dead woman wearing shoes?"

Ihara frowned. "I don't recall. Why?"

"Somebody barefoot was here."

The lieutenant was unimpressed and said that the boot prints belonged to the killer, and the dead woman had probably left the others on an earlier occasion. Akitada revised his good opinion of the lieutenant's intelligence and did not mention the small cut in one of the strips of paper on the door. He had had to bend a little to see it closely and confirm that it had been made from the outside. Someone had spied on the woman inside, someone who was shorter than either he or Tora and who had been barefoot and carried a knife.

Back in the dead woman's room, Akitada considered the destruction. It looked accidental rather than intentional, a direct result of the victim's attempt to escape her attacker. Being blind, she had kept to the walls, trying to reach the door to the hall-way, and in her struggle against the knife-wielding killer, she had knocked her trunk away from the wall and grabbed for the shelf and torn it off. And all the time, the killer had been slash-ing and stabbing at her, for there was her blood on three of the walls and finally on the interior door, where the marks of bloody fingers had left vertical smears all the way to the thresh-old. She had died at the foot of this door, her lifeblood soaking into the dirt.

Akitada looked with pity at the things that had fallen from the shelf. The woman's life must have resembled that of a starv-ing hermit. The single small earthenware bowl was in pieces but had been chipped long before, and her chopsticks were of plain rough wood. She did not own a large pot to cook rice in, but then she had no rice either. Evidently she purchased small amounts of food in the market and cooked them in a little iron pot on her hibachi. Her food stores were pitiful. A handful of dry millet had spilled from a twist of paper, and among the shards of the bowl lay a few leaves of cabbage and a tiny piece of dried fish.

He tried to remember her. She had been thin, yes, but had she actually looked starved? Surely she had had enough cus-tomers, even without adding prostitution to her labors, to live better than this.

The tangled bedding also was quite old and had been mended many times, the stitches and patches grossly uneven. It must have been difficult to work by touch alone. The more he consid-ered her struggle to survive, the more he was filled with wonder. That same spirit had caused her to fight against her killer even when it was hopeless.

He turned his attention to the trunk. It had intrigued him from the start, because it was lacquered and had once been ex-pensive. He opened it, expecting more surprises, but it was nearly empty. Only a few pieces of rough clothing, neatly folded, lay on the bottom. He had no wish to paw through a dead woman's private possessions, but made himself do a cursory check. A few cheap cotton scarves, two pairs of cotton trousers, and two cotton jackets, the sorts of clothes worn by peasant women, scullery maids, and outcasts, were all that she had owned. If she had plied a trade as a streetwalker, she had certainly made no attempt to look attractive to men. The trunk apparently also held her bedding in the daytime. How very different were the arrangements in most houses. Each member of Akitada's family had four trunks, one for the clothing of each season. And bedding had a separate storage place.

Tomoe had been very poor.

Akitada was about to drop the lid again, when he noticed a faint bulge under the bottom layer of clothes. He pulled out a small black lacquer box, a box most beautifully decorated with a design of fish cavorting among waves. The pictures were drawn in gold lacquer and the fish scales inlaid with mother-of-pearl. It was an altogether exquisite piece.

He opened the lid, and found that the inside of the box was painted with flowers of the four seasons and that it contained cosmetics. A twisted paper held powder to whiten the face, and small compartments were filled with kohl to outline the eyes and paint eyebrows, tweezers to pluck eyebrow hairs so the new ones could be painted above them, rouge for the lips, and a vial of tooth-blackening liquid. They were the sorts of cosmetics used by highborn ladies or elegant courtesans. What possible use were they to a blind street singer? There was no mirror in the room, any more than the windowless space had needed any lamps. Had she stolen the box for resale? If so, why had she not sold it long ago?

Among the twisted papers containing various powders he found another puzzle. One of the paper packages felt hard under his fingers. He undid it and saw that it contained three pieces of silver, an astonishing amount of money for someone who lived on the edge of starvation.

He showed his find to the lieutenant, who was first excited, then angry.

"Those lazy louts should have found it when they searched the room. You were right, sir. The pieces of dung cannot be trusted with an investigation. When they told me the dead woman had no money, I wondered if she'd been robbed. I suppose this proves she wasn't. So we are still working with an unpremeditated act, with a crime of passion?"

"Hmm." Akitada flattened out the paper and saw some faint characters written on it, not with ink and brush, but with something like charcoal. The characters had become smudged from handling, but he thought they were names: Nobunari and Nobuko—the first male, the second female. Was the money theirs? Or had she simply wrapped the coins in a discarded piece of paper she had found somewhere? Paper was not readily available to someone who could neither read nor write. He corrected himself. It was theoretically possible for a blind person to write, provided that person had once had sight and had been taught. But a street singer? He shook his head and put the money back in its paper and replaced it. He closed the box and handed it to the lieutenant. "You had better take care of this," he said. "It may turn out to be evidence. It either proves that robbery was not the killer's aim—or that he was interrupted before he could ransack the trunk."

The lieutenant pondered this. "I get your drift. You think your Tora arrived and the killer ran? Yes, I suppose it could have happened that way." But he sounded dubious and peered into the open trunk, tossing the folded garments around. "Not much else in here except her rags. I suppose she put her bedding on top every morning. What do you make of her having such a fine box and the silver?"

"I don't know. It's strange."

"Stolen, I expect."

Though Akitada had just had the same thought, the lieutenant's easy conclusion bothered him. "Not necessarily," he said. "We must learn as much as possible about the victim and her past and current life. Now I would like to ask the mason and his family a few questions."

When they got back to the main room, they found that the couple had crept out of their blankets and was sitting beside the central fire pit. The mason, middle-aged before his time, still wore his dusty jacket and short pants, and his hands and feet were encrusted with stone powder. His wife did not look much cleaner. Poor people had no bathing facilities, and the public baths charged too much money, but the contrast to their lodger Tomoe was striking. She had made a great effort to be clean, perhaps because her work required it, but Akitada rather thought that cleanliness had been important to her, a matter of pride.

"We are sorry to be so much trouble." Akitada squatted down near the mason, though the man's simian features did not promise much in terms of intelligent responses. After a moment, the lieutenant did the same.

"No trouble, no trouble," the mason muttered, avoiding eye contact and bobbing his head.

"The lieutenant tells me that you heard your lodger cry out and sent for help. Is that so?"

"She was screaming. It was terrible. It was like demons were tearing her to pieces. I sent my son for the constables."

Akitada thought of the blind woman struggling for her life, trying to reach the door and help. And these people had sat there, paralyzed with fear. Superstitions were common, but so were cowardice and ill will. He constrained his anger and said encouragingly. "You must have been very frightened."

"Yes. We ran outside and hid. After a long time I went to listen at the door. I heard nothing. But I figured the demon must have heard us, and we went back outside."

What a repulsive little toad this man was! In fact, Akitada felt nothing but revulsion for the couple. He looked from one to the other. "Did you hear or see anyone leave?"

They shook their heads.

"Did your lodger receive visitors in her room?"

The mason hesitated and looked at his wife. She glared back at him. The mason fidgeted and said sullenly, "I'm a busy man. I have no time to watch her."

His wife gave a snort.

Akitada said, "Yes, of course. But perhaps your wife, being in the house most of the day, may know something?"

The woman smirked. "She looked down her nose at people. Men think that makes a whore special." She snorted again. "Men are fools." She glared at her husband.

Aha, thought Akitada, so the wife was jealous of Tomoe. He considered her with interest. She was a short, dumpy female with the sharp nose and close-set eyes of a rat and a permanent scowl of bad temper. The street singer had been no beauty, but to the stonemason she must have seemed a fairy compared to the mother of his children. Had she caught her husband with Tomoe and gone after her rival with her kitchen knife? If so, the mason would be bound to cover up for her.

As if she guessed what he was thinking, she said suddenly, "That fellow they arrested. He was here before, and they argued. He said he'd be back, and she'd better do something or he'd kill her."

CHAPTER FIVE

THE SHACKLES OF LIFE

*O*f course the lieutenant's eyes lit up at this damning piece of evidence against Tora. Pressed by Akitada, she remained adamant, saying that she had been worried about her lodger and had put her ear to the door when she realized that Tomoe was arguing with a man. The lieutenant shot Akitada a triumphant glance and asked, "How can you be sure it was the same man who killed her?"

She was. Not only had she recognized the voice, but she had seen him leave right afterward.

Akitada did not for a moment believe that she had spied on Tomoe out of concern for her safety, but rather because she suspected that her husband was with the lodger. He regarded husband and wife thoughtfully and asked, "Had there been any other visitors? Or perhaps strangers who seemed interested in Tomoe?"

The mason glanced at his wife.

"Pah," she said, "a woman like that always has men. Trash! I'm too busy to watch."

Akitada took this to mean that they had not actually seen or heard other visitors, but suspected that there had been some. He said, "Tomoe complained of someone following her home from the market. Do you know anything about that?"

They shook their heads, and that ended the visit.

Outside, the constable attempted to give a belated impression of alertness. Akitada badly wanted to see Tora, but a new day was beginning and he was due in the ministry. He thanked Ihara.

The lieutenant bowed. "I'm in your debt for finding this, sir." He held up the cosmetics box.

"Not at all. You would have found it yourself." Since Akitada regretted leaving it with Ihara, he added, "Take good care of it. It may turn out to be important."

He walked back alone to the Greater Palace, watching the sky clouding over even as the sun rose with a spectacular display of fiery hues. Perhaps some rain would cool down the unseasonably hot and dry weather. The smoky orange color of the clouds looked like a bank of smoldering fires, as if a major conflagration were under way in the city. He felt an involuntary chill, a sense of impending disaster.

When Akitada passed through the main gate of the Greater Palace, he worried about Tora in his miserable cell. Had they "interrogated" him already during the night? It was likely. Even if they had not, they would not wait much longer before taking the bamboo canes to Tora's back or using other forms of torture to force an admission of guilt from him. And Tora was not about to confess to something he had not done.

Akitada decided he would report at the ministry and then go immediately to the prison. As he joined the stream of government officials, many like himself in robes and hats with rank insignia, he became nervous about his appearance, adjusting his hat and brushing at the wrinkles in his gown and full silk trousers. He had dressed too hurriedly after the night's summons and had not had time to shave. No doubt Soga would hold this against him.

The morning was gloomy, becoming increasingly cloudy. The rising sun had no chance and the ministry compound lay in the shadow of large pines so that lights still glimmered inside. Akitada climbed the staircase and entered the main hall. He expected to see Nakatoshi at this early hour, but for once Sakae was also waiting. Even more puzzling was Sakae's enthusiastic greeting. The junior clerk practically rubbed his hands as he announced that he would have his report ready by the time Minister Soga arrived.

"Very good," said Akitada approvingly and turned to Nakatoshi. "So the minister is definitely coming?"

"Yes, sir. I expect him in an hour or so."

Akitada thought. "An hour? Good. I have a brief call to make." He turned on his heel to head down the steps again.

The Western Prison was outside the Greater Palace, but only a few blocks from the ministry. Because of his official robe and rank, the constables at the prison gate passed him through to the prison supervisor, where he identified himself and his errand. This official was also cooperative and Akitada was taken to Tora's cell.

Tora was chained. He was also bruised about the face, and smears of dried blood covered his clothes and hands. When he saw Akitada, he rose awkwardly from a pile of dirty straw, rattling his chains, and tried a weak smile. "Sorry, sir. Didn't mean to make trouble for you."

"Never mind that. Are you hurt? Have you been beaten?"

"A little. It was after hours when I was brought in, and they didn't put their hearts into it." He looked at his hands and clothes. "The blood's not mine."

Akitada scowled at the guard. "This man is one of my retainers," he snapped. "Nobody is to lay a hand on him again, do you hear!"

The guard looked blank. "Yes, your honor. I shall tell them what you said."

But the screams which came from the courtyard behind the cells were not reassuring. Tora's eyes flickered uneasily.

"You may also tell them that Tora will be transferred today," Akitada said. He glanced at the dirty floor. "This place is filthy. Take us to one of the offices."

The man pondered. He was clearly torn between his duty to keep the prisoner chained in his cell and Akitada's rank. After reflection, he apparently decided the present threat had precedence over potential future repercussions. He unchained Tora and took them to a small, empty room which contained nothing but a desk and a few shelves of documents. The floor was wooden and reasonably clean. Akitada sat down and Tora followed suit.

The guard remained standing, an iron rod used to subdue unruly prisoners in his meaty hand. He listened nervously toward the corridor. "You won't be long, your honor?" he asked.

Akitada ignored him. He said to Tora, "I went to the blind woman's place, but her body had already been removed. Tell me how you found her."

Tora grimaced. "I was worried, so I went back to talk some sense into her. Not wanting to bother her landlord and that shrew of a wife, I went through the back."

"In the dark? How is it that you know your way about people's service yards in the dark?"

Tora flushed. "I've been there before. Her landlady has a vicious tongue, and I didn't want her to see me."

"Well, she saw you at some point and took you for one of her lodger's clients."

Tora just shook his head tiredly. "She's wrong. That's what I mean about her tongue. Anyway, I got to Tomoe's door and scratched. I didn't want to make much noise, and she keeps it latched on the inside. I got her to get a new latch. Well, it wasn't latched last night. The door moved when I touched it. I thought she'd left it open in case I stopped by, but then I could smell the blood." Tora shuddered. "I went in. Couldn't see a thing, so I had to feel my way about. I slipped on something wet. Blood, I think. And then I stepped on the knife. Well, I knew it was a knife as soon as I picked it up. And right after that I touched her. I was bent over, feeling for her face to see if she was still alive, when all hell broke loose. People rushed in with lights. They knocked me down and held me. Constables from the warden's office. And her landlord. And I think her landlady, too. Maybe their kids. The whole room was full of people talking and shouting. After that I couldn't get a really good look at Tomoe."

"Yes, I see. Well, just tell me what you could see."

Tora gulped. "She was near the door. The door to the main house. There was a lot of blood. I could see blood on the walls. And on the door. And on the knife I was holding. It was covered with blood." He extended his stained hands for Akitada to see. "They pried it from my hand right away. I guess it's the knife that killed her. It took me a minute to realize they thought I had done it. After that I was trying to explain why I was there so they'd take the chains off me. It was no good. They figured I did it all right. I'm sorry. It's not much help, is it?"

"Not much, but it's still early. What made you think Tomoe would leave the door ajar for you last night?"

Tora hung his head and heaved a big sigh. "When I left her in the market, I told her I'd try to walk her home. But I didn't get to. I guessed she thought I'd come later. I've been sitting here, blaming myself. For not walking her home, and for making her leave her door unlatched when there was a killer lying in wait outside."

"Nobody could have known," Akitada said, uneasily aware that he had some responsibility in the matter also.

Tora looked around the room. "I feel like a trapped beast in here. Any chance of getting me out?"

"I'll speak to Superintendent Kobe today, but the best we can hope for is a transfer across town. The case against you is strong, and it's the only one they have. The landlady says that you had threatened to kill Tomoe."

Tora stared. "That's a lie."

"You didn't quarrel the night before?"

"Maybe I raised my voice a little. Trying to get her to give me some information. She was stubborn." He buried his head in his hands and muttered, "Amida, I should have stayed with her. I should never have let her out of my sight."

Akitada bit his lip. "Tora," he asked, "were you Tomoe's lover?"

Tora lowered his hands. "No." But he looked confused, puzzled, and Akitada waited. "There was something about her. I thought a man would be very lucky to have a woman like her. I really don't know how I felt." Then, to Akitada's dismay, Tora's eyes filled with tears. "I wish she were still alive," he said brokenly.

"Tell me about her."

But Tora glanced at the guard, saw the man's avid interest, and reddened. "I really didn't know her very well," he said.

Akitada gave an inward sigh. Whatever else Tora might have said about his relationship with the dead woman would not be said here and now. "Did she have any family?"

"No. I asked her that. She said they were all dead."

"What about her customers? Could there have been a man?"

"I don't think so. Sometimes she didn't seem to like men at all. There was a lot she was keeping quiet. I know she went to a private house sometimes to sing to the noble ladies there. She looked forward to that. They paid well and were very kind to her, she said. I told you she was respectable. They wouldn't have had her there if she wasn't. And she was saving her money so she could stop working in the market." He paused and frowned.

Akitada considered the noble family. Tora had a point. No loose woman would be admitted to the private quarters of respectable ladies. "Did she mention the family's name?"

"No. She was funny about names."

"She was certainly a baffling woman. I found a lacquer cosmetics box and some silver in her trunk. Do you know anything about that?"

Tora looked astonished. "What would she want with cosmetics? She couldn't see her face."

"I know. That's why I asked."

Tora thought. "Do you suppose one of those noble ladies . . . ? No. Why would they? But the silver she must've been saving. You could see she bought nothing for herself."

"What was she saving it for? There was not enough to retire on."

Tora shook his head.

"Did she ever mention someone called Nobunari?"

Tora stared at Akitada. "No. I would've remembered. That's a gentleman's name."

"What about Nobuko?"

"That might've been one of the ladies. But I told you, she never talked about them. What's going on?"

"It may mean nothing, but the silver was wrapped in a piece of paper. Someone had scrawled the names on it with a piece of charcoal. Could Tomoe write?"

"Write? She was blind."

Silence fell. Tomoe's secrecy intrigued Akitada. "Who do you think killed her?" he finally asked.

"I'm betting on the gangsters." Tora clenched his fists in helpless anger. "The silly fool! I asked her to tell me. I told her they were dangerous and wouldn't think twice about slitting her throat to make sure she didn't talk."

Akitada pondered this. With Soga breathing down his back, he was in no position to investigate gang activities. "What about the person who followed her? You said she could smell him."

"They say blind people have a sharper sense of smell and hearing."

"Did she say what sort of smell?"

"Bad. She called it—what was that word—yes, pungent. Whatever that means. She used strange words sometimes."

"It means 'strong' or 'sharp.' Not very helpful. Sometimes people may carry the smell of a particular job. Like a rice wine brewer, for example. Or a dumpling baker."

"Nothing like that, I think. She would have said so."

Silence fell again. Akitada sighed. "Well, that's all I can think of. I must hurry back to work. Soga is expected. If I can't get you transferred today, I shall be back after work."

Tora looked contrite. "I'm very sorry, sir," he said with unaccustomed humility, "if I have caused trouble for you at your work."

Akitada smiled and touched his shoulder. "It wasn't your fault. And you're more important to me."

Tora's eyes moistened. Keeping his head down, he nodded and rose to let the guard take him back to his cell.

"Oh," said Akitada, "I almost forgot. Do you recall if she was wearing shoes when you found her?"

Tora thought. "Not sure, sir. I think so, but I wasn't really looking at her feet."

"No, I suppose not. Never mind. Don't worry."

Akitada watched him walk away. He knew about being in chains and about the willpower it took to walk upright and square-shouldered when you had recently received a flogging. He felt helpless and frustrated. Because of a superior he heartily disrespected, he had to postpone the more urgent need of Tora. He seemed forever caught in conflicts of duty, private and public.

Outside, a wind had sprung up. In the palace grounds it

stirred dust clouds from the dry streets and whipped up the
gowns of officials hurrying between buildings. Clutching his
hat, Akitada bent his head into it and tried to subdue his flapping skirts and full trousers. Dust particles stung his face and
got into his eyes. In the distance, thunder rumbled.

Of course Soga had already arrived. Impossible to slip quietly into his office, pretending that he had been there all along.
Soga was still in the main hall, glowering at the clerks, who were
blank-faced. He must have delivered himself of some tirade,
because the heads of scribes could be seen, peering curiously
around corners and over transoms.

Soga turned on Akitada with an avidity that meant he had
been the cause of his anger. "In my office," he snapped without
a greeting.

Akitada bowed and said pointedly, "Good morning, sir. I
trust you return safe and well from your trip?"

Soga did not respond. He marched into his private office
and took his seat behind the desk. Akitada followed and turned
to close the door.

"I want the two clerks in here," snapped Soga.

Tasting the familiar sour bile of helpless anger rising in his
throat, Akitada opened the door again for Nakatoshi and Sakae.
The three of them gathered around Soga's desk.

Soga did not invite them to sit. His round face was still suf-
fused with color and his pudgy hands clutched the edge of the
desk. He seemed to be trying to control his wrath. Akitada swallowed nervously, wondering what Soga had shouted in the
hearing of the ministry's staff. That it concerned him he did not
doubt. Well, he had tried to return to his duty, but fate had once
again interceded. Perhaps this was the end of his career. The
thought that he would no longer have to bow his neck under
the yoke imposed upon it by his bitter enemy should have
cheered him, but the faces of his wife and his son, of old Seimei
and the others rose before his eyes. What was to become of

them all? Tora in jail on a murder charge, his house filled with
dependents, a son to raise and see secure in some official position, perhaps other children in the future, and he had no funds
to fall back on, no outside income except for a rather poor farm
in the country.

Soga finally raised his head and looked slowly at each of
them. When his round black eyes reached Akitada, he compressed his lips and a prominent vein in his temple began to
throb. But his voice was calm.

"I have returned today to give you instructions about running the ministry in my absence. I must say what I found on my
arrival has not encouraged me to think this possible. Nevertheless, it cannot be helped. You, Sugawara, are in charge. Sakae, who
seems to have shown some initiative in your absence, can handle
the routine business of your department. Nakatoshi will assist
you. I expect daily reports. Sakae will draw these up and all three
of you will sign them. They are to be sent every night to my house
in the country. You will not make any decisions other than routine ones without my express permission in writing. That is all."

Akitada was completely taken aback. What was taking Soga
away so suddenly? And how could he, Akitada, run the ministry
with any efficiency while his hands were tied by this ridiculous
reporting system which would cause delays and expenditures?
How was he to deal with the patent insult that Soga did not
trust him to carry out the duty without constant oversight—
and that by the clerks, Sakae in particular? And how would this
affect Tora's desperate situation?

"Sir," he began.

But Soga cut him off instantly. "The clerks may leave and
tend to their duties," he snapped.

When Sakae and Nakatoshi were gone, Soga wasted no
more time. "You were late and your appearance suggests that
you have spent the night in some house of assignation. Furthermore, you were absent again yesterday," he said. "I am sure you

were aware of my opinion of your work, of your suitability for your position, and of your character before this latest dereliction. If you had not somehow impressed certain people with your exploits in places too distant from the capital to verify your outrageous claims, you would not be where you are now. As it is, I must tolerate you and, in the present emergency, leave you in charge. Let me assure you that the slightest infraction during my absence will result in my demanding not only your removal from your rank and position but also severe punishment for malfeasance in office."

For a moment, the room lost its stability. The floor under Akitada's feet behaved as in an earthquake, and the walls faded in and out before his eyes. There was a ringing in his ears, and when he tried to speak, he had lost his voice. He took a deep breath, cleared his throat, and tried to fix his eyes on Soga. "Under the circumstance," he said in a shaking voice, "I shall, of course, resign."

Soga rose. Something like triumph flashed in his eyes. "You may prepare a letter of resignation and leave it on my desk. I shall sign it upon my return. For the time being you will remain in your position and carry out your duties as ordered. If all goes well I shall not count the latest demerits against you. As you know, the annual fitness reports are due in another month, and yours is already sadly deficient. A charge of flagrant dereliction of duty would cost you the chance at another position."

"When will you return?"

"You will be kept informed." Soga glanced at his desk. "Take care of the correspondence, but pass on all private letters. And remember what I said." With that final threat, he walked past Akitada and out the door.

Akitada stood lost in a tumult of emotions until Nakatoshi's touch on his arm brought him back to reality.

"Can I bring you some wine, sir?" Nakatoshi asked anxiously.

"No." Akitada ran a hand over his face as if brushing away cobwebs and took a deep breath. "Yes, perhaps. Thank you." A cup of wine would put some warmth into his body, would thaw out the icy fury that seemed to paralyze his muscles and his brain. He walked stiffly around Soga's desk and sat down. Outside, thunder growled again, and the pines in the courtyard tossed in the wind. A gust of air stirred the papers on the desk. He got up to close the shutters and lit the tall candlesticks.

The correspondence. He looked through it. Apparently Soga had already removed anything he considered too important for Akitada's eyes. The rest was routine. When Nakatoshi returned with the warm wine, Akitada gulped it thirstily, then told him to take dictation. For the next hour, Akitada dealt with the business of the ministry.

"Is anyone waiting outside?" he asked, when the paperwork was done.

"Nobody important. It's time for the midday rice."

Akitada glanced at the closed shutters. He was not hungry. The sound of rain had been with them for a while now without his having noticed. And he had forgotten Tora. "One more letter," he said. "It must be delivered immediately. Then I shall see the petitioners."

The letter was addressed to Kobe, superintendent of the capital police. He hated to ask the man for this favor, but his concern for Tora was too great. Besides, a request to transfer Tora from the Western to the Eastern Prison was not unreasonable since Tora resided in the eastern half of the capital. The problem was that Kobe would assume other concessions would be expected later.

Then he had Nakatoshi show in the people who had waited patiently outside (some of them, as it turned out, for many months) to lay a problem before the minister of justice. He discovered that several had come bearing gifts, which he refused. The ones who had waited for months appeared too poor to curry the minister's favor in this way. This was not surprising. Akitada had always known that Soga enriched himself in his office. Indeed, most officials considered it a perquisite of their posts. Also, not surprisingly, the ones with gifts rarely deserved consideration, while the poor fellows who had lingered for months in the waiting area seemed to have legitimate cause for review. With a sigh, Akitada took down their information and sent them away until their cases could be studied. The others he dismissed brusquely. Still, hours passed in this manner until it became difficult to read the documents, because darkness was creeping from the corners of the room.

Impatiently, Akitada called for more lights. Nakatoshi came and threw open the shutters. The rain had stopped and it was clear again, but the sun had set and left behind a steamy dusk. Only now did Akitada become aware of the stiffness in his back and neck. He also realized that it was late and that he had done nothing about Tora.

"How many more?" he asked Nakatoshi.

"None, sir. And Sakae asks if he can leave."

"Dear heaven, I forgot all about him." Akitada rose, stretching his painful legs and back. "Don't tell me there is always this much business," he said with a grimace.

Nakatoshi grinned. "No, sir. A lot of stuff accumulated in His Excellency's absence. Besides, he doesn't see very many of the petitioners."

"I gathered that. There was one old man who had been here every day for the past three months."

"That would be Mr. Chikamura? The one who claims that his property has been taken by his nephew?"

"His home actually. I cannot imagine where he lays his head. He seems afraid for his life if he sets foot in his own house. I told him we would look into the matter. Have one of the scribes check the property deeds and then send someone from the police to his home to see what is going on."

Akitada walked across to his own office, where he found Sakae pacing the floor impatiently. He said, "Sorry, Sakae, but there was a great deal of work. How did you manage?"

Sakae pointed to a stack of documents. "All finished, sir. And here's the report for the minister. We've already signed."

This was so unlike the Sakae he knew that Akitada looked quickly through the papers. Not only did they seem in order, but Sakae's handwriting had improved materially. Light dawned belatedly. "I see you called on one of the scribes to assist you."

Sakae drew himself up. "Under the circumstances I thought it proper, sir."

"Yes. Quite. Very good." Akitada signed the report. "I shall see you tomorrow then?"

Sakae bowed and departed. Akitada was still looking after him, wondering what had come over his clerk, when Nakatoshi joined him.

"Sakae is a changed man," Nakatoshi said, making a face.

"I wonder why."

"Isn't it obvious, sir? Sakae wants your place when you're gone."

Akitada turned, aghast. "My place?" Then he remembered that he had offered Soga his resignation and that it had been accepted. He felt the crushing weight of worry about the future. Then shame returned. How had the clerks found out?

Nakatoshi looked embarrassed. "Before you came, the minister was speaking rather rashly about changes he intended to make. He also complimented Sakae on his fine work reorganizing the filing system. I'm afraid Sakae took this to mean . . ."

"I see."

So that was why everyone had been all ears when he had arrived this morning. The humiliation of having been dismissed in such a public, and no doubt insulting, fashion made his face burn. He turned away abruptly, saying, "Until tomorrow then," and walked out.

CHAPTER SIX

KOBE

*A*t the door, Akitada met a familiar figure just coming in: a tall, middle-aged official who had a neatly trimmed beard and wore a formal silk robe and court hat.

"Sugawara," he cried, his face breaking into a big smile. "Here I am. Don't look so glum! All will be well."

"Kobe," said Akitada weakly, coming to a stop. Little did the man know that nothing was well, or would be in the end. Still, he was touched that Kobe had come in person and seemed in a friendly mood. Becoming aware that his greeting was lacking in welcome, he bowed quickly and returned the smile. "I was coming to see you. I hope you didn't take my request amiss?"

"Of course not! What are friends for?"

Akitada regarded him uncertainly. "That is very good of you. I didn't want to trouble you, but since you know both Tora and me, I thought you might be willing to help. It's a cursed affair, and Tora was flogged before I could get to him. I was afraid using my influence would do nothing but make matters worse."

Kobe laughed—a nice, relaxed laughter. "Come, come! Why act the stranger when I expected to see an old friend? Of course I know Tora couldn't have done such a thing. It's all a mistake, though I expect Tora was meddling again. Sorry to hear about the flogging, but he was cheerful enough when I talked to him."

"You have been to see him? That was very kind of you."

"Not at all. Prisoners come to me, not I to them. I ordered his transfer. It took a while. Confounded paperwork. But you know how it is."

"Yes. I've been tied up all day myself. Thank you."

"If you're free now, shall we pay him a visit?"

Akitada hesitated. Kobe's open support might give his enemies an opportunity to charge him with favoritism. He said, "I don't like to impose further on your goodness."

"You're not. I like Tora. Come, you can tell me what you think about the case on the way."

Akitada still hung back. "What if . . . certain people use this kindness to make trouble for you?"

Kobe raised a brow. "Ah, so you've heard the rumors. Never mind that. And you, of all people, warning me about getting into trouble?"

That made Akitada smile. "Who better?"

"Nonsense. If you can break a few rules, so can I. We've been in the business of catching villains long enough to know that one has to use one's own judgment sometimes. I'm just doing my job. Besides, I'm interested."

Akitada gave up. They crossed the Greater Palace grounds together. The rain had cooled the air a little after the oppressive heat of the previous week, and there was still enough light to see by. The moist air intensified the scent of honeysuckle drifting over the wall of one of the ministries, and at the Shingon Temple, young monks laughed as they swept the water with brooms from the steps of the gate.

Suddenly Tora's situation did not seem so bleak anymore. Akitada thought of what Kobe had said and snorted.

Kobe threw him a glance. "Something funny?"

"In a way. It seems that I've finally broken the rules once too often. Today Soga forced me to resign and then had the gall to announce that he expected me to cover for him for an unspecified period of time. I'm to run the ministry until his return. I've been promoted and dismissed in the same breath."

"You're joking!"

"Not at all. And I've never worked as hard or as cheerfully. Of course, my situation is not really amusing, but sometimes it's easier to laugh at your troubles."

"But what will you do?"

"I don't know. At the moment Tora's problem is more important." He told Kobe what he had learned, and they became involved in the discussion of Tora's case. Akitada barely noticed the archivist Kunyoshi waving from the other side of street. He waved back.

Clouds of small gnats hovered in their path. Officials and clerks, on their way home from ministries or the imperial residence, tottered along on tall wooden *geta,* skirting puddles and holding up their fine silk trousers.

As they passed the main gate of the imperial residence, its thatched roofs sodden black from the rain, Kobe nodded to one of the guards, the son of a powerful family. Kobe had truly risen in the world, and Akitada felt a little less guilty about accepting his assistance.

After leaving the Greater Palace, they turned northeast. In this part of the city were public buildings and the palaces and mansions of court nobles. The Sugawaras, though sadly come down in the world, had lived here since the capital had been built.

When they saw the bleak walls and gate of the Eastern

Prison ahead, Kobe said, "A fascinating case. I shall look forward to your solution."

"It's difficult to think of it as a mental exercise when it may mean a friend's life."

"Come, come," said Kobe bracingly. "We've worked ourselves out of muddles before, you and I. Don't be so downcast. We'll have Tora free in no time."

Kobe's kindness was touching, but Akitada remained uneasy. They had never quite seen eye to eye in the past, and while he knew Kobe to be scrupulously honest and in his own way as dedicated to justice as he was, the superintendent could become very stubborn when they disagreed. Besides, there was the threat to Kobe's career. Few enough officials were both able and incorruptible. He hoped that Tora could be cleared quickly before someone took notice.

The conditions of Tora's imprisonment had improved dramatically. They found him sitting cross-legged on a clean straw mat, gobbling food from a heaping bowl and looking a great deal more cheerful than that morning. On a gesture from Kobe, the guard left.

Tora greeted Akitada with a wide grin, wiped his mouth with his sleeve, and put aside the bowl. He bowed to both of his visitors, then said to Akitada, "Thank you, sir. This is a great deal better, and the food isn't half bad either. But, as I told the superintendent, I need to get busy solving the murder. Have you had any news?"

Tora's meal reminded Akitada that he had not eaten since the night before. No wonder he felt light-headed. He said, "No news at all, I'm afraid. Soga has taken it into his head to leave the city for a while and I was trying to catch up on the work he left behind. I'm on my way home now for my evening rice. After that I'll think about what is to be done next."

"Well, well," said Tora, "I guess you may be the next minister then. And here you've been worried about losing your job."

"Actually, I shall have to present my resignation on the minister's return."

Tora's jaw sagged. Then he exploded. "Why, that dirty scoundrel! That lazy piece of dung! How dare he do that to you when you've been doing all his work for months? He's just another stinking official. Rotten to the core!"

Akitada bit his lip and glanced at Kobe.

But Kobe merely raised an eyebrow. "I'd like my men to be as loyal as yours. Of course, he had better not have the judge hear him say things like that."

"Judge?" asked Tora, blanching a little.

Kobe nodded. "I have requested that your case be heard tomorrow." He turned to Akitada. "Around midday. I hope that's convenient? Can you attend?"

"I will make time. It was very good of you to push Tora's case forward. Who is the judge?"

"Masakane."

"Oh." Akitada knew the man from past court cases he had observed, and Masakane had never liked him. But he nodded. "Masakane is fair."

Tora looked nervously from one to the other. "What will happen? There's no evidence to clear me yet. And they haven't arrested anybody else. What's to keep the judge from sentencing me?"

Akitada said, "It's only a hearing. We will ask to have the trial postponed and you released into my charge. With a little luck I hope to make a good case for further investigation. But you must be completely frank with us about your relationship with the woman."

"You know all there was. I liked her, but there was nothing between us. She didn't want that."

Akitada gave him a hard look. It sounded as though Tora had tried. What had possessed him? Tomoe hardly met his usual requirements.

Kobe remarked, "From what I've gathered, there was some mystery about this woman."

Tora said eagerly, "That's right. And I bet if we figure it out, we'll have her killer. She was different from other street people. Like she didn't belong. She was polite, but she never talked about herself. It took me two months to get her to open up a bit. And she'd never have let me walk her home if she hadn't been scared."

"Perhaps she had committed some crime," Kobe wondered.

Tora adamantly denied the possibility, but Akitada thought of the expensive cosmetics box and the silver. It was quite possible that Tomoe had worked with a gang of thieves—in which case her killer could have been one of her accomplices. He said, "Tora, you must consider the possibility. If she worked with gang members, it explains why she protected them."

"No." Tora shook his head stubbornly. "You don't know her the way I do."

"But you said yourself that she did not tell you everything."

Tora flushed. "You haven't believed me from the start, sir, but I know that she was neither a harlot nor a thief. I know that as well as I know you."

Akitada had a strong conviction that nobody had truly known Tomoe, but he did not say so. He turned to Kobe. "What do you think should be done first?"

"I can have my people check on gangs." Kobe grinned. "Now that you're running things at the ministry, my sending across police documents shouldn't raise any eyebrows."

Akitada thought of the nosy Sakae and hoped that young man was too preoccupied with filling Akitada's shoes to have any time or interest in spying on his now very temporary superior. "Thank you. That would be very helpful. There is also the cosmetics box. If it was stolen, someone may have reported its loss. And if not, perhaps that young police lieutenant Ihara might try to trace it to its maker. It was of particularly fine workmanship and seemed an odd thing for her to have."

Kobe nodded. "I know Ihara. I'll pass along the word."

"Of course, if Tora is released, he can do some work himself. He knows his way about the city and is clever about mixing with all sorts of people. Apart from having been fond of the woman, he will want to clear himself of these ridiculous charges."

Kobe grunted. "Well, I suppose that's all then. Tora's biggest problem will be convincing the judge of his good character. He doesn't have much respect for authority." But he winked at Tora.

As they walked through the prison's gate into the street, Kobe asked, "Did Soga tell you why he left the city?"

"No. I thought it was very strange, even for him."

"Well, perhaps he was afraid you'd think him a coward. He's taking flight to his country estate because there is smallpox in the capital."

"Good heaven! My wife mentioned something of the sort a few days ago. I did not believe it. Is it a serious outbreak?"

"Some cases among the nobles, and a few in the city. It's being kept quiet to avoid panic. One very highly placed person is already getting better. You know as well as I that we have the occasional case. Keep it to yourself. It seems a woman who used to help out at the Soga residence got the disease. When Soga heard she died, he decided to move to the country. He'll look very foolish when it all comes to nothing."

They parted after that, and Akitada turned homeward. He was touched by Kobe's friendship but began to fret again about his situation. Soon the news would be out that he had lost his post and had no hopes for another. Meanwhile, how would he tell his wife? Akitada had never questioned Tamako's loyalty, and she had reminded him of it just this morning. Or rather, last night—so much had happened in the meantime! But his wife was also a mother and the mistress of his household. After some reflection she would see how his loss of influence at court would hurt Yori's future. And the economizing that must follow his loss of income would soon be a daily reminder of his failure. Tamako would come to blame him for their misery.

If he could avoid serious censure from Soga, he might find a clerkship in one of the other ministries or a post as supervisor of one of the bureaus. The thought of shuffling more paperwork depressed him. Another man in his situation would turn to his friends. Akitada had made many in his time, but some were gone and others had cooled toward him. And the ones who were left and in positions of sufficient influence to help him were overwhelmed by favor seekers every day of their busy lives. He could not bear to join the throng of abject men who prostrated themselves, holding humble petitions above their heads, every time the great personage emerged from the inner chambers of his residence.

When he got home, Yori was again practicing with the straw dummy. The figure had lost most of its stuffing and no longer produced those satisfying thwacks but Yori had adjusted his style to the pitiful limp figure that sagged against the fence. He now used his sword to stab viciously at various vital parts, shouting out each target before attacking. "Slit the throat . . . slice the arm . . . slit the peach." This last accompanied by a vicious stab at the dummy's nether regions.

Split the peach? That sounded like some of Tora's gutter language.

"Yori."

The boy swung around, cried, "Father," and then dashed across the courtyard swinging his sword and shouting, "Father's home! Father's home!" He threw himself at his father with such force that Akitada had to take a step back. Picking up his son, he demanded, "Where did you learn such language?"

Yori clutched his neck and giggled. "What language? Did

you visit the market? Did you buy me something? I could use a helmet. When's Tora coming back?"

Akitada gave up on the offensive phrase. Yori spent almost all his free time with Tora and Genba. And he was a boy, after all. It would be different with a girl. So he hugged his son and said, "I hope Tora will be home soon. Maybe tomorrow even. And I have been too busy to go to the market. Perhaps later in the week. Have you studied hard today?"

Yori made a face. "That old Seimei! He's such a fuss-body. He says, 'No, no. You must do that character again. Hold your brush just so. Make the tail of the stroke curve up like the tail of a drake.' Mother always likes what I do."

His father smiled. "Now that you mention it, I believe Seimei gave me the same advice about the tail of the drake when I was your age. And it turned out, he was quite right. I could never have managed to get into the university if my character had not had the tail of a drake."

Yori looked impressed. "Truly?"

"Truly."

Genba trotted toward them from the stable, his round face anxious. He bobbed a perfunctory bow. "Any news, sir?"

At the main house, Seimei and Tamako had come out. Akitada realized that they must all be worried about Tora. Because of Soga he had forgotten to send them a message.

He told Genba, "I'll try to have Tora released into my custody tomorrow. The case looks complicated."

"That's all right then." Genba heaved a sigh of relief and grinned. "Might have known you'd take care of it, sir. Didn't know what to think when your lady told us what happened. Not that she knew very much." He looked at Akitada expectantly.

"Let me eat something first."

Genba bowed. "Please take your time and enjoy your meal."

Akitada set Yori down and took his hand. Together they walked to the main house.

Tamako murmured, "Welcome home. You have been awaited anxiously."

"Thank you. I'm sorry I could not send a message. Tora should be home tomorrow. I will tell you what happened in a little while. At the moment, I'm very hungry. If cook has anything ready, have her bring it, please."

Tamako's eyes widened with concern. She hurried away on soft, stockinged feet, her layered silk robe billowing behind her as it swept across the gleaming wood floor. Akitada admired, not for the first time, his wife's elegant bearing and grace. Tamako was the only child of one of Akitada's professors and had been raised by him after her mother's death. She could easily have become spoiled or self-absorbed, but had instead grown into a calm, intelligent young woman and, he thought, the perfect companion for a man of his temperament. The fact that her father had indulged her by teaching her things normally reserved for men—she read and wrote Chinese, for example, and was well-versed in the five classics—had proved a boon because Akitada could not abide stupidity and enjoyed talking with her about all sorts of things a man normally only discussed with other men. Now he was miserably aware that she deserved much better than a dismissed official who had not achieved middle rank yet and probably never would.

Seimei took Yori from him and promised to bring fresh tea. With a sigh, Akitada went to his study. Someone had folded away his bedding. He untied his court hat and put it away in its box, rubbing his neck where the strings had bitten into his skin. He needed a shave. And a bath. But first food and his report on Tora. And then he would have to tell them of the resignation.

Pushing back the sliding doors to the garden, he walked out onto the veranda. In the small pond, the koi rose to the surface, expecting to be fed. His whole household expected sustenance. Even his own belly demanded to be filled. How would he take care of all of them?

He could apply for a post in one of the provinces, as a secretary in one of the provincial administrations close to the capital. Taking orders from someone of his own class could not be worse than dealing with Soga's insults. And it would spare him the stares of his colleagues here. But Tamako would be very unhappy. She had not had an easy time during the bitter winter of Akitada's northern assignment, nearly losing the child she carried while they lived in fear for their lives. Here, with her own household, she had been contented. She enjoyed the respect of friends and family, and had the company of Akitada's married sisters and of her female friends. He sighed.

Seimei brought the tea. He handed Akitada a small cup of steaming greenish liquid. "It's a special blend. I added some orange zest and a little honey and a few other good things to restore your spirit and soothe your empty belly."

Akitada was touched. Seimei, like the others, had never shown him anything less than love and support. He tasted. "Excellent." He emptied the cup. "Yes. I feel better already."

Seimei, glowing with pleasure, poured again.

And the food, brought in by his wife and her maid, was even more welcome. Akitada ate like a starved man, hardly caring what they handed him. They watched him in awe. When he finally pushed the last empty bowl away with a sigh, Tamako poured some warm wine.

He looked at them all. "Thank you for being so patient. Seimei, please call Genba now."

When everyone had gathered, Akitada told them about Tomoe's murder and the case against Tora. Their faces lengthened.

Tamako said loyally, "Tora would never hurt a woman, especially not a blind one. He likes to pretend he can solve crimes like you and was simply trying to discover who was terrorizing the poor woman."

Genba nodded. "It's just like Tora to want to help someone like that."

"There is to be a hearing tomorrow," Akitada told them. "I hope to get him released into my custody until the trial. I'm afraid he must try to clear himself of the charge because I'll be tied up at the ministry. Soga has decided to move to the country for a while and left me in charge."

Seimei and Genba smiled and nodded as if this were the most natural thing in the world, but Tamako's eyes narrowed. "I don't trust that man," she said. "He's hatching some plot again. Be careful. He wants to get rid of you."

Here it was. Akitada sighed. "There was no need for any plot." He looked from one face to another, wondering what they would think of him. "I've offered him my resignation as soon as he returns."

Nobody spoke. Genba looked puzzled, his large, kindly face contorting as he tried to understand. Seimei's mouth was slack with surprise.

But Tamako nodded and said, "Good. I'm glad."

"Yes, indeed." Seimei now found his voice. "It's a pity that the minister has never given you the encouragement you deserve, sir. Master Kung warned us that without his superior's support an official will be unable to govern."

Genba, whose mind always worked along simple lines, asked, "But why did you offer, sir?"

"The minister expressed his dissatisfaction with me, Genba. It seemed proper to resign."

"And what will you do next?" Genba persisted, brushing aside the minister's dissatisfaction like a pesky gnat. "His Majesty will not announce any more appointments until the first month of next year."

"For the time being I'm still at the ministry and very busy. Later I shall have to look for another post somewhere."

Seimei gave Genba a look and said, "As soon as people hear what has happened, you will be overwhelmed with offers, sir. You can take your pick then." Genba brightened and nodded, and Tamako summed up cheerfully, "It will all work out for the best."

When Akitada was alone with his wife, he took her hand and said, "Thank you, Tamako. I know how you must worry about the future."

"Do you?" She pulled her hand from his and looked at him searchingly. "If you think so little of me, I shall be ashamed to be your wife. You used to honor me with your confidence, but lately you have distanced yourself. I wish you would tell me what I have done to deserve it."

He was dismayed. "You misunderstand. You have never done anything but what is right."

She shook her head. "You've been edgy for many months now. I have watched you push your favorite foods away with little appetite, and you've left my bed to pace on the veranda or in the corridor. And many nights you stayed away, while I waited and watched your light burn all night in your study. But you have not spoken to me about what troubled you. If I have lost your confidence, then the fault must be mine."

He said weakly, "There seemed no point in worrying you." The truth was that he had lost confidence in himself and had been too ashamed to tell her for fear of disillusioning her. But he could not say it and instead felt the hot blood rise to his face. He knew his cursed weakness only too well and had no right to beg for her sympathy. Unlike other, better men, he could not put aside his self-doubts long enough to take decisive action in times of trouble, or to find contentment in his hard-won successes. Sharing this secret would make her regard him with disgust.

She said reproachfully, "My husband's trust is never a trouble."

But the Great Sage counseled that a man had best keep his innermost thoughts to himself or risk destroying the harmony of his family. Akitada said firmly, "Never mind. I've just been overworked and tired lately. You mustn't be foolish and take my moods personally."

Tamako, who had reached out to touch her husband's hand with hers, withdrew it again. "Forgive my foolishness," she said, tonelessly. "I shall have the maid spread your bedding and wish you a good rest then." She made him a formal bow and left, closing the door softly behind her.

Akitada looked at that door for a long time, wondering why he always managed to say the wrong thing.

CHAPTER SEVEN

OLD MEN

Seimei brought Akitada his morning rice the next day. It was still dark, but for once Akitada was instantly awake and thinking about the chores ahead. He got up and sat behind his desk, watching impatiently as Seimei knelt to place the bowl of gruel just so and then poured a cup of tea. The old man's hands shook a little, and Akitada noticed how loose the skin had grown around the frail and knobby bones—as if it belonged to a much bigger person. Never a large man, Seimei had shrunk imperceptibly but shockingly. His face had lost flesh to the point that Akitada could see the hollows and ridges of the skull beneath. He was suddenly afraid.

"Are you feeling quite well these days?" he asked.

Seimei jerked and spilled a few drops of tea. He looked at Akitada for a moment, then averted his eyes. "So sorry," he muttered, dabbing at the spill with his sleeve. "Careless of me. I am very well, sir. Nothing at all the matter. You know I drink my strengthening tonic every day. No, no, I feel entirely well. And quite energetic." He rose from his kneeling position with a quickness that must have caused pain in his arthritic joints and busied himself with Akitada's bedding, as if to prove the point.

Akitada bit his lip. Seimei was much too proud to admit to infirmities. "I am very glad to hear it," he said, between sips of his gruel. "I really don't know what we would do without you. I was going to suggest that you take special care of yourself."

Seimei paused in his folding of quilts. "Thank you, sir," he said, his eyes a little moist. "It is good to be needed at my age. I would not like to be useless, though they say it is enough to do the best you can and await the will of heaven."

"That will not be for a long time, I hope," Akitada said briskly. "You've raised me and now you're raising my son. I am deeply grateful, Seimei." He saw with dismay a tear spilling down Seimei's cheek. The old man turned, dashing it away with a shaking hand. He finished folding the bedclothes and putting them away in their trunk. Only then did he return to the desk.

"Yori is a fine boy," he said, looking at Akitada earnestly, "just as you were. He will go far some day, perhaps even as far as his father. I think you have been needlessly troubled about the future and are still so even now. If you will only look up, sir, there are no limits."

Akitada was astounded. It struck him, for the first time, that there were few secrets between them. Child and man, Akitada had been guided and loved by Seimei. They knew each other's flaws and were often irritated by them, but they were bound together by bonds of familiarity and loyalty as strong as the bonds of blood. To a lesser degree that was true also of Tora and Genba. Yori was a part of this extended family, and soon other children and new servants would join his household. They all belonged to each other. He had been wrong to complain of his responsibilities. The others lived within the same bonds and seemed happy and contented.

"You are wise as usual, Seimei," he said, pushing aside his bowl and getting up to put his hand on the old man's shoulder.

How thin and bony it had grown, and how bent his back. "It is said: The world is what we wish it to be."

Seimei loved quoting proverbs almost as much as the sayings of Master Kung, and he smiled and nodded. "That is so, sir. Did you drink your tea? Why not take it out on the veranda while I brush out your robe? It will be a beautiful morning."

Akitada obediently picked up the cup and walked outside. In spite of his exhaustion the night before, he had bathed and shaved before falling into a deep sleep. Perhaps that accounted for his newfound faith in himself.

It was not morning yet. The stars still blinked and there was a new moon. It would be another clear, hot day when the sun rose, but for the moment some of the freshness of yesterday's rain still lingered and sweet scents drifted from the dark shrubs of the garden. He sipped his tea and found that Seimei had remembered and made the orange-and-honey-flavored drink again. He was a little ashamed that he had never tried to please Seimei, or even thought about him much.

A splashing in the pond reminded him of the hungry fish and he went back to get the remnants of his rice gruel for them. The light from his study showed their shapes only vaguely as they rose from the blackness of the water to snap up a morsel and then disappear to make room for another. Dim shadows of grey and silver, brown and orange moved with only an occasional brilliant glint of light on a fin in the black depths of the pond. He was seeing and yet not seeing them.

Somehow, this reminded Akitada of Tomoe. Had her blindness made her life one of unrelieved darkness, or had she found sparks of brightness in it, perhaps too brief to grasp? She had been scarred by smallpox. Probably the disease had robbed her of her sight, as it did with many it spared from death. Her life and death seemed as dark to him as the pond, but both must have been filled with the shapes of people.

Tora vehemently opposed the notion that Tomoe had sold

herself like a common streetwalker. As proof he had cited the fact that she had been invited to the home of one of the good families. Akitada would give much to know the name of that family.

On the other hand, two members of her own class, people who were in daily contact with her, the beggar in the market and the stonemason's wife, had called her a harlot. Whom to believe? Had she been involved in prostitution and a ring of thieves and gangsters? He could not make that image blend with his own memory of the woman, of her lute playing and her austere lifestyle.

Inside Seimei appeared, carrying Akitada's best robe and trousers carefully folded over his arm. Akitada said, "Not my court robe, Seimei. It's just an ordinary day in the office."

Seimei smiled. "You want to make a good impression on the judge, don't you? Besides, you have taken the place of a minister and must not shame such an exalted office."

Soga dressed far more extravagantly than Akitada, but to Akitada's mind such things had nothing to do with his performance in the office. On the other hand, he really did not want to prejudice Tora's case, so he submitted without further argument.

◆

He arrived at the ministry behind Nakatoshi, who looked startled to see Akitada so early and in such formal dress.

"I was just opening up, sir," he said apologetically. "I haven't had a chance to look over the work for today."

Akitada smiled at him. "It doesn't matter. We'll do it together." Still filled with the energy of the previous day, he even looked forward to routine paperwork, but his real interest was in the petitions. One or two promised some interesting legal work. He asked Nakatoshi if any progress had been made on the Chikamura claim.

"Not yet, sir. There might be something later today. Oh, I almost forgot. After you left yesterday, someone stopped by and left a note for you."

Akitada, thinking of Tora's upcoming hearing, hurried into the office and snatched the note from the desk. It was on standard government paper, folded many times very neatly, but not sealed. There was no superscription. It was strange that it should have been delivered in person. Akitada registered this strange combination of fussiness and lack of formality as he unfolded it.

He did not recognize the spidery hand, but the writing style was characteristic of clerks in government service. Again there was no address or signature, lending an aura of secretiveness to the missive, almost as if sender and recipient were engaged in some illegal transaction.

"In regards to the matter about which you enquired: It has come to mind that the properties in question in the province mentioned are assigned to its current governor. They were indeed at one time associated with the family—the confusion with shrine lands no doubt arising from the name itself. My deepest apologies for not having been of service when required."

Without signature, identification mark, or personal seal, the message was incomprehensible. Akitada called Nakatoshi. "Are you certain this was meant for me?" he asked, holding up the note.

"The gentleman said so, sir. He was a very elderly person."

"Strange. There is no signature. Might it be for the minister?"

"Oh, no. He gave your name, sir. I think he works in one of the bureaus. He looked a little familiar, but I can't place him. A small man in his late sixties. I assumed you had had some business with him."

Akitada shook his head. "I don't recall." But he reread the note, and this time there was something vaguely familiar about it. Name, property, land, province. Shrine lands? Of course. The Utsunomiya property. *Miya* referred to shrine. This was about

Haseo's case. That business now seemed so far away that he had completely forgotten it. Well, Haseo must certainly wait again while he sorted out Tora's problem. Akitada said, "Yes. I remember now. It must have been Kunyoshi. The archivist from Popular Affairs." He glanced at the pile of waiting paperwork. "Please send him a note—no, wait!" Kunyoshi, who was a senior archivist, had taken the trouble to come in person. He could not simply brush him off. Soga's arrogance must be rubbing off on him already. He sighed. "I'm going over to thank him for his trouble. It shouldn't take long."

As he strode quickly along the wide street past the Court of Abundant Pleasures and the Halls of State, the first light appeared where the eastern mountains met the starry sky. It was already getting warm, and his formal silks hampered his movements and made him perspire. The brief respite of yesterday's cooling rain had not lasted, and the increased humidity added to the unhealthy, sticky feeling. Akitada briefly wondered about the smallpox rumors and hoped that by now fears were subsiding. Of course, that would bring Soga back all the more quickly.

The first wave of senior officials was already arriving for duty. They, at least, had not abandoned the capital yet. Akitada passed through the gate of the Ministry of Popular Affairs, hoping that Kunyoshi was in already. He was. Akitada found him bustling about with stacks of documents, muttering under his breath. Nobody else seemed about. Nakatoshi had referred to the archivist as very elderly, and Akitada, who had thought little about it in the past, now realized that Kunyoshi must be nearly Seimei's age, though he certainly moved more easily. He called out, "Good morning." Kunyoshi did not respond but went on with his chore and his muttering. Akitada caught the words, " . . . told him to put these away . . . I'm sure of it . . ."

It was only when Kunyoshi was returning that he noticed Akitada. His face lit up. "Ah, it's you sir. I did not hear you. Did you get my note? I left it with that nice young clerk of yours."

Akitada bowed. "Yes, I came to thank you." He said it loudly, knowing that the old man was somewhat deaf.

Kunyoshi's eyes, disconcertingly, watched his lips. Then he smiled. "No need. Glad to do it. Hope the information helps."

"Well, I did have one or two questions. You indicated, I think, that some property which used to belong to the Utsunomiya family is now under the control of the incumbent governor of Izumo. A Fujiwara, I think?" It was a safe guess. Most men in position of authority were Fujiwaras. Theirs was a large clan with many branches, and the Fujiwara chancellors, as well as the Fujiwara empresses, saw to it that they had supporters in all the key positions.

"Oh, yes. Fujiwara Tamenari. Of course, he does not administer the land himself. Customarily the income from the rice harvest and other products is divided evenly between the cultivator and the government. I assume that is the case in this instance."

"When did the property become public land?"

Kunyoshi frowned and scratched his head. "Now, where did I put my notes?" He shuffled among the papers on a shelf, muttered, went to another shelf, then to his desk, and ended up standing still, with both hands rubbing his skull as if that would stir his memory.

"It does not have to be a precise date," said Akitada—though that would certainly have helped. "Can you recall anything? Was it about five years ago?"

"What?"

Akitada repeated his question.

Kunyoshi shook his head. "I would not want to say when I cannot recall. It may come to me later." He looked depressed.

Izumo Province, thought Akitada. It was too far away, on the Japan Sea, but a rich province and an important one for its ancient shrine to the gods. "Was it a large estate?"

"Oh, dear me, yes. A very rich plum for the nation. And for

the governor, who is wealthy enough himself. I must say, under the circumstances he should pay the taxes on the questionable acres. I suggested as much."

Akitada felt a new respect for Kunyoshi. Standing up to a Fujiwara must have taken considerable courage. "I hope," he said with a smile, "you have not made any enemies."

"Hah! At my age? What do I have to lose?" Kunyoshi opened his mouth and grinned so widely that Akitada could see almost every one of the few remaining yellow teeth. Like horses, men in their old age seemed to grow long in tooth, nose, and ear.

Akitada gestured at the many shelves full of documents. "The nation would lose an indispensable servant," he said with a smile.

Kunyoshi turned shy. He looked down at his gnarled fingers, rubbing them nervously. "Once perhaps," he said sadly, "but not anymore. I don't hear well and I've become forgetful. Who wants an archivist who forgets things? It's time I left."

Akitada had never liked working in the law archives of the Ministry of Justice. It was dreary, dull work that involved much climbing up and down to reach tall shelves and a great amount of dust. Surely this was very hard on an old man. "Won't you like having time for your family?" he asked.

"I have no family. It would not have been fair to them. You see, this . . ." he gestured to the shelves and documents, "was all I wanted. Just to work in my humble way at something I could do well." He added wistfully, "But not anymore. Not anymore."

Akitada was dumfounded. Such a choice amounted to a re-nunciation of the world just as much as if he had chosen to be-come a monk. The sages, who knew a great deal more than the Buddhist crowd, taught that it was a man's duty to take a wife and have children. That rule even took precedence over serving one's sovereign and superiors faithfully. Where would the world be without the family structure? It was the very foundation of life. Knowing that he had a family made it desirable for a man to work and serve his country. And now this old man, having outlived his parents and siblings, had no place to call home. Akitada said lamely, "I see. I'm very sorry. What will you do?"

Kunyoshi looked through the open doors toward the northern mountains. They were bathed in the golden light of the rising sun, and the distant roofs and pagodas of the great monasteries of Mount Hiei shimmered among the trees. "My life is short. I suppose I shall become a monk," he said without enthusiasm and smiled a little sadly. "They keep records in monasteries."

◆

Akitada returned to his own paperwork a much chastened man and persisted until Nakatoshi told him it was time to leave for Tora's hearing.

When Akitada passed through the front of the building, dozens of men and women stopped their quiet conversations and turned to look at him hopefully. "There he is," someone in the back hissed loudly, and instantly all of them knelt and touched their heads to the floor. Akitada stopped in surprise. Then he saw a few petitions being raised above the bowed heads and realized that word had spread. His receiving the rejected petitioners had encouraged others to try their luck.

He told them, "Thank you all for coming and waiting patiently, but today I must attend a court hearing and won't be back until late. Perhaps tomorrow will be a better day."

They sat up. There was a small babble of conversation until one man—yes, it was old Chikamura, back to find out when he could take possession of his home again—bowed and thanked him. The rest joined in a quaint chorus of humble mutterings. Akitada's heart warmed. Serving his emperor and his fellow subjects was the finest work a man could do.

Police headquarters bustled with activity. The red-coated figures of policemen with their odd black hats and their bows and arrows were everywhere. Akitada climbed the steps to the Metropolitan Court hall in the wake of a nun in a white cotton robe and veil. He thought that she must be young by the nimble way she skipped up and felt regret that such a young woman should have resigned herself to the emptiness of a religious life. To his mind, such a step was to be taken only in old age or after the loss of a husband. At the doors to the hall he caught up with her and thought he detected a whiff of perfume. No doubt it was only incense.

Inside, they were separated by the red-coated policemen, who took Akitada's name and directed him to the front of the courtroom. The nun joined the audience.

Hearings were held continuously. Each time a new case was called, the audience would shift and change, as those who left made room for newcomers. Judge Masakane was concluding a case. The prisoner apparently was a thief, and a number of witnesses who had appeared against him were on their way out. New witnesses assumed their places. Akitada recognized Lieutenant Ihara beside the stonemason and his wife, all waiting to be called to testify against Tora. He found a place near them.

Masakane had been a judge in the Metropolitan Court for as long as Akitada could remember. All judges were adjuncts to the imperial police, passing sentences based on the evidence submitted by police investigators on culprits arrested by police constables. More often than not, those found guilty ended up in one of the two prisons maintained by the police. The system depended on all cogs in the process operating in a fair and unbiased manner. But there was considerable oversight and, by and large, it worked better and far more efficiently than the old system under the Ministry of Justice.

Much of Akitada's early trouble with Soga had stemmed from his fascination with police work and criminal trials. He used to spend too much time observing in the courtroom and, occasionally, meddling in an investigation. Judge Masakane certainly knew him by sight and suspected him of being a spy for the ministry. That he did Akitada an injustice—Akitada admired Masakane's fairness and acumen—did not matter in this instance.

As the thief, sentenced to one hundred lashes, was dragged from the hall, a hum of anticipation stirred through the crowd. They knew the next case involved a vicious murder. Masakane, seated in the center of the large dais with scribes on either side of him to record the proceedings and the verdict, glanced up and saw Akitada. He scowled, raised his baton and brought it down sharply on the wooden boards.

"Bring in the next defendant."

The judge resembled a small, ill-tempered turtle in his old age. His fine robe of heavy green silk with its flaring shoulders looked like a shell from which a shrunken head and two small hands emerged and motioned without disturbing its rigid shape. Masakane's round skull, nearly bald now, was pale and spotted, and a beaky nose came down over thin lips and a receding chin. But his eyes were still bright and black as they watched Tora who, once again in chains, was led in between two guards and made to kneel and prostrate himself before the judge. The corners of Masakane's mouth turned down in disapproval.

"So you are the person accused of murdering a blind woman. State your name!" he barked.

Tora began to recite his name, place of residence, and service to the Sugawaras. Masakane's eyes flickered toward Akitada. "Name only! Pay attention, imbecile," he snapped. Instantly, one of the guards brought his leather whip down across Tora's buttocks.

Akitada clenched his hands. The judge had recognized him. Since he resented his presence, he would make Tora pay. It was not fair, but neither Tora nor Akitada had any recourse. Akitada certainly could not reprove a judge in his own court. He was thinking about leaving, when he felt a hand on his arm.

Kobe gave him a tight smile and said in a low voice, "Ignore his honor. He must have his little show of temper before he can proceed. Seems to feel it instills proper respect in the defendant and the crowd."

Akitada frowned. "I don't remember that. He was always very sure of himself, and there was little or no flogging in his courtroom. Why the change?"

"He thinks people take advantage of him because of his age. Rumors that he's getting too old for the job have made him bitter."

"That is bad for Tora."

"Oh, don't worry. Masakane will be fair—or at least fairer and more predictable than the others. He follows the law to the letter."

Masakane, who was listening to the reading of the charges, cast an irritated glance in their direction, recognized Kobe, and bowed. He rapped his baton twice, making the scribe break off in mid-sentence, and called out, "Make room there in front for the superintendent. And . . . er . . . for his companion also."

A shuffling and rearranging ensued as they made their way to the front and bowed to Masakane.

"Allow me to introduce my friend, Your Honor," Kobe said to Masakane. "Lord Sugawara is the defendant's master and came to speak on his behalf."

Masakane grunted, "Is that so?" and bowed slightly to Akitada.

Up close, the judge looked more human, though Akitada could not be certain if he was grimacing or smiling. Akitada said, "It is always gratifying to see justice dispensed by a superior judge, but it is true that I have a personal reason for being here today."

"Hmmph," said the judge. "Well, let's not waste any more time on pleasantries. Get on with reading the charges."

As Akitada listened, he glanced across the crowd and noticed the nun again. She was trying to get closer, perhaps to hear better, or to see the defendant. It was clear that her interest in the proceedings went beyond that of the rest of the crowd. Akitada wondered who she was. He decided to keep an eye on her, and perhaps speak to her after the hearing.

When the scribe had finished, Judge Masakane said, "Very well. Let's have the police report."

Lieutenant Ihara stepped forward, bowed, and recited the circumstances of Tora's arrest and the condition of Tomoe's body and of her room. In the crowd, the nun pushed back her veil a little and craned her head. She had a pale, very handsome face dominated by a pair of extraordinary eyes.

The coroner came forward next and spoke of the multiple stab wounds and of the slashed palms of the victim, suggesting that she had attempted to defend herself against her assailant. He also testified that the body had shown evidence of recent sexual intercourse. The nun put her face into her hands.

Even Masakane looked shocked at the coroner's report. He wanted to know if the dead woman had been raped, but the coroner could not confirm this. The crowd muttered angrily— or perhaps salaciously.

Tora was kneeling, hunched into himself, but Akitada saw that his fists were clenched on his knees until the knuckles showed white against the brown skin.

Masakane next called the witnesses. The testimony of the stonemason and his wife was as Akitada had expected. The crucial witness was, of course, the wife. She wore a clean robe today and her hair was twisted neatly in back and tied with a white ribbon. She presented the image of a respectable housewife and mother. When it was her turn, she knelt and prostrated herself, reciting, "This insignificant person is called Yuzuki, wife of the stonemason Shigehiro, of the eighth ward."

Masakane regarded her benevolently. "You know that you

must speak the truth or suffer a beating," he warned. "Now, take a look at the defendant. Have you seen him before?"

She sat up on her heels and eyed Tora. "Yes, Your Honor. He was the lover of the dead woman Tomoe, the one who killed her."

"Ah. Now we're getting somewhere. You saw him kill her?"

She giggled nervously. "Well," she said, "I've seen him when he went to her, and then I saw him later with the bloody knife in his hand, standing over her lifeless body."

The judge frowned. "And between the time that you saw him arrive and the time you saw him standing over her dead body, what happened?"

She flushed. "Why, I'm not sure. I've got my household to look after and my children to tend. We're poor and work hard. I can't watch all the time. And I couldn't know he was going to do her in, could I?"

"No, of course not." Masakane pursed his lips. "So you say you had no reason to suspect him. Tell me, had he visited the woman Tomoe before?"

"Yes. At least three times. She was the type."

"Ah. What type is that?" asked the judge, smiling thinly.

"Why, the kind of slut who brings men home and lies with them."

There was a gasp of protest from the nun, but when people turned to look at her, she ducked her head and pulled the veil across her face.

"You say she was a prostitute?" Masakane liked his testimony clear.

The stonemason's wife fidgeted. "Well, not that exactly. Not regular. She was too ugly for that."

Tora lost his temper. "You're a filthy liar, woman," he roared, "and I shall make you eat your words."

"Silence!" shouted Masakane, slapping down his baton. This time the whip caught Tora across the back. He gritted his teeth against the pain and resumed his rigid self-control.

When Masakane turned back to the woman, he studied her for a moment, pushing his thin lips in and out. Then he asked, "On the night of the murder, where were you when you saw the defendant arrive?"

She looked up quickly and then back down. "I was in the yard," she said in a rush, "taking in laundry. It was already dark and he didn't see me. He knocked on her door, and she let him in."

Tora made a derisive noise and caught another stroke of the whip. Masakane eyed him sourly. "Well, since you cannot keep your mouth shut, did you or did you not enter the dead woman's room from the yard that night?"

Tora said, "I did, but Tomoe did not let me in. The door was open. Tomoe was already dead." He turned and pointed a finger at the stonemason's wife. "That one's a liar. I don't believe she was in the yard. I think she and her coward of a husband were hiding from the real killer. Or maybe they did it themselves."

The woman burst into angry denial at this, the crowd muttered, and Tora got whipped again. But this time Masakane glowered at Tora's guard. "How dare you use your whip when the prisoner merely answered my question!" The guard knelt and muttered an apology.

Masakane asked Tora, "Did you kill the woman Tomoe or not?"

Tora looked him squarely in the eyes. "I did not, Your Honor."

Masakane turned to Akitada, "Since you are his master, do you believe him?"

Akitada was a bit startled but managed to say, "Of course. I have known Tora for many years. He is a courageous fighter but incapable of killing a helpless blind woman in such a cowardly fashion. On the contrary, Tora was trying to protect her."

Masakane raised his brows. "Protect her? From whom?"

"She had told him she feared for her life because she had

overheard plans of a crime. He went to see her that night to attempt once again to get her to tell him the details of the plan and the names of the criminals."

"Hmmph." Masakane stared at Akitada, then at Tora, who stared back at the judge defiantly. Akitada held his breath.

Masakane heaved a sigh. "Lieutenant Ihara?"

Ihara stepped forward.

"It seems that the case is far from clear. Do I understand that you are still investigating it?"

"Yes, Your Honor."

"Very well. In that case, I shall remand the defendant into his master's custody until you have completed your investigation." The judge turned to Akitada. "Perhaps you can be of assistance? I am told you take an interest in crime."

Akitada bowed. "Yes. Thank you, Your Honor."

"You understand, of course, that you are responsible for the defendant's behavior during this time and that you will produce him for trial if that becomes necessary?"

"I do."

It was over. Akitada barely waited to see the chains taken off Tora. He turned to Kobe. "There's a nun in the audience who seems to take a strong interest in the case. I want to have a word with her before she leaves."

Kobe nodded. "I saw her, too. Go on! I'll look after Tora."

But when Akitada searched the crowd for the nun, she was gone. He pushed past people and started running. Outside in the courtyard he saw only the usual redcoats and a few people arriving for the next case. No sign of a nun anywhere. He was about to curse himself for not having kept a better eye on her, when he caught a bit of white disappearing beyond the gate, and rushed after it.

Too late he realized that he had not even thanked Kobe.

CHAPTER EIGHT

THE NUN

*A*t first Akitada had no difficulty following the slender figure in white. She moved at a quick but steady pace, walking first toward the west and then turning south. In the heat of the afternoon there were few other people about, and she evidently knew her way.

This area, like Akitada's own quarter on the opposite side of the city, had been intended for public offices and the homes of court officials. Building plots were generous and the streets broad. Numerous canals carried fresh water from the river and fed into the many gardens of the area. Behind high bamboo fences or mud walls, earlier generations had laid out fanciful landscapes with bubbling streams and small lakes and built their homes among them. But the early hopes of the city planners had never been fulfilled in the western city. The decline was less noticeable in this quarter, close to the Greater Palace enclosure, but even here Akitada saw empty spaces, open fields, and groves of tangled brush and trees where villas or large compounds once had stood. But many homes, substantial and in good repair, remained and were occupied by officials or wealthy country gentry who kept a residence in the capital.

Akitada cast a knowledgeable eye around. Wherever she was going, it was not to a temple or nunnery. There were none here. She must be visiting one of the families who had held on to their family plots and maintained their homes with sufficient funds to guard against the bands of thieves who roamed the streets at night.

When she turned a corner, he increased his speed. He did not want to frighten her, but looked for a chance to catch up or see where she lived.

She was halfway up the street, walking along a plain white-washed wall without gates. On the other side of the street, three young louts lounged against a broken fence, but straightened up with interest when they saw the nun. Akitada did not like the way they looked at her, and neither did she apparently, for she walked more quickly. The three conferred briefly, then crossed the street to cut her off.

Upper-class residential quarters were generally quiet and peaceful in this part of town. Akitada's father-in-law had lived here, and Tamako still owned the land and maintained a garden where her childhood home had stood. But lately, the good people lived within walled compounds with massive, barred gates, and women emerged only in the company of male servants. Perhaps an elderly nun could have passed without attracting the attention of three hoodlums, but this one was a young and attractive woman, and the street was empty. She was about a hundred yards ahead of Akitada, who cursed his voluminous white silk trousers and the stiff, heavy robe, clothes that were not only hot but cumbersome.

Up ahead, the hoodlums stopped the nun, one barring her way and the other two closing in from behind. She backed against the earthen wall and seemed to make entreaties, which they greeted with bursts of laughter. When they began to man-handle her, Akitada started to run, shouting, "Leave her alone!"

He fell almost instantly over the loose folds of his trousers. Scrambling up, he fully expected to see the bullies take to their heels. Not only was he an awkward witness—they probably in-tended to rape their victim—but his formal court robe and hat marked him as an imperial official of rank and should have put fear into their cowardly hearts.

But nothing of the sort happened. They turned their heads to look at him and burst into laughter. Furious, Akitada gath-ered up the legs of his trousers before continuing. They laughed even harder at this and, after a brief exchange, two of them started toward Akitada. The third stayed with the nun.

Akitada stopped. The two rascals sauntering toward him with grins on their faces were not about to make a humble apology. They looked as if they expected to have some fun with this official in his stiff robe, ballooning trousers, and elaborate headgear. Akitada was in excellent condition and trained in wrestling, but a confrontation with two robbers was unwise at this juncture. He was unarmed and hampered by his ridiculous clothing. And, besides being a nuisance in a fight, his robe had cost him many months of salary and he was hardly in a position to sacrifice it to a couple of hoodlums at this time in his career. He considered slipping off the outer robe, but when he began to undo his sash, the two changed their deliberate saunter to a fast walk. There was no time.

Beyond them, their companion was now struggling with the nun. Akitada scanned the ground for something he could use for a weapon. There was nothing. Hereabout, the streets were kept clean. He shouted again for help, this time for con-stables, but all remained silent. Then the nun screamed, and Akitada resigned himself to a fight and crouched.

The two thugs stopped a few feet away, looked him over, and laughed some more. The taller one, who was missing his front teeth and whose nose had been broken a few times, sneered, "Look at that. The puffed-up little toad wants to fight."

"He, he, he," snickered his companion.

The nun screamed again. Akitada kept his eyes on the face of the big ruffian. "All three of you will be in trouble, if you don't stop your friend this instant," he announced through gritted teeth.

"What kind of trouble?" asked the big fellow, raising his brows. "You'll make us wear those big trousers of yours, maybe? Or tickle us with the ribbon on that silly hat?"

"He, he, he, he," sniggered his companion, flexing beefy hands. Apparently he lacked the gift of witticisms. Possibly— with that vacant look in his small eyes—he lacked any wit at all. But Akitada did him an injustice, because he suddenly asked in a high voice, "He looks like a puffball. You wanna play ball with him, Jiro?" They laughed.

"What business do you have, bothering your betters?" Akitada demanded, casting a hopeful glance down the street behind him. It remained empty, but he now saw that it led to a bridge over one of the canals. He decided to make a quick retreat that way.

While his would-be tormentors were still laughing at his question, he managed to cover half the distance before the big man shouted, "Hey, stop!"

Naturally, Akitada ignored him and kept backing away as fast as he could while stumbling over his trousers. They broke into a run and caught up with him at the bridge. He sidestepped the smaller and quicker of the two, who pelted full speed onto the center of the bridge, where he came to a halt.

The other man slowed in time, narrowing his eyes speculatively. There were no handy sticks or rocks lying about, but a cedar seedling grew just at the edge of the canal. Akitada reached down and pulled it up. The big man snorted with derision and jumped forward, reaching for Akitada's left arm. Akitada twisted away and shoved the bristly cedar plant straight into the other man's eyes. The bully screamed and staggered onto the bridge, holding his face. Here he collided with his companion, who had collected his few wits and was rushing to his assistance. Akitada made quick work of tipping both into the canal below by kicking their feet out from under them.

He did not wait to see if they could swim but gathered his trousers and ran up the street. The third man had the nun on the ground. Akitada flung himself on his back. The thug tried to throw him off.

"Run," Akitada cried to the nun, digging his fingers into the man's throat. She lay sprawled on the ground in a tangle of robes and silken undergowns, slender legs bare except for her white socks, long black hair tumbling from under her veil, and eyes huge with terror. She scrambled to her feet, gathered up her skirts, and took off up the street.

He saw no more, for he was whipped around and his back and head made violent and painful contact with the wall behind. The nun's assailant was choking, but he knew a few things about street fighting. With a grunt of pain, Akitada let go and slipped off the man's back.

The situation had deteriorated, for if the other two had climbed out of the canal, he was faced with three angry hoodlums who would hardly settle for robbing him of his fine outfit and the amusement of watching him run off in naked humiliation. In fact, the brute who had attacked the nun was so outraged at the interruption of the rape that he came at Akitada with fists flying. Akitada ducked, but not fast enough. His eye took the full impact of the fist. He sat down abruptly on the ground.

Lights flashed wildly inside his head. He knew he must move, must take some action, but he could do no more than raise his arms to protect his head. He fully expected a vicious beating, but instead his ears registered shouts and receding footsteps. Cautiously he lowered his arms, pushed his lopsided hat out of his face, and saw with his good eye that his assailant was running toward the bridge, where his wet companions were making frantic gestures for him to hurry. Slowly and painfully, Akitada turned his head the other way.

A very odd-looking old man with a long staff was coming down the street.

Akitada was too surprised to get up. The man was covered from head to toe in a large, extraordinary garment of many colors and patterns vaguely reminiscent of the patchwork stoles worn by Buddhist clergy, and his staff seemed to have a Buddha figure at its top. He was not a monk, because he had luxurious white hair and a full beard.

The white-beard stopped in front of him, and uttered a hoarse, "Ah!" Bending forward a little, he studied Akitada with the detached interest of a small boy who has found a strange lizard or beetle. Akitada bowed from his sitting position. The old man bowed back.

"Thank you for coming to my aid, Uncle," said Akitada, using the polite term for an elderly person of the lower classes. He thought the old fellow must be one of the poor eccentrics who lived on a few coins or a bowl of food donated by the servants of the wealthy. He was probably senile, but such venerable age demanded courtesy, regardless of condition. And he was grateful that he had come tottering along when he did.

"You are welcome," said the old man gravely.

Akitada got to his feet. He was puzzled why the thugs had run, and looked around for a constable or perhaps a soldier. But the street was empty. Various aches and pains made themselves felt. He arched his back, decided that it was only bruised, and found that a sleeve was torn from his robe. He brushed at the dirt on his skirts and inspected the tears and stains in his white trousers ruefully. He hoped his clothes could be mended but had his doubts. Still, it might have ended worse. Now that the excitement was over, he began to feel angry.

"You should do something about that eye," said the old man, bending closer and peering at him critically.

The eye had swollen shut and throbbed unpleasantly, but Akitada's good eye revealed that the old man's eccentric garment, though dirty and a bit ragged, was a patchwork of fine silks and brocades and that his staff was beautifully carved and lacquered. Wondering, Akitada asked, "Did you see what happened?"

"I see most things."

"Then you saw the nun and the three men who attacked us?"

The old face creased in thought. "Perhaps. There are many nuns about. Also robbers and thieves. Were they robbers?"

"Yes." Akitada decided that the old-timer probably could not see very well. "Do you often pass this way, Uncle?" he asked.

"I go wherever I please. Why do you ask?"

"The nun screamed for help, and I shouted also. Nobody came to our aid, even though this is a respectable and quiet neighborhood. There must have been people behind these walls who heard us. I wondered why no one came."

"You think it's quiet here, do you?" asked the old man and looked fixedly at the wall behind Akitada. "Are you looking for the quiet life? You won't find it here, young man. No, not at all. The contrary, in fact."

Akitada turned and looked at the wall also. It was an ordinary whitewashed mud wall, over six feet in height and topped with slanting tiles to let the rain wash off. Many of the noble residences in the capital had such walls. His own did, though it was not in such good repair. That fact and the length of the wall and probable size of the property beyond meant that the owner was a rich man. Surely he had many servants, some of whom should have been within hearing distance and rushed to their aid. But not a sound came from the other side of the wall.

"Really? Who lives there?" he asked the old man.

"Nobody."

"Then why do you say this is not a quiet place?"

"Quietness doesn't always signify the absence of sound, or even of human presence. Sometimes places retain the spirit of past turbulence long after its source is gone."

Akitada gave the old man a sharp look. He was a very well-spoken beggar and had, on consideration, not once shown proper respect by bowing or kneeling or asking for alms. Neither had he used a polite form of address. Akitada was not fussy about rank, but many of his acquaintances would have been outraged, and some might have had the beggar beaten. Because of the white mustache and beard, it was hard to make out the man's expression, but it seemed to Akitada that he was being laughed at.

He frowned. "Look here. I've been attacked in broad daylight by three hoodlums who were trying to rape a nun, and I intend to get to the bottom of this. Now, did you see any part of the attack or not?"

The old man shook his head.

"You did not see the nun running toward you? You must have seen her."

The old man shook his head again.

"And you don't know who owns the houses around here?"

"Oh, I know that very well. You asked me who lived here. Nobody lives there, for the owner is absent, having gone to his place in the country, but the property belongs to Lord Yasugi. And the houses across the street belong to Secretary Ki, to old Lady Kose, and to Professor Takahashi." He jabbed his staff toward the thatched roofs rising behind garden walls and shrubbery. "In the street beyond are the homes of Minister Soga, Junior Architect Wakasa, Lay Priest Enshin, and Assistant Lieutenant Akizane. Would you like me to go on?"

Akitada said weakly, "No, thank you."

How close Soga's residence was to the Greater Palace, and yet Soga had never managed to arrive at work on time. And Akitada had never been invited to his superior's house. He thought of the three thugs and wondered why Soga had not at least taken some action to secure his own neighborhood. He said, more to himself than to the old man, "Things have truly come to a terrible pass, when not even a nun is safe on these streets in broad daylight."

The beggar cackled. "There'll be worse before the year is out. Death and chaos. It was predicted and has come to pass."

Akitada stared at him. "What are you talking about?"

"Don't you read the calendar? This is a most unlucky year."

Akitada had little patience with superstitious taboos and prognostications. They got in the way of getting things done, and those who terrified the gullible with such predictions caused, in his opinion, nothing but trouble. He snapped, "Nonsense. The calendar often predicts dire events that don't come to pass."

The old man drew himself up and shook his staff at Akitada. "You fool!" he shouted. "You don't have the brains to interpret the irregularities in the motion of the planets. During the first month alone ten stars fell out of the sky. And what of the strange cloud of black smoke over the Josei Gate on the second day of the second month? Hmm? How do you explain that?"

"Such things happen independently of human affairs."

"Is it human affairs you want? Then what of all the reports that fiery souls have been seen leaving the bodies of the living? Even you should know that portends death. All the signs spell death, and deaths there shall be. The cremation fires at Toribeno shall not cease burning till half this city is empty. A few thugs more or less pale by comparison."

The old man scowled ferociously, then turned and strode away toward the bridge, his colorful robe dragging in the dust. Akitada looked after him and shivered. It was nonsense, of course. He should not have troubled the poor old man, nearly blind and no longer quite rational. Old age damaged men in different ways, Seimei as well as Kunyoshi, and Judge Masakane as much as this poor creature. Death announced its coming in their infirmities.

He turned to follow the long wall around the corner, where he found a big roofed gate and gatehouse. But the gatehouse was empty and shuttered, and no amount of pounding brought an answer. The beggar had been right about this anyway. No one was in residence.

He looked at the three tree-shaded houses across the way. The properties were smaller and the gates more modest, but the nun could have sought refuge here.

A young servant girl peered through a small opening in the gate of the first villa. When she saw Akitada's face, she started back fearfully and refused to admit him, asserting that no one had come to this house, and that no nun lived there, or anywhere else on this street.

With a sigh, Akitada passed on to the next gate. Here his knock was answered by a boy. He told Akitada that his master, Secretary Ki, had removed himself and his household to the country. Nobody had come to the house all day, and the boy had never known of any nuns in any of the houses in the neighborhood. Akitada came away, thinking that Soga's fear of smallpox seemed to have affected his neighbors.

He had no high hopes of finding anyone home at the third house either, but to his surprise, the gate was opened by the owner himself. A thin middle-aged man in a wrinkled and faded blue silk robe glowered at Akitada, and snapped, "Well?"

Akitada bowed. "Am I addressing Professor Takahashi?"

"Yes. So?"

"My name is Sugawara. A little while ago three hoodlums attacked a young nun on the next street. She got away, and I wondered if she came here for help or if you might know where she lives."

"No." The professor was pushing the gate shut, but Akitada

placed a hand against it, and said, "Just a moment, professor. Both my rank and my request entitle me to some courtesy. If you will not invite me in, at least answer my questions."

Takahashi reluctantly opened the gate again. "You can come in, if you must," he said ungraciously.

Akitada walked in, and watched his host closing and re-latching the gate behind him. Takahashi muttered, "Can't be too careful about whom you admit these days. The whole capital is overrun by criminals." He eyed Akitada's appearance sourly and added, "As you seem to have discovered."

They stood in a small overgrown front garden on stepping stones that led to a building half hidden behind trees and fronds of bamboo. Takahashi made no move toward the house.

"Did you hear anything, someone passing in the street or knocking on a gate?" Akitada asked.

"I neither saw nor heard anyone," Takahashi insisted testily. He cast an impatient glance at his house. "You had better report the matter to the police and be done with it. Not that anything will come of it. The authorities have their own concerns to look after."

Wondering if this was a sarcastic comment on Soga's flight, Akitada asked, "You live alone?"

Takahashi said, "I cannot fathom what possible concern that could be under the circumstances. If you are just making conversation, I am busy."

As if to confirm this, a young male voice called petulantly, "Where are you, *sensei*? The soup is getting cold." Footsteps approached and a young man in white silk shirt and trousers appeared from behind the screen of vegetation. He stopped when he saw Akitada in his bedraggled finery. "Oh dear," he breathed and adjusted his hair and his clothing in an almost girlish manner, "I didn't know we had company. An injured gentleman of rank. Won't you ask our guest in?"

Takahashi glared. "Mind your own business. The gentleman is a stranger who was merely asking about the neighbors. Go back and eat. I shall come in a moment."

The youth pouted, but gave Akitada a regretful smile and a graceful wave of the hand before retreating.

Looking after him, Akitada said, "Perhaps your companion . . . ?"

Takahashi interrupted him. "My student. He heard nothing. We have been at our studies. I resigned from the university and now devote myself to private teaching."

"I see. Since you have lived here all your life, perhaps you can tell me if any of your neighbors may be likely to shelter a nun."

"I pay no attention to my neighbors. The place across from me has an absentee owner. He spends most of his time on his estates. I doubt that a man so lacking in any spiritual qualities, or indeed intellectual ones, would have acquaintance with nuns or priests, but he does at least maintain his property. The others are either too young or have outlived their relatives. If that is all . . . ?"

"Thank you. You have been most obliging," Akitada said with some sarcasm.

Takahashi ignored his tone and unlatched the gate.

Back on the street, Akitada turned. "Who is that rather strange old man in a robe of colored silk patches?"

"That's Enshin. Calls himself a lay priest now, but he used to be head of the Bureau of Divination. Gone quite mad, of course." With that, Takahashi slammed the gate in Akitada's face.

So the beggar had been no beggar at all, but a man who had once held higher rank than Akitada. And he had called him uncle! Akitada hoped that Takahashi was right, and that the old gentleman had lost his mind.

He walked a little farther, found that the next block was taken up by a small overgrown park, hardly a place where a frightened nun would hide, and gave up the search.

It had been a bad day. Not only had he lost the nun, and a promising lead in Tora's case, but he had been attacked. As he made his way back to the Greater Palace, his good robe in tatters and one side of his face throbbing with pain, he became very angry.

Conditions had never been safe in the capital, but street crimes used to take place at night. These three hoodlums had attempted to rape a nun in broad daylight, and in a quiet upper-class residential area, only blocks from where Tamako tended her garden. She was supposed to take Genba or Tora along on her visits, but Akitada was by no means sure that she did.

It seemed to him a great wrong that nothing had been done to curb crime in the capital. The nobles called meetings and wrung their hands, and the robbers laughed at them. The thugs had felt secure enough to mock him, a ranking government official. The criminal element had seized the power to themselves. Little wonder conditions were bad when men like Soga simply enriched themselves and took to their heels at the first sign of trouble. A man who cannot observe order and restraint in his own conduct cannot instill order and restraint in his subjects.

But Soga was gone and he, Akitada, was now in his place—however temporarily. He had been taught that you must support rectitude if you wish to end corruption, and the Chinese masters placed the responsibility for a peaceful nation squarely on the shoulders of each individual citizen. Well, he would do something about it.

Filled with righteous anger, Akitada stormed into the ministry and his office. He hardly noticed that the sun had set. There was a light in his office. Nakatoshi knelt at his desk, sorting through the day's letters and appeals. He looked up in surprise. "I didn't expect you so late, sir," he stammered. "Everyone has gone home already." His eyes widened and he rose. "What happened to you?"

"Get your writing things," snapped Akitada, waving him

away and sitting down on his cushion. He pushed the pile of papers aside. "I was attacked by robbers, and this time they have gone too far."

"How terrible! Let me make you a cold compress for your eye, sir."

"Never mind my eye. I want you to take this down before I lose my train of thought. And get another candle. It's too dark in here." The truth was that he could not see out of his eye and the throbbing pain now extended to the rest of his head.

Nakatoshi gulped and rushed out. When he returned, Akitada waited impatiently for the lighting of the candle and the rubbing of the ink, drumming his fingers on the desk and reviewing points in his mind. When Nakatoshi was ready, he began to dictate a memorial addressed to the emperor. His anger having overcome his natural diffidence, the words flowed from his lips so rapidly that Nakatoshi had a hard time keeping up.

The memorial was a long one. It recited the history of outrages which had occurred in recent memory as well as events from more distant history. Akitada outlined the mistakes which had been made in the past and linked them to their dire results. He spoke of unenforced and unenforceable laws, of poorly trained constables, of the inadequacy of the police force to deal with the rampant conditions of lawlessness in all parts of the city, and of the sweeping imperial pardons which all too frequently released even the most violent criminals to prey again on the inhabitants. He cited past administrations that had dealt with unrest and crime effectively, touched on the present conditions, and proposed new methods of law enforcement and punishment to address them.

Finally he suggested to His Majesty that here was an opportunity to be remembered forever as the sovereign who had brought lasting peace and prosperity to his capital and nation by ending a legacy that had made his officials the mockery of every low criminal roaming the streets. How long, he asked, would it be before foreigners saw the nation's weakness and invaded the country?

When he was done, Nakatoshi laid down his brush and rubbed his hand. He stared at Akitada with shining eyes. "That was magnificent," he said. "Will you really send it?"

Akitada found he had a fierce headache and massaged his neck. "Of course. Tomorrow. As soon as I fill in a few missing dates and polish it a little. I'm too tired now." He rubbed his eyes and winced.

"Will that be entirely wise, sir?"

Akitada looked at the young clerk in surprise. "Wise? I don't know if it is wise. I only know it must be done and you and I must pray that His Majesty will listen."

"But, sir, you cannot have thought how this will sound to His Majesty and his present administration. You as much as tell him that he and his ministers are responsible for the present unrest."

Akitada frowned. "Hmm. Mistakes have been made by previous administrations but, yes, I suppose I do suggest that. The worst abuses have been going on for fifty years or more. They could have done something, anything. Of course, the emperor is still very young, but I'm counting on the fact that this memorial will pass through the chancellor's hands first."

"I'm afraid it will."

Akitada suddenly grinned. "Why are you so worried, Nakatoshi? I'm nobody. If it were not for the fact that I shall be sending this under Soga's authority, nobody would bother to read it."

Nakatoshi's eyes widened. "Surely you won't sign the minister's name to it?"

"Of course not. It will bear my name and my seal, but be transmitted through channels under Soga's cover."

Now Nakatoshi grinned also. "The minister won't like that at all."

"You mean he will demand my resignation?"

They both laughed. Akitada was tired and in pain, but he was also filled with great excitement, suddenly seeing a thousand things he could do, must do, looked forward to doing. He glanced at the stack of papers on his desk—Soga's desk—almost longingly. But he was too tired tonight and could not concentrate as he should. And revising the memorial would require a clear head. Then there was Tora's case to look forward to. Or Tomoe's murder, rather. He thought of the nun. He would find her, but not tonight.

Akitada left the ministry happier than he had felt for a long time and walked into a cheerful gathering at home, where his family was celebrating Tora's release with a special feast. His swollen eye caused a brief outcry. He had to submit to the application of herbal packs prepared by Seimei and to a scolding from the old man because he had ruined his best robe.

He told them about the mysterious nun and the three thugs and his memorial to the emperor. Then he ate and drank some wine, listening drowsily to Tora's plans, Yori's chatter, Seimei's discussion of herbs to reduce swelling, and wondered only once why Tamako was so quiet.

That night he slept very well.

CHAPTER NINE

FORTUNE TELLING

*W*hen Seimei quietly entered the next morning, he found his master already awake and sitting at his desk, surrounded by books and documents, and making rapid notes by the light of a candle.

"Good morning, Seimei," Akitada said absently, dipping brush into ink and writing some more. "Is Tora up? I must see him before I leave for the office."

Seimei set down his oil lamp and came over to peer at Akitada's face. "Umhum," he muttered. "That still looks very bad, sir. Is it painful? Can you open the eye at all?"

Akitada paused in his writing. "It hurts and I cannot open it. So what? Life does not come to a halt because of a black eye. There is a great deal of work to be done the next few weeks."

Seimei frowned. "Perhaps the eye itself is damaged. We should call a physician."

"Nonsense." Akitada bent to his task again.

"At least go in a little later this morning and let me apply more compresses."

"No. Now go get Tora and my morning rice."

Seimei left, shaking his head.

Akitada was at last filled with excitement and hope. In the past hour or so he had gathered data and quotations from the library of chronicles, law books, and Chinese classics that he and his ancestors before him had collected. The memorial was the most momentous work he had ever been engaged in. In addition, there were several other exciting and important projects in hand and, for once, he had the freedom to engage in them. He hoped fervently that Soga would stay away for a long, long time.

Tora came in, wearing the clothes of a poor day laborer. His shirt and short pants were of cheap cotton, he had tied up his hair in an old rag, and he was barefoot. He was followed by Seimei carrying a tray with a steaming teapot and a bowl of gruel. Seimei cast disapproving glances at Tora's attire.

Akitada washed out his brush and said briskly, "Sit down, Tora. Seimei, please pour tea for both of us and then you may leave us for a little while."

Tora grinned. "No tea for me, sir. I had some wine with my morning rice. Wine warms the blood and encourages proper digestion." He cast a sly look toward Seimei.

"What complete nonsense," Seimei cried. "As I have told you before, wine overheats the blood and sours the stomach. It is for that very reason that it should be avoided in the morning. Tea has the opposite effect. You will be sorry in another hour when you start belching and getting drowsy."

"Stop the wrangling," Akitada interrupted. "There's work to be done. Tora, I have to be at the ministry this morning, and possibly into the afternoon. You must begin the investigation alone. I suggest you seek out Lieutenant Ihara and discuss what progress he has made. Perhaps you can work together on checking known gangs and their activities." He saw that Tora looked mulish and asked, "What is wrong?"

"I don't like Ihara. Besides, I work better alone."

"Don't be silly. He may have learned something important in the meantime. And a police officer has certain prerogatives that you don't have."

"Not with crooks."

"You have a point. But at least make sure that you speak to him first. And be pleasant. He could have made your release much more difficult. Why are you wearing those clothes?"

"I thought it might be better if I blended in with the crowd this time."

"Ah. Quite right. You do look more like those toughs yesterday. But Ihara first."

Tora sighed. "All right. Anything else?"

"The vendors in the market may know about Tomoe's regular visitors."

Tora nodded. "I was going to start there."

Akitada drummed his fingers on the desk and thought. Should he send Tora back to the street where the nun was attacked? No, better not. Tora had improved past all recognition during his years of service with Akitada, but his manners were not quite up to dealing with the people who lived there. Of course, Professor Takahashi might welcome the very handsome Tora. Foolish thought. Tora definitely could not handle a proposition from Takahashi with diplomacy.

"What's so funny?"

"After my run-in with the thugs yesterday, I spoke with one of the neighbors—a retired professor who offers private tutoring to handsome boys. I was wondering if you might have better luck with him than I."

Tora chuckled. "I doubt it, sir. I bet it was only your bruised face that turned him off. In a couple of days, you'll be as handsome as ever and have him eating out of your hand." He gave a snort and added in an undertone, "Or whatever."

Akitada ignored the coarse suggestion and said, "It's too bad that I'm so busy at the moment. That nun knows something . . ." He broke off, his mouth open with surprise. "Great heaven! She wasn't a nun at all."

"No nun?" Tora looked interested. "You mean she was an ordinary girl in nun's clothes? Was she pretty?"

"Not an ordinary girl. A noblewoman, I think, and quite pretty. And wearing perfume. I was so preoccupied with the brute who slammed me against the wall and very nearly blinded me that I forgot the silk she wore under the nun's habit. And her veil had slipped. I think her hair was long."

Tora whistled. "What luck! Silk underclothes. Brother, how I wish I'd been there!"

Akitada regretted his words and said sharply, "Really, Tora. The point is she came to your hearing in disguise. That means she's respectable, belongs to the upper classes, and certainly undertook that errand without the approval of her family and, as it turned out, at considerable risk. Why would a young woman of that class take such a chance?"

"Well, it wasn't for my sake, so it figures it was for Tomoe. Bet you she's one of the ladies Tomoe used to sing to."

"Perhaps, but she wouldn't take such chances just because she felt sorry for a blind entertainer. No, I think she knows something of Tomoe's past, or she's involved in the same dangerous game which cost Tomoe her life."

Tora thought. "She'd hardly be working with a gang. If she knows the killer, he wasn't a thug. Maybe we're looking in the wrong place."

Akitada sighed. "We must find her. Whatever she knows is both secret and dangerous. As soon as I can get away from the office I'll go back and talk to the neighbors again. This time I'll ask about a young woman who is probably married and part of a family in that quarter. Meanwhile, you'd better see Ihara and then go into the city. Good luck!"

◆

Tora spent the best part of the morning looking for Lieutenant Ihara. Tora's poor clothes were no help in getting information from the constables. Finally, one of them sent him to the Eastern Prison. When Tora got there, a guard recognized him and, unaware that Tora had been released, thought he was escaping and tried to throw him back into a cell. The confusion was finally cleared up, but not until Tora had gathered more bruises. Ihara was not there and was not expected.

In an increasingly rebellious mood Tora retraced his steps.

This time he took up his stand in the courtyard of police headquarters and asked every red-coat passing by for Ihara. They ignored him until a burly sergeant came to investigate. "If they told you he's not here, that's where he is," said the sergeant with confusing logic. "We're too busy to talk to every lout who walks in here with questions. Go away or I'll have you thrown out."

Perhaps he would have been treated better if he had worn his neat blue robe and black cap, but that had proved a distinct disadvantage when dealing with the criminal classes. Tora retreated to the gate and fumed helplessly, until he saw Kobe arriving. The red-coats stood to attention, and Tora blocked his way.

"Sir," he cried, bowing to the superintendent. "I wonder if *you* might help me."

A collective gasp went around the constables. Two of them jumped forward, shouting, "Your pardon, Honorable Superintendent," and grabbed Tora to drag him away.

Tora shook them off. "You see," he said to Kobe, "all of these bas—er, constables—claim they don't know where Lieutenant Ihara is, which is surely a strange thing in a well-run police department. I wouldn't trouble you, but my master insisted. They've already sent me clear across town to the Eastern Prison. When I got there, no Ihara, but the guards tried to lock me up again. And just now the sergeant told me to get lost."

Eight or ten grim-faced policemen with metal prongs and chains moved in on Tora. They waited for the order to seize the troublemaker and teach him some manners.

But instead Kobe put a hand on Tora's shoulder in the friendliest manner and said, "Well, let's see what I can do for you, Tora." The policemen looked at each other and retreated a few steps. They hid their weapons and pretended to form a sort of honor guard through which the two men passed.

In the courtyard, the plump sergeant hurried toward them. Kobe said loudly, "I'm surprised that you had difficulties. Most of our men are well-trained. They know that I expect them to treat everybody with courtesy and to show eagerness when assisting the public."

The sergeant stopped. Tora saw his sheepish face and grinned. "That's good to know, sir. If I need a job, I might want to give your sort of work a try. I've got a certain talent for it, and you could use able people. Seeing as there are so many bandits loose in the city."

Inside the building, Kobe sent for Lieutenant Ihara and then invited Tora to sit down and explain his talents to him.

Tora looked around Kobe's large and well-appointed office, noting with approval that a constable appeared quickly with hot wine, and that another policeman asked if he should take notes. His master's imminent loss of employment had quite determined him to find a job, and police work might be the very thing. He enjoyed investigating crimes, and heaven knew, Kobe must be desperate to replace the dolts outside. That brilliant red uniform was nothing to sneeze at either. Girls liked that sort of thing.

So he took a deep breath and began with his strong physique, moved on to his military service, glossing over the fact that he had been summarily cashiered for insulting his superior, and outlined with great satisfaction his adventures during his service to Akitada. Tora was not given to modesty, though he stopped short of outright lies.

When he was done, a straight-faced Kobe said, "You are a most amazing person, Tora. I don't think we have a position worthy of your talents."

Tora waved the objection away. "Never mind. I'll be glad to make myself available as a consultant or advisor whenever you have a tricky killer or a case your people can't solve. I expect there are many such, enough to keep me busy. But at the moment I have Tomoe's murder to solve. Maybe we'll talk again some other time?"

Kobe choked and was still coughing when Lieutenant Ihara entered and saluted. Tora and Ihara exchanged slight nods.

"Tora was looking for you," Kobe informed the lieutenant. "He plans to begin his investigation into the blind singer's murder today and thought you might share your findings with him."

Ihara's jaw dropped. For a moment, he looked both shocked and disgusted. Then his face congealed. "I was under the impression, sir," he said stiffly, "that this man is a suspect in the case and under house arrest."

"Tora was placed in the custody of Lord Sugawara until the investigation is complete. There's a difference. In fact, it was Lord Sugawara who sent Tora to you."

"But, sir, the training manual, *Instructions to Officers of the Metropolitan Police,* states specifically that details of an ongoing investigation must not be shared with the public, let alone the accused."

Kobe's fingers gently tapped the desk. "Judge Masakane instructed Lord Sugawara to assist in this investigation. That changes the situation, because the *Instructions* also remind you to follow legal procedures as outlined by a proper judge. Lord Sugawara is busy at his ministry during the absence of his superior and has delegated a part of the work to Tora. Tora assures me that he has experience in criminal investigations and is eager to assist. Now, do you have any other objections, or can I get on with more pressing business?"

Ihara blanched. "None, sir." He bowed, then nodded to Tora and headed out the door.

Tora looked after him and made a face. "Thanks for your confidence in me, sir. I wasn't really looking forward to this even before the lieutenant expressed his feelings, but my master asked me to do it, so I suppose I'd better." He got to his feet and bowed.

Kobe smiled. "Good man!"

Ihara was waiting outside. "Follow me," he snapped.

They passed through the main hall and out into the courtyard. Constables saluted Ihara and stared at Tora. Ihara entered a low barracks and took Tora to a tiny office which contained little more than a battered bamboo shelf stacked with papers, and a small, stained writing desk with brushes and a worn inkstone.

"Sit!" Ihara pointed to a small grass mat near the writing table.

Suppressing a sigh, Tora obeyed. "If you could just fill me in about anything that didn't come out during the hearing, I'll be on my way. I'm thinking about that lacquer box, for example. Any success tracing it?"

Ihara had a sheaf of notes in his hand and frowned down at them. Turning abruptly to Tora, he asked, "Can you read?"

Tora only looked at him and extended his hand. The truth was that his reading skills remained poor, but he was not about to give this arrogant bastard of a police officer the satisfaction of admitting it. He looked through the paperwork, an assortment of notes taken down by different people. Some seemed to be interviews, transcribed by police department scribes and fairly legible, but many were notes dashed off by Ihara and other policemen. Tora pursed his lips. "These," he said, holding up some of the latter, "are badly written."

Ihara flushed. "We are very busy and must often note things down in a great hurry and without adequate equipment or light. The one on top concerns the box."

"Ah," murmured Tora and tried to read it. "What is that bit about Nara?"

Ihara snatched the paper from his hand and scanned it. "Oh, that. It's nothing. Lord Sugawara wanted me to find out where the box came from, in case she had stolen it somewhere. We've asked all the lacquerers here, but nobody recognized it. What's more, they didn't think it was local work. This one man said he thought it had been made by someone called Tameyoshi in Nara. But they all agreed it was very fine and must've cost a lot of money. Clearly stolen."

Tora glared. "Not by Tomoe. Maybe it was a present from that family she visited."

Ihara gave a shout of laughter. "Don't be ridiculous. Who would give a blind woman an expensive cosmetics box? For singing a few songs?"

Tora shook his head stubbornly. "There's bound to be an explanation. Tomoe didn't steal and she wasn't a whore."

"Maybe she was no whore. I'm inclined to believe her land-lady was lying about that. Let's face it, with those pockmarks, she'd have had a hard time giving it away."

Tora flared up, "Watch your tongue! She had more class than you and I together. It's not her fault she was poor and blind and had a few scars on her face. I thought you people were sup-posed to protect us, not drag our names into the mud when we can't help ourselves any longer. The superintendent said so."

Ihara bit his lip. "Sorry. I shouldn't have said that." He stared at Tora. "It hadn't occurred to me that you and she . . . might've been close."

Tora scowled, his fist clenching around the papers. He decided that he would not tell Ihara about the nun who was no nun. In fact, he had no intention of sharing any information with the man, now or ever.

"Here! Watch what you're doing. I need those," yelped Ihara, pointing at the papers.

Tora eased his grip and smoothed out the crumpled sheets. He glanced at the rest quickly, then handed them back to Ihara and got up.

"Well? See anything interesting?" Ihara asked.

"If there is, you should know."

"What're you going to do?"

"Talk to people." Tora made for the door.

"Be sure to report to me."

Tora grunted and let the door slam behind him.

He hoped he would never have to lay eyes on Ihara again. No wonder women were attacked on the street in broad daylight and hoodlums dared to lift their hands against his master. With the exception of Kobe—Tora was willing to give the superintendent the benefit of the doubt—the police were incompetent, ignorant, and lacking in manners. He no longer wished to join their ranks and hoped Ihara would make a fool of himself.

Tora strode out briskly, so infuriated by his encounter with the snooty lieutenant that he was oblivious to his surroundings until he passed through the market gateway and was greeted by the sights, sounds, and smells of the place. People bustled about or bargained, shop boys cried out their wares, and on dozens of small stoves simmered soups, filled dumplings, and fried fish. Dodging shoppers, vendors, and merchandise, Tora made for the tower.

Tomoe's place had been taken by the soothsayer who used

to occupy one of the steps on the other side. Draped in a colorful new shawl, he seemed to be doing a good business in his
new, elevated location. Tora did not like the speed with which
he had taken Tomoe's place, but he knew well enough that in this
world of commerce each vacancy was instantly filled by some
other creature trying to scrape up enough coppers for a day's
food, while hoping to make his fortune before it was too late.

Tora preferred an honest death in battle to this futile struggle in the marketplace. Even a farmer could die contented,
knowing that he had grown rice for his own family and many
others besides. Poor Tomoe had gained nothing from her struggle. Tora wondered how she had managed to get her choice location. He walked around the tower. The soothsayer's place was
now taken by an amulet seller in a pilgrim's straw hat and white
robe. He was doing an even better business than the fortune-
teller. Tora looked around for other regulars. There was that
filthy piece of dung, the beggar, pulling at the clothes of one of
the amulet seller's customers. And the storyteller had his usual
group of wide-eyed maids with young children in tow. Tora
walked past a straw sandal maker who was measuring the feet
of a boy as his mother haggled over the price. Beside him a
young girl was selling paper fans. He didn't see the noodle soup
man at his corner across from the tower, but it was still early in
the day. The *mochi* seller was just coming into view, moving
through the crowd of shoppers with his large basket of rice
dumplings strapped to his back, calling out, "Sweet dumplings,
savory dumplings, fresh dumplings, bean paste dumplings."

The sun was high and many hours had passed since Tora's
morning rice. He decided to treat himself to a dumpling while
asking a few questions. The *mochi* man in his short pants and
jacket had a prematurely lined face, and his arms and legs were
sinewy and brown from walking around the market all day and
kneading dough and baking his dumplings at night. His lean

face broke into a smile when he saw Tora. He stopped his chant and swung the heavy basket down to the ground.

"How are you, Brother?" Tora greeted him. "One of the bean paste dumplings, please. No, make that two, and wrap up the second. My master's little son is fond of them." Genba was too, but Genba was getting fat, and besides Tora was low on funds at the moment.

The vendor exchanged the dumplings for some coppers, and watched Tora take a big bite out of his while tucking Yori's into his sleeve. "You hear about Tomoe?" he asked.

Tora wiped rice flour from his mustache and nodded. "I'm the one that found her."

The vendor's eyes grew large. "You don't say? Was it as bad as they say? Blood everywhere? Like some wild animal got her?"

"It was an animal all right," said Tora, looking at his half-eaten dumpling and then tossing it toward a sleeping dog. He had lost his appetite. "But a human animal."

"Here," said the vendor, "what was wrong with that dumpling?"

The dog, startled awake into a growl, devoured the unexpected gift and licked his chops. "Nothing," muttered Tora. "You shouldn't have reminded me."

"Oh. Well, watch it. If people see you tossing my dumplings to the dogs, it'll hurt my business."

"Sorry. You happen to have any idea who killed her?

The vendor chewed his lip. "We've been talking, some of us in the market. Seemed weird. She had nothing. Was she raped?"

"They don't know for sure." The question reminded Tora that he should have asked Ihara for the coroner's report. The bastard probably wouldn't have given it to him, but he should have tried. Then he had the uneasy thought that the report might have been among the papers he had returned without reading. He sighed. Maybe he had better sit in on Yori's lessons.

The dumpling man said, "If she wasn't raped, your guess is as good as mine. People here liked her. She worked hard and we all felt sorry for her."

"Somebody didn't. How long had she been working here?"

"About three years. She just stopped in the middle of the market and started singing. The guards fined her for working without a proper permit. After that she paid. Didn't do much business at first. People paid no attention. Then the soothsayer gave up his place on the tower platform to her, and she started drawing a nice crowd."

So the soothsayer had merely taken back his old place after Tomoe's death. Tora turned to look at him and asked, "Did she have any special friends? The soothsayer, maybe?"

He got no answer. Three youngsters had come up, and the vendor was busy selling them dumplings. When he was done, he said, "I wouldn't know about her friends. She kept to herself. I've got to move on or the guards will fine me."

The *mochi* man only had a permit for walking about with his goods. Stationary vendors paid more and did not like competition next to their spaces or stands. Tora strolled back to the tower and stopped at the line of customers in front of the amulet seller. "What's the big attraction?" he asked a woman, while giving the pretty girl in front of her a wink and a smile.

The girl giggled, but the woman said fervently, "His amulets are direct from Ise Shrine. The God has blessed them. It's a lot of money"—she opened her hand, and Tora saw that it contained about twenty coppers—"but I'm scared. My little boy— better he should live than eat *mochi*, right?"

Seeing her poor clothes and her work-worn face, Tora asked, "Is he sick?"

"Not yet. Amida be blessed! But the sickness is everywhere. Only last week the neighbors' baby died. Covered with hundreds of boils she was! Terrible!"

Tora began to grasp the run on amulets. A smallpox panic seemed to have started, and people were buying the small wooden tablets to protect themselves against that terrible plague. Tomoe had been pockmarked and blinded by smallpox. Once, no doubt, she had been just as pretty and lively as the giggling girl in the queue.

Tora turned away—he did not have enough money for an amulet in any case. Every time he thought of Tomoe, something twisted in his belly. His master had asked him if he had loved her, and he had said "no." But love is not such a simple thing to explain. With Tomoe it had not been lust. He had not wanted to lie with her—even the thought made him uncomfortable. But he had wanted to hold her close, to protect her. Many times. And he mourned her death and convinced himself that the pain he felt for having failed her might ease when he found her killer.

He glanced up at the tower platform where the soothsayer sat importantly before a red silk cloth on which he cast people's fortunes. Tora wanted to know why he had given up his spot to Tomoe.

He got in line behind a fat merchant and sat on the steps while the fat man whispered his questions and the soothsayer rustled his yarrow stalks and clinked coins. Bits of their exchange drifted back to Tora: "That's a 'yes' on the travel, but the direction is not auspicious . . ."

"Ssh! Not so loud." Whisper, whisper. "Profit?" Whisper. More rustlings and stirrings.

"Ah! Yes, a prosperous undertaking if you . . ."

Down at the bottom of the steps, the beggar had hold of a woman's skirts. She hit him with her full basket, and he let go, shouting an obscenity after her.

The fat merchant pulled out a string of coppers and paid the soothsayer, leaving with a happy smile. Sometimes Tora wondered if soothsayers passed along only good news in hopes of a generous tip and return visits. But he believed in dreams and omens himself and thought that at least some of the diviners spoke truth. So he bowed politely to the long-faced man with his stiff black hat and the colorful shawl about his shoulders before squatting down.

The diviner looked at him carefully with rather sad eyes. "Ten coppers if by coins," he said. "Twenty if by stalks."

"By coins," said Tora quickly, fingering the sad remnants of the money in his sash.

"I remember you," said the soothsayer. "You knew Tomoe."

Tora nodded. "I don't suppose you could find her killer with your divining, could you?"

"My method can only give a 'yes' or a 'no.' You have to have the name of a person."

Tora sighed. "I haven't got one. Besides, it wouldn't be good evidence in front of a judge anyway."

The long-faced man raised his brows. "Oh, I don't know. There was a murder case where they found a man guilty on the say-so of a medium. He confessed when she pointed the finger at him. Fate never lies."

"I heard you gave this spot to Tomoe when she first started her business three years ago."

The soothsayer nodded, still studying Tora's face.

"Why are you looking at me like that?"

"Your face is interesting. That forehead and chin! Hmm. And the way your ears are placed. Yes. You will have a fine future."

Tora was pleased. "You read faces, too? I thought soothsayers only used the stalks and coins."

The soothsayer smiled. "I'm of Korean descent and my father passed some of the old skills on to me. There is not much call for it, because few people have fortunate faces. Especially lately. Yours is the first in a long time. Most faces are ordinary, and this year too many have death written on them. I warn them, and they go to buy an amulet." The soothsayer sighed. "As if it mattered."

Tora was puzzled by this, but decided to stick to his purpose. "About Tomoe. Why did you give her your place?"

"She bought it. Paid me handsomely for it."

"Did you ask her where she got the money?"

"I didn't have to. She told me she sold her mirror, since she wouldn't need it any more. A great pity." He shook his head. "She was a beauty."

Tora stared at him. "A beauty?"

"Oh, yes. The bones of the face don't change even when disease destroys the skin. I see beyond the outer shell. She was both beautiful and good. But I could tell that she was marked by death all the same."

"You saw that?"

"Oh, yes. About a week ago. I told her to go away, far away. She believed me, but she said she needed two more pieces of silver before the end of summer."

"What for?"

"She didn't say."

Tora pondered this while the diviner rearranged his divining stalks and the three copper coins. There were two people waiting. He must hurry. "Sorry to take up your time. Just one more question. Tomoe was afraid of somebody. Do you happen to know what that was all about?"

"No. She never mentioned it." The soothsayer looked sharply at Tora, then added, "You knew her better than I. Many bad people come to this market. One kept watching her, a tall man. He looked dangerous, like a soldier, or maybe a highway man. He had a very bad face. I don't think she knew."

Tora fished ten coppers out of his sash. "Well, thanks anyway." He made a move to get up.

"What about your fortune?"

"I really came about Tomoe. Besides, you already told me about my face."

"No. You shall have your fortune. A friend of Tomoe's is a friend of mine. Poor people must help each other. What is your question?"

"Well then, will I find Tomoe's killer?"

The soothsayer picked up the three copper coins and showed them to Tora. "See, they have characters on one side only. If I toss them, like this, some fall face up, some face down. Face up means it's *yin* or even, with a value of two. Face down is *yang*, or odd, with a value of three. Added up, the first throw gives us a 'yes' or 'no' answer. If the total adds up even, it's a 'yes,' if odd, a 'no.' "

Tora stared at the coins. "That's a 'yes,' isn't it?"

The soothsayer nodded and smiled.

"Good!" Tora was immensely pleased. His master had never trusted the predictions of diviners and soothsayers. It was always right to do what was needful when it was needful, he used to say, whenever someone urged postponement because the time was inauspicious or the direction of a journey was forbidden. Now Tora would not only prove him wrong, but solve a murder without his master's help.

The soothsayer said, "I think you may have unexpected troubles on the way. You must be careful."

Tora grinned. "Don't worry. Nothing can happen to me. You told me I have a great future."

The soothsayer did not return his smile. "Let's consult the gods." He took up his bundles of yarrow stalks, separating them and placing them in strange combinations between his fingers, then laying them down and starting the process again. Tora ventured to clear his throat.

"Don't interrupt!" growled the soothsayer.

Tora sat, wondering what was happening and wishing he could leave.

After a long time, the soothsayer sighed and gathered up his stalks. For a long while he sat looking at Tora without speaking. Then he said, "It is good and not good. You will succeed, but terrible things will come to pass."

"What things?"

"There will be great grief. More I cannot say." He sighed deeply. "These are evil days for many." He scooped up Tora's coppers and bowed. "Be safe, Tomoe's friend."

CHAPTER TEN

THE HIDDEN GARDEN

When Akitada arrived at the ministry with the notes for his memorial to the emperor, he found the number of petitioners grown so large that they were sitting two deep along the walls of the reception hall. He stopped in dismay. It was impossible to deal with all of their petitions today unless he was given an additional staff of ten clerks. Besides, there was the draft of his memorial to the emperor. He wanted to polish and dispatch it this very day. As he stood there, considering these things, he saw that they looked even more disappointed than he felt. He wondered if he was properly dressed and checked to see if his hat was askew. He was wearing his comfortable everyday robe again. But still they whispered and looked troubled. Ah. It must be his black eye. Relieved, he smiled and said, "I'm glad to see you. Please, do not let my black eye worry you. I assure you I can read and write well enough. But there are too many of you to . . .".

To his surprise, one after the other of them rose, bowed, and left until there was only a handful still waiting. He shook his head and went into his office. Nakatoshi followed and closed the door.

"Why did they leave so quickly?" Akitada asked him.

"I'm not sure, sir." Nakatoshi was also looking at Akitada's eye. "Perhaps they left because you said there were too many."

Akitada snorted. "If so, they are the most humble and polite group of litigants I have ever seen. Do I look particularly frightening?"

Nakatoshi flushed. "Not to me, sir."

Akitada laughed. "The eye looks worse than it feels. Let's get to work." He glanced at the draft of his memorial and the stack of new paperwork beside it, rubbed his hands, and sat down behind his desk.

Soga's desk. With his hand already extended toward the top document on the pile of ministry business, he looked up. "Any news from the minister?"

"No, sir."

"I don't recall signing the daily report Sakae was to prepare. What happened to that?"

"We sent only one."

"Why only one?"

"The messenger came back with a note. We're not to send anything else from the capital until the minister asks for it."

"Strange."

"Yes. There was no explanation."

A brief silence fell while they considered Soga's peculiar order.

"Hmm," said Akitada finally. "Well, let's get started on this. And then I want to see the people who are waiting. That old fellow—what was his name?—the one whose house was taken over by his nephew. Is there any news on that case?"

"Mr. Chikamura. We verified that he is indeed the owner of record and sent some constables to tell the nephew and his friends to depart."

"Good. I wonder what he wants now. Well, I expect he'll tell me." Akitada took the first letter from the stack and read it. After discussing its contents with Nakatoshi, he dictated a brief answer, and moved to the next document. From time to time, as they worked their way through the daily allotment of bureaucratic paper shuffling, he glanced longingly toward his memorial.

It was midmorning before Akitada had time for the petitioners. Fortunately there were only five left, four men and an elderly woman. Leaving aside Chikamura, theirs were all complaints against a neighbor for infringing on their property rights. Akitada dealt with them quickly. Then he saw Chikamura.

"Welcome, Mr. Chikamura," he said with a smile, when the old man had fallen to his knees and knocked his head on the floor. "I'm told you are now in possession of your home again?"

"Yes, your honor. I came to thank your honor for throwing out my nephew, whose heart and guts a thousand demons should gnaw for his unfilial behavior."

"I trust he and his companions left quietly?"

"Oh, yes. The cowards didn't dare argue with policemen. But he was very angry with me. He said I'd be sorry for what I'd done."

Akitada frowned. "That's bad. He might bring his friends back with him to take revenge. Do you have a way to protect yourself?"

Chikamura grinned toothlessly. "He won't dare. I'll run out the back door and shout for the constables."

Akitada smiled back. "Excellent. But be sure to report any further threats."

Mr. Chikamura bowed deeply again and prepared to withdraw, when Akitada thought to ask him, "Do you happen to know why all those other people left when I arrived?"

"Oh, they're fools. They saw you come in with that black eye and wearing that plain robe, so they figured you're in trouble already."

The perversity of this made Akitada laugh, but he realized that Seimei had been right in the matter of his clothes. Being simpleminded, the common people measured power by its visible signs. Since he had stopped wearing his luxurious court robe, they thought he had lost his rank and position. Perhaps they had also assumed his black eye was due to a beating for some malfeasance.

The rest of the morning passed as he dealt with the new petitions, and it was midday before Akitada could reach for the draft of his beloved memorial. He rubbed fresh ink as he read, saw a number of phrases that needed strengthening, and, feeling again the surge of excitement and happiness, dipped his brush into the ink.

But his pleasure was short-lived, for Nakatoshi showed Kobe in before he had made much progress. Remembering his obligation, Akitada suppressed his annoyance and thanked the superintendent for interceding on Tora's behalf.

Kobe waved his gratitude away and asked, "What in heaven's name happened to you?"

"Oh, I forgot." Akitada chuckled. "I seem to be more than usually scatterbrained. After I left yesterday, I followed that nun and managed to stop three hoodlums from raping her in a residential area west of the palace. She got away, but I did not."

"You reported this to the police?"

"No. I tried to find the young woman who, by the way, was no nun. It became apparent that the people in the area were afraid to talk to strangers. I was so outraged at the conditions in our capital that I came back here to draft a memorial to his majesty and everything else slipped my mind."

"A memorial?"

Seeing Kobe's frown, Akitada added lamely, "I've also had a great deal of ministry work."

"You should have reported the crime immediately. Such

conditions persist because people do not report crimes to us. Where exactly did this attack take place and who was involved?"

Akitada told him. As Kobe probed, Akitada realized that he had almost done an unforgivable thing. His memorial would destroy Kobe, who was an excellent official, a fair and honest administrator, and a genuine friend—all in the name of registering an official protest to His Majesty and perhaps furthering his career. Shame crept up his neck and made his ears burn, and he could hardly look Kobe in the eyes.

He had dwelt on the gross failure of the police to control crime in the capital. Kobe's enemies would not care that Kobe had inherited a problem beyond his meager resources, and that all his efforts were undermined by the continuous sweeping pardons issued by the Imperial House. They would use Akitada's memorial to remove him.

He hardly knew what he said in answer to Kobe's questions, and listened with half an ear as Kobe told him that Tora had been to see him and had talked to Ihara. Kobe relaxed a little when he mentioned Tora, but Akitada was aware of a new distance between them, of a withdrawing of good will, and of a guarded wariness in its stead. Eventually Kobe fell silent and rose to leave.

"Perhaps I had better not proceed with the memorial," Akitada said awkwardly. "It's not the right time."

Kobe said coldly, "Many a career has been made by a timely and well-written memorial. You must do what is best." He turned and left without a smile.

Akitada sat for a long time, unhappily remembering Kobe's manner and skimming through the draft Nakatoshi had written. He shuddered at how close he had come to submitting this. And yet there was a great need for change, and it was certainly his duty as an official to bring such gross defects to the emperor's attention. Many a timely reform had died in its conception because a man's duty had come into conflict with obligations of friendship or family. It was not easy to follow the right path, and not even the Great Sage would have had a simple solution to his dilemma. But he would have been steadfast and held to the rule that an official must always serve his country first of all. Sometimes there was something a bit inhuman about Master Kung.

As Akitada could not put aside his feelings of friendship, he knew himself once again inadequate to his office and powerless to effect even small changes in the administration. With a sigh, he tore up the pages. Nakatoshi had been right: They were good, quite the best thing he had ever written. Then he tore up the notes he had made in the predawn hours—those eloquent phrases, well-chosen citations, and sound solutions. Some day, he hoped, he might mend the breach with Kobe.

He no longer had any appetite for the midday meal Nakatoshi had procured and left instead for police headquarters to make his belated report. It was a sign of Kobe's new coldness that he had not offered to dispatch a couple of constables to Akitada's office to take down the information.

The sergeant at police headquarters seemed efficient. When Akitada described the three thugs who had assaulted him and the nun—he decided not to confuse the man with the fact that she had been no nun—he nodded.

"Are you familiar with them, then?" Akitada asked.

"Two of them, sir. The idiot and the big lout. They work together. Small stuff usually. A lot of robberies and thefts. They threaten their victims, but usually don't attack them."

"Well," said Akitada, "they certainly attacked this time. The newcomer had the nun on the ground when I interrupted him. He's responsible for the damage to my eye. The others tried but did not have a chance to maul me."

The sergeant raised a finger. "Ah, yes, but there you are, sir.

You fought back. If you'd just left them alone, you wouldn't have been hurt."

"Look here, sergeant," snapped Akitada, outraged by this rationale and still upset over having destroyed his memorial, "if I had not resisted, the nun would most certainly have been raped."

The sergeant flushed. "It was very brave of you, sir, but such things happen. Women should not go out alone."

"No," said Akitada bitterly. "Not when we have a police force that does not enforce the law because it does not care about crimes against women unless it is a case of murder."

"Sir," protested the sergeant, appalled, "it's not true that we don't care. We don't have enough men to go after any but the most dangerous criminals."

That was true enough, but should they accept the fact without making an effort to change it? Akitada rose, too angry to listen to more excuses and explanations. "Do you or your fellow police officers have any notion where these three thugs might live?" he asked with heavy sarcasm.

"Of course we do, sir," the sergeant cried. "Allow me to get the information for you." He rushed from the office. Akitada studied the bare walls and worked up more fury. When the sergeant returned with a slip of paper and explained that they might have moved elsewhere, he said scornfully, "Well, I must try my best to find them for you and perhaps I had better plan to take them into custody also. Are you willing to put them into a cell if I bring them to you?"

The sergeant gaped. "Er, sir, it's not a good idea for an ordinary citizen to attempt arrests. These men are known to be dangerous."

"Are they? And yet you leave them free to rape, rob, and terrorize the ordinary citizens."

Akitada stormed out of police headquarters.

◆

The street where Akitada had last seen the young woman was empty. He was walking along the wall where the third man had thrown down the woman when he heard the music.

The sound was very faint and came from the other side of the wall, from the property that was said to be uninhabited. Someone was playing a zither. Akitada stopped. The faintness, he thought, was due to the fact that the musician was plucking the strings very softly. He was momentarily enchanted and stood there on a warm and scented afternoon, listening, imagining a beautiful woman daydreaming of her lover.

But he had business to attend to. If someone had returned to this residence, he would ask his questions there before calling on the neighbors again. He quickly walked around the corner and to the main gate, where he knocked loudly.

As before, there was no reply. The gate remained stubbornly closed. He listened. The music had stopped. He stepped back and looked at the gatehouse. Like the gate it was an elaborate structure with a sweeping, tile-covered roof and carved beams and shutters. On the street side, a wooden grate allowed the gatekeeper to see who wanted admittance. The room behind was dark and had seemed unoccupied, but now Akitada thought he noticed a slight movement there. He went closer and peered through the grate. "Open up this instant. This is an official matter," he called out.

In vain. No answer came from the gatehouse, except the soft sound of a door being closed. Then, silence. He waited a little longer, angry and suspicious. Then he crossed the street to knock at the gate of Lady Kose again.

The same little maid looked out and recognized him. To his surprise, she unlatched the gate immediately and admitted him to a crowded courtyard filled with many large and small containers in which small shrubs and trees were growing. She bowed and said, "This insignificant person humbly apologizes for stupidly turning the honored gentleman away yesterday."

"Ah. Well, you were no doubt frightened by my appearance."

She risked a sideways glance. "Yes, sir."

"May I speak to your lady today?"

"Yes, sir. Please come."

Akitada followed her, looking bemusedly from her tidy little figure to the many potted plants she was skirting with the practice of familiarity. "Someone here is a fine gardener," he commented.

"My lady takes great pleasure in her plants."

Lady Kose was seated on her veranda, wrapped in a large shapeless grey garment that he took at first for a nun's robe. His heart skipped, but then he saw that she was surrounded by snippets of greenery, bits of wire, small knives, and assorted pebbles, hard at work on a miniature azalea bush growing from a shallow earthenware dish.

"This is the gentleman from yesterday, my lady," announced the little maid.

Lady Kose looked up. She must be in her eighties, Akitada thought, her skin pale and almost transparent, marked with a million fine lines of age so that it resembled very costly paper with thin bits of dry grass embedded in it. Her eyes were still sharp, though.

And so was her voice. "I am so glad you returned. I told Kiko it was quite unconscionable to turn away a wounded man, but the girl is very protective of me. Please accept my apologies."

Akitada smiled, bowed, introduced himself, and was invited to take a seat on the veranda. Lady Kose offered him refreshments, which he politely refused. He responded by paying her compliments on her work with the azalea. She was inordinately pleased by these, hiding her smile behind dirt-stained fingers. "I dabble a little in making my small world appear larger," she said and gestured at the garden. Akitada saw that its size was

modest but appeared to encompass a wide and varied landscape. The only full-sized trees belonged to Lady Kose's neighbors. They stretched their enormous limbs over her garden
walls as if they were reaching greedily for the toy-like cushions
of clipped azaleas and the miniature moon bridges that spanned
a tiny stream. The flowering camellia trees had already dropped
their petals in the recent heat, but late azaleas still bloomed in
shades of rose and crimson. Dwarfed black pines, maples, and
cypresses grew from small hills and mountains, and the stream
wound, like a diminutive river, between them and flowed into a
tiny pond that reflected the cloudless sky above. Small birds
seemed to feel at home here, and somewhere a cicada sang. Lady
Kose's retreat looked unreal—an island of peace surrounded by
a threatening world.

Convention required more expressions of interest and small
courtesies. Eventually the old lady signaled a return to the purpose of Akitada's visit. "I trust you are not unduly troubled by
your injury?" she inquired politely.

"No. It will soon heal. However, I have been trying in vain
to find the young woman who was the cause of it."

Lady Kose's eyes widened. She dropped the knife which had
been trimming an azalea twig. "You were attacked by a female?"
Her tone and expression showed how deeply shocked she was.
"A fox spirit or a goblin, surely."

Akitada laughed. "Not at all. The damage was done by a
very real thug, and the young lady was also as substantial as you
and I. I happened along and interfered when three hoodlums
waylaid her not far from here."

She clapped her hands. "Oh, just like the brave Sadamori
who captured a gang of robbers all by himself."

"Well, not really. They got away. And I also lost the young
lady in the process. I wondered if you could help me find her
again."

Lady Kose was overcome with emotion. She clasped her hands together and, forgetting to cover her mouth, smiled at him with blackened teeth. "What a romantic tale!" she cried. "Young lovers separated by fate and yearning for each other. It's Lord Narihira and the Ise Princess all over again. I must remember to note it down later. Oh, how I hope you will find her and live happily ever after."

Akitada was beginning to feel a little out of his depth. "Er, I am afraid the lady is a stranger to me. I am investigating a murder and think she may have some information."

Now Lady Kose was nearly quivering with excitement. "A murder? Perhaps a crime of passion or a feud between families? And the killers attacked this young woman also? How terrible! But you came to her rescue and, like Yorimasa, you will slay the monsters."

This conversation was becoming difficult. The old lady seemed determined to make up her own fantastic story. Akitada said firmly, "Thank you for your good opinion of me, but I must make a start first. This young woman was dressed as a nun, but I have reason to believe that she is really a married woman who may live in one of the houses nearby." Heaven only knew what she would make of this.

But Lady Kose made an abrupt return to the real world. "A young gentlewoman, you say? Hmm. It wasn't Kiko or I, of course." She giggled. "Secretary Ki's wives are all of middle age, though his first lady has been talking of taking the veil. I believe Secretary Ki is becoming difficult these days. Older men, you know. Then there is Professor Takahashi. But of course he is a bachelor. No women in his house at all." She twitched her nose. "And Wakasa has sent his family to the country, as has Minister Soga. His Excellency Enshin is a widower, and Assistant Lieutenant Akizane keeps his place only for amusements. His family lives elsewhere. Lord Yasugi, who owns the large villa across the street, comes for an occasional brief visit, but he has returned to his estates. I am afraid there are no young gentlewomen hereabouts."

"I think somebody must still live in the Yasugi house. I heard a zither when I passed. When I knocked at the gate, someone was peering out at me from the gatehouse, but nobody opened."

She stared at him. "Hah!" she said. "I wonder."

"Could someone be hiding in the villa?"

"You mean the young woman who was dressed up as a nun?"

"Yes." It sounded far-fetched and he added, "Or someone who may have seen her."

Lady Kose turned. "Kiko!"

The little maid appeared. "Yes, madam?"

"Do you remember telling me that Lord Yasugi left for the country with his whole family?"

"Yes, madam. It was last week. Three carriages he had, and four wagons for servants, and many, many porters."

"Ah. Did all his ladies leave with him?"

"I think so, madam. All the servants left."

"Yes, of course. Nobody would stay without servants. Thank you." Lady Kose turned back to Akitada. "There you have it. Kiko knows all the servants around here. There is nobody across the street. Perhaps the music came from another house?"

Akitada did not think so, but he said, "Perhaps." Lady Kose had no more information. With a sigh, he rose, bowed, and said, "Thank you for your kindness and for allowing me to see your wonderful garden."

She looked disappointed. "Must you leave so soon? I wished to ask more questions about this interesting young woman of yours. You see, I write stories. Kiko seems to think they are good. And I could tell you more about the family across the street."

Akitada hesitated, then took his seat again.

"A pity they are gone," she said. "There are all sorts of ladies there when they are in town. Yasugi has three wives and two grown daughters. His third lady is not much older than the daughters. It was a very romantic marriage. They say he took pity on a young widow, but I think he lost his heart. Like the *Tale of Lady Ochikubo,* though she was no widow. But both ladies were in very straitened circumstances, and both gentlemen very rich. It is a wonderful thing that men are so passionate. Now that the daughters are young women, I think we shall soon have page boys running back and forth, carrying love poems." She raised a hand to her mouth and giggled.

"You have been very kind," said Akitada firmly, "but since the family is gone, I really don't see how they can be involved in this." Afraid that she would trap him into more of her romantic fantasies, real or imagined, Akitada bowed again, and retreated quickly.

"Please come back," she cried after him.

Across the street loomed the long wall and gatehouse of the Yasugi residence. The unseasonable heat made the air above the tiles shimmer against the green trees and blue roofs like iridescent silk. He marveled that a wealthy man would leave such a valuable property unattended. Someone was inside, and that someone was hiding. He thought of the three ruffians.

But would robbers play the zither? Not likely!

He decided to walk around the perimeter of the property and look for another entrance. The northern boundary wall adjoined a small wood of pines and cedars. It was thickly overgrown, but Akitada found a footpath that followed the wall and seemed to be a shortcut to the next street. The wall was solid, but on the next street there was a small secondary gate to the service area of the Yasugi property. This gate was locked from inside and nobody answered his knock. The next cross street was the one where the attack had occurred, and Akitada knew that wall was blank. He returned to the footpath. When he turned the corner, he caught a glimpse of a man who seemed to disappear into thin air before his eyes. The path lay empty, and yet he was certain that a moment ago a figure had been there.

Halfway down the path, a crippled pine leaned toward the wall. One sturdy branch reached over its top. All a man had to do was to pull himself up, crawl along the branch, and jump down on the other side. The man had gone over the wall.

Akitada took off his outer robe, wrapped it around his waist, and tied up his trousers. Then he pulled himself up quickly and stood on the branch, looking down into an elegant garden. There was no sign of the intruder.

If a man had climbed the pine and jumped into the Yasugi garden, he was there for no good purpose. That left Akitada little choice but to follow and try to stop whatever was about to happen.

He nearly slipped off the branch when he caught sight of the man again. He was moving along a path, not thirty feet away. The burly shape, the checked shirt, and the bandage across his face were unpleasantly familiar. It was the thug who had come for him at the bridge the day before. He had inflicted some damage when he had rammed the small tree into the man's face, but his presence here was not only ominous but dangerous: Akitada was not armed and did not know if the man's companions were with him.

There was nothing like surprise reinforced by bluff. Moving out along the branch, Akitada jumped down into the garden and found the path. Putting on his robe again, he untied his trousers. Then he stepped from the cover into the path and walked casually toward the man. "Hey," he shouted. "You there! What are you doing here?"

The fellow started and turned. His good eye almost popped out in surprise when he saw who was coming.

Akitada pretended to recognize him also and scowled dreadfully. "You again!"

Putting his hands to his mouth, he shouted, "Tora, Genba! Thieves! Come quick!"

The ruse worked. The thug made a frantic dash into the garden, with Akitada in hot pursuit, shouting, "Robbers! Call the constables! Get your bows. Quick!" and making as much noise as he could. The man disappeared into the shrubbery.

Akitada's shouts should have brought out any Yasugi retainers, but nothing stirred in the compound. The service buildings— stables, storehouses, and a kitchen—looked deserted. Akitada moved quietly on his soft soles, peering around corners and through windows into buildings. He found all doors firmly locked. Where had the fellow got to?

Too late he heard the clicking of a latch. He swung around and saw the gate to the back street closing with a thud. The man had got away.

With a sigh, Akitada walked back to the main residence.

The path skirted an artificial lake, much larger than Lady Kose's miniature puddle. The separate pavilions were connected to each other and to the largest building by roofed galleries. He crossed a small moon bridge over a narrow arm of the lake and looked down at floating water lilies with pale yellow starlike blooms. Speckled *koi* rose sluggishly to inspect the sudden intrusion of a human shadow into their quiet world.

The house was closed up, its heavy wooden shutters securely locked into place. The only sound Akitada heard was the crunching of the gravel under his feet and the occasional chirping of a bird somewhere. He inspected each building. The number of pavilions suggested that Yasugi's wives and his daughters each enjoyed their own quarters. It was not until he had almost finished that he noticed the first sign of life.

A pair of women's sandals, large and well-worn, stood at the bottom of the veranda steps. Not bothering to remove his own shoes, Akitada climbed the steps and turned the corner of the building. And there a wooden shutter had been pushed aside and a sliding door was open to the interior. He took a cautious step forward and peered in at thick grass mats, a clothes stand with women's garments draped over it, and a painted screen. Various articles lay about nearby, all of them belonging to an upper class woman: a fine bronze mirror stand with its round mirror; a comb box and a cosmetics box, both finely lacquered; books; papers; writing utensils; and, near the veranda, the zither he had heard.

He cleared his throat, but all remained still. The stillness was strangely breathless, a silence filled with . . . what? . . . fear, anticipation, or perhaps danger?

"Is anyone here?" he asked.

The silence became heavy and suffocating. The image of the bloodstained room of the street singer flashed through his mind. He was suddenly afraid that he had come too late after all and crossed the threshold quickly.

It took a moment for his eyes to adjust. They fell first on the mirror and cosmetics box, and he felt a surge of excitement. The box was the twin of the one owned by the dead Tomoe.

He made a move toward it, when he heard a soft rustling. Half turning, he saw a figure silhouetted against the brightness of the sunlit garden beyond the door—a large sword raised in both hands.

He took a desperate leap as the long blade hissed down.

CHAPTER ELEVEN

THE BOY

𝒯ora left the soothsayer, greatly troubled by his prediction, and almost fell over the beggar who was crouching at the bottom of the steps. The screams of pain jerked him out of his abstraction.

The beggar was rolling in the dirt in apparent agony. "Oh, my back," he groaned. A small crowd gathered. "My rib's broken. Aaah! Fetch a doctor, quick. He kicked me! Oh, Amida, the pain!" His scabby knees drawn almost to his chin, the beggar rocked back and forth in the dust like a large ball of rag and bone, his face contorted and his arms clutched across his middle. Both his face and arms were covered with assorted scratches.

Tora did not believe for an instant that he could have injured the man—or that a man with broken ribs would roll around that way. He knew this for what it was: a ploy to extract money from an unwary shopper. The broken rib was an outright lie.

A crowd grew with a speed that proved the spectacle of human pain was of greater interest than shopping for food, eating, or even standing in line to buy amulets against disease. True, some of the regulars lost interest when they saw who was writhing on the ground, but others remained to see how the beggar's victim would react.

Tora glanced at the crowd. Some people were glaring at him. One woman shook her fist, and somebody shouted, "You young hoodlums think you can walk all over us. Just you wait!"

It was not clear what he was to wait for, but Tora bent and hissed into the wailing beggar's ear, "Cut that out and I'll stand you some wine."

The beggar brought the noise down to a soft whimper and whispered back, "How much? And how about some food?"

"Very well, a meal with a flask of wine in the restaurant by the gate. But I want some information." Louder, he said, "Let me help you up."

The beggar unwrapped himself and staggered to his feet. Tora made a show of checking him over for injuries, a process which involved some very realistic groans and squeals from the beggar. Then he put an arm around him and said, "You'll do, but let's get you something to eat."

The crowd parted, murmuring encouragement, the regulars smirked, and Tora and the beggar staggered to the restaurant. There a waiter barred the door.

"Not in here!"

Tora considered: The beggar was filthy and he did not look much better. He pulled out his last coppers and held them up. "I'm buying."

The waiter scowled and pointed to the outside benches. "You can sit there. What do you want?"

"Give him a bowl of soup and a flask of your cheapest."

"Hey," cried the beggar, "you promised me a full meal and some decent wine."

The waiter spat and disappeared inside. When they were

seated, Tora looked around to make sure that nobody paid attention, then leaned across to grab the beggar by the collar and jerk him close. "Listen, you stinking piece of garbage," he snarled, "don't think I don't know what you pulled back there. I watched you do the same stunt before. You're here because I want some information. And if you ever try that trick on me again, I'll see to it that you get a public whipping."

The beggar squeaked. When Tora released him, he rubbed his scrawny neck, where the scratches started bleeding, and grumbled, "Don't threaten me. I know you, even in those old rags. You're the one used to hanker after that blind slut. What happened? Lost your job?"

Tora glared. "Watch your mouth when you speak of the dead, turd. As for my clothes, I'm undercover. I'm working with the police on her murder." It was stretching the truth a bit, but that couldn't hurt with scum like this.

To Tora's surprise the man's face turned pasty white and his eyes boggled. "Here, I know nothing about that," he stammered, jumping up.

Tora grabbed him by the arm and flung him back on his seat. "Not so fast!" He eyed him with disgust, then reminded himself that beggars shied away from police matters because all too often they made convenient scapegoats. The beggar gulped, ran a grimy hand through the greasy strands of hair that hung to his shoulders, and hitched up his ragged shirt, revealing that he had not bothered to wear a loincloth. He looked like a living piece of garbage. Worse, he stank like garbage, and fear had intensified the aroma.

Tora moved downwind and kept his eyes on the creature's face, but found this equally nauseating. The shifty eyes squinted everywhere but at Tora, and the thick lips were cracked and had traces of dried white spittle in the corners. "Relax," Tora said, "you're not in trouble. I just want to ask some questions."

The beggar croaked, "You sure don't look like police."

"I told you, I'm in disguise. Tell me what you know about Tomoe's regular customers. Especially those engaged in illegal activities."

"Engaged in illegal activities?" mocked the beggar, who was getting his nerve back. "And what might those be? I'm just an ignorant bastard, you know."

"Don't jerk me around. You know what I mean: gambling, robbery, burglary, selling children into prostitution, and cheating old people."

Tora had heard that criminals looked at their work as a kind of trade and formed guilds or families that were run by a boss, or father figure, and staffed with members who were ranked as officers, soldiers, and apprentices. He figured that Tomoe had tangled with a gang boss.

The beggar's expression turned shifty. His eyes moved constantly—like black flies crawling on a moldy dumpling—from Tora, to other restaurant patrons, to the passing crowd in the market, then back to Tora again. "I wouldn't know, but if you're looking for her killer, you'd better check the toms she took home with her. She put out to anybody who paid enough. That back door of hers might as well have been a curtain. I figure one of them felt cheated and cut her up a bit. They say there was a lot of blood." The beggar licked his lips and grinned. "Maybe he even liked doing it."

Tora narrowed his eyes, but there was nothing to be gained by hitting the beggar now. Better let him talk.

The waiter came and slapped food and drink down on the bench between them. "Ten coppers. You pay now."

Tora suppressed a grimace. That left him with only three coppers, and he had a long day ahead of him. He paid, then snatched the wine flask from the beggar's greedy fingers. One of them was missing the tip. "Talk first!" he snapped.

The beggar stuck out his tongue and reached for the soup bowl.

"I said, 'Talk first!'" Tora shouted and pounded the flimsy bench. Some of the soup splashed out.

"Now see what you've done," complained the beggar. "Oh, all right. She used to sing to a guy owns a training school on the other side of town. They say that's not all he does. He comes here with his friends: a big, mean-looking guy and a young kid. I don't know their names."

"Is his name Kata?"

Surprise flashed in the beggar's eyes, but he said, "How should I know? He didn't introduce himself to me."

Tora reached for the soup.

"All right. It may have been."

Tora relaxed. He was pretty sure now that the beggar knew Kata. He pushed wine and soup toward the man and thought about the interesting implications. Not only was he looking forward to getting his hands on that sly fellow Kata, but there was also the Haseo look-alike. And that one had been seen near the watchtower, not far from where Tomoe worked. He hoped they would not recognize him in his rags but planned to apply a handful of dirt to his face before paying his visit. Impatient now to be gone, Tora watched with ill-concealed irritation as the beggar slurped his soup and drank his wine. The sight turned his stomach. Getting up, he told the filthy creature, "Stay out of trouble or else!" and walked away.

Kata's training school was in session again, but the crowd outside seemed much smaller than last time. They hardly gave Tora a second glance; he was one of them, a shabby, dirty fellow without a job and nothing better to do on a fine day than to watch some fighting. Tora squatted next to a scruffy youngster and scanned the training hall.

Kata was demonstrating a sword technique to three older students. It looked like an aggressive move against two or more armed fighters that involved a quick and fatal outcome. Kata was certainly not training for contests, and Tora appreciated the usefulness of his technique. Having been a soldier, he did not like to play games with a sword.

Stick fighting was another matter, and Tora was remarkably skilled at that. A long bamboo pole could kill if handled a certain way, but it was primarily a weapon of defense. The idea was to disarm the other guy or perhaps incapacitate him by breaking an arm or a leg. In a case like that, a man could afford to toy a bit with an opponent. He saw that Kata's stick fighters were rank beginners, and an idea began to form in his mind.

An elbow poked his side. "You new here?" asked his neighbor.

Tora eyed the skinny kid. He was maybe twelve, stringy, and wild looking. He probably had no family and lived on the streets on what he could steal from food stalls and shops, or from people's houses if they were careless enough to leave them unattended. There were thousands of hungry, homeless boys like this in the streets of the capital and they were always a nuisance.

"None of your business, brat," he growled and turned his attention back to the lesson. Kata being a gang boss certainly made sense. As a training master, he could conduct his business practically under the noses of the authorities. Haseo's double was absent, but he surely had some link to the organization. Tora smiled with grim satisfaction.

"Bet I could tell you what you want to know," squeaked the youngster beside him.

His voice was changing and made Tora jump a little and wonder if he had underestimated his age. He turned to look him over more carefully. The boy cocked his head and touched his nose in the manner of someone who has information for sale.

"What could you know? You're barely weaned from your ma's tits," Tora said.

"Hah!" The scruffy youngster stuck out his bony chest and announced proudly, "I work for him," jerking his head in the direction of the training school. "That's how I know. Bet you came looking for a job."

Tora gaped in mock surprise. "How d'you know that?"

The boy grinned. "You're the type. You like fighting and you look like a soldier out of work. They always come and pretend they're just watching. Then, pretty soon, they offer to work for food."

Tora glanced at the students again. The ones in front were practicing the "whirlwind" defense, which involved turning rapidly in a circle while slashing about with the sword. They were coming dangerously close to wounding each other with their wooden swords, wheeling about the training hall like demented tops. He snorted. But the boy might be useful. Tora asked, "D'you think he'd take me on?"

"Might." The boy squinted at him. "You been in the army?"

"Yes. And I'm better with a sword than those fools."

"Good. Got a good army record?"

Tora shifted uneasily. "Well . . ."

The boy grinned and slapped his shoulder. "Don't worry. That's good, too. Just so long as they're not looking for you."

"They wouldn't be looking for me here anyway."

"Where you from then?"

"The North Country."

The boy clapped his hands. "Kata will like that. He says they've got tough fighters up that way. Yes, I'd say you've got a good chance. Mind you, he expects loyalty. Me, I've worked for him almost two years now. I'll soon be a regular and get my lessons for free."

"What sort of work?"

"I'm a runner now. The fastest there is because I know my way around. And I keep my mouth shut. That's important in this business."

I bet it is, thought Tora. "You're a bright kid. You'll go far."

The boy nodded. "I know. And I'm not afraid."

"Well," said Tora, "if you can help me get the job, I'll make you a deal."

"What kind of deal?"

"You tell me how to act and who to talk to, and if all goes well, I'll give you some lessons to get you started. I can use a sword and a pole better than any of them."

But the youngster balked a little. He cast a nervous glance toward Kata, who was shouting at an unfortunate student. "Are you really good?"

Tora jerked his head toward the alley behind the school. "Let's go back there and I'll show you."

The alley was deserted. One side was the mostly blind wall of the training school, and the other a long line of half-broken fencing separating the alley from the backyards of poor dwellings. A few empty sake barrels rested against the wall, and a pile of kitchen garbage had gathered near a wooden shed. Tora waited. In a moment the skinny youngster opened the back door and emerged, carrying two wooden swords.

Tora extended his hand for one of the swords. "Just a little sample. That move your master was teaching just now? It's called 'The Whirlwind,' and it should be done like this." He demonstrated with an explosion of movement that made his arms and legs a blur, causing the air to whistle around his outflung sword arm. He finished with a sudden jump that brought the point of the sword against the boy's throat.

The youngster shrieked and fell backward into the dirt. Tora grinned down at him. "Like that, see? You slash at as many as you can, making some room for yourself, and then you go for the leader. That stops the rest, but if it doesn't, you kill the bastard and start over again. I've never had to do it more than once. By then they've got the message and run."

"Amida." The youngster got to his feet, his eyes big with

wonder. "I've never seen Kata *Sensei* move like *that*." Then he added loyally, "But I figure he could."

Tora doubted that Kata would teach that particular trick, because he had just invented it. The problem with it was that it left your back unprotected when you stopped whirling to attack a single opponent. But the youngster would not know that. So he grinned lazily and perched his backside on one of the up-turned barrels. "Now it's your turn. What's your name?"

"Kinjiro. And you?"

"Tora."

"Tora?" The boy looked impressed. "If they call you Tiger, you must be famous."

Tora said modestly, "Nah. Would I be looking for a job if I were?"

Kinjiro said fervently, "Well, I think you're great. And if you aren't famous, you will be."

Tora nearly blushed at so much admiration and began to wonder if this young sprout of a cutthroat might be salvageable after all. But he doubted that his master would take on another obligation just now, especially one of such dubious promise, and put the thought firmly from his mind. He said, "Thank you. Someday you may have such a name, too. You know a lot already. Speaking of that, can you tell me about a big fellow with a trimmed beard? He was with your boss. Nicely dressed. About forty, I'd say. We had some words. I didn't like his manner and I doubt he liked mine. Who is he?"

"Uh, oh! I bet you messed with Sangoro." The boy clapped his hand over his mouth and looked over his shoulder. "Don't mention that I called him that. He wants to be known as Matsue *Sensei*."

"*Sensei*? Is he a teacher like Kata?"

"Matsue *Sensei* is a master swordsman. He doesn't waste his time with ordinary fighters."

"Or so he says."

The boy grinned. "Maybe you'll show him, eh? I don't like him, because he beats me. But he's the boss's friend. Maybe he's in the business. I wouldn't know because I'm not allowed in the meetings." His face lengthened. "Matsue *Sensei* might make trouble for you. The best thing to do is to talk to the boss when he's not around. Once you're in, show the boss what you can do. Matsue *Sensei*'ll have a hard time getting rid of you then."

Tora gravely thanked him for the advice.

The youngster asked, "Will you show me how to handle my sword now?"

The impromptu lesson was inconvenient, because someone might come at any moment, but a deal was a deal, and Kinjiro had passed on some useful information. Tora picked up the sword again and showed Kinjiro various stances. His private opinion was that the slight, bandy-legged boy would never develop the muscles, height, or weight needed to handle a heavy sword. But the exercise reminded him that he had become rusty himself. They used to have sword or pole practice every morning in the courtyard—he, the master, and Genba. But lately the master rarely had the time, and when he did, he practiced with Yori, who had become very enthusiastic about swords. Genba had turned into a lazy slug. Perhaps signing up with Kata was not such a bad idea. There was some small risk that Kata would recognize the ragged, unshaven Tora as the companion of the official who had asked nosy questions about Matsue, but Kata had never seen him close up. Tora felt his chin. Perhaps in a day or so he could grow enough of a beard to be safe. The temptation of getting inside the gang was too much to resist.

"Tora?"

Not much harm in teaching the kid a few tricks. He might need him in the future. "Pay attention, Kinjiro," Tora said. "There's more to being a fighter than learning moves. Think about it: Every time two men meet with swords, one will be the winner and one will be dead. Never get into a quarrel lightly."

"I don't plan to lose," said the boy with a toss of the head. "And if I do, I deserve to die. That's a fighter's fate."

"Hmm. Yes. But always keep death in sight. If you forget it, you'll make a mistake and death will rudely remind you."

The boy nodded. "That's very good. I shall remember it. Now show me what I must do."

Tora sighed and assumed his position. "Watch me. You must train your body to obey you perfectly, and most especially you must think to protect yourself. So, first of all, always stand sideways to your enemy. See? He's got less to strike at that way."

The boy watched and followed Tora's example.

"Crouch down a bit more. Make sure your shoulders are no higher than your enemy's sword hand. No, put your weight on the forward knee. Right. Now stretch the other leg out behind you. That allows you to lunge, twist, or retreat instantly." He demonstrated.

The boy grinned and lunged. Tora twisted aside and, lashing up with his sword, easily disarmed him.

"Ouch!" Kinjiro rubbed his wrist. When he tried to pick up his sword again, his hand would not obey.

"What's this?" drawled a lazy voice behind them. "How dare you injure this child?"

Kinjiro cried out, "It wasn't like that, Matsue *Sensei*. Tora was teaching me."

Tora turned and saw two men. Both were tall. One—a stranger—was as thin and lanky as a scarecrow; the other was Haseo's double. Tora finally had a good look at their mysterious stranger. Matsue did the same with him. His scrutiny was unfriendly. "Tiger?" he sneered. "You look like a mangy cat."

Matsue bore a certain superficial resemblance to Haseo. It was probably greater at a distance and due to the way he walked and held himself. His face was actually quite different. The eyes were smaller and colder, more calculating than Haseo's. Haseo had not had much to smile about, but when Tora had met him, the joy of having escaped and the thrill of holding a sword again had lit up his face like the sun. This man's smile was tight, contemptuous, and spiteful. Tora reacted with instant loathing. He cocked his head and snapped, "I may look like a mangy cat, but I got claws for rude bastards like you."

Kinjiro pulled his sleeve. "No, Tora. This is the master's friend, the one I told you about."

Tora already regretted his rash words and was seeking some way to gloss over them, when Matsue took a step toward the boy, spun him about by the arm, and slapped him so viciously across the face that he flew through the air and landed in a whimpering heap in the dirt.

"Hey, why'd you do that?" Tora cried, clenching his fists.

"He talks too much. People have lost their tongues for doing that."

The boy uttered a choking moan and crept up to cower behind Tora, clutching his shirt and peering around him at Matsue. "Please, Matsue *Sensei*," he wailed, "I've said nothing I shouldn't. I only told Tora what a great swordsman you are."

Matsue lost some of the cold fury that had marked his attack on the youngster. He growled, "What business is that of his? Your job is to send scum like him on their way."

"But, Master, he wants to sign up. He's from the north and a very great fighter. He's almost as great as you."

Silence fell. Tora was still glaring at Matsue, aware only of an intense, burning hatred for the man. He strove for self-control, forcing his breathing to become shallow and gradually relaxing the tension in his body.

Kinjiro's words had caused Matsue to shift his attention to Tora. As they locked eyes, Tora almost lost his control again. He felt a strange shock and thought: He can see right into my head with those mean eyes. He knows what I'm thinking. He knows what I'm here for. Maybe he's the one that killed Tomoe.

Matsue broke the spell first. He spat. Then he drawled, "Let's go inside and see how good you are, mouse catcher." He turned toward the training hall and held open the backdoor for Tora to enter.

Tora hesitated. Matsue was heavier, especially in the shoulders. That should make him slower, but his strokes would carry all his weight and would be hard to parry. Besides, Matsue had a reputation as a swordsman, and Tora had little training, had only used a sword in battle, and was badly out of practice. On the other hand, here was his chance to show the bastard who was the better man. In front of Kata and his men. In front of a crowd who believed Matsue superior. It was tempting, but Tora knew he must not do this if he wished to gain information.

Kinjiro gave him a little push from behind. "Go on. Show them what you can do. You'll be in for sure." The boy's cheek was red and swelling. Tomorrow he might even have a black eye. Tora remembered the bean-filled rice cake in his sleeve. No telling when he'd get home. He fished it out and handed it to the boy. "Here. I'm sorry you got hurt on my account."

Kinjiro looked surprised. "Thanks. It was nothing," he said and took a large bite.

Tora walked quickly past Matsue and the thin man into the hall.

Matsue interrupted class.

Kata frowned. "What's this?" he demanded, staring at Tora, who still held his sword. "Since when do we invite vagrants to join a class?"

Matsue said, "This one's been outside talking to the kid. Apparently he's been bragging that he's some great fighter from the north. I thought he might show us his stuff." He gave a derisive snort.

Kata eyed Tora. "Have I seen you before?"

"Maybe. I came once just to watch a little. I'd heard about you in the market, Master Kata. Thought I'd ask for a job, but you were busy."

Kata's eyes narrowed. "In the market? Who sent you?"

"I don't know his name. A beggar. I tripped over him near the tower."

One of the students guffawed.

Kata relaxed. He nodded, smiling. "We know him."

"He can start with the students," Matsue said. "That should give them some confidence."

Kata turned to one of the students. "You, Seijiro. You can use the practice."

Seijiro flushed. Younger and smaller than the others, he looked nervous, but took his stance. Tora eyed him and decided that he had been matched against the weakest student in the school. Feeling the insult, he crouched and attacked, disarming the other fellow almost instantly.

Turning to Kata, he said, "You haven't got very far with this batch, have you?"

Kata did not answer. He called a name, and another student assumed his position.

This time Tora toyed with his opponent. He let him attack, offering openings that the other man did not see and bungled. In the end, Tora disarmed him without much effort. "Come on," he said impatiently, "how about a better opponent, *Sensei?*"

But Kata, after exchanging a glance with Matsue, shook his head. "They need the practice, and I can see how you handle yourself with them. If you do well, I may give you work."

Matsue was leaning against a wooden trunk, looking bored. He was the opponent Tora wanted, but there was nothing he could do about it if he wished to be accepted by Kata. He decided to put on a good show.

His third opponent was quick. Tora found himself moving a great deal with this one. Jumping about and twisting in this warm air made him sweat. The fellow eventually tried the new whirlwind move, and Tora ducked under the flailing sword, tripped him, and placed his sword against his throat. "Always wait until the master has taught you the right defensive action in case the whirlwind doesn't blow away your opponent," he admonished his victim with a grin.

Kinjiro applauded enthusiastically, but Kata shouted, "Silence!"

A fourth student stepped forward. Tora wiped the sweat from his face and saw with relief that this man was considerably older. Surely he would not jump about like a mad flea.

He did not. But he was a very deliberate defensive fighter, and this bout lasted four times as long as the last. When he had finally disarmed the man, Tora was tired. He realized he was badly out of shape, but expecting him to fight one opponent after another without allowing him rest periods between bouts struck him as unfair. By now, his thin shirt and trousers were glued to his sweating body, and he kept having to wipe his sword hand on his clothes to get a firm grip. He saw with some satisfaction that the students he had fought looked worse than he.

The last student was his own age. If the past performances had been anything to judge by, this must be the star pupil. He was. The student executed several aggressive moves perfectly. Tora decided to use caution. He concentrated and paid attention to his defensive moves while waiting for an opening for a surprise attack. This paid off, because he managed to trick his opponent into an ill-considered lunge, which allowed Tora to twist and seize the other man's sword hand, bending it back at the wrist. The student screamed and dropped his weapon.

As he bowed to his shamefaced opponent and then to Kata, he heard Kinjiro applaud again. This time, reluctantly, a few students joined in.

Tora expelled an audible sigh of relief. He was drenched in sweat, and the muscles in his calves and shoulders ached and throbbed unpleasantly. "Well, *Sensei*?" he asked Kata with a grin. "Are you satisfied? Will you take me on? I work cheap. Food and shelter to start with. But I can use some sword practice, so I'd like a few private lessons, too."

"Do you now?" Kata cocked his head. "And what other sorts of work can you do?"

"Well," said Tora with a laugh, "I draw the line at sweeping up after everybody, but as I'm pretty good with my sword, I could take care of any troublemakers, or collect money that's owed to you, or generally just keep an eye on you and your business." He went to place his practice sword on the trunk Matsue was leaning against.

Matsue straightened up and seized Tora's wrist. "Not so fast, mouse catcher. Maybe you did scare a few of the little pests, but I'm not done with you. After the tiger roars, he'd better prove that he has teeth and claws. You call yourself Tora; let's see if you can fight like a tiger."

Tora stared at him. He had just fought five bouts and was exhausted. Sweat was pouring off him. He said, "I'm tired. Some other time. Tomorrow, maybe? Or later tonight?"

Matsue smiled unpleasantly. "What? Are you no tiger after all? After filling the boy's ears with your boasts, you now claim fatigue because some puny students practiced their pathetic skills on you? And you expect to become a useful member of this training school? Pah!"

Tora flushed with anger. Matsue had planned this from the beginning. He bowed. "As you wish."

Matsue took another practice sword from the wooden box. It was beautifully tapered, slightly longer than Tora's, and almost black in color. He performed a couple of sharp slashes, then assumed his position.

When Tora had taken his place, Matsue, small eyes flickering with malicious joy, bowed. Tora returned the bow. His hand and the grip of his sword were slippery with his sweat, but he made an effort to put this complication from his mind and think positively. He would not allow Matsue to taunt him into confusion or, worse, fear. Instead, he would make his move quickly and end the contest before it was too late.

Focusing his eyes on Matsue's center, he waited. When Matsue lunged, Tora parried, saw his chance, and instantly took a large step forward to side kick Matsue's leg. It was a soldier's trick of overcoming an attacking adversary quickly. But the move failed miserably. As Tora's leg shot forward for the kick, the foot carrying his weight slid out from under him. He slipped on the wet boards where one of the students had tumbled earlier and was already falling when Matsue's sword came hissing down.

A fierce, hot pain exploded in Tora's skull, and the world disappeared.

CHAPTER TWELVE

THE BEAUTIFUL LADY
YASUGI

As he jumped to avoid the downward slashing sword, Akitada crashed into the clothes stand, which toppled, covering him with a pile of scented silk garments. A woman screamed piercingly, "No!" Momentarily blinded and helpless, he knew his attacker was striking again. He attempted to roll out of the way of the blade, but was tangled in the garments. This time, miraculously, the blade caught the wooden frame of the stand, and he only felt a sharp blow to his shoulder. The woman screamed again.

Heaving up clothes and stand with a single violent movement, Akitada regained his feet and vision. Even in the semidarkness, he took in the scene quickly. Two women were in the room, one cowering on the floor and sobbing hysterically, the other, massive as a figure carved from rock, standing protectively in front of her, her broad face a mask of snarling determination. The woman on the floor was his "nun," though she was no longer wearing the veil and habit. Her protector was a servant, a peasant woman of extraordinary size.

The sword lay on the floor between him and the two women. Akitada bent to take it up, seeing with surprise that it was very beautiful. The hilt was gold inlaid with colored enamel and pearls, and the blade was incised with patterns filled with gold and silver. He touched his thumb to it. It was as dull as a wooden practice sword.

"Very pretty," he said, "but since swords like this are meant for ceremonial wear only, it's not very useful as a weapon. Still, you might have killed me. Do you always attack visitors who have announced themselves outside your door?"

The maid still simmered with hostility. "You have no business here," she said. "I was protecting my lady. Go away or I'll call the constables."

Akitada ignored this. "This is Lady Yasugi then, I assume? She can tell you that calling for constables does little good in this neighborhood. We met yesterday in the street outside."

The woman on the floor got to her knees and bowed. "This foolish person apologizes for the mistake. We thought you were a robber."

She had a lovely, cultured voice. Akitada returned the bow. "A reasonable mistake. I was passing your house when I saw a man climbing over the back wall. I scared him off, but decided to have a look in case someone else lurked about. My name is Sugawara Akitada, by the way. I serve in the Ministry of Justice."

The maid could no longer contain herself. "You met my lady in the street? And someone was climbing our wall? Amida! What is going on?"

Her mistress said sharply, "Be quiet, Anju," and told Akitada, "I am Hiroko, my Lord Yasugi's third wife."

"Ah. I was told that Lord Yasugi had left with his entire family days ago. Why are you here alone?"

Her eyes flickered to her maid before she answered. "I fell ill.

My lord left me until I would be well enough to travel. I shall join him soon. We are expecting an escort any day."

Akitada did not bother to keep the disbelief from his voice. "Lord Yasugi left two women here alone?"

She flushed and lowered her eyes. Akitada saw now that she was a remarkable beauty. The nun's habit had hidden her best features: an oval face framed by thick, long hair; large eyes and sweetly shaped lips enhanced by touches of paint; a graceful body flattered by the thinnest of silks in many layers and in exquisite shades of rose and lilac. No man in his right mind would let such a treasure out of his sight for long.

She spoke again, in a pleasant soft voice that nevertheless put him in his place for implying criticism of her husband. "We could not be certain that I had not contracted smallpox. My lord left two male servants, but one has gone to nurse his sick mother, and we have sent the other after my husband to tell him I am now well enough to travel."

Smallpox again. Apparently it seized people's imaginations to such a degree that they abandoned their loved ones. Akitada was shocked at the husband's inhumanity. He looked from her to the servant, who stood stolidly beside her mistress, watching and daring him to doubt what he was being told. Then he laid the sword on a clothes chest, bent to pick up the rack, and set it upright again.

"Oh, please do not trouble," cried Lady Yasugi. "I have forgotten my manners. Forgive me. Anju will do that. Anju, a pillow for Lord Sugawara and see if there is some wine."

Akitada found the cosmetics box under the pile of silk robes and picked it up. "This is very beautiful," he said. "The design of a master. There cannot be very many like it."

Lady Yasugi glanced at the box. Twisting her hands in her lap, she murmured, "Thank you. It is nothing. A gift from a relation. Bring the wine, Anju."

The maid gave her mistress a look of reproach but left the

tumbled clothing she had been replacing and went out. They were alone, a situation that was not merely unorthodox but quite improper between a married woman and a strange male visitor. Akitada wondered about the relationship between this beautiful creature and her wealthy lord and master.

She leaned forward a little and said urgently, "I have not thanked you for saving me yesterday. You injured your eye?"

Suddenly Akitada felt self-conscious about his appearance. "It's nothing. I'm glad you are safe." He cast another glance around the luxurious furnishings of the large room and then went to sit on the cushion the maid had placed for him. The cosmetics box he set on the floor between them, where the slanting rays of the sun made the gold inlay shine and the mother-of-pearl glimmer in a rainbow of colors.

She glanced at it nervously, and then at him, but did not comment. Instead, she made an effort at polite conversation. She smiled and said softly, "Forgive me for not thanking you earlier, my lord, but I did not want Anju to know what happened. She worries so."

Akitada raised his eyebrows. "She's quite right to worry. This is no longer a safe neighborhood and you should never go out alone. Why didn't you take your maid with you?"

Turning her head away, she said pettishly, "Oh, I am so tired of being watched all the time. I thought it would be safe to walk to the palace in the middle of the day. And I put on the nun's habit so nobody would bother me."

She was lying. Akitada firmed his resolve. "I see. You disguised yourself because you thought it would be safer?" She nodded, giving him a quick glance to see if he believed her. "Why was it so important for you to attend the hearing on the murder of the blind woman?"

Her eyes widened at his directness, but she must have expected the question, and that meant she knew he had been at the hearing and had followed her. "What? Oh, you know about that? No particular reason. I meant to go to the palace and watch the guards at their practice. When I passed police headquarters, people were going in and I decided to find out what was happening."

"Come," he said, "you can do better than that. I was there and watched you during the proceedings. You either came because of the victim or the accused, and as the accused is my retainer Tora, I know you weren't there on his account."

She flushed, with anger this time, and burst into defiant speech. "You are wrong. Why shouldn't I go to a hearing out of interest? I have seen too little of the outside world. Women of our class rarely have an opportunity to see life the way men see it. We are kept like prisoners in our fathers' houses, and when they die, we are under our brothers' control, or that of our husbands. And when we finally become old and have neither husbands nor brothers left, our sons keep us locked away unless we cut our hair and take the veil. Only nuns and peasant women escape their prison." Her eyes flashed with emotion. "Not a day passes when I don't wish I were a nun. I keep the habit for the moment I can cut my hair and escape this cage."

The maid, returning, overheard her words. She said sternly, "The master does not like you talking that way. You have a good life here. Why trouble yourself with ugly things when you have fine clothes, good food, your books, and your toys? You can play your zither, paint, or walk in the garden whenever you please."

Her mistress buried her face in her sleeve.

Akitada looked at Lady Yasugi and wondered. He had gathered that her desire for a religious life had nothing to do with spirituality and a great deal with spirit. He did not approve altogether of too much spirit in a female. It was true that noble women spent most of their lives inside their homes. Most preferred it, because going out would bring them into contact with the ragged, diseased, and unsavory poor. They would be accosted by beggars, prostitutes, thieves, and robbers. Lady Yasugi had certainly learned that much on her recent excursion. But of course she had lied. It had all been an elaborate lie. A casual stroll to satisfy her curiosity was not the real reason she had left the dubious safety of this house. He turned to the maid. "Anju, did you know Tomoe was murdered?"

The woman's large chin sagged. "Amida." She stared at him. "That's why you're here?" Turning on her mistress, she cried, "There. I told you. Now see what's happened. What will the master say when he finds out the police are asking questions?"

This was not quite the reaction Akitada had expected, but he settled for it. "Do I take it that Lord Yasugi is unaware of your relationship with the blind street singer?" he asked the mistress.

Lady Yasugi's hands were clenched so tightly that the knuckles showed white against her creamy skin, and her eyes looked frightened. But she said calmly enough, "I have no idea what you are talking about. Anju is confused."

Akitada turned back to the maid. "You understood very well, didn't you, Anju?"

The maid flushed. "No, no. I must have misheard you, sir." Seeing his disbelief, she stammered, "I . . . I thought . . . you said Tonomo. Yes, Tonomo. He's one of the children. Always in trouble . . . er . . . we didn't want the master to find out. That's all."

Akitada greeted that feeble explanation with a derisive laugh, but the maid's foolish attempt at a lie was not funny, at least not to Lady Yasugi, who was quite pale and on the verge of tears. He was more confused than ever about the connection between this wealthy, elegant woman and a poor singer from the slums. After a moment's hesitation, he tried appealing to her conscience.

"Lady Yasugi, I'm not with the police, but I'm helping them on this case. This poor woman was brutally murdered in a small room she rented. Being blind, she had no way to protect herself against her killer. I have seen the room. There must have been a terrible, bloody struggle." He noted with satisfaction that she gasped and pressed her hand to her mouth. "I'm sorry to upset you, but I need your help. My retainer Tora knew Tomoe and was worried about her safety. He found her dead and was arrested for a murder he did not commit." Akitada decided to play his hunch. "He told me that Tomoe used to come here to perform and that you befriended her." When she only stared at him without making a protest, he knew he had guessed correctly. "I beseech you, both for Tomoe's sake and for Tora's, tell me what you know about her. The motive for the crime may lie in her past and nobody seems to know about that."

Was it his imagination or had she relaxed? She opened and closed her mouth, but finally said only, "How terrible!"

Exasperated, Akitada asked, "Do you know Tomoe or not?"

She glanced at the maid, then nodded. "Yes. She did come here. To sing to me, as you said. Anju did not approve because my husband would have objected to having a street singer in our quarters, but I felt sorry for her and thought a little extra money would help someone so sadly afflicted. The servants told me about her murder. So sad! When I saw her name on the board in front of police headquarters and read about the hearing, I went in to find out more. Out of pity and curiosity, that's all."

The maid cried, "You went into police headquarters yesterday? A place full of criminals and rough men? Only a prostitute would go there unattended. The master won't like that at all."

Lady Yasugi gave an exasperated sigh. "I only wanted to find out what happened to the singer, Anju. Nobody knew who I was. There is no need to trouble my lord with such a trivial thing. He will only blame you."

The maid clamped her mouth shut and folded her arms across her chest. "I should have told him from the start and none of this would've happened," she grumbled, but her mistress had won her point.

Akitada gave Lady Yasugi a long look, which she met calmly enough, but he saw that her fingers were locked tightly and was convinced that she was still lying. Why? Because the maid was present? He picked up the cosmetics case and opened it. It was filled with salves and paints as Tomoe's had been, and the designs inside and out were as exquisite as those on hers, though not quite the same—different plants and flowers, he thought. But he was certain it had been made by the same artist. He was about to ask his name, when Lady Yasugi said sharply, "Anju, don't just stand around doing nothing. This wine is quite cold. Go and heat a fresh flask. And try to find some pickled vegetables or plums. There must be something left." Her voice was tight with impatience and the pretty forehead wore a frown. The maid took up the flask and left the room.

They were alone again. The sun had moved and taken with it the broad band of golden light that had made the box sparkle and cast a soft radiance over the room and its occupants. It must be getting late. Akitada attempted to separate his admiration for this beautiful and troubled woman from his suspicions.

She listened to the receding steps for a moment, then said urgently, "Please do not pursue this matter, sir. Anju must not know any more. Everything depends on it."

Astonished, Akitada protested, "I regret but I cannot do this. A crime has been committed and Tora may lose his life over it. If you know anything, you must speak."

She wrung her hands. "My husband . . . you do not understand . . . please . . . there are children and I cannot risk their lives and happiness. Besides, it is a family secret that cannot have anything to do with the murder."

Satisfaction washed over Akitada. Finally they were coming to it. He leaned forward. "If this has nothing to do with the murder, I shall not reveal your secret, but you must speak."

She shook her head. "You cannot know . . . I beg you, have pity."

Feeling heartless, he said, "My dear lady, there is too much evidence of a very close connection between you and Tomoe to support your allegation that she merely came here to sing. For one thing," he raised the cosmetics box, "there is this. Tomoe's box is a twin to yours. Such an expensive and beautifully made article should not, by rights, have been in the possession of a poor blind woman."

She began to weep softly, raising a silk sleeve to hide her tears. "Oh, dear heaven." she moaned, "if my husband finds out, it will destroy me."

"I have given you my word that I will keep your secret if it doesn't affect the case."

She lowered her sleeve. Even tear-stained and reddened, her face was still lovely, her eyes awash with pain. Increasingly distracted by her anguish, he made a conscious effort to remain in control, but before he could speak again, she shocked him utterly.

"Tomoe was my sister," she said, new tears welling over and spilling down her face. "My older sister. Now are you satisfied?"

He was dumfounded. "Your sister?" This beautiful and elegant creature and the ragged, pockmarked blind woman from the market could not be sisters. "How did such a thing come to pass?"

She dabbed at her face and looked toward the door. Her fear of the maid was palpable. When she spoke again, she did not look at him, but the words tumbled from her lips. "My sister made a bad marriage. When our parents did not approve of the man, she went to be with him, and they disowned her. Then she got smallpox and lost her eyesight, and her husband divorced her. I knew nothing of this until I went shopping for silk one day and found her working in the market like a beggar. Anju was with me and we could not talk freely. I offered her money, but she was too proud to accept charity. Tomoe was always proud. And stubborn. There was little else I could do because my husband would not have allowed it—he is . . . very strict about the company I keep—but she came to visit several times. We pretended it was to sing to me. She sang, and we talked little, hardly like sisters, because we were never alone. I'd give her some money for the . . . for her work, and she would leave again." She raised tragic eyes to his. "So you see . . . it cannot have anything to do with her murder."

It was a tragic story, but such things happened when daughters rebelled against their parents' wishes and made their own choices. Wisdom resides in the soul, not the mind or the body. The parents, no doubt, had felt that their daughter had proven unworthy of family membership. Perhaps they had even lost her without feeling much regret—not so much as they might have felt for a lost ox or chicken. Akitada felt very sorry for the two women, but he knew that Tomoe had chosen her fate. Tomoe had committed the ultimate sin; she had defied her parents and run away.

Akitada looked into the melting eyes of the beautiful woman across from him and decided that rebellion must be something of a family trait, for Lady Yasugi disobeyed her husband and had expressed strong feelings about her lack of freedom as a woman; only a day earlier she had almost paid a high price for her lack of decorum.

Truly, women were difficult to understand. Tamako had always shown a proper respect both for her father and for her husband. Tomoe, and perhaps to a lesser degree her sister, were excellent examples of the suffering women brought upon themselves when they did not subordinate their foolish notions to the wiser counsel of men. Seimei would quote the Great Sage on that subject: "If retainers obey their lords, children their parents, and wives their husbands, peace and tranquility will reign." And yet, there was something very attractive about a spirited woman.

Lady Yasugi broke into his thoughts. "You won't mention this to anyone, my lord?"

He started to tell her that he must find Tomoe's killer and for that reason needed to know more about Tomoe's family and her husband, but she drew in her breath sharply. "Shh! Anju is coming."

The maid gave them a suspicious glance, then poured more wine for Akitada. She offered him a small bowl of pickled plums. To justify her errand, Akitada drank and took one of the plums. Both wine and plums were excellent. He recalled Tomoe's poor room and the few bits of coarse food she had subsisted on.

There was little more he could do under Anju's watchful eye. An idea occurred to him: If he could bring Lady Yasugi to his own home, it would be much easier to separate her from her maid. He said, "You're not safe here. I chased off the thug who climbed the wall, but he may return. If you consent, my wife will make you welcome in my house until your husband sends for you."

The maid snapped, "The master wouldn't allow it." She looked belligerent, her arms folded again and her chin thrust out. "I'll keep watch. She'll be all right."

Lady Yasugi nodded. "Yes, it is better so. Thank you for your offer, but I should like to stay here."

Foiled, Akitada said, "In that case, I shall send you one of my men to keep watch until your own people come. Genba is a gentle giant who used to be a wrestling master before he came into my service. You may trust him completely."

There was a short hesitation as mistress and maid exchanged glances. Then Lady Yasugi bowed. "Thank you, Lord Sugawara. We are very much indebted to you for your warning and your kind offer. I trust we won't deprive you of your man for very long."

It was a signal that the visit had come to an end.

She rose to accompany him to the veranda. The setting sun had dipped behind the trees and left a soft radiance behind which flattered both inanimate objects and living beings. For a moment they stood looking out across the garden as Anju hovered behind them.

The third Lady Yasugi's private garden was enclosed by the outer wall, two other pavilions, and a covered gallery leading to the main house. The scent of the flowering wisteria growing against her veranda hung heavy in the warm evening air, and late bees still buzzed about the long, pendant white blooms. It seemed very peaceful here, but beyond the wall lay the violence of the western city, and even in the buildings around them evil might lurk.

Akitada glanced down at the zither. "I heard you playing earlier, a very charming sound. The street is just beyond that wall. I knew the house must be occupied and wondered why no one answered my knocking at the gate."

She blushed a little. "We heard your knocking. Forgive me, but two women alone cannot receive visitors. And we were afraid. I should not have played my zither, but time passes very slowly here."

He could imagine her loneliness in this deserted villa and understood her frustration with a life that tied her to an autocratic husband who had deserted her at the first suspicion of smallpox. Her beauty was more pronounced here than in the half light of her room, though Akitada saw that she was not as young as Lady Kose had suggested. He guessed her to be Tamako's age. On an impulse he asked, "Do you have children, Lady Yasugi?"

She went very still for a moment. Then she said tonelessly, "No. I have disappointed my lord in this also."

"I'm sorry." Producing a number of male heirs was a wife's primary responsibility. On this rested her standing in the household. If Lady Yasugi had proved infertile, it might account for her husband's neglect and her own unhappiness in her marriage. Many a man divorced a barren wife because of the overriding duty to ensure the survival of his family. Still, she was a very desirable woman. Akitada glanced at that pure profile with the gently curving eyebrows and the elegant hairline. Few women of her class dared to be seen in the bright light of day. He said, "Surely fortune will soon bless you."

"Thank you." She gave a shiver and changed the subject. "It seems strange to feel fear in this beautiful place."

"Genba will take care of that when he gets here."

"You are very good."

A brief silence fell. No doubt she wished him gone, but Akitada still hoped for something more, some small piece of information he might use to find Tomoe's killer. "May I ask your father's name?" he asked.

She stiffened. "It cannot matter. I bear the Yasugi name now."

So she still tried to protect her secret. He could not probe further and bowed to her. "Thank you for your hospitality," he said formally. "If you permit it, I shall take another stroll about the garden to make sure all is well. Genba should arrive at your front gate within the hour. He's a big man with a large smile."

She murmured her thanks, and he stepped off the veranda and onto the garden path. The events of the day had finally managed to give him a headache. He looked forward to a hot bath, food, and bed. Retracing his steps, he checked the gardens and service buildings, visited the back gate again, finding it securely locked, and explored the shrubbery underneath the troublesome pine branch. Eventually he made his way to the front gate, where he found Anju waiting for him.

She said ungraciously, "I have to let you out. The gate can only be locked from the inside."

He nodded. "Keep an eye on your mistress. If you can find a sharper weapon than your master's sword, use it. As soon as Genba arrives, you can relax."

She bowed. "I'm sure the master will be much obliged."

The two wings of the big double gate were barred by a ponderous beam that it would take two sturdy men to lift. But a smaller gate was cut into one of the panels. This was bolted by two sliding bars. A short chain led from this gate to a bamboo rattle. Nobody could pass in or out without alerting the household. He waited for her to open this gate, but she stared at him, almost as if she were still trying to decide if he was friend or foe. Then she made a strange sound, something between a grunt and a chuckle, and slipped the bars back. The small gate flew open with a loud rattle of the bamboo sticks, and he stepped through.

"It's Murata," she said.

He turned, but the gate slammed shut with another rattle, and he heard the bolts slide into place and her footsteps recede.

For a moment he was confused. Murata? Had he misheard? What had she meant by it? Then it came to him that she must have given him Lady Yasugi's family name. Most helpful, of course, but why had she done so in defiance of her mistress's wishes?

Perhaps Anju had a purpose of her own. Her mistress had made it clear that, far from being her devoted servant, Anju was her watchdog, loyal only to Lord Yasugi. But this was surely not in her master's interest. Akitada wondered again about the relationship between the wealthy lord and his third wife. Perhaps, being elderly and uncertain of his power to attract a pretty young woman, Yasugi was filled with jealous suspicions.

Lady Kose had said he had taken pity on her because she had been a poor widow. Strange, he had almost forgotten that. As she had not given Yasugi any children, her position was especially weak. It lent some credence to her claim that she was afraid to have Yasugi find out about Tomoe. But was any husband so unreasonable as to hold a harmless meeting between sisters against his wife? No, it was more likely that she feared the connection because of some past indiscretion. And Anju? Why was she making trouble for her mistress?

He was suddenly exhausted. Rubbing his throbbing head, he cast another glance at the Yasugi villa's imposing gates, many tiled roofs, and well-kept walls, and went home through the evening dusk.

Genba admitted him with the news that Tora had not returned yet. He was chewing, and Akitada was tired and irritated. He said sharply, "Why are you always eating? For heaven's sake, at least put the food away and empty your mouth when you answer the gate."

Genba hung his head. "Sorry, sir. My supper. Your lady is sending me out on errands and I grabbed a bite while I could."

"Hmm . . . I'm afraid I have another, more important assignment for you."

Genba looked nervous. "Her ladyship needs ink, paper, and brushes to teach the young master. And cook wants more rice and some dried fish."

"I don't care what they told you," Akitada snapped. "You have no time for silly errands. You're to go to a villa in the western city. I found two women there alone and had to chase a ruffian away who had climbed into their garden. Heaven knows what would have happened if I hadn't come along. He was one of the men who attacked us yesterday."

Genba broke in, "You found the nun?"

"Yes, but she's no nun. She is Lady Yasugi, wife of a wealthy provincial lord, and she has only a maid with her. They expect an escort to take them to their country estate, but meanwhile they're in desperate danger. Take your bow and arrows and a short sword. And hurry. It's growing dark already, and those thugs will probably return at nightfall." He gave Genba directions and then went into the house.

Tamako and his son were in her room, sitting close together, looking at a scroll of pictures and poems by the light of a tall candle. Yori scrambled up, crying, "Come and see the fine book

Mother found. There are pictures of rabbits and foxes, and of frogs and birds. And all of them are dressed like people."

Akitada swung his small son up into his arm and went to look. Tamako greeted him with a smile. "Welcome home. Your eye looks much better."

He doubted that, but nodded. "You make a charming picture reading together. How is Yori's reading coming along?"

"Oh, exceedingly well," she said brightly.

"I hate reading," Yori informed his father. "I'd much rather practice with my sword."

His mother flushed and shook her head at Yori. Something about that small message between mother and son irritated Akitada.

"Come, Yori," he told the boy, "let's sit down and you can read to me what it says next to these pictures."

Tamako said quickly, "It is in grass writing and too difficult for a child of Yori's age."

Akitada glanced at the book. The writing looked pretty simple to him. "Why? He has been studying with Seimei for two years now. At least he can guess at some of the words. Here, Yori. What is it that the frog says to the rabbit?"

Yori bent over the page and giggled. "'Why don't you jump into the pond, silly rabbit?' And the rabbit says, 'I don't like to get my fur coat wet!'" He giggled again and rolled the scroll to the next picture.

Akitada firmly returned to the picture and said, "That's not at all what is written here. Try again."

Yori stuck out his lower lip. "I don't want to. I like my story better."

"Yori," said his father sternly, "you cannot always have things the way you want them. We must learn to read and write so that we can carry out our duties to the gods and our emperor when we grow up. Now read!"

But Yori could not or would not. He ran to his mother and hid his face against her shoulder.

"Why is he refusing a simple request?" Akitada asked his wife.

Tamako sighed. "Yori is still practicing his Chinese characters and cannot read grass writing yet. He tries, but it's very difficult. I well remember how I struggled and how ashamed I was when my father . . ." She stopped when she saw Akitada's face and said, "He's still very little."

"He is nearly five. I could read when I was his age. Girls are not expected to learn as quickly." A sharp pain shot through Akitada's head. "It seems to me that you pamper Yori too much. Seimei tries to make him do his work, but you only sit and look at pictures with him and so, of course, he runs to you when he should be hard at work. I'm not pleased with his progress." He glared at Yori in his mother's protective embrace. The realization that Yori preferred her company rankled.

"Oh," Tamako cried, "I do try. It seems to me if you make a child hate learning, he'll never make an effort, but if you show him how entertaining it can be, he'll be much more open to instruction."

"Nonsense," snapped Akitada. "Such an attitude merely turns him into a weakling and a dawdler. He can look at pictures after he has practiced his characters. This trifling must stop."

"We would have practiced writing," Tamako said, "but there was very little paper left, the ink cake is almost gone, and a brush broke. I have sent Genba to get more."

"Genba has more important things to do. How can this household be out of paper and ink? Yori?" The child looked at him. "Did you waste the paper and ruin the brushes?"

Yori's eyes filled with tears. "I didn't mean to, Father."

Tired and with a pounding head, Akitada suddenly felt overwhelmed. "Why must I keep an eye on the smallest details of this household?" he demanded. "And where's Seimei? Why is he not teaching the child? Heaven knows I am too busy to do everything myself."

Tamako pulled the sobbing Yori into her arms, irritating her husband further. "Seimei was not well today. He was feverish. I made him lie down in his room."

"Oh. That's another matter," Akitada conceded, wondering just how ill Seimei was.

Encouraged, Tamako added, "I worry about smallpox. What if he has it? Yori must not go near him until we're certain it's not."

Akitada finally lost his temper completely. "I have told you before that there's no truth to this imaginary epidemic. Don't you think I would take precautions if I feared for your safety? Do you doubt my word in everything?"

Turning his back on them, he lit a small pottery lamp and stalked along the dark corridor to Seimei's room. To his surprise, this was in darkness also. The old man was dozing, his thin frame wrapped in a quilt, his elbow propped on an armrest, and his head supported in his hand. He had not heard the sound of the sliding door or noticed the flicker of the oil lamp. Akitada sat down beside him. The room seemed excessively warm and stuffy because someone had closed the shutters to the outside. No wonder, he thought, that he is feverish in this hot room, wrapped up in layers of wadding-stuffed blankets. He reached out and touched the wrinkled hand. The skin felt hot and dry, and Seimei jerked awake.

"Oh," he said, his voice hoarse and cracking, "you are home, sir. Sorry, but I must have dozed off for a moment." He began to peel back the quilt and tried to get up. "Your tea? Shall I make it for you?" he quavered.

Akitada restrained him. "No, Seimei. I came to see how you are. My wife told me that you felt ill."

Seimei shook his head. "It was nothing. I'm quite all right. Just a touch of tiredness, that's all." He swallowed and started to shake. "How cold it is all of a sudden," he said through trembling lips.

Akitada was beginning to feel concerned. He touched the old man's forehead and found it burning with fever. "You're ill, old friend. You treat all of us for the slightest complaints, and yet you do not treat yourself. How is it that you didn't read the symptoms and prescribe the correct remedy?"

"It is nothing," Seimei said again.

Akitada looked around the room. It was as neat as only a man with lifelong habits of tidying up after others could keep it, but there was not a single sign of anyone else having visited with tokens of concern. No small brazier heating water for his tea stood by his side, no flask of wine, not even a water pitcher to refresh the feverish tongue.

A sudden and violent anger seized Akitada. Apparently the panic about smallpox had seized Tamako to such a degree that she had neglected a sick old man whose devotion to the family deserved her loving care. At least Yasugi had left his wife a maid before deserting her. The shock of this discovery made him physically ill.

He leaned forward and, raising the lamp, gently undid the front of Seimei's robe to look for telltale spots, but there was nothing.

Seimei croaked, "No, not smallpox. I would not have stayed."

"Then I would have had to tie you down, old man," snapped Akitada. "What utter nonsense. You belong here. I'm glad it's not the disease, but you're quite feverish." He carefully covered the shivering old man again and got up to bring Seimei's medicine box to him. "I want you to tell me what medicines are indicated and how to prepare them."

Seimei revived a little as he fingered through his box, pulling forth this twist of paper and that container of salve. Eventually he instructed Akitada in the preparation of an infusion and the addition of other ingredients to a bowl of watery rice gruel.

Then he attempted to get up for a trip to the privy. Akitada caught him before he could stagger out the door and supported him to the outdoor convenience and back again. The trip exhausted Seimei and he agreed to be put to bed.

With Seimei settled in his blankets, Akitada left for the kitchen. Tamako hovered in the corridor outside Seimei's room.

"How is he?" she asked.

Akitada said coldly, "Very sick, but you can relax. It's not your dreaded smallpox," and brushed past her.

"I'm glad it's not smallpox," she cried after him. "Where shall you eat your evening rice?"

His stomach twisted again at the thought that she would have let the old man die rather than expose herself and the child to the disease. "I shall eat with Seimei," he said over his shoulder.

In the kitchen, the cook greeted him with complaints about the lack of foodstuffs and the absence of both Tora and Genba. He ignored her and instead barked commands about hot water and gruel at her.

The rest of the evening he spent tending to the old man. When Seimei had drunk his hot infusion of herbs, claiming that he felt great relief, he ate some of the gruel. Akitada had tasted this in the kitchen and almost choked on the bitterness. They sat together after that and Akitada told him about Lady Yasugi, but speaking was painful for Seimei and eventually Akitada offered to read to him instead. Seimei demurred, but then pointed to the "Sayings of the Sage," a ragged and much-thumbed scroll he kept nearby. Master Kung's brilliance notwithstanding, Seimei eventually dozed off, and Akitada put away the book and went to his own room.

He could not remember when he had felt this miserable. He was dazed from the headache and tiredness and deeply distressed. As he lay under his quilts, the words of the Great Sage kept passing through his mind. "A man who does not plan against the future will find disaster on his doorstep." Tonight he had found disaster, and tomorrow morning he must speak to Tamako, to make clear to his wife, before it was too late, what he expected of the mistress of his household and the mother of his son. But even though her heartlessness had deeply offended him, he must be mindful that angry words would arouse resentment. He thought of the beautiful Lady Yasugi, who lived in constant fear of her husband. "Severity," Master Kung advised, "must only be directed at oneself."

CHAPTER THIRTEEN

THE STOREHOUSE

*W*hen Tora woke the first time, he thought he had the worst hangover of his life. The world gyrated blearily before his eyes, which hurt almost as much as his head, and when his stomach heaved, he rolled quickly to avoid vomiting all over himself. After that he passed out again.

The next return to reality began the same way, but the vomiting produced only dry heaves and he remained conscious. He put a hand to his throbbing head, touched sticky blood, and reconsidered his condition. An injury? Cautious investigation confirmed that he had a large wound on his scalp, and a lot of dried blood not only on his head, which was too tender to explore thoroughly, but also on his face and neck, and on some ragged clothes he seemed to be wearing. The clothes brought back memory.

He was lying on a dirt floor, propped against a wall inside a storage shed. Bars of sunlight fell through the spaces between the boards that formed the walls and roof. In a corner lay a pile of sacks and boxes. Otherwise the shack was empty. It was day-time, but probably not the same day he had fought Matsue. That bastard!

Wondering if he was a prisoner, he crawled to the door and stood. For a moment the shack spun madly while the floor heaved under his feet. Afraid of falling, he got back down on all fours. The door was not locked, but he was exhausted and crawled into the corner with the sacks, rested his aching head on them, and closed his eyes.

He must have dozed off, because he next felt someone shaking his arm.

"Tora? It's me. Kinjiro."

"Wha . . . oh." He struggled to a sitting position. "What's going on?" he managed.

"I brought you some water and a bit of food. How are you feeling?"

"Thanks. Not too bad," Tora lied. He took the pitcher and drank it nearly empty. After that he felt a little better, but he did not want the food, though it looked like good rice and vegetables. Kinjiro gobbled it down hungrily.

"I guess I made a fool of myself," Tora said bitterly.

"No, you didn't. They're talking about how good you were. You slipped, that's all. Matsue shouldn't have struck you like that."

Tora was grateful. Really, there was hope for this kid. "So what now?" he asked. "I don't guess I'll get the job."

"There was talk last night. Kata *Sensei* and Matsue *Sensei* arguing. I couldn't hear all the words. Matsue *Sensei* doesn't like you, but Kata *Sensei* was very impressed."

"He can't be too impressed after what happened," said Tora. "Who brought me here?"

"Two of the students and me."

"Thanks. What about the students?"

"They think you should stay." Kinjiro grinned. "They figure

they can learn to beat you. Matsue *Sensei* won't waste his time on them."

Tora snorted and touched his sore head. "I guess he's done me an honor then. That makes me feel a lot better."

"Matsue *Sensei*'s a bit fanatical about being the best. You want to wash? There's a lot of blood on you."

"Make myself presentable to express my thanks for the welcome, you mean? I don't think I've got the strength yet to deal with all those students who're planning to challenge me."

Kinjiro laughed. "You're funny. I like you."

Tora reached across and tousled the boy's hair. "I like you, too. Thanks for bringing the water and food."

Kinjiro flushed. "It was nothing," he said gruffly.

Tora eyed him thoughtfully. "Tell me about yourself while I try to stop my head from acting like it's about to burst open like a ripe melon."

"There's nothing to tell. What you see is what I am."

"Not much then. But in time, with some proper food, you may fill out."

"Yeah. I'm not stupid. They feed me here."

"And they didn't at home?"

The boy spat. "Home!"

"No parents? No brothers and sisters?"

"I wish!" This was said with such venom that Tora raised his brows.

"Oh?"

"I don't want to talk about it." The boy moved impatiently. "What about you?"

"Oh, my family's nothing special. They were peasants. We had a small bit of land at the end of the eastern highway. They're all dead now."

"How come?"

Tora said nothing for a moment, then, "They starved."

"Starved? Farmers? You'd think a farmer wouldn't starve."

"They do when they have a few bad harvests and the tax collector takes all their rice for taxes. You can get through the winter gnawing a few roots and leaves left in the fields, but if your seed rice is gone, there'll be no harvest the next year. But the tax man comes anyway, and if you can't pay, he takes what you have and makes everyone work off the debt on one of the lord's pet projects. In my case, I got to be a soldier. When I got back from fighting, they were all dead."

"Oh." Kinjiro thought about it, then said, "I've never been out of the capital. My father was a scribe. We lived in a nice house a few wards north of here."

"A scribe? That's a pretty good job, isn't it? Practically a learned man. How come you end up here?"

"He died."

"But . . . ?" Tora swallowed the rest of his question. The boy had turned his head and was plucking nervously at his shirt.

"I don't care," he said fiercely. "I can look after myself. I don't need anybody. Someday I'll show them all."

"Is your mother dead, too?"

The boy kicked a heel viciously into the dirt. "No such luck! The bitch had better things to do. She got married again."

Tora was appalled. After a moment, he said, "I guess her new husband didn't want to adopt a whole family. What about brothers and sisters?"

"She kept my baby sister. And it wasn't her new husband got rid of me. It was her. She tried to sell me to a post stable where they beat me every day. When I ran back home, she had to return the money. That made her mad and she said I had to get out. The filthy bitch." His voice broke and he jumped up, kicked the door of the shack open, and disappeared.

The door clattered shut, and Tora stared at it. Poor kid. He had at least been a grown man when his parents died. Kinjiro's mother was either heartless or without choice in the matter, and the boy was taking her rejection hard. No wonder he had joined a gang.

Tora rested a little more and was just making up his mind to walk home, when Kinjiro returned. "You're in," he cried. "Kata wants to talk to you about the job." Before Tora could ask for details, he was gone again.

Tora got up and walked out of the shed. The bright sun blinded him, but most of the dizziness was gone. He found a well. Kneeling on the stone coping, he lowered the wooden bucket by its old rope and pulled up water. It took three more buckets before he had rid himself of most of the caked blood in his hair and on his skin. His skull seemed to be in one piece, though it hurt like the devil. He washed out his shirt in the last bucket and draped it over the fence behind the training school to dry. He would stay long enough to find out what the job entailed.

Wearing only his short pants and hoping that the old scars on his upper body would look more impressive than a ragged shirt, he walked into the training hall. Kata stood talking to some students and ignored him. Tora did not see Matsue and went to sit on the trunk. After a while, the boy showed up with a paper-wrapped bundle.

The thought of working for Kata was still tempting. Of course he would have to get his information quickly, before Kata decided to send him out on a burglary or hold-up. He had an uneasy feeling that he should have planned things better.

Thinking made Tora's head hurt worse. He decided to go back to his shack and take a little nap, but as he was shuffling away, Kata called out, "Hey, you. Tora."

Tora turned and said humbly, "Yes, *Sensei?*"

Kata dismissed the students, then said, "Come here."

Tora obliged and submitted to a close inspection of his wound. Kata tsked and shook his head. "How do you feel?"

A little surprised by the solicitude, Tora managed a grin. "Like I've a beehive in my head and the bees are trying to get out."

Kata chuckled. "Matsue shouldn't have struck so hard, but it was an accident."

Tora's grin faded. "It was no accident."

"These things happen," said Kata vaguely. "Anyway, you can have a job helping me in the training hall. I've seen you handle a sword. How are you at kickfighting and wrestling?"

"Not so good, but I can beat anybody with a pole."

"Really?" Kata waved to the boy. "Kinjiro, get two poles."

Tora bit his lip. His head pounded like blazes every time he moved. But he accepted the bamboo pole and took up his position. It was a short bout. After a few turns, Kata stepped away. "Yes," he said, "I can see you're good. You can teach me a few things." He tossed the pole to Kinjiro, went to pick up the paper-wrapped package, and thrust it at Tora. "Put these on. The boy'll take you to a house where you can stay tonight."

Tora was so astonished by all this that he made Kata a deep bow. The pain that shot through his head added a touch of unintended emotion to his expression of gratitude.

"Never mind," said Kata. "You'll be useful. Maybe later I'll let you help with some other business. How do you feel about the police?"

Tora stepped back and glowered. "I won't have anything to do with them." His memory of Lieutenant Ihara made him embellish a bit. "Those crooked devils treat poor bastards like filth while the rich can do no wrong. Greedy merchants rob their customers, and then they turn around and rob their workers by sending us away without wages. And if we complain to a constable, he'll lock us up and beat us half to death for making trouble."

Kata nodded. "I know. Police brutality. I noticed the fresh stripes on your back. We feel like you do and protect each other. That means we don't talk about our business to anyone outside the family. How do you feel about that?"

"It's an excellent rule."

Kata laughed and patted his shoulder. Then Kinjiro took Tora's arm to pull him away. Tora was nearly blinded by the agony inside his skull.

Tora changed in the shed, putting on a pair of full cotton trousers and a plain blue shirt. The jacket had been made for a man who was both shorter and much fatter than Tora, but it was comfortable.

"I got the best," Kinjiro informed him. "Old Gunzaemon buys his used clothes only from the best people. Got a nice selection. Lots of people dying this year."

Tora grunted. The stick-fighting bout had made him sick again and he did not feel like talking. He did not feel like walking either and shuffled along glumly, until Kinjiro had to grab his elbow when he veered and almost fell into a ditch. "Here," cried the boy impatiently, "watch where you're going."

They crossed Suzaku Avenue, turning into the business quarter, and soon passed the market.

Emerging from his haze of pain, Tora stopped.

"Kinjiro," he asked, "did you ever come here with Kata?"

Kinjiro looked impatient. "Kata *Sensei*."

"Sorry. Kata *Sensei*. I'm not at my best today."

The boy relented a little. "Yes, I'm here a lot. Why?"

"I think I saw Kata once. At the tower."

"Listening to the blind woman, I bet."

"Yes. Do you know her?"

"I know everybody. She got murdered. Kata *Sensei* was in a terrible temper when he heard. We all stayed away from him."

This was puzzling. Had something gone wrong with an order Kata had given? "Why was he mad?"

But Kinjiro clammed up. "You ask too many questions. Forget it."

After a moment Tora tried again. "How many people work for him?"

The boy looked at him suspiciously. "Why do you want to know that?"

"An important man's in more danger. I was wondering how best to guard him."

"He's important. We keep our eyes open and our mouths shut. You heard what he said."

Tora nodded. If Kata had a big operation, he might take drastic steps to stop a blind female from talking about his activities. "Good. I'll be useful then. Where are we going?"

"Just a place."

Tora sighed inwardly. This was like dipping water out of the ocean with an acorn shell. He decided it was his turn to be resentful. "Sorry I asked," he said huffily.

The boy gave him a sidelong glance. Tora compressed his lips and looked straight ahead. After a moment, the boy said, "It's just a house. Kata's borrowing it."

Tora said nothing.

"What's the matter?" the boy demanded.

"Never mind. I thought we were friends," said Tora heavily, "but I see you don't like me. You don't trust me either. I'll be better off working elsewhere."

"Don't say that," the boy cried. "I didn't mean it. It's just . . . you'll get in trouble if you know too much."

Tora pointed to his head. "I feel awful and I'm just trying to learn about the job."

"I'm sorry. I want to be your friend, Tora. Honestly."

Tora looked up at the sky. "Hmm."

The boy caught his sleeve. "Please, Tora. I don't have any friends. The others treat me like a kid. We could help each other. I'd look out for you and you for me."

"We . . . ll . . ."

"Please?"

"Friends trust each other."

"I trust you."

"All right. Let's see if you do. If I'm going to work for Kata *Sensei*, I'd like to know as much as I can about him and his people."

Kinjiro's eyes flickered. "I don't know everything. And we're not supposed to talk."

"I thought I was one of you now. See, you don't trust me. Never mind."

"What do you want to know?"

"How do you like the boss?"

"I'd die for him. He makes sure I get plenty to eat and sometimes he tells me I've done well. He's like a father. He looks after us. He finds us places to stay, and buys our food and wine. And if we get hurt, he gets a doctor. He sent me for new clothes for you when I told him how bloody you were. We all belong to Kata *Sensei*."

"What about the work—anybody ever get killed?"

Kinjiro hesitated. "You mean us? Not so far. A few got arrested. It beats starving in the streets."

"Hmm. And what does Matsue *Sensei* do for the boss?"

"They're friends. Matsue *Sensei* is a great sword fighter but he can be mean."

"I know." Tora touched his head and grimaced. "But you say they argue. And he doesn't teach. Why does Kata need him?"

"I'm not sure. Sometimes I think Matsue *Sensei* can lay his hands on money. Or maybe he knows something about Kata *Sensei*."

"Ah. When Kata *Sensei* lost his temper about the blind woman's murder? Did he argue with Matsue about that?"

"Maybe. Kata *Sensei* liked her a lot, but Matsue *Sensei* hated her."

Tora stared at Kinjiro. "Kata liked her? And Matsue hated her?"

"Matsue *Sensei* would not go near her. He'd just stare at her from a distance. Weird. Like he didn't think she was really blind.

Once Kata tried to make him talk to her. He got so angry he walked off. Matsue *Sensei* is very strange."

"Right." Tora lost interest. The long walk had been too much. He was so exhausted he could barely see where he was going.

He was spared racking his painful head for more questions when they reached the quarter of the Eighth Street Gate, a quiet and respectable neighborhood where the houses were old and solid. This time of day the streets were empty and the shop fronts closed. Apparently everybody was at their evening rice. The place they sought was at the end of a block, a large one-storied house. It presented windowless walls to its neighbor and the side street, but had sliding doors and shutters in front.

It seemed a strange hideout for Kata's thugs. Surely the neighbors would not keep quiet about the comings and goings of shady characters. Tora decided that it must be a temporary refuge. Criminals tended to move from place to place, though Tora had never known any to live so well.

Kinjiro gave four quick taps to the door. A panel slid open, and then the door slid back with a squeak, revealing a scruffy-looking individual who nodded to the boy and eyed Tora suspiciously.

In the dim light from some high windows, Kinjiro led Tora down a stone-paved hallway past the empty raised shop front and into an equally empty kitchen. Here a strange mix of aromas greeted them: food, both fresh and stale, sweat, smoke, and—all-pervasive—the clean scent of aged wood.

The boy lifted the lid of a rice cooker. A white cloud of steam escaped and filled the air with a rich smell. "You hungry yet?"

Tora sniffed. "I could eat something. Where is everybody?"

"They'll come later. After work." Kinjiro found two bowls and filled them with rice from the pot. He located a tray of salted vegetables, ladled them on top of the rice, then fished some pickled radish from a barrel on the floor. Handing Tora one of the bowls, he said, "Come," and headed farther along the dark corridor.

Tora followed. They walked in the dusty footprints of others past an interior garden, and stepped up into the main room of the house. It had once been the best room of a prosperous merchant family. The wooden beams and walls had darkened over the years, and many stockinged feet had polished the raised wooden boards to a deep luster, now dulled by dirt and scuff marks. In one corner the floor was charred black. Someone had either lit an open fire there or spilled burning charcoal and left it. It was a miracle the house had not burned down. Spills and food stains marred the floor where it was not covered with the abandoned belongings of prior occupants. Clothing and bedding lay about in heaps wherever they had been kicked.

"Whose house is this?" Tora asked, surprised. "Where are the servants? The family?"

Kinjiro went out on a narrow veranda overlooking the small garden and sat down. "It belongs to Buntaro. He's second in command. No servants. Just an old man." He started eating with the greedy appetite of a growing boy.

It was much lighter outside than in the house and Tora looked curiously at the plants and small fish pond that filled the enclosed space. The fish in the pond were dead, bloated forms that floated on the surface, and the plants needed water. He sat down and looked dubiously at his food. He had not eaten for more than a day, but the sight of the dead fish made him feel queasy again. He took a small bite of the vegetables. It was good, and he tried some rice. "But there must have been women and servants once," he said between mouthfuls.

"Don't know. We haven't been here long." Kinjiro did not bother to empty his mouth but talked around the food. "There was nobody here but the old man when we came. The old man's gone away on a trip."

Tora had an uncomfortable feeling about the place. His encounter with the vicious Matsue had been bad enough. Now he was involved with a gang of thugs and thieves who would not think twice about killing him if they found out what he was up to. Though he was not precisely working for the police, the criminals would certainly see it that way.

And then there was a chance that the police might be tipped off by a neighbor and decide to raid this place. The guard was not at the door for nothing. If Tora, already a defendant in a murder case, were caught living with a gang so soon after his arrest, he would not have a chance in hell to prove his innocence. But it was a little late to back out now. He reminded himself that he was on the trail of Tomoe's killer.

Kinjiro departed with his empty bowl and returned with a large pitcher of wine and two cups. Tora, who was making little headway with his food, refused the wine. His head pounded until he was nearly cross-eyed with the pain. What he needed was water. He watched the boy pour down several brimming cups in quick succession. "Are you allowed to drink all that?"

"Sure," boasted Kinjiro, belching. "It's the best. Kata *Sensei* gets it from one of his clients. Here! Try some."

"I need water," croaked Tora, staggering to his feet, "and the outhouse."

Kinjiro got up. "I'll show you."

They passed down another dark corridor and through a back door into a fenced service area with several smaller buildings. Kinjiro pointed out the latrine, but Tora made straight for the well. When he reached it, he ran out of strength and sat down heavily. Kinjiro pulled up a pail of water, dipped a ladle in and offered it to Tora. "You don't look too good," he said needlessly.

Tora drank and handed the ladle back. "I'll be all right in a minute," he muttered, closing his eyes.

"Are you sure? Because I can't stay."

Tora's eyes flew open. "You're leaving?" he yelped. He had visions of a gang of bandits jumping on the strange intruder and asking questions later. "Who's going to explain to the others what I'm doing here?"

Kinjiro narrowed his eyes. "You aren't afraid, are you?"

Tora flushed. Of course he was afraid, but he could not disillusion his only ally. "Don't be an idiot," he snapped. "I want to get some sleep and I don't want every fool who trails in to shake me awake because he's never seen me before."

"Oh." The boy relaxed and grinned. "I'll tell the guy at the door to warn them. See you in the morning then."

Tora nodded and watched him disappear into the house. Actually, the situation was not without interest. He was alone in a robber's den—well, alone except for the character at the street door, and he would hardly leave his post except for an emergency, such as a trip to the outhouse. Tora eyed the latrine and decided to use it himself.

When he emerged, he investigated the service yard. It was nearly dark by now. Wishing he had a lantern, Tora poked around in the large shed. It held houschold goods. He made out firewood, tools, spare buckets, a ragged broom, a coil of rope, a couple of braziers, a ladder, and an abandoned bathtub filled with sacks of beans, strings of onions, root vegetables, and a lot of other unidentifiable household goods.

A storehouse stood in the middle of the yard. It was the most substantial of the outbuildings, covered with plaster and roofed with tiles. Storehouses protected family valuables from the fires that often consumed the wooden dwellings, and this one was securely locked. No doubt the gang kept its ill-gotten gains in it.

Night was falling rapidly and already the unfamiliar place was full of black shadows and eerie sounds. Something knocked and something else scrabbled. When Tora thought he heard a groan, he retreated into the house.

It was even darker there. Suppressing irrational fears about ghosts and goblins, Tora felt his way down the dark corridor to the main room, where he could barely make out the piles of bedding. Helping himself to one of the quilts, he curled up in a corner and went to sleep.

He slept fitfully because he was nervous and because his head bothered him. At one point he thought he heard voices and steps, but nobody came to disturb him. Toward morning he fell into a deeper sleep and did not wake until well after daylight. To his surprise, he was still alone.

He sat up and gave a tentative shout, but no one appeared. After rolling up his bedding and tossing it back on the pile, he went to take a look around, but the rest of the house was as empty as the main room. Even the guard had disappeared.

This last discovery made Tora very uncomfortable. Where had the guard gone? And why? And why had he been left behind? He could not rid himself of a sense of impending disaster. Did they expect a raid? Perhaps he had been left to be arrested for some crime the others had committed during the night. He listened for the pounding boots and whistles of police constables, but all remained still.

Much too still! The sun was up. Where were the normal sounds of a neighborhood waking to another work day?

The urge to run warred with Tora's curiosity. He stood uncertain for a moment, then decided that he would at least do a quick search of the rooms first.

In the kitchen he found evidence that someone had visited the house during the night. The rice pot was empty and on a shelf was a paper containing two square rice cakes and a lot of crumbs. Tora helped himself to the cakes, then checked the rest of the house. He found little of interest, apart from some spare clothing and one or two weapons of the type common among criminals, until he opened the door to a room that was furnished better than the rest. It had thick grass mats on the floor, its own small garden court, and a few pieces of well-made furniture. Apparently it was used as a guest room for an honored visitor.

Among the furnishings stood a large ironbound chest of the type used by traveling merchants to carry precious goods. Tora checked it. It was locked. The police would force the lock, he thought, and listened again for the sound of their pounding feet, but the same eerie silence prevailed. He was about to open a clothes chest, when he heard an odd little bump in the corridor outside. He peered cautiously out the door. The corridor was empty. Deciding he must have imagined it, Tora turned back to the clothes chest. And here he finally made a discovery, though what it meant was more than he could understand. On the bottom of the clothes chest, underneath the folded jackets, shirts, and pants, he found some documents. They seemed to belong to Matsue. Tora had no wish to be caught rifling through that character's private property and quickly flipped through them. Some were about his training and qualifications as a swordsman and some were old travel permits. But two pieces of paper made him whistle softly in surprise.

One was a formal transfer of rice land in the Tsuzuki district between a Lord Tomonari and his maid. The other was the title of ownership to a small farm. Tora was familiar with such legal papers, because his family had once owned a farm. This particular farm was slightly larger and probably on much better land, and it belonged to someone called Sangoro.

Sangoro was the name Kinjiro had used for Matsue before correcting himself quickly. Nothing unusual about that. Many an aspiring swordsman changed his name for any number of reasons. Perhaps Matsue wanted to hide his peasant background. What startled Tora was another word that jumped up at him from among the lines of spidery writing. It looked like the family name of the dead Haseo: Utsunomiya.

Tora was still trying to decipher this paper when he heard a distant squeaking noise followed by the clicking of a latch: the street door. Slipping the document inside his shirt, he hurriedly replaced the rest of the papers and closed the trunk. Then he stepped out into the corridor and listened. The house was as still as before. He checked the main room and then the entry, but found nobody. Belatedly it occurred to him that the door could have been closed by someone leaving the house. The thought that he had been watched made him nervous. Tora opened the door, verified the squeak, and looked up and down the street. Nobody. The neighborhood lay deserted.

Remembering the service yard, he went back to check there. It was as empty as the house. A couple of sparrows were bathing in the dust beside the storehouse. Tall walls screened out all but the roof of the neighbor's house and some treetops. Tora pulled up a pail of water, drank thirstily, and splashed some on his face and head. His headache had dulled considerably.

The silence made him jumpy. He should have been hearing the voices of children and the sounds of men and women at work beyond the fence, but there was nothing but the soft twitter of small sparrows and the cooing of a few pigeons on the roof. He listened, then heard another sound. It was very faint, a sort of scrabbling accompanied by a whimper. Only a dog, he decided. It must be locked up somewhere. Perhaps it was thirsty. He filled the bucket again and left it on the well coping while he looked around. He peered behind the latrine and into the storage shack. No dog, but the whimpering continued. That left the storehouse. Storehouses were windowless because they were not intended for habitation, human or animal, yet it was from inside the storehouse that the sounds came.

Who would lock an animal in a storehouse? It was dark and airless in there. Was the dog being punished? Or was it supposed to guard some particularly costly haul the thugs had hidden there? He grinned at the thought of robbers afraid of being robbed. Poor beast, but he could do nothing about it.

As he turned away, he remembered the eerie groan the night before. Come to think of it, this faint wailing did not sound like a dog. Tora pressed his ear to the storehouse wall and gasped. Whatever was wailing in there did not sound human, either. He recoiled from the wall, a slow horror building inside his chest and taking his breath away.

It must be a ghost—the ghost of somebody the robbers had killed. That's why they had taken to their heels without their clothes and valuables. Tora backed away slowly.

Another faint but horrible wail struck his ear, and he reached for his amulet before remembering that he had left it at home.

Home. That's where he should be. Tora feared ghosts much more than a whole army of cutthroats in the flesh.

But it was broad daylight, and he had second thoughts about this particular ghost. What if the man inside was still alive?

He approached the storehouse again and checked the lock. It was heavy and unbreakable. Inside, the wailing stopped. A cracked voice called out, "Buntaro?" Tora skipped back a pace, thought about it, and decided that a ghost would not get his name wrong. And this Buntaro was one of the thugs, the owner of this place.

Relieved that he was not dealing with the supernatural, Tora put his mouth to the door, and shouted, "I'm not Buntaro. What are you doing in there?"

The voice inside broke into an agitated and incomprehensible babble and he heard fingernails scrabbling at the door.

"I don't have a key and can't understand you," Tora shouted.

The babbling rose a few decibels but was still too agitated to make out. He thought he heard the word "police." Did the person inside want him to get the police? A gangster, no matter how desperate, would never make such a request.

This cast a different light on the situation. It was one thing if gangsters dealt harshly with one of their own, but if they held an innocent person in there, Tora had an obligation to help him.

He considered the storehouse. Like all such buildings, it was made of very thick plaster walls, its roof was tiled, and its single door was of thick wooden planks. It had been built to withstand fire and robbers, and the lock was hopeless without a key.

He was taking another look at the lock when the door behind him flew open and someone cursed. A tall, thin man stood on the threshold. "What are you doing there?" he bellowed, adding another curse for emphasis.

Tora remembered him now. He had been the one with Matsue when they had found him giving the boy a lesson in sword fighting. Tora had nicknamed him the "Scarecrow" because he was ugly and his clothes hung like rags on his thin frame. The situation was awkward, but at least the fellow would remember him. He said quickly, "Oh, hello. I wondered where everyone was. I thought I heard a dog in there. Must've been mistaken."

In reply, the Scarecrow pulled a knife from his jacket and started across the yard. Tora stepped back and crouched to defend himself, but the thug only checked the lock, then glared at him. "You'd better not be making trouble," he shouted, pounding his fist against the door for emphasis, "if you know what's good for you. Kata *Sensei* doesn't like meddlers and neither do I."

Tora straightened up. "Don't worry, I don't care what you keep in there. The emperor's treasures, for all I care. I was washing myself at the well when I thought I heard a dog whining."

The other man looked at the bucket and at Tora's wet hair. "All right," he said grudgingly, shoving the knife back into his belt. "Just keep your nose out of our business in the future. You'd better come along now. Kata *Sensei* wants you." He took Tora's arm, but kept the other hand on the knife handle.

"Where's everybody gone to?" Tora asked, allowing himself to be dragged along.

"Moved to another place."

"Why?" He remembered the ironbound chest. Why had they left their loot behind? Not to mention their prisoner.

The Scarecrow opened the street door and pushed Tora out. "Smallpox," he said. "Next door and a few houses up the street and behind us. Almost everybody's gone from this quarter. We found out this morning." He locked up and motioned for Tora to start walking.

Smallpox.

Tora thought of the amulet seller in the market. It must be spreading fast. He wondered about the man in the storehouse. Maybe he had been locked up and left to die because he had smallpox. Tora shivered. "Why didn't someone tell me?"

The Scarecrow snapped, "I just did. Shut up and get your legs moving."

Stupid question. They hadn't cared what happened to him. It was Kata who had sent the Scarecrow back for him. And that might be an ominous sign, too.

The street lay deserted, but when they passed the neighbor's house, Tora saw the paper seal with the official warning on the door. A faint sound of chanting could be heard. Someone was dead or dying inside. He felt sorry for the family.

But then, he was not exactly on his way to a celebration himself. And what was he to do about the poor wretch in the storehouse?

CHAPTER FOURTEEN

BROKEN TIES

Akitada felt more like himself the next morning, but Seimei
was still feverish. Akitada had more medicinal gruel and herbal
infusions prepared, helped the old man again to the latrine, and
then got dressed for work. He was already late. The sun was rising and he should have been at the ministry hours ago. After
checking again to make certain Seimei was comfortable and
giving the cook instructions about his care, Akitada sought out
his wife.

Tamako was waiting for him in her room. The bedding had
been put away, and she knelt fully dressed in the center of the
room, her eyes downcast and her hands folded in her lap.

"Good morning," he said formally, making her a slight bow.

"Good morning," she answered, bowing also.

"I wished to speak to you before I leave," he said, feeling ill
at ease before such calm expectancy.

She bowed again. Since she did not raise her head, he could
not make out her mood.

He sighed and sat down. "I was disappointed in you yesterday," he said. "It seemed to me that you were neglecting both our son and a sick old man. I have heard your explanations and cannot accept them. Therefore I thought it best to explain how I wish my family's affairs conducted in the future."

She said nothing, but bowed her head a little more. In the uncertain light it was hard to see, but he thought she looked pale. He decided on a gentler approach. "Tamako, I know you have been past reason worried for our son's life because of the rumors of another smallpox epidemic." She looked up then and opened her mouth to speak, but he raised his hand. "No, let me finish. You cannot know what happens outside this house. You spend your life here with our child and hardly ever see anything of the world." He remembered Lady Yasugi's impassioned protest of such a cloistered life and went on quickly. "I realize that this limits your awareness, and such ignorance can greatly multiply one's fears, but you must trust me in this. I have been both in the Greater Palace and in the city. Your fears are groundless. Besides, our lives are in the hands of the gods and there is little we can do to guard against fate."

She raised her chin defiantly. "I have been told that the disease is even among the highest ranking nobles; that, in fact, His Majesty has contracted it."

"Nonsense. Who has said such things?"

"I may spend my days here," she said, a little tartly he thought, "but I receive visitors. Yesterday, your sister Akiko stopped by with Lady Koshikibu. Lady Koshikibu was the empress's nurse, and it was she who told me the news from the imperial household. Akiko came to tell me that she is making preparations to leave for the country with her children. I meant to tell you last night, but . . ." She compressed her lips.

He had stormed out of the room, furious that his son could not read yet and worried about Seimei. Now he covered his compunction with bluster. "That is dangerous gossip indeed.

Lady Koshikibu must be deranged to pass along such information. You are not to pass it further." He envisioned the panic
that would strike the capital—no, the nation—if such a thing
became known. "Furthermore," he added, "it cannot be true, or
I would have heard."

Tamako looked away. "As you wish."

"Very well. Now there's the matter of Seimei. He's still feverish this morning. I wish him to be cared for in my absence. If
you're too afraid to visit him, you may delegate one of your
maids to tend to his needs, but someone is to watch over him all
the time. If his condition worsens in the slightest, you will send
for me and for a doctor."

She bowed. "I had intended to do so," she said stiffly. "He
sent us away yesterday and we were afraid to disturb his sleep,
or you would not have found him alone."

It might have happened that way. Seimei was very stubborn
about accepting help. Akitada unbent a little more. He would
give Tamako the benefit of the doubt. "I'm very glad," he told
her. When she did not react, he added, "I did not know what to
think yesterday when I found him in an overheated room without so much as a drop of water. I couldn't imagine how my
family could have forgotten their obligation to Seimei, of all
people. He has served my family from his childhood and has
been like a father to me. He's part of my family."

Tamako's eyes had widened. "Oh," she said, "now I see. You
thought I would let Seimei die for fear of infection."

Aware that he had somehow offended again, he said briskly,
"Well, I'm very glad I was wrong. Let's say no more about it. And
when Seimei is well again, he can take Yori's lessons in hand."

"There is another problem. I am told that both Tora and
Genba are occupied with your errands. We are out of supplies
and I had sent Genba for them last night when you counter-
manded my orders."

He realized that she was very angry with him. Perhaps he

should have explained the situation. "You know what Tora's doing. I had to send Genba to stand watch at Lady Yasugi's villa. She is the young woman who was nearly raped. Yesterday I caught one of her attackers creeping into her home. Since she is young, beautiful, and alone except for a maid, her need was greater. Send your maid to the market for today. Genba should be back soon."

There was a pause. Then she said, "Very well."

He felt relief at having settled the matter so easily and was about to rise and leave for the ministry, when Tamako spoke again.

"Perhaps," she said, her voice as tight as the clenched hands in her lap, "as you have lost all confidence in me, it is time for you to consider taking a second wife. It would be a wise thing to do. You no longer trust me to supervise your household or to teach our son, and I have not given you any other sons, which you must wish for when life is so uncertain. You and Yori are the last of your father's line and . . ."

Seized by a sudden rage, Akitada bounded up. "No!" he shouted. "I do not want another wife or more children. I want order in my household." And he stormed from the room.

All the way to the Greater Palace, he muttered under his breath.

Women! The very idea of having to deal with more than one. The Great Sage had warned men against over-familiarity because it made females dictatorial. Tamako was punishing him for his just reproof of her behavior by threatening to withdraw her affections. For that was what the suggestion of taking another wife amounted to. Go ahead and see if I care, was what she had implied. He stalked along, rehearsing in his mind what he would tell her that night, and became more and more miserable in the process. He could not recall a time in their years of marriage when they had had such a quarrel.

Tamako had changed. She no longer cared for his company

as she had in the days before Yori had begun to capture all her attention. Perhaps he had been more abrupt lately than usual, but there had been many serious matters on his mind. A wife should make allowance for a husband's greater responsibility. He felt alone and hurt by her words, and that angered him some more.

Sakae awaited him at the ministry. "Have you heard, sir?" he cried. "The emperor is sick. He may die." He was practically hopping about in his excitement.

Akitada stopped. "What do you mean?" he demanded. The emperor was barely thirteen years old, and a healthy young man. The possibility of his dying seemed completely remote.

"He has smallpox."

Akitada sucked in his breath. Could it be true? Could the disease really have entered the sacred inner palace itself and infected the emperor? He glared at Sakae. "How do you know this?"

"Someone working in the chamberlain's dormitory told someone in the headquarters of the inner palace guards. The page who carries messages between bureaus stopped by this morning and told us. It was still quite early." This last Sakae added to show that they had been at work long before Akitada arrived.

"You are a clerk in the Ministry of Justice," Akitada said sharply. "I would have thought that you might have learned about the unreliability of hearsay evidence. Until we receive official word about His Majesty's condition, I will not permit you to bandy about such dangerous gossip. Do you understand?"

He brushed by the gaping Sakae and went into his office. Nakatoshi was bent over the usual pile of correspondence. He rose and bowed. "Good morning, sir." He added with a smile, "You look more yourself today, sir."

Akitada touched his eye. It felt normal. He had almost forgotten about it. It seemed a long time since he had tangled with the three thugs. The thought gave way to the vivid image of

Lady Yasugi lying on the ground, her clothing tangled about her legs. At the time he had been preoccupied with the villain who had meant to rape her. Now the image suddenly became powerfully erotic. He curbed his imagination firmly, smiled at Nakatoshi and said, "Good morning, and thank you."

"Has Sakae told you the news about the emperor?"

Akitada felt the smile fade on his face. "Surely there is no truth to that?"

"His informant wasn't the only one, sir. I was told the same story by the senior clerk of the crown prince's office. I'm afraid he's a very reliable source. It's disturbing news, not only because of His Majesty's life being in danger, but also because there are apparently already plans for change in case the worst happens."

Though Nakatoshi's words referred to matters of national importance—how the next emperor would deal with matters of government and who would take the most cherished positions upon his accession—Akitada's first thought was that he had once again put himself in the wrong with Tamako. And to be fair, if even the sacred person of the emperor was not safe from this terrible contagion, Tamako could be forgiven her fears. "Dear heaven," he muttered and sat down, staring blankly at the pile of paperwork awaiting his attention.

"I mentioned it, sir, because Minister Soga would have called at the palace to present his wishes for His Majesty's recovery and to offer prayers on his behalf at the temple."

Of course, and Soga would have been thrilled at the opportunity. Or would he? With smallpox in the imperial household, Soga would surely have made his excuses. Akitada was struck by an unpleasant suspicion. "Surely I'm not expected to fill in for him?" Access to the imperial residence was restricted to nobles of the fifth rank and above, and he did not qualify.

"I'm afraid so, sir. I've taken the liberty to send a message that His Excellency is away and that you're taking his place. I expect that you'll be given special permission."

"Dear heaven," said Akitada again and glanced down at himself. "But I cannot go like this." When Nakatoshi did not reply, he got to his feet. "I suppose I'd better go home and change into my court robe."

"I shall take care of business here, sir." Nakatoshi gave him an encouraging nod, perhaps because Akitada's lack of enthusiasm was so manifest.

Akitada reentered his home less than an hour after he left it. The first person he encountered was Tamako. She looked pale and drawn and—shockingly—very sad. Bowing, she asked, "Is anything wrong?"

He tried to gauge her mood. Had she been crying? "It appears the emperor is really ill. I must change into my court robe and call at the palace."

"How terrible," she murmured. "I hope he will recover. Allow me to be of assistance."

Feeling guilty, he protested, "That's not necessary. Seimei . . ." But Seimei was ill. There was no way to avoid her company. The court robe was a very awkward costume to get into and out of.

She said, "Seimei is resting. I believe he is better, but not well enough to get up. I am sorry that I can offer only my own clumsy services."

Tamako was not clumsy about anything she did. Such phrases were common in polite exchanges between married people who merely tolerated each other. He felt his stomach twist with misery. "Thank you."

In his room, he undressed silently while she lit incense in a long-handled burner. The room filled with the heavy aromatic scent of expensive male perfume. Akitada wrinkled his nose at it. She lifted the court robe, the train, and the full white silk trousers from their trunk and spread them over a wooden stand.

"I tore the trousers and the robe," he said. "Did someone mend them?"

"Yes." She took the incense burner by its handle and passed it back and forth under the stand, letting the faint spiral of scented smoke rise into the folds of the clothing. "It was not too bad. The robe only needed re-stitching, and the tears are hardly noticeable in the fullness of fabric."

"Thank you." He stood there, feeling helpless and uncomfortable in his underrobe and stockinged feet. Belatedly he remembered his cap. Risking a glance at the mirror, he winced, took off the cap, and studied his eye. The bruises, though they had faded, were still there and made him look like a hooligan.

"I have some cosmetics," she said. "They should hide those bruises."

"I'm not wearing powder and paint," he said, shocked by the notion.

She bowed her head. "I am sorry. I should not have suggested it."

They fell silent again as he waited for her to finish perfuming his clothes.

After a long while, he said, "I should not have spoken so harshly to you earlier. Especially when it turns out that you were quite right about the emperor."

"It does not matter," she said listlessly.

She held out the silk trousers, and he put his hands on her shoulders as he stepped into them. Their physical closeness was an irritant, and he stepped away from her as soon as he could. Feeling guilty, he searched for something else conciliatory to say. "Let Yori practice his reading until we can buy more paper and brushes."

"As you wish." She helped him with the gown and seemed to avoid touching him, then turned to get his sash, his elaborate headgear, and his baton of office. Kneeling before him, she placed these articles at his feet and bowed. "Do you wish for anything else?"

"N-no. Thank you." He watched as she rose and left the

room—so silently that he was aware only of the softest rustle of silk and the slightest whisper of her feet on the polished boards. The door closed noiselessly. It was as if his wife had dissolved into air. Putting on the sash by himself was a struggle.

His progress on the way back was awkward, as always when he was forced to wear formal dress. Nakatoshi awaited him with the official pass that would admit him to the Imperial Palace. Sakae hovered in the background, looking smug. Akitada took the opportunity to apologize for having doubted him earlier. Sakae's smug expression turned into a smirk. He accepted the apology with a humility that was as excessive as it was false.

At Kenreimon, the central gate to the Imperial Palace, Akitada presented his pass to an officer of the palace guard, a man much younger than he and well above him in court rank. He was waved through without so much as a curious glance. No doubt a stream of well-wishers had already paid their respects, and Akitada was of less significance than any of them.

Before him lay the inner wall and another gate, Shomeimon, nicknamed the "Bedroom Gate." It was thatched with cypress bark and only slightly smaller than the outer one. He climbed the three steps, had his credentials and costume inspected by two stern-faced officials, and descended on the other side.

He now stood in the South Court of the Imperial Palace. The Audience Hall, known as the Purple Sanctum, rose directly before him. It was very large but as simple as a Shinto shrine, unpainted and roofed with thick cypress bark. A wide staircase led up to its veranda.

To his right and left were other halls, and beyond the Audience Hall rose more roofs in bewildering succession. Akitada looked around the courtyard, scene of many imperial festivities and sacred rituals, and at the famous cherry and orange trees on either side of the grand staircase. These things he had only heard about. Then he gazed at the people in the courtyard, some walking, others standing about in groups. They were either not afraid of contagion or valued the opportunity to show their devotion more highly. Palace servants in white with tall black hats mingled with courtiers and senior Imperial Guard officers carrying bows and arrows.

Akitada caught some surprised glances at his own robe and retreated nervously. He saw now that the inner wall was a double covered gallery that led off to the east and west, but he did not know where to turn.

One of the officials at the gate had waved casually toward the left. Akitada began to walk that way along the covered gallery. Men passed him, giving him curious stares; he was a stranger here. All of them outranked him, and he did not dare ask them for directions. When he reached another set of steps into the courtyard, he saw that the gallery continued into a separate enclosure and stopped. He looked doubtfully at the two halls ahead. Most visitors seemed to be headed toward the second of these. Akitada followed them into the graveled courtyard and walked under the trees, looking for one of the palace servants. Alas, there were none.

He had just made up his mind to risk interrupting one of the small groups of nobles, when he recognized a face. His old friend Kosehira stood chatting with several others, his pudgy hands fluttering and his round face unusually serious. Akitada stopped.

One of the men with Kosehira noticed him and said something. Kosehira turned, cried out, "If it isn't Akitada!" and rushed over. Good old Kosehira. He had always treated Akitada as a friend, even if he had long since outstripped him by several ranks.

They embraced. "What did you do to your face?" demanded Kosehira. "Been in the wars again?"

"Just a disagreement with a thug. How are you, Kosehira?"

"Never better. My family grows and my garden is beautiful just now. You must see it. I have moved the waterway and built a charming poetry pavilion in the far corner. It's so inspirational that even you would have poetry flowing from your lips there. When will you come?"

"Kosehira," said Akitada nervously with a glance at his friend's companions, "surely this is not the time and place, when His Majesty is so ill. And aren't people afraid to come here?"

"Oh, that. Well, we're not likely to be admitted to his presence. Everyone is very concerned, but I hear he is not too bad. Young people seem to shake these things off so easily. They say he's hardly marked at all. Dreadful disease, of course. A lot of people have left for the country. All is well at your house, I hope?"

"Yes," Akitada said, bemused, "and yours?"

"Of course. I've added three more children to my brood. Two sons and a puny little girl. I seem to spoil my little ladies more than the boys. And how fares your family? Any new lovely ladies?"

Akitada smiled. "No. Both Tamako and Yori are well."

Kosehira cocked his head. "Only one child? In all those years? Come, that is too bad of you. I know of any number of well-born young women who would eagerly join your household and provide you with a large family. As a matter of fact, one of my own cousins . . ."

"Please, Kosehira, not now. I'm here to pay my respects and have no idea where to go."

Kosehira looked puzzled. "But how did you get in?"

Akitada produced his pass. "I'm representing Soga."

"Is he ill or dead?" Kosehira asked hopefully. He knew Soga, and he also knew of Akitada's troubles with the minister.

"Neither. He's gone to the country."

"Pity."

"How serious is this epidemic?"

Kosehira's face lengthened. "Serious. Kinnori has died and now his son and two of his wives have it. The great minister of the left has moved to his second wife's home, because his first wife's father and uncle are both ill. The crown prince's mentor is at death's door and has taken Buddhist vows. And there are others. It's hard to tell who's sick and who's in hiding; they just don't come to court or they have left the capital. It's said that Takaie brought it back with him from Tsukushi when he returned to court early this year. His retainers and servants have spread it among the common people. Apparently the young get it first."

Akitada stared at him. This passed belief. "But what about all these people here? And why haven't there been announcements and proclamations? Why just let the disease spread without so much as a word?"

Kosehira raised his thin brows. "You must have heard something about it."

"I didn't take it seriously. Not until I was told about His Majesty's illness today."

"Actually, the place is pretty empty today. You should see it when all is well." Kosehira sighed. "We're all in the hands of Buddha."

They fell silent. Akitada wondered if Tamako worried that he would bring the disease back with him. She had expected him to take his family to their farm in the country. But Seimei was too ill to travel, and Akitada could not leave the ministry. Worse, Tora had disappeared, and Genba was at the Yasugi mansion.

Kosehira slapped his shoulder. "Come, cheer up. You're safe enough. All will be well. Now go and take your wishes for His Majesty's complete recovery to the chamberlains' office. I'll show you the way. The head chamberlain is on duty now; he will receive you."

Kosehira left to explain matters to his friends and then walked with Akitada to the chamberlains' office. Akitada felt a shiver of awe. He had never set foot in the Imperial Palace, let alone penetrated as far as the handful of nobles who associated daily with the emperor in his private apartments. But he had prepared his speech and must deliver it. It was now part of his duties.

"I'm not looking forward to it," he confessed when they stopped at the bottom of the steps.

Kosehira laughed. "You're only the hundredth visitor today. They won't pay much attention. Just say your bit, and creep back out. Backward, mind you."

Yes. He had almost forgotten about that. Much depended on his not placing a foot wrong or neglecting proper protocol. He felt the sweat breaking out on his forehead. Better get it over with before he started dripping all over the chamberlains' shining floors. He started up the stairs.

As it turned out, Kosehira was right. When he gave his name and purpose to a guard at the door to the chamberlains' office, he was conducted into a large room where three formally attired nobles awaited him. He entered, knelt before the one in the center, and touched his forehead to the polished wooden boards.

"You are Sugawara, acting Minister of Justice?"

"Acting Minister of Justice" sounded very grand, but Akitada felt thoroughly inadequate to the present situation and merely murmured his assent.

"Why have you come?"

At this he sat up and delivered his prepared speech. He managed to do so without stammering, then bowed and immediately returned to his previous position.

"Very dutiful, Sugawara," said one of the great men—Akitada was not sure who any of them were—"Your wishes will be delivered to His Majesty. He is grateful for the prayers of the nation."

Akitada did not know how he was to respond to that and therefore remained perfectly still. There was a brief silence, then another voice said impatiently, "That is all. You may now proceed to the temple."

Akitada rose to his knees, bowed again, and retreated backward, hoping he would not miss the doorway and fetch up against the wall. A hand touched his shoulder, and the guard motioned him to rise and depart. The worst was over.

Kosehira waited outside. "I'll come with you to the temple," he said. "It never hurts to pray."

A practical attitude. They walked the short distance together, exchanging news about their families and their work. It was a measure of Kosehira's worry that he was unusually subdued.

No monks were sweeping the steps of the temple gate today. All was quiet and neat until they had crossed the temple garden. When they were climbing the steps together, they heard the soft hum of sutra chanting. They stepped into the shadowy solemnity of the temple hall and the heavy scent of incense. The only light came from the tall tapers that burned before the monumental figures of three golden Buddhas. Smaller statues of the celestial generals danced in front of them. Each of the Buddhas wore swirling gilded robes and stood before a large gilded nimbus. By a trick of the flickering candlelight and the haze of incense against the shimmering gold, it seemed as if the statues were alive. The generals turned and dipped and the Buddhas smiled as they emerged from the divine fire.

The chanting monks—dark-robed and seated in the shadows—were almost invisible against the side walls, but a gorgeously attired priest in purple silk and a rich brocade stole occupied the central mat before the altar. He sat cross-legged, apparently in prayer. Kosehira approached him, bowed a greeting and murmured, "My friend Sugawara and I came to pray for His Majesty." The priest turned his head, gave Akitada a long glance from under heavy lids, and nodded.

They knelt side by side on another mat, performed the cus-

tomary obeisances, and then assumed the posture of medi-
tation.

Akitada had been raised in the faith and was familiar enough
with its rituals, but his true spiritual center was with the ancient
gods of Shinto. At heart, he did not approve of the foreign faith,
though it was not wise to say so when it was practiced with such
devotion by those in power. He listened to the hum and throb
of the chant and stared up at the image before him. Judging by
the small jar of ointment in the statue's left hand, this was
Yakushi Nyorai, the Buddha of healing. Akitada concentrated
on saying a prayer. After all, he was praying for the sovereign
and he wished the young emperor well. Indeed, he had been
glad to hear he was not dying.

But his mind drifted to worldly matters. He would have to
go home to change again, and that meant meeting Tamako to
report on the emperor and discuss the problems of sending her
and Yori into the country. The complications involved were beyond him. She would leave without him, and he could hardly
stop her. Given her feelings at the present time, this separation
was likely to deepen the breach between them. As he thought of
her words again, they seemed to him a rejection of who and
what he was. He could not bridge the distance between them
without changing himself into someone he did not want to be.

Defeated, he turned his mind to Tomoe's murder. Lady Yasugi's stunning confession that they were sisters had opened new
possibilities. He considered their conversation. Something was
wrong about it. Her sadness—and there had been a very deep
sadness behind their strange exchange—troubled him. Even
grief for her sister did not account for it. Besides, he was not
convinced that the two women had been very close. They had
only met again recently, and Tomoe's way of life must have
shocked the fastidious Lady Yasugi. And why the fatalistic ac-
ceptance of a joyless marriage in so young and beautiful a
woman? Yasugi was a much older man. Could she truly be so

attached to him that his coldness caused her hopelessness? Akitada did not think so. He decided to pay her another visit and ask more questions. There was, for example, Tomoe's husband who had abandoned her because of her blindness. The sisters had been very unlucky in their husbands. As had been the parents who had raised their daughters to be dutiful. Neither girl had turned out to be the meek, obedient creature they had envisioned. If he approached the past carefully, Lady Yasugi might confide in him.

Perhaps they could walk together in the garden. She was a woman of great beauty and grace and capable of strong affections. Her defiance of her husband in order to help her sister proved that. When looked at in that way, her rebellious spirit seemed admirable. She had certainly shown courage. He smiled at the memory of the noble beauty dressed in that unattractive nun's garb and mingling with the common crowd in the courtroom.

A touch on his sleeve brought him back to his surroundings. Kosehira signaled some warning. He glanced up at the image of the Buddha and then over to the priest. The priest was glaring at him. Puzzled, Akitada looked at Kosehira.

"You are smiling," whispered his friend.

Akitada guiltily rearranged his face, but the priest still glowered. Putting on a rapt expression, Akitada said in an audible undertone, "I thought I saw the Holy Yakushi nod his head. No, I'm sure of it. I take it to mean that he has heard my prayer."

The priest cleared his throat. "Blessed be Amida. A sign! Thank you, young man. You must have a very pure mind to break through the barrier and receive an answer. I have only once been blessed in that manner. What was your name again?"

Akitada stuttered his name.

The priest nodded. "A good omen. A Sugawara praying for His Majesty. A very good omen."

Akitada quickly performed the closing obeisances. He and

Kosehira left after bowing to the priest, who graciously bowed back.

Outside in the temple garden, Kosehira doubled over in laughter. "You liar," he gasped. "I know you too well. Do you know who that was?"

Akitada glanced back nervously. "No. I just assumed he was someone important. That fine robe . . ."

"It was the late Emperor Sanjo's brother, the present emperor's uncle."

"Dear Heaven. No wonder he looked outraged."

"You made a good recovery. He was impressed by your spirituality." Kosehira burst into more giggles. "And by the fact that the great Michizane's descendant is praying for the emperor. If he remembers, chances are excellent that he will put your name up for promotion."

"Don't be ridiculous." It was true, his ancestor was routinely blamed for every catastrophe. The notion that he had broken the curse made Akitada laugh also, and they passed out into the street in a lighter mood. Akitada asked, "Kosehira, do you know any Yasugis? This one seems to own vast estates somewhere but spends part of his time in his mansion here in the capital."

"Yasugi? Fat old fellow who looks apoplectic?"

Akitada was pleased with this description. "I've never met him, but I, er, ran into one of his wives. The youngest. Apparently he left town without her."

Kosehira's eyebrows almost met his hairline. "You ran into one of his wives? After her husband left her behind? Come, there's a story there. If it's the man I'm thinking of, she's said to be a beauty." Before Akitada could deflect his curiosity, he clapped his hands in delight. "So that's what's been on your mind. Would that explain the smile? Pure thoughts indeed!" He roared. "You philanderer! Better watch out, though. Yasugi controls some very influential people and maintains a small army on his estate in Tsuzuki."

"Nonsense." Akitada flushed and, aware of it, made matters worse. "We only met once and she had a maid with her, an ill-tempered, hateful woman loyal to the husband."

Kosehira grinned. "Ingenuity gets rid of troublesome servants."

"Please be serious, Kosehira. Tsuzuki is just south of here, isn't it?" Akitada calculated, with some dismay, that Yasugi could already have fetched his wife home.

"About thirty miles from here. Come to think of it, someone mentioned his going home. Afraid of the disease like everyone else. Strange he would leave one of his wives behind." Kosehira regarded Akitada thoughtfully. "Will you be . . . meeting her again?"

Akitada snapped, "This is no romance. I'm investigating the murder of a blind woman, her sister's, as it turns out."

"A murder? You don't say." Kosehira seized Akitada's arm. "I can't wait to hear. Will you come to my house tonight? We can have a quiet dinner with some good wine, and you'll tell me all about it. It will be like old times."

Akitada regretted thoroughly having mentioned the Yasugi name. "I'm sorry, Kosehira. I can't. The case is urgent, and I am tied up at the ministry every day. Besides, Seimei is ill—no, not the smallpox—and Tamako is afraid to stay in the capital with Yori. I will come as soon as I can."

Kosehira looked disappointed. "I could help," he offered hopefully.

Akitada hesitated. "Well, do you know the Murata family? The parents of the two women?"

"Murata? Bureau of Divination?" Kosehira shook his head. "Not really. Yasugi's third wife was said to come from humble circumstances. Some scandal, I think. I can ask around."

Akitada looked at his friend gratefully. "Would you? And I promise to tell you all as soon as I can."

They parted then, and Akitada turned toward home. He

had not gone far when a voice hailed him. Kunyoshi, the archivist, was running down the street, his skirts flapping around his skinny calves. He seemed in an almighty hurry to catch up. Akitada wondered what he could want now.

Kunyoshi trotted up, puffing. "Sorry," he gasped, "didn't want to miss you."

He took a few rattling breaths while Akitada patted his back and said loudly, "Take your time. I'm in no hurry."

Kunyoshi gestured at Akitada's court robe and said humbly, "You are very kind, my lord. It was rude to shout and run after you, but I'm afraid this foolish old person has made a mistake." He paused to catch his breath again, peering up at Akitada from rheumy eyes. "I thought, how dreadful if Lord Sugawara should set out on such a long journey and then find out that it was all a silly mistake made by a senile old fool. I was quite desperate to find you when I happened to see you just now outside the temple. It was as if the Buddha himself had answered my prayers."

"Surely you exaggerate. What mistake?"

Kunyoshi wrung his hands. "Do you recall asking about the Utsunomiyas?"

"Yes." How remote that seemed now. Tora had been charged with murder, a smallpox epidemic was raging, and his family was in turmoil.

But Kunyoshi knew none of this. He stood there, trembling with anxiety. And now tears were beginning to course down the sunken cheeks. People cast curious glances at them.

"Kunyoshi," said Akitada, taking the old man's arm and leading him aside, "I was not going anywhere, so no harm is done. What exactly did you remember?"

"I told you that the land was in Hoki Province. Do you remember?"

Akitada frowned. "Izumo, I thought. Something about the shrine being involved in the land dispute. I could not have gone there in any case. It's much too far."

"I am glad you did not go, but I was afraid you would. I could see it meant a great deal to you. And people say that you always solve a mystery."

Akitada was getting a little impatient. "So, if the land is not in Hoki or Izumo, where is it?"

Kunyoshi was wringing his hands again. "That is what I cannot remember. I know it was to do with a shrine. A very important shrine. Only it was not Ise or Izumo." He wiped away tears. "I'm getting worse. My mind remembers nothing. I'll have to resign." He heaved a ragged sigh, bowed to Akitada, muttering, "So very sorry," and stumbled away.

Akitada looked after him. Poor old man. Everything conspired to bury Haseo's past and there was nothing he could do about it, at least not now. He must go home and deal with more urgent problems.

CHAPTER FIFTEEN

CAUGHT

The Scarecrow pushed Tora into the training hall. They arrived in the middle of some sort of celebration. Tora relaxed a little; surely they would not be quite this happy discussing methods of killing him.

Kata waved and shouted, "There's a general amnesty."

The Scarecrow gave a whoop and pulled Tora into the gathering. "That'll mean three, four more men, and times are good. Lots of empty houses."

"I make it six," said Kata. "Denzo and Kiheiji sent word they're coming to us."

Tora tried to look cheerful. If the emperor had called for an amnesty—and because of the epidemic it was all too likely—the jails would be emptied immediately. The gang had reason to celebrate, but heaven help the decent citizens in the weeks and months to come. As for hoping to have the police arrest Kata and his men for their crimes, the thought was ludicrous. His masquerade was not only dangerous, it had also just become pointless. Tomoe's death would not be avenged lawfully.

But at least there was no immediate danger. One or two of the men, the Scarecrow among them, still scowled when they looked at him, but Kata seemed friendly enough. The Scarecrow had taken Kata aside to report right after they arrived, but the conversation ended with Kata firmly shaking his head and the Scarecrow slinking off.

Kata was in excellent spirits, smiling broadly and joking with his men until it was time to push back the sliding doors and begin the daily lessons.

For the first time Kata put Tora to work drilling students. Hoping to pick up a little more information before drifting away from the place for good, Tora complied. He worried about the man in the storehouse. During one of the breaks, he asked Kata about the epidemic.

"Good for business," was the only comment he got.

"The Scarecrow said we're moving to another place. Where are we going?"

Kata waved him away. "Back to work. You'll find out soon enough."

The morning passed slowly. Tora was not yet up to continuous sword practice, even when it was not competitive. He tried to conserve his strength, but felt Kata's watchful eye on his back. He was also wary of Matsue, but his archenemy did not show up. In fact, the other gang members left, leaving only the students, Kata, Tora, and Kinjiro.

At midday, the lessons stopped. The morning students departed and Kata also disappeared. Tora collapsed against a wall and closed his eyes. Rest was blissful until his stomach began to growl.

With a sigh he fished out his last three coppers and looked at them dubiously. Kata had not mentioned pay. Still, he could not complain: He had offered to work for room and board, and that had been provided. The trouble was, he had eaten little the night before and only two small rice cakes that morning. He glanced toward Kinjiro, who was replacing the wooden swords in their rack. "Hey, Kinjiro? You want to go to the market for some noodle soup?"

Kinjiro stopped. "Can't. I'm supposed to watch the place till they get back. You go ahead."

Tora put his coppers away. He wondered why the boy seemed subdued today and got to his feet. "No. I'll keep you company. Too much food makes me sluggish anyway."

Kinjiro grunted and went to get a broom. Apparently cleaning the training hall between sessions was part of his duties. Tora watched him for a while, then said, "Wouldn't you rather do some other work? You could be an apprentice . . ." His voice trailed off. Honest trades, like mat weaving, cloth dying, paper making and so forth, would not appeal much to the youngster after the exciting adventures promised by Kata and his men. The danger in a criminal career was part of the thrill. Kinjiro probably dreamed of moving up through the ranks until he became an officer himself, maybe even someone like Matsue.

Kinjiro gave a snort of derision. "Too late for that."

This surprised Tora. "What do you mean?"

The boy shot him a pitying look. "No tradesman's going to take me on. I've got a reputation." He said it almost proudly.

"You've been stealing," Tora accused.

"That too. But mainly I collect the money."

Tora opened his mouth and closed it again. Of course. Kata was taking protection money from merchants in the market. Tora could not recall who had told him. For a weekly fee, Kata's hoods were supposed to protect the merchants from other gangs. If a man did not pay up, they would demonstrate the foolishness of such behavior by ransacking his business themselves. And Kinjiro was sent to collect the money. Naturally he could not now apply for honest work.

Tora had developed a soft spot for the boy. Kinjiro had fallen into a life of crime because he had been abandoned and nothing else had offered. He was trying to make the best of it, but apparently he was not such an enthusiastic gang member after all. Maybe his upbringing in a decent home by a respectable father had something to do with that. Or maybe he lacked the selfish cruelty and bovine stupidity which made for contentment in a life of crime.

"If you could be anything in the world, what would you be?" Tora asked.

Wielding his broom viciously, Kinjiro swept some debris out into the street. "His Excellency, the chancellor, of course," he sneered. "He's got more wealth than anybody and tells the emperor what to do."

"No, seriously."

The boy leaned on his broom. "I'd want to be what my father was." He immediately began his sweeping again. "And you?" he asked. "You think you'll have it easy here? Just drill the students for a few hours every day? Maybe walk to the market with Kata *Sensei,* watching out for his enemies? You're a bigger fool than me. If you had any sense, you'd leave now and never come back."

The last was said so fiercely that Tora's uneasiness returned. He got up and grasped Kinjiro's arm. "What do you mean?" he asked. "What's happened?"

Kinjiro shook loose. "Nothing. I'm just talking," he muttered and went for an old rag, which he put under his broom to dust and polish the floorboards to pristine cleanliness before the afternoon's lessons.

"Kinjiro, you heard something. They talked about me, didn't they? I know Matsue's trying to get me. He almost did. And now the Scarecrow thinks I'm spying on him. I can't seem to do anything right."

Kinjiro glared at him. "Maybe they've got reason. You've been snooping."

Tora's heart plummeted. He looked around nervously. If they suspected him, surely they wouldn't leave him here with just the boy. He locked eyes with Kinjiro. There was not much point in protesting his innocence. "What are they going to do?"

"How should I know? But I wouldn't hang around to find out if I were you."

It was good advice. Unless they were lying in wait outside. "Are you supposed to keep an eye on me?" Tora asked suspiciously.

"What if?"

"You'd be in trouble if I ran."

Kinjiro stared at him. Then he said, "You're a fool, Tora. Go! What do you care what happens to me?"

"I care. I don't treat my friends that way."

Kinjiro said fiercely, "Then go ahead and get killed. Because that's what they'll do as soon as they figure out what you're up to." When Tora made no move to leave, he cried, "They'll probably do it slowly. An ear first, then another. Then your nose and your tongue. After that, a hand, a foot, your privates. You aren't going to know about the rest." He was practically in tears.

Tora took the boy by his bony shoulders and shook him. "If you know all this about them, what are you doing here? What would your father say?"

Kinjiro tried to free himself. When Tora held on, he cursed and kicked and punched him. Tora ended up wrapping both arms around the thin, gasping figure and holding him until he calmed down. Kinjiro shook with sobs.

He released the boy then but left his hands on his shoulders. "I think we'd both better get out of here," he said.

Kinjiro sniffed and wiped his nose on his sleeve. "I could go back to the post stable," he said miserably. He put away the broom and rag and brushed off his clothes. "All right. I'm ready. Let's go before they get back."

But they were too late. The peace of the midday hour was broken by the sound of a large number of people approaching outside. They looked out and saw the gang. Led by the Scarecrow, they walked close together with an air of grim anticipation. It took Tora only a moment to realize the magnitude of the trouble he was in; the group parted and revealed in its midst a lopsided creature who was grinning malevolently at him. The beggar from the market.

Tora thought of making a dash for it. In fact, he had taken a few steps toward the back door, when it opened and Matsue and Kata walked in.

After that, things moved quickly. The gang entered from the street and slid the doors shut. They formed a circle around Tora. Cut off from the outside world, the hall had become dim and secretive. Nobody talked.

The Scarecrow took the beggar by the arm and led him to Kata. "He's got quite a story to tell," he announced grimly.

Kata let his eyes slide to Tora, then told the beggar, "Talk."

The beggar bowed deeply and whined, "Important information, Master. Worth at least a gold coin."

Kata raised a fist. "I pay you, scum. You work for me."

Tora felt sick. He had been a fool to trust the beggar. Who better to keep an eye on the market and Kata's clients than he? And the bastard was even missing a finger, often a sign of gang membership.

The beggar knelt, crying, "Yes, yes. Of course, Master. Right away. Only you'll see, it's of the greatest importance to you. All I ask is that you remember the service this insignificant person is doing you. I'm a poor man ... Aiihh!" He squealed as the Scarecrow's booted foot connected with his ribs.

Kata pointed to Tora. "You know him?"

The beggar nodded eagerly. "Yes. Yes. He abused me not two

days ago. When I cried for help, he tried to bribe me to tell him about you. I didn't tell him, but he already knew something. He works for the police. When the others told me he was passing himself off as one of us, I knew right away you were in danger and came to warn you."

Kata looked at Tora. "You disappoint me," he said sadly. "I liked you. But I don't like being made a fool of. I don't like liars. And I especially don't like police informers."

Tora's mind raced. "The scum is lying. I would never work for the police. That's a serious insult to a man's character. The crooked little bastard tried to extort money from me, claiming I kicked him. I took the slug aside and gave him a drubbing, and now he's getting his revenge by telling lies about me."

Kata's eyes narrowed. "Why should I believe you?"

"Look at him! He'd kill his grandfather for a few coppers. And if the bastard lies about me, he'll lie about you. Today he's selling me; tomorrow it'll be you. Remember, he's the one that told me about you in the first place."

Kata looked confused by this logic, but he turned on the beggar, "What did you tell him about me?" he growled.

The beggar shrunk away. "Nothing. I swear. He was asking about the blind singer. He thought you'd killed her."

Kata's jaw sagged. "Tomoe? He thought I'd killed Tomoe?"

"Yeah. Just like a stupid policeman." The beggar tried a conciliatory grin.

Kata turned to Tora. "What do you know about Tomoe's murder?"

Tora decided his safest bet was to claim ignorance. "Nothing. He's making it all up."

This brazen denial outraged the beggar, who began to jump up and down. "You threatened me. You said you were police. You said you were investigating her murder. You wanted to know who the gang boss was that had been talking to her. You choked me and made me tell you—"

Kata's face turned an angry red. "So you did talk." He back-handed the beggar so viciously that he went flying into two of the gang members. Then he turned back to Tora. "You told the truth about that, but everything else was a lie, wasn't it?"

"I'm not with the police," said Tora, trying to bluster. "And I'll not be insulted and called a liar. I have my pride. You can have your job." He turned to walk off, but the circle of men closed against him. Tora clenched his fists. "Tell your goons to let me pass. You can't keep me here against my will."

Matsue spoke for the first time. He drawled, "Search him!"

Tora tried to make a break for it, but instantly five knives were inches from his throat and he could smell the bad breath of the thugs who crowded around him.

Matsue laughed. "What can you do now, mouse catcher? If you are who you say you are, nobody'll miss you. And if you're working for the police, you're guilty. Either way, you're a dead man."

Tora hoped he was wrong, but then Kata said, "Search both of them."

Of course they found Matsue's document. They passed it to Kata, who glanced at it and passed it to Matsue.

Matsue stared at it and then at Tora. "So," he said, "you're a snoop *and* a thief. There's more to this than looking for the blind bitch's killer. I'm going to enjoy getting the truth out of you before I kill you."

The beggar was next. He squealed with outrage when they took away the pouch he carried on the rope that held up his pants. The pouch contained a large number of coppers and two pieces of silver. Kata was about to put them back when he looked more closely at one of the silver pieces. "Matsue," he said, "have a look."

Matsue looked. "Two characters are missing. Is that the one you gave her?"

Kata nodded. He kept the coin and threw the pouch back at

the beggar. Then he turned to Tora. "You're not stupid, whoever you are. You know we can't let you go." He gestured and the men around Tora stepped back.

Tora scanned implacable faces. Only Kinjiro cowered in a corner, his eyes wide with terror. "What're you going to do?" Tora asked hoarsely.

Nobody answered. The others, even the whimpering beggar, had become very quiet. The silence was heavy with anticipation. Tora had witnessed it only once before when he was a soldier and had attended the execution of a deserter. Just like the condemned man's comrades, they all knew what was next. He saw it in their faces. They looked back with avid eyes, moistened their lips, waited for his futile panic when Kata or Matsue would give the signal.

But instead the silence was broken by a knocking on the street doors. "*Sensei?*"

One of Kata's men cursed; another said, "It's the students."

Kata gave brisk orders. "Tie them both up and lock them in the shed until tonight. I want a watch kept on them."

When the beggar tried to protest too loudly, Matsue knocked him out with a brutal blow to the temple. Tora allowed himself to be bound. They hobbled his legs and tied his wrists behind his back, looping the rope around his neck in such a way that he could not move his arms without strangling himself. Then they took him and the bound and unconscious beggar to the small shed where Tora had been left earlier. This time they locked the shed door and left a guard outside.

Tora did not waste time on self-recrimination. He considered his options. The trouble was, there did not seem to be any. His movements were restricted by the rope around his neck, and outside a guard was leaning against the locked shed door. The beggar was either dead or still unconscious. If the latter, he would come around soon and certainly raise an alarm if he saw Tora attempting to escape. Tora wondered why they had not been gagged, but realized that the guard outside could cut off any noise before it would disturb the neighbors who, probably knew better than to pay attention to the goings-on here.

The shed was flimsily built and old. No doubt a board or two could be loosened someplace, but how was he to accomplish this? And what was the alternative? To lie here, waiting patiently for the lessons to be over so the cutthroats could kill him without attracting too much notice? What with the amnesty and the raging epidemic in the city, nobody would bother to investigate two more bodies left in a ditch somewhere.

Tora decided to work on his bonds. The worst was the rope around his neck. He had to find a way to loosen that enough to allow himself some freedom to work on his wrists. He tried various contortions, but he only tightened the knots even more.

Breathing hard, he rested and thought about his bonds. He might get more slack in the rope if he knelt and arched his body backwards. Perhaps he could then reach the knot at his ankles. He managed to kneel, but there was not enough give to allow him to move his bound hands, though he could breathe a little more easily. On the other hand, the pain in his back, shoulders, and neck got worse.

They had tossed him down near the pile of sacks and boxes. He shuffled over on his knees to investigate it. The boxes were useless, but there was something hidden under the sacks.

How to move the sacks? Eventually he used his teeth and a slow and painful backward shuffle to drag off one sack at a time. The rope cut off his breath, choking him, and his neck and arm muscles went into spasms so that he had to rest several times, but he persisted and uncovered a large earthenware water jar. Such useful utensils are not abandoned in derelict sheds, but this one appeared to have sprung a leak. A thin crack ran down one side to the bottom.

Unfortunately, the jar was no more help than the boxes or sacks. If it were broken, it might be a different story. Shards had sharp edges and could be used to saw through rope. Tora was not sure how he could manage such a thing, but it was a moot point since he had no way of breaking the jar.

Defeated, he flopped down across the sacks to think about his chances of escaping once they came for him. Short of a miracle, they were nonexistent. He was forced to consider the jar again. He had neither tools nor the use of his hands, and his feet were hobbled too closely to allow him to kick the jar apart. But he could try to break it with his weight.

He checked on the beggar, who had not moved.

Getting up on his feet—not an easy thing to do—he shuffled into position and backed up. Then he sat down with as much force as he dared use with the guard outside. Pain stabbed his back and posterior, but the jar survived. He suppressed a groan, checked the beggar's motionless figure, and scrambled up again to repeat the process. After the fifth attempt, he heard a faint cracking. On the next try, the jar collapsed. For a moment it felt as though a dozen knives had been stuck into his back and backside. He gritted his teeth and listened. The guard outside had taken to walking back and forth. He was muttering under his breath but appeared unaware of activity in the shed. Tora rolled off the jar and waited until some of the pain receded. The jar had become a pile of smaller pieces, with one large shard pointing upward from the flat bottom. He ignored the warm wetness seeping through his pants and maneuvered the shard into a corner by pushing it with his head, then backed up and brought his wrists up against it.

He needed to rub the rope against the upright shard until it parted—easier thought of than done. The shard kept moving and tipping. Since he could not see it, he had to turn around each time to check what had happened and to reposition it. Meanwhile, the rope—a strong new one—gave no signs of parting. The shard caught his skin more often than it did the rope until his hands were slippery with blood.

To make matters worse, the beggar started muttering and moaning in his corner.

Suddenly there was a scratching against the back wall of the shed, and a soft "Ssst." Tora hissed back and waited. After a moment, Kinjiro's voice whispered, "Tora?"

"Yes." The beggar seemed to have drifted off again.

"Can you get loose?"

Tora could not, but whispered, "I'm working on it."

"I'll try to get rid of the guard."

Tora did not know what to say. What could Kinjiro do? More to the point, what would they do to him if he were caught? He whispered, "Be careful," but the boy had already gone.

He worked his wrists up and down feverishly. Outside Kinjiro was striking up a conversation with the guard. "Kata *Sensei* says to cover for you if you want to relieve yourself."

"Kind of him," grumbled the man. "I'm about to burst. That snack I had in the market didn't agree with me. I've been stepping from one foot to the other forever."

His rapid footsteps receded.

Tora heard Kinjiro working the lock. The lad seemed to be trying out keys. There was not much time. If Kinjiro could not open the shed quickly, the guard would be back, and their chance would be lost. He leaned into his labors with total concentration, ignoring the pain in his wrists, ignoring the choking halter around his neck, ignoring the cramping muscles in his arms and back. Outside Kinjiro cursed. Things were not going well. Tora made one more desperate effort, and this time he thought he felt the rope ease a little. Once more, and yes, a definite easing! Then several strands parted. He was almost there. He glanced at the beggar. The man's eyes were open and watching him.

At that moment the rope parted. Tora was drenched with sweat and his breath was coming in gasps. He loosened the halter around his neck, straightened his painful back, and brought his arms forward. His wrists were a bloody mess, and he grimaced as he undid the rest of the knots with his teeth. Then he untied his feet.

Just in time.

"Hey," shouted the beggar. "Someone quick! He's escaping."

Cursing under his breath, Tora pounced on him and knocked him out again, stifling the man's shriek. He felt no compunction and had no time to worry about the evil little toad.

Outside, Kinjiro had stopped working the lock and was wrenching at the door instead.

"Back away," Tora shouted and delivered a mighty kick to where he knew the lock was. The door flew open and he shot out.

"Hurry," Kinjiro cried, his voice squeaking with panic. "The bastard's going to be back any second. We've got to run for it."

Their luck ran out immediately. When they rounded the corner, the guard was strolling toward them. His jaw sagged comically; he let out a yell. Tora barreled into him, knocking him down, the boy slid past, and together they ran for the next corner, dimly aware of shouts and pounding feet.

After that they ran for their lives. They dodged piles of refuse, sprinted past a funeral procession, knocked down a small child who had stepped into the street to stare, dove down alleys, and zigzagged through two wards to throw off their unseen pursuers. They did not slow down or look behind them until they reached Ninth Avenue, a busy street marking the southern perimeter of the capital. Here they attracted curious stares. Tora caught up with Kinjiro. "Slow down," he gasped, "or we'll have the constables after us, too."

Kinjiro nodded, but he kept looking over his shoulder. At the intersection with Suzako Avenue, he turned toward Rashomon, the gate leading out of the city.

"Not that way," Tora said. He pointed to the large temple on the other side of the street. "Quick, in there!"

The Eastern Temple was an ancient complex adjoining Rashomon. It had been designated "Temple for the Protection of the Land." A steady trickle of people moved through its large gate. The epidemic had brought them here to offer their prayers for relief. Tora and the boy joined the worshippers and climbed the steps to the temple gate. An elderly monk stood there, holding a large collection bowl, his eyes unfocused and his head bobbing rhythmically as each visitor dropped his offering. Tora parted with his last three coppers as they passed through. Instead of following the others to the main hall, he and Kinjiro cut across the courtyard toward the pagoda.

As Tora had guessed, they were the only visitors to the small altar room whose walls and pillars were covered with paintings of the two Buddhist worlds. Exhausted, he collapsed on the steps that led to the floors above.

"Well," he told the boy, who was inspecting the pictures, "we did it. Thanks for your timely help."

"Don't mention it." The boy suddenly turned and grinned. "That was very good. I can't remember when I've had more fun. Don't you wish you could see their faces? Bet they're running around like a bunch of ants back there." He chortled and came to sit beside Tora. "We've got to leave town. How much money have you got, Tora?"

"I just gave the baldpate my last coppers."

"Stupid."

"Hey. Remember where you are. You want to go to hell?"

Kinjiro grinned. "Too late to worry about that. We'll walk a few miles and offer to help a farmer for a meal and a dry place to sleep. Just so we get out of the capital."

Tora shook his head. "No, we can't. There's unfinished business."

Kinjiro sat up. "Are you mad? You want to go back there again? They'll kill you. You heard Kata. And Matsue won't put it off this time."

"Yes, I know. That's the point. What we know about Kata and his gang is not much good unless we tell the police."

Now Kinjiro was on his feet, his face filled with shock and disgust. "You work for the police. The beggar told the truth." He clenched his fists and cried, "And I trusted you." He made a sound between a sob and a curse, and rushed out. Tora went after him, groaning when his much abused muscles refused to cooperate. He stumbled down the pagoda steps after the boy, who was already halfway across the courtyard. Tora had visions of his running to warn Kata. He was not afraid that the gang would escape the law, but that they would take their revenge on Kinjiro for letting Tora go. By dint of superhuman effort, he managed to catch up and snag the boy's shirt just as he was dashing through the temple gate. They fell sprawling at the feet of the gatekeeper. People stopped to see what was happening.

The monk was not amused. "What are you doing?" he demanded sternly, hauling the boy up by the scruff of his neck, and glaring at Tora. "And you a full-grown man, too. Aren't you ashamed to behave this way in a holy place?"

"Er—" said Tora, quickly hiding his bloody wrists and hands in his sleeves, "ah, well, my son here got frightened and tried to run away. He doesn't like temples, you see. Says they're full of ghosts and goblins. I've been trying to show him that there's nothing to be afraid of, but he's very stubborn. Don't let him go, please."

The monk, who had been about to release Kinjiro, got a firmer grip on him. "Is that so?" he asked, looking from one to the other. Kinjiro glared at Tora and attempted a kick at the monk's shins. "Yes, I see what you mean," the monk said, giving the boy a shake. "Now, son, if you don't obey your father, I'll have to lock you up. There is nothing to be afraid of in a temple. Ghosts and goblins don't dare enter sacred places. Who has told you such silly and blasphemous tales?"

Kinjiro snapped, "My mother."

"Amida!" The monk shook his head. "You both have my sympathy. Women are evil and corrupt creatures and will never enter the Pure Land. That is why they spread such tales. Don't believe their wicked tongues."

Kinjiro stared at him, then said with feeling, "You're right. They *are* evil. I won't ever believe one again."

"Then you'll go quietly in with your father?"

"Yes." Kinjiro nodded fervently, and the monk released him.

Tora immediately put a protective arm around the boy, smiled at the onlookers, and bowed to the monk. "Thank you for your wise counsel. May the Buddha bless and reward you."

The monk nodded graciously, and they walked with the others into the courtyard and ascended the steps to the main hall. Tora, who kept his arm firmly around the boy's shoulders, became aware that they were shaking and that tears seemed to be running down his cheeks. Then he realized that the boy was not crying but laughing. They entered the Buddha hall side by side and found a dark recess near the doors. Up ahead a huge Buddha figure presided over prayer services for the protection of the capital. People knelt and monks chanted, but they were alone in their corner.

"That was so funny," the boy choked out.

"It was not." Tora was tired, sore, and irritated. "I almost lost you and I bruised my knees and elbows. You never give a person a chance to explain, do you?"

Kinjiro was still laughing. "That monk must've met my mother. Explain what?"

"Promise not to run again?" The boy nodded and Tora removed his arm. "I'm not with the police. I'm trying to clear myself of a murder charge."

Kinjiro stopped laughing and asked suspiciously, "How come you're not in jail?"

"My master got me out on his pledge to have me back in court for the trial. He convinced the judge that the police didn't

have a strong enough case against me. You see, I found the murdered woman and was arrested in her room. She was a friend
of mine."

Kinjiro considered this. "The blind singer from the market?
The one that got knifed? And you joined the gang because you
thought Kata killed her?"

"Exactly."

"Well, you're wrong about that. Kata didn't do it. She was
his good luck. Since she's been murdered, he's been complain-
ing how nothing turns out right any more. I bet he thinks your
getting away is just the final blow."

Tora remembered Kata's astonishment that Tora should
suspect him. Perhaps Kinjiro was right. He frowned. "So maybe
he's out of it, but that still leaves the others. What about Matsue? You said Matsue didn't like Tomoe."

Kinjiro thought about it. "I don't know. I don't see high and
mighty Matsue *Sensei* sneaking after a street singer. He'd send
somebody else."

"I think you're wrong. He'd do it himself so Kata wouldn't
find out."

The boy considered it. "Maybe. But you can't go back there.
It's too dangerous. Let the police figure out who killed the blind
woman."

"We have another problem. They've got some poor bastard
locked up in the storehouse."

Kinjiro looked puzzled. "Are you sure? He isn't one of us and
I would've heard if they'd been in a fight with another gang."

"I'm sure. I think it's an old man, and he may be sick. He
called out for Buntaro."

"Buntaro?" Kinjiro's face lengthened. "Oh, my," he said. "It
may be his uncle. Oh, Buddha! He told us the old man had gone
to visit relatives in the country. And they did have a bad quarrel
the day before."

Tora was shocked. "Why would he lock up his own uncle in

a dark, hot, airless place like that?" Buntaro was the Scarecrow. He remembered the man's anger when he had found Tora tampering with the storehouse lock. And then he had pounded on the door and shouted a warning about not making trouble or it would be the end of him. It had been meant for the old man inside as well. "What was the quarrel about?" he asked the boy.

"Oh, the same old thing. It's the uncle's place and he didn't want us there. When the old man fetched the police, he scared the wits out of us, but all the constables did was order us to leave. Kata was in a terrible temper. He made us stay away for a day, but then Buntaro said his uncle had left for the country and we went back. I guess the old man never left."

"Do you know where they keep the key?"

"I know where there are some keys."

"Good. Come. We're wasting time," Tora said. "We've got to get him out before his nephew gets rid of him permanently."

Kinjiro caught his sleeve. "You can't. They'll be checking the place. Matsue keeps his stuff there."

"They'll do more than check if we don't hurry."

CHAPTER SIXTEEN

PURPLE AND WHITE
WISTERIA

Kosehira was not the only one of Akitada's friends who was puzzled by his monogamous state. The fact that Akitada had resisted taking secondary wives to make certain of a large number of sons—hedges against the many diseases and mishaps that killed young children—fascinated Kosehira. He enjoyed all of his wives and his large brood of children and considered Akitada's arrangement not much better than monkish abstinence.

He thinks me a dull dog, mused Akitada as he walked homeward. The beautiful profile of Lady Yasugi leapt into his mind, and he wondered what it would be like to make love to her. To his shame, he felt a surge of desire. Except for a single lapse, he had been faithful to Tamako, but lately he missed the easy friendly companionship they used to have. People grew apart after several years of marriage, and certainly that was when some men took secondary wives. Often such an arrangement was welcomed by the first wife because it meant that she was no longer plagued by her husband's physical demands or continuous pregnancies. In fact, had Tamako not voiced that very thought only this morning, even though he had not been unduly demanding in his visits to her room? Her rejection had felt both cruel and disloyal. The breach between them was intolerably painful, and he tried to ease the hurt with angry resentment.

The truth was that he wanted affection, not many children. He wanted to come home and lose himself in some gentle cosseting, some laughter, and only afterward in the arms of a pretty wife.

As he left the Greater Palace enclosure, he saw a small silent group gathered around the notice board and went to see what had happened. It turned out to be the first official warning by the Great Council of State about the smallpox epidemic. A little late, thought Akitada bitterly, when half the officials and a good portion of the populace had already fled. The notice advised against contact with those who were suspected to have the disease. It also listed symptoms and recommended treatments. Such announcements were, of course, intended for those who could read. It was assumed that they would explain matters to the rest of the populace.

A young official, rumored to be both capable and ambitious, recognized Akitada and came over. "Ah, Sugawara," he said with a smile, "I hear you've taken on Soga's job. How exciting for you. Is he still alive?"

"Certainly he is," said Akitada coldly, "and expected back any day."

The younger man looked amused. "You don't know Soga then." He gestured at the proclamation. "All this good advice about taking boiled onions and ginseng when we all know that doesn't work. Soga, like many others, has taken to his heels to save himself, leaving those of us behind who are willing to risk our lives in hopes of benefiting from the flight of others." He gave a barking laugh, slapped Akitada's back, and walked away.

Akitada stared angrily after him. Was that what people

thought of him? That he had remained because he hoped for promotion—as if he had the glimmer of a chance at Soga's rank and title. He turned away from the proclamation and walked home in a glum mood. Not far from his house, he encountered a funeral, an important one to judge by the long and solemn procession, on its way to the cremation grounds at Toribeno. It was not yet dark, and that meant that the fires at Toribeno must be burning day and night. Apparently the nobles who had remained for whatever personal reasons were paying a heavy price for their decision, and so were the ordinary people who had no choice in the matter.

He could risk his own life—the possibility of dying of smallpox still did not strike Akitada as very likely—and he must do so because of Soga's absence, but he had no right to endanger others. Tamako and Yori must leave the city. If Tora had returned, he could take them to Akitada's sister. Or if Lady Yasugi had left for her husband's home, Genba could do so. If neither was available, he must go himself. He shook his head at the problems that would cause at the ministry.

Yori opened the gate for him, proud of his new role as gatekeeper, and Akitada's heart lifted. Swinging the boy up in his arms, he said, "I see you're making yourself useful. That's a very good thing. I may have to rely on you to look after the whole family."

Yori clung to him. "That's what Mother said. She said you didn't have time for us anymore."

Akitada put the boy down abruptly. "That's not true," he said harshly.

Yori gave him a frightened look. "I'm sorry," he said in a small voice.

Akitada tried to control his anger. Apparently Tamako had wasted no time letting the child know his father cared more for others than his family. Then he saw Yori's eyes fill with tears, and something twisted inside him. Crouching down to bring his face level with his son's, Akitada said, "No, Yori. *I* am sorry. I know I haven't had much time for you lately, but there have been so many worries. Seimei is sick. Tora's in danger of going to prison. A lady was attacked by evil men and I had to send Genba to watch over her. People are falling ill and dying everywhere in the city. I've had a great deal of work. You do understand, don't you?"

The boy nodded, but then said, "Do you have time now?"

Akitada rose with a sigh. How could you make a five-year-old understand? He took the boy's hand. "Yes. Will you help me change out of my court clothes first?" Yori brightened and nodded eagerly. "Then let's walk through the garden, and you can tell me what you've been doing lately."

His reward was a broad smile and an excited and disjointed report on varied activities. Yori had caught a mouse, but the mouse had bitten him and he had dropped it. He showed off a tiny red mark on a finger and was praised for his courage. He had also helped the cook to make dumplings and his mother's maid to shake out the bedding. Then he had fed the fish in Akitada's pond. Akitada thanked him gravely. He had tried to practice with his sword, but the straw man had fallen apart and neither Tora nor Genba were there to fix it.

"And have you had your lessons with your mother?" asked Akitada, who was wondering what mood Tamako might be in.

"Oh, Mother said I didn't have to do them. I wanted to go to the market with cook, but she wouldn't let me. She won't let me go anywhere. Will you take me with you sometime?"

Akitada felt sorry for Yori, cooped up for days now without playmates or anyone in the household paying attention to him. He tried to explain about smallpox and how people could pass it to others. Yori gave him a worried look and asked, "Have they passed it to you, Father?"

"I hope not."

The boy gently removed his hand from Akitada's and stepped away a little. "Is it a very bad illness? Is it like what Seimei has?"

Akitada did not attempt to take the boy's hand again. Fear raised walls between people, and this one had been thrown up between them by Yori's mother. "It's bad," he said, "but not at all like Seimei's. How is Seimei, by the way?"

"All right. Can we have some sword practice?"

"Perhaps later." They had reached the center of the garden, and Akitada—at a loss for words to make his son understand— looked around him. The last light of the sinking sun still gilded the treetops, but below the bright colors had softened. Spring was gradually passing into summer, and the warm air was filled with the scent of a thousand blossoms. His was an old garden and had become somewhat unkempt in the exuberance of its new growth and recent neglect. He tried to find some hope in this proof of burgeoning life and beauty, but knew that beyond these walls and towering trees there were men, women, and children tossing with the fever of the disease or dying in dark incense-filled rooms, surrounded by chanting monks and weeping families.

Or perhaps, given the general fear of infection, they suffered and died alone.

Within his house, things were not much better. No one was dying, but he was alone all the same.

Akitada paused outside his room to look into the fish pond. The koi, replete with an overgenerous feeding by Yori, rose sluggishly to the surface. "Thank you for feeding them," Akitada said. "I'll understand if you would rather not help me with my clothes."

Yori looked stricken. "If you would like me to help, Father, I will. I'm not afraid."

Akitada smiled and tugged his son's hair. Yori, like all children his age, wore his hair parted and looped over each ear. He was a handsome child, with perfect skin, large long-lashed eyes, and dimples when he smiled. He was smiling now, and Akitada's heart melted. "Come inside then," he said. "I have not been near anyone who is likely to be infected. Besides, we must not let our fear drive us away from each other."

"No, Father." Yori took his father's hand and together they climbed the steps to the veranda and went inside.

But as they entered Akitada's room from the garden, Tamako came in from the corridor.

"Oh," she cried, her eyes on Yori. "I was busy and missed your return." She made her husband a formal bow. "You are welcome."

Seeing her worried glance at Yori, who was clinging to his robe, Akitada doubted the last, but he bowed in return. "Do not trouble yourself. Yori has offered his assistance."

"But I'm here now. Yori, please go and read to Seimei."

Yori clung harder and cried, "I promised."

Akitada disliked subterfuge. "Why can't he stay?" he asked his wife. "Are you afraid that I might infect the boy? And if so, are you not afraid for yourself?"

Her eyes blazed. "Sometimes it's wiser to keep our thoughts to ourselves. It seems to me that lately we have both said more than was wise . . . or kind."

Akitada seethed, but Yori tugged at his sleeve. "Please don't be angry again."

Akitada made an effort to smile at his son. "I'm not angry with you. Here, you may help me take off the train and hang it up neatly on the stand." He began the laborious process of untying, unwinding, and peeling off the many layers of stiff silk.

Tamako stayed, but said nothing else. When Akitada was putting on his ordinary robe, she asked tonelessly, "You are staying in the city?"

He did not bother to turn around. "Yes. I gather neither Genba nor Tora have returned?"

"No."

"I think it best for you to take the whole household to stay with Akiko in the country. If neither Tora nor Genba is available, I will accompany you. Perhaps you could be ready to leave tomorrow?"

There was a long silence, and he turned to look at her. Her face was pale and expressionless. "You will not stay with us at your sister's?"

"You know I cannot leave my post."

He watched her eyes move from his face to Yori's. "Let Yori and the others go," she said. "I will stay here."

The notion was ridiculous. He frowned and said, "I cannot imagine what good that will do. In the country you and Seimei can continue with Yori's lessons and you can be a companion and help to my sister. We cannot just saddle her with a child and an old man, not to mention two servants who won't know what they're supposed to do in a strange household."

She lifted her chin stubbornly. "I shall stay."

"Absolutely not." He turned his back on her and left his room, furious at her defiance of his orders.

He found Seimei on his veranda, sitting placidly in the last rays of the sun and sipping tea. Thank heaven, the old man looked much stronger. Seimei was instantly apologetic for taking his leisure. "I had planned to begin lessons with the young master again," he said, "but your lady insisted that I must rest today."

"Quite right." Akitada sat down next to him. "I want you to be well enough to travel to the country tomorrow. My sister has enough room, I think, and you'll all enjoy a little vacation."

Seimei blinked at him. "Is the smallpox so very bad then?"

"Yes, I think so. I hope Tora's all right. It's not like him to be gone this long. Two days and two nights without a message."

Seimei smiled. "Ah, Tora is like the flea between the dog's teeth. He will come to no harm."

Akitada had seen enough in his much shorter life to distrust

Seimei's optimism, but it was good to see the old man in better spirits. On an impulse, he said, "I must stay here, of course, but it seems that Tamako fears the disease, yet refuses to leave."

Seimei nodded complacently. "Man is the pine tree, and woman the wisteria vine."

There was certainly nothing of the clinging vine about Tamako. At least not nowadays. There had been a time when they had exchanged love poems tied to flowering wisteria branches and Akitada had planted a wisteria in his garden for Tamako. The plant was enormous now. He could see a part of it climbing through a pine tree outside her pavilion. It was purple, like the one in her father's garden had been.

The one in Lady Yasugi's garden was white, a much rarer plant, its long, glistening blossoms almost ethereal among the feathered leaves.

He rose abruptly. "I'm glad to see you are better, but I must go now. There is a great deal to do and I have promised Yori some sword practice."

Seimei nodded with a smile. Akitada did not go back through the house but through the garden again. He found his son waiting in the courtyard.

◆

The following day, Akitada dealt with paperwork at the ministry. The claimants in the front hall were few these days, a very good thing because most of the scribes were absent. Sakae continued in Akitada's old capacity—no doubt in hopes of promotion, like that other ambitious young man at the notice board—and Nakatoshi was Akitada's usual faithful attendant. By midday he had finished most of his work and decided to check on Genba.

The Yasugi mansion lay silent and somnolent in the warm sun. Here the troubles which had befallen the city seemed remote, and Akitada inhaled deeply the scent of flowers drifting over the wall. His heart started beating faster and he wished foolishly that he could hear the sounds of the zither again. He pictured her, seated under the fragrant blossoms of the wisteria, slender, graceful, her oval face bent over the instrument, lips curving into a smile.

And then, as if by magic, he did hear the zither and stopped. He knew the tune, had played it himself not too long ago on his flute. It was "Dream of the Night," and the words expressed a woman's yearning for the lover who had just left her bed. When the music ended, he swallowed hard and went to knock on the gate.

Genba peered out, then opened the small door. He looked guilty, but that had become Genba's ordinary expression lately. And he was eating again. When Akitada stepped through, he saw Lady Yasugi's unpleasant maid standing there with a silly smirk on her round face. Two folding chairs had been set up against the wall of the gatehouse, and a basket filled with food and wine flasks stood between them.

"Hmm," Akitada said pointedly, giving Genba a frown. "Anything to report?"

Genba gulped down a mouthful of food and croaked, "Nothing, sir. All quiet."

Akitada turned to the maid. "And your lady rested well?"

"Yes, sir. She's in the garden." She shot Genba a glance, then led the way. As soon as they stepped out into the sunshine of the garden, she pointed, "Over there," and left to continue her tryst with Genba. Akitada decided to forgive Genba, and walked toward the woman who had so quickly taken possession of his thoughts.

She was leaning over the railing of the small bridge, tossing bits of food to the fish below, making a charming picture in spite of her severe gown of dark grey brocade and the fact that her hair was looped up at her neck in a rather matronly fashion.

When she heard his steps on the gravel, she jerked around,

her face pale and her eyes wide with fright. The fear passed quickly into a rosy blush. She had not painted her face today and looked more delicate.

Perhaps his surprise at her appearance showed, for her hands flew to her face and hair, and she gasped, "Oh. I did not expect to see you again, my lord."

"I'm sorry I startled you. I only came to make certain all was well." His eyes drank her in hungrily.

"Thank you. I expect my husband any moment." An expression almost of despair passed over her face and she looked down. "You must want Genba back. There is no need for him to stay any longer."

"I have not missed him at all," lied Akitada. She looked up then, and he became lost in the faint pink flush just beneath her pale skin. Before he could stop himself, he said, "This morning you are as lovely as the roses." To his delight the color deepened and her eyes widened with pleasure.

Instinctively they moved closer to each other. "You have been very kind to me," she said softly, her eyes searching his face as if she were trying to memorize it. "I had almost forgotten how kind a man can be." Her eyes filled with tears. She turned and started walking away from him.

"Wait," he cried, his voice hoarse and the words tumbling out without thought. "I came to speak to you, to ask you to trust me. I know you fear your husband. I saw the look in your face when you thought I was he. There is a way for you to escape that bond . . . if you wish."

She stopped, but did not turn around. Shaking her head, she said, "No. Please do not press me. I cannot leave my marriage, and you must not speak to me this way."

He went to take her by the shoulders and turn her toward him. "Why not?" he asked. "I'm only a senior secretary in the Ministry of Justice, and not at all wealthy like your husband, but my family is old and respected. I offer you my protection. My love." He felt strangely lightheaded at having spoken words he never intended to say. He marveled how suddenly he had made this drastic change in his household arrangements, in his life, and in the lives of his family. And he waited, holding his breath, for her answer.

She stared up at him, frozen in surprise. Then her color deepened again and her eyes softened. "Oh," she whispered, "if only I could." Her hand crept up to touch his cheek.

Feeling triumphant, he pulled her against him. "It's simple. Just say 'yes,'" he murmured against her hair, thinking how much he liked her scent, the feel of her body against his, her caressing hand on his face.

For a moment they clung together, then she began to fight free. He saw that tears were running down her face and released her. "What's the matter?" he asked anxiously. "A woman may leave her husband in the same way in which a man may divorce his wife. You need not even see him again. Come with me now. You can write to him, and I can see to it that everything is made legal. I'm quite good at law," he added with a smile.

But she shook her head and looked at him through her tears. "It cannot be. Now or ever." She snatched his hand and pressed it against her wet cheek. "My dear Akitada, you have given me the strength to go on, and for that I shall always be deeply grateful. If you care for my well-being, please do not ask again." She released his hand gently.

He opened his mouth to protest, to argue, but such an expression of intense pain came into her face—still so beautiful even with tears glistening in her eyelashes and sliding down her cheeks—that he could say nothing.

"Please give me your word," she insisted.

He hesitated. "If you promise to call on me when you need help."

She nodded. "But," she said, "we must not meet again. It is dangerous for you to be here now. My husband may arrive at any moment."

"What could he do? Surely he doesn't beat you?" demanded Akitada angrily.

She sighed. "Sometimes. But he has better ways to punish me."

"How can you stay with a man like that?" he raged.

She gave him a reproachful look and he relented, consoling himself with the conviction that she would soon enough be driven into his arms. He knew now that she was not indifferent to him.

He could not take his eyes off her, and after a moment he realized that she wanted him to go. Casting about in his mind for ways to prolong the meeting, he recalled that other matter, her relationship with the murdered blind woman, her sister. But he did not know how to question her about their parents and asked instead, "Will you miss the capital?"

Her eyes softened. "I was once very happy here as a child, but that was a long time ago. I married and moved away, and for a short while I was happy then also. Now there is only grief."

"Yasugi's estate is in the Tzusuki district, I think?"

She looked a little taken aback. "You are well-informed."

"I care about you. And I'm not convinced you'll be safe with him."

Her face paled. "Oh. You must not follow me. Promise you won't!"

"I cannot promise. You may need me."

She stamped her foot, eyes flashing. "No. I forbid it. I shall deny knowing you."

She was very beautiful in her temper, and he laughed. "Very well," he said. "When we meet again, I shall not admit knowing you unless you give me permission."

She relaxed. "Thank you," she murmured with a look that was almost flirtatious.

He stood gazing at her, wanting her, and trying to think of something else to say. But there was no more time. The maid came rushing down the path, shouting and waving her arms.

"Dear heaven," breathed Lady Yasugi and looked around frantically. "My husband is here. He must not see you. What shall we do?"

They had no chance to discuss the matter, for the maid arrived and poured out her excited report. From the gate building came the sounds of horses and the shouts of men.

"I must go," Lady Yasugi cried, and before Akitada could stop her, she had gathered up her skirts and was running back toward her room. At that moment, her husband set foot in the garden and took in the scene with a sweeping glance.

He gave a single roar. "Hiroko!"

She faltered and stopped as abruptly as a deer hit by an arrow, then walked slowly toward her husband, her head lowered and her hands folded against her breast. When she reached him, she knelt. Akitada could not hear what they said to each other, but he knew from her husband's gestures that he was angry, and from the way she hunched her shoulders that she was desperately afraid.

Enough! Seeing her like this was unbearable. Setting his face, Akitada went to meet the man whom he already hated with every fiber of his being.

Yasugi, a short, squat figure in a fine blue hunting robe and white silk trousers, awaited him, his broad face flushed with anger. He was said to be in his early sixties, but age had not been kind. He had too much soft, lax flesh: a misshapen belly, small hands with fingers like fat white worms, and heavy jowls that pulled down the corners of his mouth before joining a triple chin. He straddled the narrow path and scowled, as if to signify that the master of the mansion had returned and caught the adulterers red-handed.

Bristling inwardly, Akitada bowed. "Do I have the honor of making the acquaintance of Lord Yasugi?"

Yasugi glared. "What are you doing here? And what have you and my wife been up to?" His voice was loud and insulting.

Akitada was offended and decided to show it. His own pedigree was much better than this man's, and money was not everything. He drew himself up and said coldly, "I beg your pardon. I must have made a mistake. Please direct me to your master."

Yasugi stared for a moment. Then he growled, "I'm Yasugi. Your man says your name is Sugawara. That does not explain what business you have with my wife and in my home."

"Ah," said Akitada, raising his brows. He let his eyes travel over the figure of his host, then remarked coldly, "You really should take better care of your property. I had the good fortune to protect your valuables and your lady from an attack by bandits yesterday. I came back today to make sure the villains had not returned, but now that you have finally found the time to see to matters yourself, I shall be glad to be on my way." He nodded to Yasugi, whose eyes had narrowed, then bowed to his still kneeling wife. "I wish you a safe journey, my lady."

Without raising her head, she murmured, "Thank you, my lord."

Apparently her husband had second thoughts. "Perhaps I've made a mistake. I've had a long and thirsty ride. Will you join me in a cup of wine?"

Akitada said stiffly. "Thank you, sir, but I have neglected my own affairs too long and shall not trouble you further. Your maid will explain what happened." He brushed past Yasugi, who had to move aside, and walked quickly back to the gate, where Genba was helping with the horses.

"Leave that!" he shouted, glowering at Yasugi's men, and stalked out through the gate.

When Genba caught up, his face was anxious. "Is something wrong, sir?"

"That man's an unmannered brute," Akitada raged. "We're well rid of him and his people."

But not all of his people. Not the slender woman who had knelt on the gravel path before her monster of a husband and trembled at the brutal punishment awaiting her for having entertained a man in his absence. Akitada clenched his fists in impotent fury. Why had the cursed man arrived just then? Another few minutes and she would have agreed to come with him or he would have been gone.

Perhaps fate was punishing him for the sins of a past life—though he had enough fresh ones to choose from. If he had not pursued her for his own pleasure, she would not have to suffer now. Instead of protecting her, he had exposed her to even more vicious treatment.

Genba trotted behind him, puzzled by his master's mood. After a while, he said timidly, "I hope I haven't done wrong in striking up a friendship with the maid, sir. I thought she might have some information."

Akitada stopped and turned. "Really? That was good thinking. I owe you an apology. What did you learn?"

Genba flushed. "No need to apologize, sir. I enjoyed the food she offered. Her name's Anju and she's worked for Lord Yasugi all her life. Her grandmother was his wet nurse. She's very loyal to him, but . . ." Genba paused, giving Akitada an uncertain glance, "she doesn't like her mistress much."

"I gathered as much. Come, let's walk on while you report. Did she reveal any private matters between her master and mistress?"

Genba's color deepened. "Matters of the bedchamber, you mean?"

"No, of course not," Akitada snapped, though he had meant that also. "I refer to their daily life together. Her position in the household. Do they live together like a normal couple?"

It was badly put and Genba said instantly, "I wouldn't know how normal couples behave to each other, but according to the maid, this lady is disliked by everyone in the household, and her husband is often angry with her. The servants think she's either been unfaithful or refuses to . . . give him a child. Anju says the lady drives her husband crazy with her bad moods. Sometimes she makes him so angry that he shouts and beats her."

Genba paused when he saw his master's bleak face.

"Go on."

"That's all. It must be a terrible life for both of them, sir. Why do you think they are still together? Why doesn't he divorce her?"

Akitada said bitterly, "More to the point, since the man beats her, why doesn't she leave him?"

"I don't know, sir."

Akitada sighed. "I don't know either, Genba. I was hoping you could explain it."

He was in an impossible situation: She would or could not leave an abusive marriage, and he had promised not to interfere unless she asked for help. He could only hope for a future when she would change her mind and come to him.

They were approaching a private home, when its gate opened suddenly, and a harried servant appeared. "There you are, doctor," he cried. "Come in quickly. The master's having the bloody flux, and the third lady is covered with boils."

Akitada said quickly, "I'm no doctor," and pulled Genba away.

"This smallpox is a terrible disease," offered Genba, looking back at the servant who stood wringing his hands and looking up and down the street.

"Yes. Tomorrow you will take the family to my sister's country place."

"People have been leaving in droves. I hope they have wagons and oxen left at the rental stable."

Akitada had not thought of that. "Do the best you can, but be careful whom you deal with. If you see someone in ill health, leave quickly and go elsewhere. Tora's not back yet, and I'm worried about him." He stopped at the corner of Suzako Avenue. "I have another errand, but will be home soon."

◆

Akitada's errand concerned Lady Yasugi's parents and took him to the administrative offices of the capital, where he asked to see records of families with the surname Murata. Since he now knew that Hiroko had been raised in the capital, he planned to contact her parents for information about her sister Tomoe. He also hoped to get their support in a more personal matter: to free their other daughter from a hateful marriage and to take her as his wife.

But when he finally located the information, he faced a more disturbing problem than he could have imagined. Her father was the late Murata Senko, hereditary master of *yin-yang* and one of the scholars who devised the annual calendar that listed all the taboo days, directional prohibitions, auspicious days, and planetary conjunctions that governed most people's lives. He had been a middle-rank official and had worked for the Bureau of Divination in the Greater Palace, so Kosehira had been quite right. Murata had sired only two children, a son and a daughter. The son had died in infancy. The daughter's name was listed as Hiroko. Since by marriage she had passed out of the Murata family, the records did not bother to give her husband's name. Her mother was also dead. The Murata family had ceased to exist.

Which raised two questions: Who was Tomoe? And why had Hiroko lied about her?

CHAPTER SEVENTEEN

TO THE DEATH

Tora and Kinjiro made their way to the Scarecrow's house by such a circuitous route that the sun was getting low by the time they reached the quarter. They need not have troubled. Most streets were empty. When they got close to the house, they moved even more cautiously, but all looked quiet and deserted.

"There may be somebody inside," Tora said. "Is there a way in from the back?"

Kinjiro looked Tora over. "You're big," he said, "but you may be able to do it."

It involved climbing the rear fence at a corner, and then walking like a rope dancer along the narrow top of the wall for a distance of about twenty feet, before jumping to the roof of the large shed.

Kinjiro demonstrated with the ease of someone used to the route. Tora shuddered. He doubted the flimsy wall would support him, and anyone walking along the top and on the shed roof would be visible from several streets and houses.

"Kinjiro," Tora hissed.

The boy paused, swaying back and forth, and grinned down at Tora. "Nothing to it."

"It won't hold me."

"It'll hold you if you walk quickly."

"People will see us."

Kinjiro cast a glance around. "It's the hour of the evening rice. There's nobody out. But if you stand there and wait, somebody may need to take a pee or something. Hurry up!"

With a sigh, Tora pulled himself up, tested the top of the wall, which was rounded and narrower than his foot, and found that it cracked and shifted alarmingly when he put his weight on it. He peered down into the service yard and at the back of the house. The area was deserted. The neighboring house also looked empty, but a thin spiral of smoke proved that someone was still living there and cooking the evening rice.

Kinjiro practically skipped along the wall and took a graceful leap to the shed, where he sat down to wait for Tora.

Tora began the balancing feat, arms outstretched, placing each foot carefully before the other. It did not seem too bad. Then he heard a door slam somewhere and Kinjiro waved to him to hurry. Tora slipped and almost fell. He caught himself, took two or three running steps, and just as he prepared to jump, the top of the wall gave under him and he fell. With a crack and a rumble that must have carried clear across the quarter, an entire section of the wall collapsed, and Tora descended in a deafening rattle of ripping and falling laths and chunks of dirt. He ended up in a pile of rubble, covered with dust and scrapes. He waited until the dust settled, his eyes on the back of the house, expecting Kata's people to come pouring out in force to investigate the racket.

"Now you've done it," Kinjiro sneered from the roof of the shed, rubbing in the obvious. But miraculously, all remained silent. Not even the cooking neighbor put out his or her head to stare at the large hole in the common wall between their properties. Tora struggled up, removed a rather large splinter from his right buttock, and limped toward the storehouse.

"Old man?" he called through the door, "Are you still in there?" There was no answer. "We'll try to get you out. Are you all right?"

Kinjiro joined him. "Hey, Uncle Chikamura? It's Kinjiro. Is that you in there?"

There was no response, and Tora said worriedly, "Maybe he's dead. Or maybe he's got the disease and can't talk."

They looked at each other. "You're going to look, aren't you?" Kinjiro asked.

"Yes, but you needn't be here when I get the door open."

"Needn't be here? Why not?"

"In case he's got the disease. Aren't you afraid of catching it?"

"Who? Me?" Kinjiro spat. "I'm young and tough."

Tora let it go. "In that case, let's get those keys," he said, his eyes scanning the pile of rubble, the gaping hole, and the neighbor's yard beyond. How long till someone would come out to investigate?

They entered the house quietly, moving on the balls of their feet and listening for sounds. The house seemed empty, and Kinjiro got tired of the precautions. Saying in a normal voice, "Nobody's here. I'm starving. I wonder if there's any food left," he headed for the kitchen.

"First the keys," Tora snapped.

Grumbling, the boy turned into the main room. It looked as before, with clothes and bedding strewn about and a general air of abandonment. Kinjiro opened a small wooden panel in the wall. Inside were some papers and a small pile of keys. He scooped up the lot and dropped them into Tora's cupped hands.

Tora returned to the storehouse by himself. All was as before. He tried all the keys, but none worked. And there was still no sign of life inside. Well, they had come this far and had made a considerable amount of noise in the process, so there was no point in being careful any longer. Remembering the stuff in the shed, Tora went to look for something to force the lock. He returned with the broom and the ladder. The ladder he leaned against the storehouse, in case he had to resort to breaking in through the tiles, and the broom handle he inserted between the lock and the door and twisted hard. The broom handle broke, but this time Tora thought he heard a faint moaning from inside. "We're getting you out," he shouted. "Just be patient." Then he headed back into the house.

"Kinjiro?" His voice echoed strangely down the dim hallway. Outside, daylight was beginning to fade. All the more reason to hurry. He had to release the old man and then take a look at what was in the locked chest in Matsue's room. A pity Matsue got the document back. Tora had looked forward to presenting it to his master. Where was that boy? He started toward the kitchen. "Kinjiro! Where the devil are you? I need your help."

And then it struck him that there was something very odd about this continued silence. He stopped and held his breath. Had the boy run into trouble? Almost certainly. Tora remembered the assortment of weapons the gang had left lying about, but he had no way of getting to them, and no doubt they were by now in the hands of their owners. He was unarmed.

He reviewed in his mind the contents of the service yard and the shed, but came up with nothing except the broken broom handle. It was a pitiful weapon against a sword or even a knife, but he dashed back to get it.

Broom handle in hand, he reentered the silent, shadowy house, where someone probably waited to kill him. He did not know how many of them there were, but he had to get to the boy.

Slowly he crept along the wall, checking each room to make sure it was empty before moving on. Opening doors took time and nerve. Even the slightest squeak set his teeth on edge, and each time he expected to be jumped. In this manner he made it all the way to the main room. It was empty, but the hidden compartment which had held the keys, and which he remembered closing now stood open. Beyond lay the corridor that led to the kitchen.

Tora brushed the sweat from his eyes, gripped the broom handle more firmly, and started forward. He had taken a few steps when he heard the boy cry out something. It was a brief sound, quickly stifled and followed by a groan. Baring his teeth, Tora rushed forward and burst into the kitchen, lashing out wildly with his broom handle.

"Ah! Finally." The Scarecrow greeted him with a grin of satisfaction. He was standing across from the door and had an arm around Kinjiro and a knife at his throat. A trickle of blood from a fresh cut was seeping into the boy's shirt. Kinjiro stared at Tora with wide, frightened eyes.

"Let him go!" growled Tora.

To his surprise, the thin man obeyed. He flung the boy aside and started toward Tora. The room was small, but Tora thought that he might be able to disarm the other man before he could do any harm with that knife: It was fortunate that the Scarecrow was alone.

But no, he heard the scraping of a boot behind him. Swinging around, he saw the ill-featured thug who had guarded the front door on his last visit. He, too, had a knife and a grin on his face.

The Scarecrow snapped, "What're you waiting for, Genzo? Get him!"

When confronted by two men with knives, it is best to use delaying tactics until one of the opponents makes a mistake, but in this case Tora was given no time. The man behind him jumped and slashed at Tora's back.

Tora flung himself aside, heard the hiss of the knife slicing through the fabric of his shirt and jacket, and then felt pain sear from his shoulder to his waist. He ignored it. There was no time. His evasive move had trapped him with his back against the kitchen wall. His attackers were now in front and moving in from two sides. Tora thought fleetingly of the whirlwind move he had demonstrated to Kinjiro, but the kitchen was too small for such acrobatic tricks, and fending off two knives with nothing but a broom handle was pretty hopeless. He steeled himself for the inevitable—at the very least some bad knife wounds. Of the two, the Scarecrow was the more dangerous, being in an excellent position to slash and stab at Tora; his companion was hampered by the fact that he was on Tora's left and had to reach across his own body to score a hit. Tora kept his attention on the Scarecrow.

When the Scarecrow lunged, his knife aimed at Tora's belly. From the corner of his eye, Tora saw Genzo closing in and preparing to strike also. Tora swung up the broom handle, felt it make contact, heard the Scarecrow's curse as his knife arm came up. Tora snatched for the knife, but the Scarecrow jerked away sharply. There was a hiss and something clattered on the floor. The Scarecrow started forward again.

At that moment the odds changed. Tora became aware of strange choking and gurgling sounds, and the Scarecrow took his eyes off Tora to glance toward his companion. Tora saw his eyes widen and instantly twisted toward what he thought was an attack. But Genzo just stood there, eyes bulging strangely, mouth gulping for air like a fish, and both hands clasped tightly to his neck.

Then Tora saw the blood. It seeped from between the man's fingers; more and more of it welled forth until it ran down his body in great gouts, covering his chest with glistening, steaming gore, and dripping to the ground. The hot, sweet smell hung sickeningly in the air, and time seemed to stand still. Tora wondered how a man could lose so much blood so quickly, yet still keep to his feet, still move his lips and roll his eyes. Genzo tried to speak, but only a smacking sound emerged, along with a great gush of blood. And then finally his knees buckled and he fell to the ground.

The Scarecrow stared stupidly down at the body. "What—?"

Tora snatched up the dead man's knife from the floor and said, "Thanks, stupid. That evens things up a bit."

The Scarecrow finally realized that it had been his own knife that had slashed his companion's throat and came at Tora with a roar of fury.

He was no trouble after that, and Tora felt no compunction about killing him. He slammed the knife into the man's chest, watched him fall, wiped the bloody blade on the Scarecrow's jacket, and looked around for Kinjiro. The boy was vomiting into a corner. Tora went to the wine barrel and dipped out a large helping. "Here," he said. "Drink that and pull yourself together. We've got work to do. The others may be on their way."

Kinjiro's face was white in the gloom, and he shook a little, but he nodded and drank. Some color seeped back into his cheeks. Tora dipped out more wine, watched him drink this also, then helped himself to some.

"Very well, let's get on with it," he said. "We need a metal tool to break open the lock. The keys don't fit."

The boy nodded, stepped over the Scarecrow with a shudder, and reached into a box of kitchen tools. He pulled out a set of iron tongs. Tora nodded.

As they left the kitchen, they had to step around the large puddle of blood forming around Genzo's corpse. The boy was still shaking badly.

Outside, the broken wall had not yet attracted notice, and Tora began to work on the lock. The nails were set deeply and had rusted, but they were no match for the sturdy tongs. In time they loosened, and the lock swung down.

Tora flung back the door. A nauseating stench greeted him. At first Tora thought the pile of clothing was too small to contain a body. He looked beyond, saw an empty bowl and the skeletal arm and hand that grasped it. He cursed with pity and anger at the inhuman monster who had confined an old man here without food or water. He was afraid to touch the body because it looked so lifeless, the arm and hand as frail as some ancient mummified limb, but Kinjiro pushed him aside and knelt on the floor.

"Old man? Are you awake? It's Kinjiro," he said—his first words since the fight in the kitchen. He put his hand gently on the clothes. Miraculously, the fingers on the bowl twitched a little.

"He's alive," Kinjiro said. "Help me get him out of here. The place stinks like an outhouse."

Tora knew all about the smell of a close prison and much preferred it to the stench of decomposing flesh or fresh blood. He stepped in and scooped up the small body, which weighed little more than a bundle of dirty laundry.

They brought the old man to the main room of the house, where Kinjiro spread some of the bedding on the floor. In the sparse light that came from outside, Tora saw the old man more clearly. His flesh had shrunk from his bones with age or suffering. Where it was not covered by thin white hair or stubble, his skin resembled yellowed paper, and his eyes lay deep in their sockets. They were closed, but his mouth gaped on a few yellow teeth.

"He's in bad shape," said Tora, shaking his head. "Fetch some of that wine."

There was no answer.

Tora started to curse the boy's laziness, then remembered the scene in the kitchen and went himself.

The Scarecrow and Genzo were as he had left them. A few lazy flies buzzed up from the blood. As he filled a pitcher with wine from the barrel he wondered what the old man would make of his nephew's death. When he came back into the main room, the boy was bending over the old man.

"How is he?"

"Coming around. He's trying to say something."

Tora knelt. The old man's eyes were open now and moving around. A grating sound came from his throat. Tora said, "I brought you something to drink. Don't try to talk."

The old man drank a little of the wine, then shook his head and croaked, "Water."

Kinjiro rushed away. Tora brushed a few thin strands of white hair from the old man's face. His skin felt hot and dry. "I'm sorry they locked you up, grandfather," he told him. "The boy and I will look after you now. My name's Tora, by the way."

The skeletal hand crept from the bedding and seized his. It also was hot and dry, the bones like those of a small bird. "Chi . . . Chikamura," the bloodless lips mumbled. As if that had been too much of an effort, he closed his eyes with a sigh.

Kinjiro came back with the water. Putting his arm under the slight shoulders again, Tora lifted the old man while Kinjiro helped him drink. He drank for quite a long time, and Tora laid him back down. He seemed to go to sleep.

"Poor old man," Tora muttered.

"What will we do with him?" Kinjiro looked nervously down the dark corridor. "We've got to get out of here."

"We'll take him with us. It's getting dark, and that's good. Go and light those oil lamps over there. I want to have a look at the trunk in Matsue's room before we leave."

"There's no time," the boy squealed. "They'll come and kill us. Haven't you spilled enough blood?"

Tora almost felt sorry for the kid, but there were more important things at stake. "You should've thought of your aversion to blood before you joined a gang," he said coldly, then went to light the lamps himself. "What did you do with those tongs?"

"M . . . me? Nothing. I guess they're still outside. You want me to get them?"

"Never mind. Just keep an eye on old Chikamura and give him some more water from time to time. He's probably not had any for days."

Carrying one of the flickering oil lamps, Tora found the tongs, somewhat bent from cracking the storehouse lock, and made his way to Matsue's room to repeat the process on the long ironbound chest. He managed to loosen part of the iron fitting near the lock, inserted the tong, and twisted. The fitting gave some more and the wood cracked, but the lock held. A hatchet would do the job more quickly, but he had none. He worked up a sweat, twisting and bending and prying. Each time, the metal gave a little more. Salty perspiration ran into the fresh cut on his back and started to burn. He had forgotten about that, so it could not be too bad. And then the lock popped open.

The trunk held treasure all right. Bars of gold were stacked next to bags of coin. The bags were filled with silver. The difficulty of carrying off this wealth—a considerable weight, even if it did not take up much space in the trunk—occupied him for a moment, until he saw the sword. Though it was swathed in silk, he knew it for a sword right away. Tora lifted it out and unwound the silk. He saw a scabbard covered with some soft white material, a green-silk wrapped hilt, and green silk cords. The sword guard was decorated with gold. It was a special weapon, and when he drew the blade, it slipped easily from the scabbard. Matsue had cared well for it. And then Tora remembered.

Before he could wonder what the sword was doing here, a shrill scream cut through the silence of the house. Kinjiro! Tora whirled and charged back to the main room, drawn sword in hand. He heard Kinjiro sobbing, "I don't know what happened. I found them like that. The old man, too. I swear it."

Another voice cut in viciously, "You lie, snotty brat. Where is the bastard?"

So Matsue had come back for his property and caught the boy. Tora hesitated, wondering if he was alone, but Kinjiro screeched again.

When Tora burst onto the scene, Matsue was headed his way, sword in one hand and a lantern in the other. There was a look of grim determination on his handsome, cruel face. Behind him, in the uncertain light of the oil lamp, Tora saw the motionless shapes of Chikamura and the boy lying on the floor like scattered rags.

Matsue stopped when he saw Tora. An unpleasant smile twisted his mouth, until his eye fell on the scabbard that Tora still clutched in his left hand. The smile faded, and he took a step backward. Baring his teeth, he hissed, "So."

Tora's heart was pounding. If the bastard had killed the boy and the old man . . . but that would have to wait. They were facing off again, he and Matsue. Only this time they both had real swords. They were on equal terms, and this fight would be to the death. Tora had no intention of losing again.

"Thief!" Matsue's voice grated with suppressed outrage. "Give me my sword, or I'll slice you in half like a ripe melon."

Tora grinned. It was a stupid request, not worth replying to. He moved a little to the left to avoid the light. As he moved, he kicked bedding aside so they would have a clear space to fight in.

Matsue's eyes narrowed. He nodded his understanding and moved to block Tora. "Did you kill the two in the kitchen?" he asked in a casual tone.

"Yes."

Matsue spat. "Fools and weaklings. You won't be so lucky now. And these are not wooden swords."

Tora watched the light dancing along the steel blades. "I won't slip this time, coward."

Matsue set down the lantern and took his position. They circled cautiously. Whichever way Tora faced, one of the lights distracted him so that he could not see his opponent's face well. Matsue flexed his shoulder, and Tora tensed for an attack. Matsue snorted. "Ah, you're afraid, mouse catcher. Nobody has ever beaten Matsue, and you're nothing but a miserable foot soldier with a big mouth." He demonstrated his superior skills with a few rapid lunges, slashes, twists, and thrusts, which Tora, expecting a trick, responded to with quick evasive or defensive moves. Matsue paused to fling back his head and laugh. "You know the way a cat plays with a mouse before it eats it? You're the mouse now, and I'm the cat."

Doubt nagged at Tora's confidence. Could the man be really as good as his reputation? There had been all those certificates in his trunk. Matsue had received formal training and had proved himself to be an expert in the art. Except for a few pitiful tricks he had adapted from stick fighting, all of Tora's experience came from fighting and killing. He wished he had not bragged to poor Kinjiro about his tricks. When it came right down to it, he had none—just a burning desire to rid the world of this man.

Tora went into his attack. A few feints and lunges and he caused Matsue to bound backward a few paces. Pleased, Tora took advantage of this to adjust his position so he no longer had the light in his eyes and could read Matsue's expression. Much depended on recognizing the moment of attack in his opponent's eyes an instant before it happened.

Matsue had not tried to stop him, and a flicker of the other man's eyes explained why. Tora now had the open doors to the veranda at his back, and Matsue planned to drive him backward until he stumbled off the veranda and fell into the small garden below. There he would impale Tora as he floundered on the gravel like a beached fish. Perversely, Tora gained new confidence from this: It was good to know the other man's mind.

And then Matsue attacked. He came with an enormous

roar: "H-o-o-o-o-u!" Tora waited, watching the pointed blade coming toward him, feeling the vibration of the other man's pounding steps in the soles of his feet. He waited until he saw in Matsue's face the dawning realization that Tora was not retreating, that he might kill him then and there, watched him adjust his grip to the new target, firming and aiming his sword differently, saw the triumph of the kill light up Matsue's eyes just before he put all his power into the final lunge.

And then Tora stepped aside.

It was a very small step. They were so close that he felt the blade brush his arm, smelled Matsue's hot breath as he shot past him, heard his feet hit the veranda floor, and turned to deliver the fatal stroke to his enemy.

But Matsue had not gone over the edge to fall prone on the gravel. He had leapt down instead, landing on his feet, and he instantly swung into another charge. Propelled by the fury of having fallen for a child's trick, he bounded back onto the veranda in one great leap. Tora could not stop the speed of this onslaught and moved aside again. But this time, Matsue had known what he would do and slashed at Tora's leg. He was past and back in the center of the room before Tora felt the burning pain and the hot blood trickling down his thigh. He had no time to check the wound, but knew that the blood loss would weaken him quickly and make the floor slippery underfoot. The odds had changed again.

It was very still in the room. Tora could hear his breathing and that of Matsue, an occasional rustle of fabric, and the sound of their bare feet sliding across the floor as they moved and counter-moved, seeking the right place and moment to strike. Tora began to inch toward Matsue, keeping his eyes on the other's face. Matsue feinted toward the left—Tora had guessed it from the flicker of Matsue's eyes and ignored it—and then Matsue lunged toward the right, where he expected Tora to be. Only Tora had by then moved the other way, raised his sword,

and brought it down with a hiss of air and a shout drawn deep
from his belly.

There was a clatter, a grunt, and Matsue backed away, staring at the bleeding stump that had been his sword hand. His
sword lay on the floor, in a splatter of blood and severed fingers.
With a roar, he tried to snatch at the sword with his left hand,
but Tora put his foot on it and placed the tip of his blade at
Matsue's neck.

"It's over," he said, almost sadly. "You'll never fight again."

Matsue slowly sank to his knees. His face worked dreadfully.
"So kill me and be done," he shouted hoarsely.

"Not yet. Did you kill Tomoe?"

Matsue gave a bitter laugh. "A swordsman doesn't dirty his
blade on women. Only scum does that." He looked up at Tora
with a frown. "What are you waiting for? Kill me. I fought honorably. I deserve an honorable death by the sword." He paused
and pointed. "By that sword."

"Maybe you fought honorably this time, but you didn't the
last time."

"That was no fight. I was teaching you a lesson about re-
specting your betters."

Killing Matsue might save trouble in the long run, but Tora
believed now that Matsue had not killed Tomoe. Besides, he
hated killing a defeated man. Matsue was finished as a fighter,
and since that part of his life mattered more to him than anything else, he was punished enough. Perhaps he might bleed to
death, but if he bandaged his arm tightly and found a doctor at
this time of night in a city full of smallpox, he would live. Either
way, he was no longer a threat.

Tora scooped up the fallen sword and broke it between two
boards of the veranda. The hilt he flung as far as he could over
the adjoining wall. Then he went to look for Kinjiro and the old
man. To his surprised relief, the boy had disappeared. That
meant he was alive and not badly hurt. More relief washed over

Tora when he found Chikamura hiding in a corner. The old man peered up at him from under his bedding and whispered, "Is it over?"

"Yes. Where did the boy go?"

"He ran away."

Matsue still sat motionless, perhaps waiting to die. Tora called, "Kinjiro?" but got no answer. The boy was probably far away by now. The events of this day had been enough to give a grown man nightmares. Suddenly Tora felt alone and exhausted. His knees threatened to buckle and he sat down heavily on the edge of the veranda.

The moon had risen and the night was no longer so black. In the distance a temple bell rang. Only a few hours ago they had sought refuge in the temple, and Tora had pretended he was Kinjiro's father. What would become of the youngster now?

A sharp female voice broke into his brooding. "Hey, you rascal. What's going on? Who knocked down my wall? Where's Chikamura?"

Tora looked around wildly and realized that the voice had come from the other side of the garden wall. Someone was in the yard.

Then came Kinjiro's voice, in a loud whisper. "Sssh! It was an accident. Don't worry. It'll be fixed." Kinjiro sounded nervous.

"I don't believe you. Come here."

Kinjiro squealed.

With a muttered curse, Tora jumped up and ran back into the room. Matsue had not moved. His eyes were closed, and he was white from shock or loss of blood. Old Chikamura was sitting up. Tora cried, "Keep an eye on him and call me if he tries anything," then dashed down the corridor.

In the moonlit yard, he found a large woman who stood with her back to him and had a grip on Kinjiro's ear. When the boy saw Tora, his face brightened. He cried, "Make her let go of me."

The woman gave her prey a sharp and painful shake and rasped, "You won't fool me with that old trick, you little bastard. I'm past putting up with you lying, thieving rogues over here. I want to see Chikamura now."

Tora hid his sword behind his back and cleared his throat.

She let go then and swung around to glare at him. "So there's more of you bastards. I'm not afraid of you either." Advancing on Tora, she said defiantly, "Come on, you big villain, I dare you lay a hand on me."

Tora stepped back quickly. "No, no, madam, you've got it all wrong. I'm not with those crooks. The boy and I came to free the old man. His nephew locked him in the storehouse and left him to die."

She looked from him to the open door of the storehouse. The broken lock and empty water bowl seemed to convince her, but she was still suspicious. "The boy's one of them," she said, shooting a venomous glance at Kinjiro, who was rubbing his ear and sticking out his tongue at her. "I want to see Chikamura."

Before Tora could answer, a weak shout came from inside the house. "Look," he pleaded, "that was Chikamura. He isn't well. I've got to go."

"I'm coming, too."

"No, don't," Tora cried, raising his bloody sword. She goggled at the sword and backed away. With a little scream, she turned to stumble across the rubble of the wall.

Tora did not wait to watch her go, but rushed back inside. Chikamura was still sitting there, but Matsue had gone. Chikamura cried, "Hurry! He's run away. Out the front door."

Tora sighed and sat down abruptly. "Never mind," he said tiredly. "Let him go. We've got to leave. Your neighbor's going to call the constables down on us." He stared at the stained blade of his sword, and reached for one of the rags to clean it. The scabbard was lying in a puddle of Matsue's blood. He went and got it. The blood had stained the white covering. Tora dabbed at the spot and then inserted the blade. He hoped the swordsmith could clean it properly. Then he looked at his leg. The cut was in his upper thigh, deep but clean. It had bled copiously earlier, but hardly oozed now. Taking off his shirt, he tore it into strips to make a thick bandage for his leg.

Kinjiro crept in. He stared at the puddle of blood and Matsue's fingers. "You didn't kill him?"

"No. But he can't fight anymore. His sword hand is useless."

"Wrong," said the boy. "You should've killed him."

Tora straightened up and looked at him. "It takes more than killing someone or winning a fight to be a man. There's been enough killing here. Now you can help me get the old man away before any more of Kata's thugs show up."

"Where are we going?"

"Home. Go get the ladder. We'll put the old man on it all wrapped up. If a constable tries to stop us, we'll pretend it's his funeral. I'm the son and you're the grandson. He'll keep his distance."

"No," squeaked old Chikamura, scrambling to his feet. "I'm not dead. I can walk. We'll get the police. They'll arrest the crooks. Look at what they've done to my house. This time I'll lay charges against Buntaro and his rotten friends."

"Ah, hmm," said Tora, "there's something I forgot to tell you. There was a fight earlier. I'm very sorry, old man, but I had to kill your nephew."

Chikamura stared at him. Then he said, "Good riddance. Never could stand him. Nothing like the rest of the family. I swear my brother's wife must've lain with a demon."

Tora breathed a sigh of relief. "All right. Let's go then."

The old man shook his head. "I'm not going to Toribeno. I'm not dead."

Tora began to pull at his hair. "We're not going to Toribeno.

We're going to my master's house. He's Lord Sugawara. You'll be safe there, and old Seimei will mix you one of his tonics to make you feel like a young man again."

Chikamura's eyes widened. "The great and wise Lord Sugawara from the Ministry of Justice?"

"That's the one. Now will you come?"

CHAPTER EIGHTEEN

THE EVIL OMEN

𝒯he great and wise Lord Sugawara was at his wit's end. Tamako had consulted a fortune-teller, and when he got home, she was pacing the floor and ringing her hands.

"Our son will die," she greeted him, "and you are to blame."

Akitada, having barely had time to slip out of his shoes before being faced with this latest crisis, wished himself elsewhere. "Tamako," he said wearily, "Genba is making preparations to take you to Akiko in the morning. All will be well."

"All will be well?" she cried. "All will be well? The soothsayer says this house is under a dark cloud and he sees death. And right after he left, a letter from your sister came; she thinks one of their servants has the illness. But you won't care. You never cared for anything but your work."

Akitada sighed. "Poor Akiko. I hope she's wrong. Of course you cannot go there under the circumstances, but you may still go to our farm if you don't mind the discomfort. Or, since you had planned to stay here in any case, you may want to take your chances . . ."

"What chances? It's too late." She burst into tears. "Oh, it is too late. My poor Yori will die. My boy, my only child." She collapsed on the floor and wailed.

Akitada had never seen Tamako, or any other woman, in hysterics. He was so shocked that he looked at his wife of six years with the eyes of a stranger. Was she possessed? Feverish? Near madness? Perhaps it was her anger at him which had brought on this violent and uncharacteristic outburst. The best policy was to withdraw from her presence to his study as quickly and quietly as possible.

But he could not do it. Instead he went to her, knelt, and gathered her to himself. "Ssh," he soothed, stroking her disordered hair and rocking her shaking body against his. "Ssh, my dear. These are frightening times, and you worry about Yori, but surely he's well, isn't he?"

Her sobs subsided a little and she nodded.

"There, you see. He is a very healthy, strong child. I'm surprised you would allow a fortune-teller to upset you so much."

She sat up a little and wiped her face with a sleeve. "It wasn't just the fortune-teller. I had a dream," she said brokenly. "Not once, but several times. The first time I dreamt you and I were in mourning clothes. It was nighttime at Toribeno. There was a pyre and the flames were licking upward. I woke up weeping."

Akitada could imagine how vivid that nightmare had been. They had attended two funerals together: his mother's and her father's. He said soothingly, "I am sorry, my dear, but you are fearful for Yori and that has brought back memories of your father's death."

She shook her head. "No. There were two more dreams. I was back at Toribeno, but I was alone. I went to place the familiar things into the coffin and to offer a final meal. But when I looked I had Yori's sword in my hand, the wooden one you bought for him, and his favorite jacket, and . . . and a tray of jam-filled cakes." She buried her face against him again and began to weep anew. Akitada held her, miserable that he did not know how to help her. They sat there, she weeping her heart out and he glumly contemplating the troubles which seemed to have befallen his family.

Much later, she detached herself and said in an almost normal tone, "After dreaming for the third time, I sent for the fortune-teller. I hoped he would tell me my dream meant something else. But he merely looked sad, muttered the words about the black cloud, offered some condolence, and left. Oh, Akitada, I'm so afraid."

Feeling a great sense of pity, Akitada got up and extended a hand to her. "Come. You're overtired. We will go to your room and see what's to be done."

She clutched at his hand and got to her feet. "Then you do think it will come true?" she cried, eyes widening with new panic.

Akitada put an arm around her. "No, I do not," he said firmly, walking her toward her room. "I think your fears have destroyed your peace of mind and I'm anxious to have my normal, sensible, cheerful wife back." He looked to see if that had raised a smile or word of acknowledgment, but she detached herself abruptly and said bitterly, "I must seem a dreadful burden to you."

He sighed inwardly. "No more than I am a burden to you, my dear. We are husband and wife, after all. It's proper that we should care about each other." It occurred to him that Tamako had not shown the slightest interest in his troubles for a long time now, but he put the thought aside.

She paused at the door to her room and brushed a limp hand over her forehead. "I have a headache," she said dully. "Perhaps I'd better try to rest. Thank you for your concern. You must have many other things on your mind." Without looking at him, she disappeared inside, closing the door gently but firmly in his face.

So that was that. For a moment he had felt close to his wife again, and the idea of first sharing their worries and then perhaps her bed had been on his mind, but it was not to be. Disappointed, he went to his study. He felt utterly alone and neglected. Seimei brought him some tea, and Akitada was ridiculously grateful for the small gesture.

"I'm very worried about Tora," he confessed to Seimei. "It's not like him to stay away so long. I think I must go to Kobe and ask if the police have any news." He did not add that if they did it would be bad.

Seimei understood and said, "Surely the superintendent would have informed you." But instead of commenting as usual on Tora's indestructible good luck, he murmured something about distressing times.

Akitada thought of his last meeting with Kobe. "The trouble is, I'm afraid I have offended the good superintendent."

This disconcerted Seimei. "How is that possible? You have always had great respect for him."

"I did. I do. It was all a misunderstanding." How little his proud memorial mattered now.

"In that case, you should certainly clear up the matter immediately," Seimei said firmly. "Remember, a man's actions will return to him."

Akitada sighed. He had only just got home and was tired, and the prospect of making an apology was very unpleasant. But he got to his feet obediently. "You're quite right, as always. I'd better go now before he leaves for the day."

◆

The sun was setting over another hot, dry day. As Akitada crossed the Greater Palace grounds, a golden haze of dust hung over the curved roofs and mottled the green of the trees. At this hour the palace streets were usually crowded with officials and clerks on their way home, but not today. There was some activity around the emperor's and the crown prince's residential compounds, but this was mostly an increased presence of guards. Few officials walked between offices, and in the Shingon Temple a prayer service was being held. The Greater Palace was so quiet it made Akitada think that the government took no notice of the troubled city beyond its gates.

The atmosphere was very different at police headquarters. Here the courtyard bustled with red-coated constables and police officers, and small groups of unsavory-looking men stood about chatting. Akitada stopped a harried young policeman who took him to the superintendent. Kobe was in a large hall, bent over a table covered with papers and maps. Lower-ranking officers sat at desks, reading documents or writing reports as constables carried messages or stacks of documents between them. Kobe did not look up when Akitada reached his side. He asked impatiently, "Yes, what is it now?"

Not an auspicious start. Akitada cleared his throat apologetically. "I'm sorry to interrupt when you're so busy, but I need some assistance."

Kobe raised a drawn face, grimacing when he saw who it was. "You and the rest of the world. Is your need greater than theirs?" He made a sweeping gesture with his arm, encompassing the room with its policemen, piles of documents, sheets of city maps, rosters of staff, and assorted unidentifiable matter.

"Er . . . has something happened?"

Kobe glared. "Yes, something has happened all right. There are people dying in this city at a rate which is beyond the wardens, the police, or the monks. If you cast a glance out the door toward Toribeno, you'll see the thick clouds of smoke from the cremation fires. They are burning day and night now. And in the poorer quarters, people just toss their dead into the street. The houses of the sick and dying are an open invitation to thieves, and robbers are attacking people brazenly, knowing that the wardens don't have enough people to stop them. We have five new murders. The markets are empty because farmers no longer come to sell their produce, and people are going without food. Tomorrow I'm supposed to supervise the distribution of rice to the hungry, but I don't have enough men to prevent a riot. Now, what is your problem?"

Akitada was aghast. "But how can this be? It was only yesterday that the Grand Council gave its first public notice of an epidemic. How can the situation have turned desperate so quickly?"

Kobe sneered, "You've been an official long enough to know that procrastination is a fine art in our government. They've known of the danger for weeks and done nothing, hoping it would go away or thinking to prevent a panic. And then their first action was to release more criminals into the streets of the city. My own troubles started with the amnesty. But I really don't have time to discuss it. You may wish to compose another memorial to the emperor on the subject of inadequate law enforcement during epidemics. And be sure to mention that general amnesties are counterproductive in times of crisis."

Akitada flushed. "I owe you an apology. Believe me, the memorial was not intended to criticize but to give you additional support. In any case, I tore it up when I saw that it might be misinterpreted."

Kobe shook his head, his eyes cold. "It doesn't matter in the least. I really cannot take the time now for an exchange of civilities."

Akitada knew then that he had lost a friend. He made himself meet those hostile eyes. "Yes. I can see that I came at the wrong time." He hesitated, then gave up, defeated by the other man's implacable face. "It was just that I was worried about Tora, but never mind." He turned to go.

"What about Tora?" snapped Kobe.

Akitada paused. "He left three days ago to investigate the

murder of the blind woman and never returned. It's not like him to be gone so long without sending word. I'm afraid something's happened to him and wondered if you had any news."

Kobe frowned. "No, no news. He came here that day, I think. Wanting to speak to Ihara. Perhaps he told him what he planned to do."

"Yes, he might have done that."

"You haven't seen him since?" When Akitada shook his head, Kobe clapped his hands. The harried young policeman responded. "Call Ihara," Kobe ordered.

"Lieutenant Ihara has reported sick, sir."

"Sick? Was he sick yesterday?"

"No, sir. He seemed all right. Just . . ." The young man hesitated, looking nervous.

"Well? Just what?"

"He was unhappy that he was expected to go among the sick people and even to touch them, when the emperor himself has ordered us to avoid them."

Kobe scowled. "I see. Thank you. That's all."

When the young man had scurried off, Kobe said angrily, "You see how well the Grand Council has planned? Now my men are refusing to do their duty."

"Perhaps he's really ill," Akitada said.

Kobe snorted derisively. "Ihara looks out for Ihara."

"I think I shall go ask a few questions in the city. Tora thought the blind woman had connections with criminals."

Kobe's eyes narrowed. "She worked in the Eastern Market, didn't she? Someone is extorting money from the merchants there. If Tora has tangled with that gang, he may well be in trouble. But in any case, you cannot do this alone. I have no men to spare tonight and it will soon be dark. Leave it till tomorrow and I'll give you a couple of constables."

Akitada had not expected even this much. He bowed and thanked Kobe.

Kobe nodded, then said, "Wait. If you haven't spoken with Tora, you haven't discussed the coroner's report."

"No."

"It was at first thought that there had been no rape, but you may recall that the coroner did find evidence of sexual intercourse. It doesn't help Tora's case, but I thought you should be aware of the fact."

Akitada said angrily, "It was not Tora. I have his word for it. How do you know it wasn't the murderer raping her?"

Kobe sighed. "I don't know, and neither does the coroner. She was no maiden. In fact, he says she had given birth."

Akitada left with a heavy heart. Tora was in danger, and the murder of Tomoe haunted his memory. There had been so much blood. Blind and helpless, she had tried to escape a monster who had chased her, slashing at her all the while. Had he raped her first or when she lay dying?

Outside in the courtyard a band of the ragged men were leaving through the gate, trotting at the heels of a red-coated constable. Akitada turned to a policeman. "Who are those men?" he asked.

"Sweepers, sir."

"Sweepers?"

"They spread throughout the city after dark. Looking for trouble, checking empty houses, gathering abandoned corpses, and reporting crimes in progress."

"Those men?" Akitada raised his eyebrows. Picking up smallpox victims was not exactly desirable work, but even so. "They look like criminals to me."

"Yes, sir." The policeman grinned. "It's the amnesty. Most of the convicts have no money or jobs, so they'll do anything for a few coppers and a hot meal."

"Good heavens!" Shaking his head, Akitada left police headquarters. With conditions in the city in such dire straits, he had no intention of waiting to look for Tora until the following day.

When he reached home, his wife was still in her room, Yori and Seimei were having a calligraphy lesson, and the evening meal would not be for another hour. Akitada told Seimei what he planned to do and instantly met with objections.

"It's not safe, sir. People say criminals are running around everywhere, and some of the sick lose their minds and go roaming about in the streets."

"I know, but I must find Tora. I shall take Genba."

Yori jumped up and snatched his father's hand. "Can I come, too? Please, Father? I want to find Tora, too."

Seimei, who knew how strong the bond was between his master and Tora, said, "Your father will need his wits about him. You can help by staying here and out of trouble. Besides, think how upset your mother would be."

Yori accepted this, but Akitada felt some of the old resentment again; Tamako no longer cared about his safety—so long as he did not bring smallpox home with him. Once it had been different between them.

He headed for the kitchen, where he had the cook fix him a snack. After eating, he changed into comfortable old clothes, slipped his identity papers in his sleeve, and fastened his sword to his belt. Then he went in search of Genba.

◆

Four hours later, right after the bell from the palace had sounded the hour of the rat, a loud knocking sounded on the gate of the Sugawara residence. Seimei, who had been dozing in the front of the house, was instantly up, his heart pounding with anxiety.

When he stepped into the courtyard, he saw that the night was very dark. The knocking was more impatient than before, and a man's voice called out. Seimei answered, "Coming!" With shaking hands he lit a lantern and hobbled barefoot across the gravel to lift the heavy latch and peer out.

When the gate swung open, he saw three ragged people,

swaying slightly with their arms around each other's shoulders. He almost slammed the gate shut again, thinking them drunk or, heaven forbid, raving with smallpox. But he raised the lantern for a better look and recognized the tall fellow in the middle. At least the bloody, filthy creature grinned at him with familiar white and perfect teeth. "Tora?" Seimei gasped.

"I brought a couple of friends," Tora said. "Hope the master won't mind."

The friends looked, if anything, worse and thoroughly disreputable to boot. One was a ragged boy, small and half-starved looking, the other a foul-smelling old man who seemed to be gasping his last breath. Pity for their condition overruled other considerations. "Come in, come in," cried Seimei, throwing the gate wide. "Oh, the master will be so glad you're back, Tora. He and Genba have gone out to look for you."

They staggered in. Tora let go of the other two and turned. "I'd better go back then," he said unenthusiastically.

"Certainly not," Seimei snapped, slamming the gate shut and latching it. "What is the matter with your leg?"

"Sword cut." Tora stumbled to the well and dropped down on the coping. "Meet Mr. Chikamura and Kinjiro, Seimei."

The old man sagged to the ground. Seimei, aghast at their condition, ran from one to the other in a distracted manner, but managed to get all three to his own room, where he scurried back and forth some more, looking for salves, bandages, herbs, and someone to brew a strengthening tea for old Mr. Chikamura. In between his mutterings, he managed to establish that Tora had been wounded in several places in a number of fights and accidents, that Kinjiro had been beaten and was badly bruised, and that the old man had nearly died of thirst and starvation while locked up for days in a hot storehouse. For Seimei that was enough. His mind was on treatments, not on the three bags filled with clinking coins or the sword that Tora treated so tenderly.

When his patients had been cleaned up and bandaged, Seimei went to the kitchen and woke the cook to brew tea and heat some food.

◆

Akitada and Genba found Kata's training school locked up and the neighborhood deserted. They went in search of the warden of the quarter. The man was asleep and ill-tempered at being woken. He knew nothing about anyone called Tora and there had been no trouble in his quarter. Akitada did not necessarily believe that, because the man also insisted that Kata ran a respectable business, but there was nothing else he could do here.

They went next to the house of the stonemason Shigehira, on the theory that Tora might have gone there to ask more questions about Tomoe's visitors. Here, too, everyone was asleep. The wife came to the door and shouted abuse through a crack. When Akitada asked to speak to her, she threatened, "Go away, or we'll call the warden."

Genba's booming voice cut in. "Woman, open up this instant. Lord Sugawara wants to speak to you and your husband."

The door slid back far enough for a suspicious eye to peer out at them. After a moment, she opened it fully. Her husband hovered timidly behind her. She did not invite them in but stood on the threshold and demanded, "What is it then? It's the middle of the night, and I'm sick of being bothered about that slut. We're hardworking decent people."

Genba growled, "Mind your tongue, woman."

She shot him a glance, taking in his size and bulk, and clamped her lips together.

"Mrs. Shigehira," Akitada said, "we're looking for Tora. Was he here recently?"

"Him?" She folded her arms across her broad chest and stuck out her chin. "No. We don't deal with murderers. Stinking garbage!"

Genba, who was usually the gentlest of men, now stepped forward and bent to push his large face into hers. "Woman," he growled, "I've warned you. One more insult like that and you'll wish you'd not been born."

She backed away, stepping on her husband's toes. "Well," she cried shrilly, "I saw him with the knife and I smelled him, didn't I?"

Genba raised his fist, but Akitada pulled him back. "Just a moment," he said. "What do you mean, you smelled him? When was that?"

She got some of her nastiness back. "When we broke in and saw him standing over her corpse, that's when. There was a bad smell and he had the bloody knife. And now he's loose to kill more people. What's the world coming to? The nobles cover up for their own and harass the poor working man. But the gods know. Oh, yes, the gods know. They sent the sickness to punish them. Beware of the wrath of the gods!"

Genba muttered angrily, but Akitada raised his hand to silence him. "Never mind that," he said to the woman. "What sort of smell was it?"

"Garbage. Rotten food. Filth."

"Ah." Akitada smiled at her. "Thank you. That was very helpful. Is there perhaps anything else you have remembered? Such as who was spying on Tomoe?"

She frowned. "Spying on her?"

"Someone had been watching her through the cracks in her back door. She knew about it, because she glued paper strips to the inside."

The woman gaped. "Those? I thought that was to keep the cold out."

"No. The man, or woman, simply made a new spy hole through the paper."

She swung around to her husband. "You piece of shit. So, that's what you've been up to every night, ogling her through the cracks in the door. And telling me you're just going out for a pee." He protested his innocence, then raised his arms in front of his face as she laid into him with feet and fists, shouting abuse. The stonemason was a big man, and his trade had made him strong, but under the onslaught of his fat and unattractive wife, he cowered against the wall and whimpered denials.

"Pitiful," said Genba disgustedly.

Akitada considered. The mason could have killed his lodger—or perhaps the wife had killed her in a jealous rage, and the coward was too afraid to speak—but on the whole he was inclined to think that the Shigehiros were innocent of anything except cruel abandonment of the blind woman to her murderer. And now there was the wife's puzzling mention of the stench. Tora had always been very clean in his habits.

In any case, they would not get any more information here. Akitada took Genba's arm and pulled him away.

"Where to now?" Genba asked, as they walked away through the dark, silent streets.

Akitada shook his head in frustration. "I have no idea. It's too late to knock on people's doors and the market has closed down because of the disease. Where do criminals hole up at night?"

"They work at night and sleep by day. In abandoned houses, in temples, under gates, and sometimes in the house of a comrade."

"We could check the charity hospitals, but I would rather not risk that unless we have some information that he's there. Let's go home and see what we can do in the morning with the help of the police."

At that moment, several dark figures detached themselves from the shadows and jumped them. Akitada, who had only caught a sound and brief glimpse of their attackers, was thrown facedown in the dirt. Someone knelt on his back, cut the sword off his belt, and hissed into his ear, "Your money or you're dead."

Akitada was conscious of a strong smell of garlic and furious at himself for letting a mere footpad disarm him so easily.

Curses, the sounds of kicks and moans, and Genba's roar told Akitada that the much bigger Genba had to deal with more than one attacker. Akitada tried to unseat the man on his back by bucking upward and rolling. A foolish effort! His instant reward was a blindingly painful blow to the head with his own sword. At this point it seemed wisest to pretend unconsciousness, and he let himself go limp. His attacker rolled him on his back and searched his clothing. Akitada was dimly aware that Genba had fallen ominously silent. He could hear the robbers muttering to each other. Then a whistle sounded not far away, and in a moment they were gone. Akitada sat up. Genba was lying motionless a few feet away. He crawled over to him.

"Genba?" It was too dark to see much, but there was blood on Genba's face. Helpless fury filled Akitada. The police were completely inadequate to the conditions prevailing in the capital—his capital. Nobody was safe in the streets any longer.

Genba stirred under his probing fingers. "Wha—where . . . ?" He moaned.

"We've been attacked by robbers. Where are you wounded?"

Genba sat up slowly and felt himself. "By dose seebs to be broken. Thass all. I'b sorry, sir. It happe'd too fast."

"Never mind. I know." Akitada got to his feet and felt the lump on his head. At least it was not another black eye. Of course, the string of coppers and handful of silver coins he had carried were gone. More importantly, he had lost the Sugawara sword, a family heirloom. A fresh fury seized him. He would get it back, whatever it took.

A light appeared in the distance, and a large group of people approached. Akitada quickly pulled Genba into the dark recess that had hidden their attackers. The man in front carried a burning pine torch before a silent group of shuffling, shadowy creatures. In the light of the smoking, spluttering torch, the leader's robe was a blaze of red against the column of black ghostlike shapes that followed.

Akitada stepped into their path. For a moment the torch swung violently, then a sword pointed at his throat. Akitada blinked against the brightness but stood firm.

"Who are you and what is your business here?" barked the man in red.

"I'm the official Sugawara Akitada. My retainer and I have just been attacked and robbed."

The torch came a little closer until Akitada could feel its heat on his face, but the sword was withdrawn.

"Sorry, sir. It's not safe in this area after dark. How many of them were there?"

"Four, I think. They beat us and took our money and my sword. When they heard a whistle—yours?—they ran. Please take the torch out of my face."

The policeman obeyed, and after a moment Akitada could see that he had been speaking to a middle-aged sergeant who looked tired and unenthusiastic. The dark figures behind him were some of the sweepers he had seen earlier at police head-quarters. And that gave Akitada an idea.

"How many sweepers did you bring with you?"

"Fifteen. Why?"

Akitada scanned the dark figures behind him. "I make it eleven now. What happened to the other four?"

The sergeant turned and counted. He cursed. "The lazy bas-tards have run off again."

"You're missing four men, and we were attacked by four," Akitada pointed out.

The sergeant looked blank, then cursed again, more vio-lently this time. He marched down the line of his followers. "All right. I want answers. Who saw the bastards leave and when?"

Nobody spoke.

"If you don't tell me, I'll have every last one of you curs whipped and see to it that you get no pay."

A ragged individual stepped forward. "They were some of those from the jail. They took off just a few streets back. I think this is their neighborhood."

"Show me!"

They all trooped behind the sweeper, who eventually stopped and pointed down an alley. "They ran down there."

Akitada murmured to the sergeant, "Tell your patrol that there will be a reward for the man who finds the four who robbed us. Promise him two pieces of silver."

The policeman drew himself up. "There's no need for that. They will obey my orders."

"Good, but it may make them more eager."

The man passed along the offer and divided his sweepers into groups of three or four. They would spread out over a four-block area and call out if they found anything suspicious.

Akitada and Genba waited impatiently with the sergeant and one constable. Shortly there was a shout, and they ran to a house where two sweepers stood watch. One of them pointed to a neighboring house. "The old woman over there says four men went in a little while ago."

"Secure the back," commanded the sergeant, then blew his whistle. The other sweepers assembled. "All right. We're raiding the place. Be ready to defend yourselves. They're armed."

They kicked in the front door and poured into the house. Shouts, thumps, and the sounds of breaking furniture came from inside. Akitada waited a moment, then borrowed the sergeant's sword and followed with Genba. They walked into chaos. Sweepers were fighting sweepers swinging cudgels and metal prongs, the two policemen were shouting orders nobody paid attention to, and several characters were slipping away toward the rear of the house. Akitada and Genba skirted the combatants and went after them. Whoever was supposed to secure the back had ignored the order.

Three men were walking rapidly down a dark alley away from the house. Akitada and Genba caught up with them. Two of the men were unarmed, but the third had a sword.

"Halt!" shouted Akitada. "You're under arrest."

Lights came on in a house nearby. The two unarmed men immediately bolted, but the tall one with the sword turned to face them.

To Akitada's surprise, he was Haseo's double. In the dim light and with the sword in his hand, the resemblance was eerie. Akitada gasped, "Who are you?"

"None of your business, dog official." The other man bared his teeth and raised his sword threateningly. A window opened in the house, and a man stuck out his head. When he saw armed men, he withdrew it quickly and slammed the window shut.

Akitada had got a good look at his opponent. Something about his stance and his sword hand was not right. Then he saw that, unlike Haseo, this man was left-handed. Or rather, he was using his left hand because his right was wounded. A thick bloodstained bandage covered most of his forearm.

"That is my sword," Akitada snapped. "You attacked me and stole it."

"You're a liar. I've no need to steal swords," said the other.

On second thought, the man who had taken the sword had certainly had the use of both hands. It was an impasse. Akitada wanted his sword but he also wanted to know if this man was related to Haseo. "You look like a man I once knew," he said. "His name was Haseo."

The other man's face froze. His sword arm dropped to his side and the sword slid from his hand. He took a couple of steps backwards, then turned and ran.

Genba went to pick up the sword. "It's not yours, sir. Funny. For a moment I thought he'd attack. I guess he just didn't trust himself with his left hand," he said.

Akitada went to inspect it. It was an ordinary weapon, the kind a military officer might be issued. Feeling both foolish and disappointed, he pushed it in his belt and said, "Somehow I don't think that was the reason, but his reaction was certainly strange."

They returned to the raided house, where the sergeant had given up the uneven battle and was gathering his few remaining sweepers. "No sign of your sword, sir," he said in a disgusted voice, when Akitada returned his weapon. "We'll let you know if it turns up."

Akitada doubted it and told Genba, "Come, we'd better go home before something else happens."

CHAPTER NINETEEN

HASEO'S SWORD

It was nearly dawn when they reached home, but lights were blazing in the Sugawara residence. The gate was opened by the cook, a woman who liked her sleep and certainly never bothered with gates.

She was in a temper. After a perfunctory bow to her master, she told Genba, "I don't know what Tora can be thinking of, arriving in the middle of the night with two sick strangers, and demanding that I cook for them. And you look terrible, too."

Akitada, who was already crossing the courtyard to the house, swung around. "Tora's back?"

When she nodded, they ran into the house, too relieved to consider the rest of the cook's speech.

Tamako met her husband in the corridor. The meeting reminded Akitada unpleasantly of an earlier one when she had thought that Seimei might have smallpox. She held a lamp, and in the flickering light her eyes glittered.

"How could you permit this?" she cried, her voice shrill with panic. "Cook says Seimei admitted sick strangers to this house."

Akitada was also uneasy about these unexpected guests, but he tried to calm her. Putting a hand on her shoulder, he said, "I doubt there's any need for concern. Tora wouldn't bring anyone who has smallpox. Where are they?"

She stepped back, letting his hand drop away. "In Seimei's room. He's treating them. You must make them go away. There are charity hospitals."

All was quiet in Seimei's room, but a thin line of light showed around the door. Akitada cleared his throat.

The door opened immediately and Seimei peered out.

"Oh, it's you, sir," he whispered. "Returned safely, may the gods be thanked."

Akitada stepped in and saw three sleeping figures under quilted covers. He found Tora and gently shook his shoulder.

Seimei had followed him. "He was wounded in a sword fight," he said anxiously.

Tora stirred, blinked against the light and slowly sat up, rubbing his face. "Ah, you're back, sir," he said with a yawn. "I meant to go looking for you, but Seimei wouldn't let me." He yawned again. "And the truth is, it's been a long day and night."

"I'm sorry to wake you." Akitada squatted beside him. "How badly are you hurt?"

Tora grinned and whipped back the cover to reveal a thickly bandaged thigh. "Just a flesh wound. Seimei cleaned it and put some stinking salve on it. Feels better already."

"And the others? Lady Sugawara is worried about smallpox."

"They've just been knocked about a bit. The kid, Kinjiro, saved my life. The old man was locked up without food and water for days, but Seimei says he'll come around."

"Good." Akitada hesitated. "Do you feel like talking now, or would you rather rest first?"

"Now. I've got to tell you. You'll never believe it. That sword the swordsmith Sukenari lost? Matsue had it all along. And a lot of gold and silver besides." Tora fumbled in his bedding and produced the sword.

Akitada glanced at it and laid it aside. "But what about the murder? Did you find out who killed the blind woman?"

Tora's face fell. "No. I know who didn't kill her. I figured it was Kata, but she was his good luck charm and he thinks his business is doomed now." He gave a dry chuckle. "He may be right. It will be. He's a gang boss."

Genba came in and crouched on Tora's other side. "How are you, brother?" he asked anxiously.

"I'll do. What happened to your nose?"

"I put it where it didn't belong." Genba grinned. "Well, did you have any luck?"

Akitada said, "Apparently not. At least the court is not in session at the moment. The sickness has given us extra time. That reminds me. I'd better explain to my wife about our guests."

Tamako still hovered in the darkness of the corridor. Akitada closed the door behind him and said, "They don't have smallpox. Just assorted wounds and bruises."

"Thank heaven." She came a little closer. "You are quite sure?"

He was not, could not be certain that they did not have the seeds of the sickness inside them, but he said "yes" as firmly as he could.

"But to bring strangers here in the middle of the night. What can Tora be thinking of?"

"Since Tora has some serious wounds and lost a good deal of blood, I thought I'd ask for explanations later. He says the boy saved his life."

"Oh." She brushed a hand across her face, as if sweeping away the fears that had clouded her usual consideration for others. "How badly is he hurt?"

"I imagine he'll be fine in a day or so."

"I'm glad. Who are the others?"

"I know nothing about them, but they're our guests until they can care for themselves. We must honor Tora's word."

"Yes." It was dim in the corridor, but he thought he saw her flush. "Yori is . . . I'll get a room ready for them." She slipped away before he could thank her or wonder what she had started to say.

When Akitada returned to the others, Genba was pressing a smelly poultice to his nose and blinking watery eyes. Akitada grinned and went to look at the two strangers. The old man was asleep, curled up under his covers, and Akitada had to lift the quilt to see his face. He looked sick and fragile and vaguely familiar. The boy, a scrawny creature of twelve or thirteen, was awake and staring up at him.

"I'm Sugawara Akitada," said Akitada with a smile. "I understand you did Tora a great service."

"It was nothing. Tora told me about you. He thinks you're one of the heavenly generals come back to earth."

Akitada chuckled. "I doubt even Tora would accuse me of that. Do you have a family, Kinjiro?"

"No." The boy scowled and sat up. "And you might as well know I've been working for Kata. Collecting his dues from the merchants every week. Don't worry. I won't stay long." He said it defiantly, as if he expected Akitada would throw him out of the house.

"Kata was running a protection racket," Tora said helpfully.

"Oh, I see." Akitada sighed. The boy was a member of a criminal gang. He hoped Tamako would not find out. "I trust you've left Kata's employ."

Tora said, "He did. He's a good kid. Couldn't help himself. His father's dead and his mother threw him out."

"I can speak for myself," muttered Kinjiro.

Akitada looked at his thin body and sharp features. Kinjiro was at the age when a child just begins to want to be a man, and this child had been plunged into the worst kind of adulthood before he was ready. He said a little more warmly, "I'm very sorry for your troubles, Kinjiro. Since Tora vouches for you, you're welcome here and I will do my best to help you make a better start."

"He wants to be a scribe like his father," suggested Tora.

The boy swung around angrily. "I said . . ." But he did not finish. Instead he turned back to Akitada. "My father taught me to write, sir. I'm not very good yet. I think it would please him if I became what he was. If you could help me find a teacher, I'd work for you for nothing—for the rest of my life."

Akitada was moved and amused by the offer. "Well, we must try to accommodate you then," he said with a smile. "Now get some rest."

Tora looked tired and in pain, but was blessedly alive. Akitada sat beside him and said impulsively, "Thank heaven you're back with us. I was so worried."

Tora grinned. "I know. I saw your face when you came in."

They smiled at each other, while Seimei busied himself with Genba's nose, and Kinjiro looked away.

"The sword I brought back," Tora said after a moment. "Will you look at it? I think it's the Sukenari sword. I wonder why Matsue had it."

Akitada frowned. "Who's Matsue?"

"Oh, didn't I say? He's the guy we're looking for. The one that looks like Haseo. Only not up close. He's Kata's partner and a master sword fighter. He wounded me, but I cut off his fingers so he won't ever fight again. He's a nasty bastard. Enjoys hurting people." Tora grimaced and rubbed his head.

Akitada stared at him. "You surprise me. I met him tonight. He acted very fierce in spite of his wounded hand, until I mentioned Haseo. Then he panicked. There must be some relationship between them."

"There is. His real name's Sangoro. There were papers in his trunk. Sword-fighting certificates mostly, and a couple of other things. He's got a farm in Tsuzuki district. But I found another paper that had the word 'Utsunomiya' on it. I was going to give it to you, but they caught me before I could get home, and Matsue snatched it back. He was livid. Like I'd caught him in some crime or something."

"They caught you? You mean Kata's gang?"

Tora nodded. "That snake of a beggar from the market told them I was a spy for the police. When Matsue found his paper on me, I figured it was all over. They meant to kill me. Kinjiro saved my life by helping me get away."

"You took a terrible and foolish risk."

Tora nodded. "I know. But I did get the goods on Matsue."

Knowing Tora's limited reading skills, Akitada wished he had the piece of paper Tora had found. He sighed and looked at the sword. "It seems to be the right sword," he said doubtfully.

"Look at the tong."

Akitada unfastened the blade and read Sukenari's name and the date. He also saw faint traces of blood. "Yes," he said, "you're quite right. Sukenari will be very glad to have it back. It needs cleaning."

"I'll get some oil in a moment. It's a very fine blade. Sliced right through Matsue's sword hand."

Kinjiro piped up, "You should've killed him. Real fighters always fight to the death. Matsue would've killed you."

"If you prevailed against a great swordsman, Tora, then the gods were truly in it," said Akitada. "I must give them my special thanks."

The boy said, "You're very lucky to have a man like Tora, sir."

"I know."

"Pah." Tora looked embarrassed. "It was the spirit in the sword. Besides, he wasn't such a great swordsman after all to lose to a mere soldier."

The door opened and Tamako came in, followed by her maid. They carried trays of food and flasks of wine. Akitada jumped up. "Thank you, but we can serve ourselves," he said, hoping the women would leave quickly.

Tamako peered over his shoulder. "Oh, Tora," she cried, "how very sorry I am that you have been wounded."

Tora covered his bloody bandage and tried to make her a bow. "It's just a little scratch, my lady."

"If you feel at all feverish, you must let me know. I have some herbs that are supposed to be particularly good when a wound becomes infected." She passed the tray to Akitada. "Please make our guests welcome."

The maid put down the wine, and the two women left.

"The old man seems very familiar," Akitada said, setting the tray on the floor and nodding toward the sleeper.

"Mr. Chikamura says he knows you." Tora reached and helped himself to a bowl of stewed fish and vegetables.

"Mr. Chikamura?" cried Akitada in surprise.

"Who's calling?" muttered the old man and sat up slowly. He blinked, rubbed his eyes and broke into a toothless smile. "My lord," he said. "What great kindness and honor you show a poor old man! You won't believe it, but that depraved nephew of mine came back with his villains and they locked me up in my own storehouse because I threatened them with the police. I thought I was a dead man. I'd just about given up and assigned my soul to Amida, when Tora rescued me. May Amida bless both of you." Wheezing with the effort, he got on his knees and knocked his head on the floor a few times.

Akitada said quickly, "Please don't exert yourself. I'm very sorry for your ordeal and will see to it that your nephew is locked up instead. Now make yourself comfortable. Here is food. Come Seimei, and you too, Kinjiro."

Mr. Chikamura crawled closer and accepted a bowl of rice from Kinjiro, "No need to bother about Buntaro," he told Akitada. "Tora killed him."

Akitada's jaw sagged. He looked at Tora. "You killed a man?"

"He killed two," Kinjiro corrected proudly. "He tricked the Scarecrow—that's Buntaro—to slash Genzo's throat from ear to ear, and then he took Genzo's knife and rammed it all the way into the Scarecrow's chest. They bled buckets of blood on the floor."

"Heavens," murmured Akitada. "You have been busy, Tora."

"He's a great warrior," cried Mr. Chikamura, who had eaten with good appetite and was becoming talkative. "After he fought Matsue, he went out to get rid of my nosy neighbor, and then they put me on a ladder, along with the bags of money, and carried me most of the way. When some constables tried to stop us, they told them I was dead from smallpox and they were gonna take me to Toribeno." Mr. Chikamura emptied a cup of wine and giggled. "The constables just backed away and covered their noses." He held out his cup, drank down the refill, and continued, "This smallpox—they say it flies through the air and if your Karma is bad, it'll enter your body. Maybe they should beat a drum to scare the flying devils away."

"We must hope that we're safe," said Akitada with a smile, but he was concerned. Seimei passed around more food and poured wine for Akitada and Tora, but he only gave tea to Kinjiro, who drank very little and ate nothing.

Akitada saw that Tora looked tired and drawn. He felt guilty but asked, "Did you learn anything about the murdered woman?"

Tora made a face. "Not much. She may have been Kata's good luck charm, but Matsue hated her. Kinjiro says he used to watch her in the market." The boy nodded listlessly. "I'd made up my mind to kill the bastard for Tomoe's murder, but he said he didn't do it."

Akitada raised his brows. "And you believed that?"

"I'd just cut off his sword hand. He figured he was a dead man, so why lie?"

"And nothing else turned up?"

Tora shook his head.

Akitada sighed. "All this trouble, and we're back where we started." He got up. "I've plagued you enough for tonight. We'll talk again tomorrow, and I'll see to Sukenari's sword. Get some sleep now, Tora."

Mr. Chikamura had listened and now piped up, "That sword is Matsue's. He told Buntaro it belonged to his family, and he's the last of them. Everybody else is dead."

Tora said tiredly, "Then he lied," and lay down and closed his eyes.

In Akitada's room a candle shed unsteady light on his desk and shelves of books. The doors to the garden were open, the blackness beyond silent and unfathomable. Tamako had spread out his bedding for him. He was not sure whether to be grateful or take it as a signal that he was not welcome in her room. He laid a square of cotton across his desk, placed Sukenari's sword on it, and got out the cleaning materials. His father had kept these in a fine old sandalwood box and had taken pains to teach Akitada to care for swords. Sometimes it surprised Akitada that a scholar like the elder Sugawara had never forgotten respect for the military traditions of their ancestors. In later years he had come to be grateful for his father's teachings, though he would never feel love for his stern and cold parent. Even now, as he laid out the stoppered bottle of clove oil, the small silk bag containing the fine whetstone dust, the batch of thick cleaning papers, and the small picks and mallets, he cringed inwardly at the memories of his boyhood.

But the cleaning of swords had become such a habit that he soon lost himself in the activity. He thought of his own sword. It had become his after his father's death. Anger at the thieves who took it helped ease the unpleasant feeling in his belly that memories of his father always brought. Unlike his father, he had used the sword, and in that he found a sense of validation, almost as if he were still competing with a dead man.

The Sugawara sword was longer than Sukenari's and a good deal heavier, but it had a very good blade nevertheless. He intended to get it back, though perhaps Yori would some day decide to order another, more modern sword. Soon it would be time to initiate his son into the secrets of taking proper care of a real sword.

Akitada wondered if Yori would approach the lesson as fearfully as the young Akitada had. Unwelcome memories of tearful battles over Yori's poor writing skills came to his mind. Was Tamako right? Had he been asking too much of the child? Was he repeating his father's sins? He had meant it for the best. A father had a duty to equip his son for the challenges of adulthood. Thanks to his own father, Akitada had known how to face danger and hardship when he met them.

Suddenly his eyes burned with unshed tears for the lost chance to thank his father. Oh, how to bridge the chasm between father and son? Yori loved Tora, and Akitada had noticed that Tora became like a child when he was with children. Why could he not be more like Tora?

He sighed and looked at Sukenari's sword. The blood stains on the scabbard were beyond him, but the blade must be cleaned before it rusted. Blood was as damaging as water to a fine blade. Tora had wiped off the worst, but he must make certain that none was left under the hilt. With one of the small tools, he removed the peg that held the blade inside the hilt and slipped it free. Matsue had cared well for the stolen sword. Whatever his background and current occupation, the robber had loved this weapon. As he rubbed on the cleaning oil, Akitada looked at the master's signature. The date was six years ago, one year before his dead friend's life had fallen apart. Strange that Sukenari should have made a sword for another Haseo.

With the last trace of the bloody encounter between Tora and Matsue removed, Akitada lightly dabbed cleaning powder on both sides of the blade and used a fresh piece of paper to polish it. The blade was beautifully made, and he was very tempted to order a new sword for himself. In the flickering light, the lines produced by fusing the layers of steel began to undulate and shimmer along the deadly edge. How very close were art and violence! The moment of creation already contained the seeds of death. And the gods governed both.

Akitada shivered. A cool breeze blew in from the garden. When he turned, he saw that the trees rose dark against a faintly lighter sky. If he hurried, he could get an hour's sleep before going to work. Turning back to his chore, he applied the fresh oil carefully and then reassembled blade and hilt. The sword guard was very finely made. He looked at the gilded pine branches and the thatched roof of some dwelling. What had Sukenari said? Pines and a Shinto shrine. Family emblems of some sort. Yes, it was a shrine roof. And then he had the oddest thought. The words for pine (*utsu*) and for shrine (*miya*) would sound like the name Utsunomiya! Could it be? Was this Haseo's sword after all?

Sukenari had known and liked a man called Haseo. Akitada searched his memory, but could not recall that man's family name. Five years had passed since the day his friend had died in his arms on a distant island. Akitada had asked the dying man for his surname. But perhaps Haseo's mind had wandered already on that dark path? He had suffered a deep and dreadful wound to the stomach and was bleeding to death and in great pain. Heaven knew Akitada had not been very rational himself.

The awful memories came flooding back then, and with them the awareness—often acknowledged but never acted on—that he owed a great debt to the man who had saved his life and then lost his own.

Akitada fingered the sword guard. The emblems had been important to its owner, whatever his name had been. No wonder none of the official records had turned up any trace of anyone called Utsunomiya Haseo. For all Akitada knew, Haseo's story had always lain there among the dusty trial records on the shelves of the Ministry of Justice and in one of the document boxes of old forgetful Kunyoshi.

His heart beating with excitement, Akitada replaced the sword in its scabbard and rose. There was no time for sleep now. He must see Sukenari right away.

◆

A short time later, without having bothered to change his robe or eat his morning rice, Akitada strode down Suzako Avenue with the sword slung over his shoulder. He probably made a strange and frightening sight, unshaven and bleary-eyed from lack of sleep, in an old robe and armed. It did not matter. At this cool and slightly misty hour of the morning, the wide street was abnormally empty, and the few people he saw looked worse than he did. Dawn broke splendidly over the many roofs of his beloved city, gilding the roofs and sparkling off the distant tops of the twin pagodas of the Eastern and Western temples. Before him stretched the lines of willows in full leaf, their long branches sweeping the ground and reaching for the waters of the wide canal. But no children fed the ducks from the arched bridges that spanned the canal. No idlers rested under the trees. A monk and a few frightened creatures hurried on some urgent errands, keeping well clear of each other, and a solitary horseman headed for the palace. The city itself seemed to be sickening.

To his relief, Sukenari was awake and untouched by the disease. He welcomed Akitada with formal courtesy. Only a flicker of his eyelids showed his surprise when he saw the sword on Akitada's back. He asked no questions until he had seated his guest and offered him a cup of warmed wine.

Akitada accepted gratefully. He presented the sword and explained how Tora had found it. Sukenari received it with a delighted smile and a bow. He immediately pulled the blade.

Akitada said quickly, "I cleaned it, but perhaps not as well as

I should have. Tora had to use the sword against the man. He cut off the man's fingers."

"Ah, did he? It looks fine, just fine," said Sukenari, turning it lovingly this way and that. "Yes, it is my sword—or rather, it's not mine. I wonder if I can find its owner."

Akitada tried to restrain his excitement. "That's why I came so early. It just occurred to me . . . that is, you mentioned someone called Haseo. Was it his sword by any chance?"

"Yes, indeed. A very nice young man and a fine swordsman. He came to the capital to study swordsmanship, and when he thought he was worthy of a good sword, he came to me. After that he returned once or twice to let me polish the sword, but he's not been back for many years now. I have forgotten where his home was, but it was near a famous shrine. That's why he wanted the decorations. The shrine for a pure life and the pine for a long one. A family tradition, I believe."

Akitada leaned forward. "What was his surname?"

"Tomonari." The smith looked curious, but was too polite to ask.

"Tomonari. Yes." Akitada sat back with a small sigh of satisfaction. "I think I met your Haseo. I thought he was telling me his name, but the detail on the sword guard makes me think that he was referring to a family motto. Did your young man say anything about his people?"

Sukenari was fascinated. "He didn't explain, but he insisted on the decoration. We ask our clients what designs they want on the sword guard and the scabbard. But what happened to him?"

"He died in exile in Sadoshima."

Sukenari became very still. "In exile?" he murmured. "But how could that be? He was a good man. Did he use this sword to kill someone?"

"I don't know the circumstances of his crime yet, but he insisted that he was innocent. My friend was a big man, with broad shoulders and a strong black beard, but he wasn't young.

I would have judged him to be a little older than I am, perhaps in his forties."

Sukenari looked dazed and sad. "Yes. He probably was. He had no beard then. I thought of him as young because he acted like a boy sometimes. He smiled and laughed a great deal, and he walked and moved with such energy—well, he seemed young to me. How very sad to suffer such a fate for no reason."

"He saved my life."

"Ah, at least he did not die in vain. Poor young man."

Sukenari persisted in calling Haseo young. Akitada's memory had been of someone who was both mature and joyless. Haseo had hardly spoken until the last few days of his life, and he certainly had not smiled until the moment when he had realized that he might see his family again. Akitada said, "Did he talk about his family? There were three wives and five children, I think."

Sukenari shook his head. "Wives and children? How pitiful! No, we only talked about swords and sword handling. Once, early on, I got the feeling that his visits to the capital didn't meet with his family's approval. Sword fighting often becomes a passion. Men have been known to abandon their families for it."

"Perhaps, but I don't think Haseo did. The one who had his sword seems to be such a man, though. His name is Matsue, I believe."

"Ah, I've heard the name. He has a bad reputation, that one. How did he come to have this sword?"

"That I must find out." Akitada rose and bowed. "I've taken up too much of your time. Thank you for your help and hospitality."

Sukenari said quickly, "But the sword. It's not mine. Will you take it? Perhaps it will help you find Haseo's family."

Akitada hesitated, then accepted and slung the sword across his shoulder again.

From Sukenari, he went to the ministry and found it was a day for more surprises. The main hall was deserted, though it was broad daylight by now and working hours had started a long time ago. Not even a scribe or attendant seemed to be in the building. He passed through the hall to his office and heard muffled voices behind the closed door. When he opened it, he found Nakatoshi and Sakae in deep conference at his desk. They both jumped up and stared at him.

He frowned his disapproval. "What are you doing?"

Nakatoshi bowed first. "Good morning, sir," he said. "Sorry about using your office, but we didn't want to be overheard."

"Really? Why? Nobody else seems to be working today," Akitada said peevishly, "and you two looked surprised to see me."

They exchanged glances. Nakatoshi flushed, but Sakae was made of sterner stuff. He said excitedly, "We just had a messenger, sir. Minister Soga has died. Of smallpox. It seemed best to discuss the matter in private." He extended a piece of paper.

Akitada stared at him, then at Nakatoshi, who nodded. The letter appeared to be from some abbot. It was addressed to the person in charge at the ministry and contained the brief announcement that the minister had succumbed the evening before. "To be reborn into the western realm," the abbot had concluded. Perhaps the sickness in his village had prevented him from adding more detail.

"Did either of you know that Soga was ill?" Akitada asked, looking at the clerks sharply.

They shook their heads. Nakatoshi said, "You may recall, sir, that they refused to receive our messenger. I thought it very strange since his Excellency had demanded daily reports. I think he must have become ill very shortly after leaving here."

Sakae was smiling to himself. Akitada cleared his throat pointedly, and his clerk adopted a mournful look. "We wondered," he said, "if the Great Council has been notified. Now that you are here perhaps I could carry your message to them?" When Akitada looked at him in astonishment, Sakae added, "To save you changing into proper attire, I mean."

Akitada glanced down at his old robe. He had neither slept nor shaved, and his clothes were by now dirty. He could hardly make an appearance in the highest office of the government looking like this. No doubt Sakae also had ulterior motives: It could not hurt one's career to make oneself known to the chancellor and his staff. Akitada had intended to send Nakatoshi, but he could spare Sakae more easily. He had to see Kobe to tell him that Tora had returned, and he wanted to begin a search of the archives. So he nodded and sat down to write the short cover letter, impressed his seal, enclosed the abbot's note, and handed the whole to Sakae.

Nakatoshi looked after Sakae and sighed.

"I would have sent you, but I need you to be here this morning," said Akitada by way of an apology. "I have some urgent business to attend to."

Nakatoshi's eyes flicked over Akitada's rumpled appearance and stopped at the sword that lay across the late Soga's desk. "But," he stammered, "the death of the minister . . . how shall I manage, sir?"

Akitada knew that his behavior was eccentric and inappropriate, but he was thoroughly tired of more problems. He had spent a night being attacked, had dealt with a hysterical wife and unexpected house guests with assorted wounds, and had tried to make sense of all the startling and puzzling revelations about Haseo and the villain Matsue. At the moment his duties at the ministry—and there could not be many while the epidemic raged in the city—were the least of his worries. He snapped, "What you have done all along. Receive messages and relay them to me. Don't tell me that Soga's death will change the routine. Sakae was eager enough to step into my shoes. Perhaps you can cover for the late minister for an hour or so."

Nakatoshi turned red. "Yes, sir. Only, what will happen to us? Will they send someone else to take the minister's place?"

"No doubt in time."

Nakatoshi hung his head. "Yes, sir. I wish it could be you, sir."

Akitada gave a sharp laugh. "Good heavens, what an idea! Ministers hold at least the senior fourth rank. I'm not likely to achieve that illustrious status in my lifetime." He saw Nakatoshi's dejected face and said more kindly, "Thank you for your high opinion. For a moment there I was afraid I'd lost it. I'm not exactly my usual self today because I've had no sleep. In fact, there was no time for a shave or to change my robe before coming here."

"I hope all is well at your home, sir?"

"Yes, so far. Tora got into some more trouble. I'm on my way now to speak to Superintendent Kobe. I assume there's no urgent business here?"

There was not, and Akitada left for police headquarters. But Kobe was not in. He had gone to supervise the rice distribution in the market. Since the markets had closed, the people in the capital, many of whom lived from day to day on food purchased in the market, were starving. Akitada felt a pang of guilt. Kobe was dedicated to his official duties, while he was occupied with a private matter. Even Nakatoshi disapproved, and Soga would have enjoyed proving his senior secretary unfit. Soga's death meant a reprieve for Akitada, but how long before Soga's successor would take exception to Akitada's unorthodox behavior? Akitada left a note for Kobe, telling him that Tora had returned after doing battle with several gang members in Chikamura's house. That should send some constables there who could deal with the bodies and secure the property. Then he returned to the ministry.

Two of the scribes had shown up late and were listening openmouthed to Nakatoshi's explanations about Soga's sudden death. When they saw Akitada, they fell to their knees. He scowled at them. How quickly people learned to abase themselves when they feared a new boss!

Brushing past them, Akitada went straight to the archives. It was a familiar and hated place. He had spent years here, condemned to doing worthless research in semidarkness among thousands of old records of legal cases, because Soga wished to humiliate him or punish him for having once again "disobeyed" by solving a murder in the city. But Soga was no longer alive. And Akitada would not have to resign.

The dreary work of the past paid off in one respect. He knew exactly where the records of criminal cases were and located instantly the shelf which held those from five years ago. Taking down the boxes one by one, he lined them up on a low table, and began to sift through them.

Halfway along, he found the case against Tomonari Haseo. It had been tried in the capital, because the crimes had taken place in the same province and were of such a heinous nature that the government had taken an interest in their disposition. Frowning with impatience at the vague comments, Akitada leafed quickly through the fat bundle of documents, looking for a description of the crime.

When he found it, he had to read the charges twice, so shocking were the murders and so solid the evidence against his dead friend.

One summer day, after a violent argument over control of the family estate, Haseo had slaughtered both his parents in the main hall of their mansion, and the deed had been witnessed by his own nurse.

CHAPTER TWENTY

HASEO'S CRIME

*A*s Akitada read the trial records, he felt the cold finger of death touching the back of his neck. Haseo's fate was sealed from the start. He never had a chance at escape. The evidence against him looked unshakable.

The nurse, Yasura, testified that a quarrel had taken place between father and son, one of many, because the elder Tomonari had forbidden his only son Haseo to leave for the capital. The son had become angry and demanded control of the estate. Outraged, the father had berated the son, who had then drawn his sword and killed the father.

The noise of the quarrel had brought Haseo's mother to the scene, and when she screamed and cursed him, he had killed her also. At this point, the nurse fled in fear for her life.

Akitada raised his eyes from the crabby script of the court clerk to stare at the shelves of documents. To his shame, he knew only too well that a son could come to hate a parent so bitterly that he wished him—or her—to die. But to make the leap from wish to deed a man would need not only anger but such self-importance that all other considerations vanished. The man he had met five years ago in Sadoshima was nothing like that. In fact, it seemed as if two different characters were involved, one the man in Sadoshima, the other a stranger in Tsuzuki.

The only way to get at the truth was to proceed from the assumption of Haseo's innocence and refute or discredit every piece of testimony that had led to his being found guilty. The nurse must have lied. At least, Akitada thought, she had lied about witnessing the quarrel. It was unlikely that she, as a female servant, was present during a private meeting between father and son. More probably she had arrived with Haseo's mother at a later time. Why had she lied?

Whatever had caused her to accuse Haseo of such a crime must have been a matter of vital consequence to the woman. Normally the bond between master and servant was a strong and mutual one. In the case of a nurse, maternal feeling and a desire to protect her charge would make that bond even closer. It was precisely this relationship that had made her testimony so devastating.

He bent over the documents again and found that the presiding judge had been Masakane, the same man who held Tora's future in his hands. The coincidence was not really surprising; Masakane had held his position for well over a decade now.

Masakane's sentence had been banishment for life, loss of family name, and confiscation of property by the state. Such a sentence was entirely proper for the crime of murdering one's parents. Evidently Haseo had been the only son and, with both parents dead, the government did not feel that the parricide's descendants should benefit from his crime. No doubt administrative greed had also played a part in this. The emperor always welcomed land that would produce income or could be given to faithful subjects in recognition of outstanding service. And so Haseo's wives and children had become homeless paupers overnight. Only the class they belonged to saved them from becoming slaves. The documents did not concern themselves with their future. For that he would have to seek out Kunyoshi again.

Akitada put back the document boxes and was gathering up the records of Haseo's trial when Sakae came in with two court officials. Akitada did not recognize them, but got a sinking feeling in his stomach when he saw their rank colors and the satisfied smirk on Sakae's face.

"Their Excellencies came to consult with you, sir," Sakae announced. When Akitada still looked mystified, he added helpfully, "You remember? The death of Minister Soga was announced this morning?"

And that, of course, made him look not only foolishly forgetful in the eyes of the two visitors, but also incompetent. Before he could save some of his dignity, the older of the two stepped forward and asked in a tone of disbelief, "*You* are the senior secretary? You are Sugawara?" He eyed Akitada's appearance with manifest astonishment.

Akitada felt the blood rise to his face. He knew he looked like a derelict, or at least like a man who had been carousing all night and not bothered to change. He made a bow and said, "Yes, I am Sugawara. May I ask who gives me this honor?"

They exchanged glances. The one who had been speaking said, "I am Yamada of the Censors' Office, and this is Lord Miyoshi of the Controlling Board of the Left."

This was truly awkward. They were senior officials whose faces he should have recognized if he had been attending all the court functions. Akitada bowed again, more deeply this time. "How may I serve Your Excellencies?"

"Do you have an office?"

Flustered, Akitada led the way. Sakae, smirking more widely than ever, trailed behind.

"A bright young man," commented Miyoshi after they were seated in Soga's office and Sakae had furnished them with cushions, wine, and an offer to take notes. The last was refused, and the helpful Sakae departed.

"I see you have moved into Soga's office already," Lord Mi-yoshi said, staring disapprovingly at Haseo's sword, which still lay on top of the documents.

"It seemed more convenient, since most of the ministry's current records are kept here," Akitada said.

"Hmmph. Naturally you cannot stay permanently. Some-one will be appointed to serve provisionally."

Lord Yamada added, "As quickly as possible."

So much for his being given the provisional appointment as he had hoped. Akitada bowed.

"Meanwhile," said Miyoshi, "we have no choice but to let you carry on. But we shall return and expect you to present a more suitable appearance. You are to make no decisions on your own without our express approval."

They left after that, but the visit boded ill for his future ca-reer. They had made it abundantly clear that they did not trust him to run the office. With a sigh, Akitada took up Haseo's sword and decided to stop in at the archives before going home for a bath and change of clothes.

Kunyoshi was the only one working in the archives. Both the sickness and the fear of getting it seemed to have affected the younger officials in much greater numbers. The others, Akitada included, remembered previous epidemics and had perhaps even contracted the disease in a milder form. For some reason, people only suffered smallpox once in their lives, and if they survived it, they were safe. But a greater reason was that this old man lived for his work. Poor man, he had suffered much from Akitada's mistake. Akitada raised his voice and called out a greeting.

Kunyoshi looked up and came quickly, eager to be of ser-vice. Then he recognized Akitada and hesitated, especially when he took in his appearance and the sword. "Have I forgotten something else?" he asked nervously. "I don't recall . . ."

"No, no. It's my turn to apologize, my dear Kunyoshi. I gave you the wrong name. I am very sorry to have caused you so much worry."

Kunyoshi brightened. "Never mind," he said with a laugh, "these things happen. And do you have another name for me now?"

The name Tomonari produced happy enlightenment. "Of course," Kunyoshi cried, clapping his hands. "Tomonari! That's what I was thinking of all along. Such an interesting case. You mentioned that the land was confiscated because of a crime. Dreadful story. And it did have something to do with a shrine, only it was the Iwashimizu Shrine, of course. Hah, hah!" He laughed with delight, his memory not only tested but confirmed to be excellent.

Iwashimizu was so close to the capital that the emperors themselves worshipped there. The shrine also had special significance for warriors because of its connection to the war god Hachiman. That must be why Haseo had chosen it for his symbol. Things were beginning to fall into place, and Akitada's spirits lifted, as they always did when he found himself on the right track in a murder investigation. They smiled at each other. "Do you suppose I could have a look at the family record?" Akitada asked.

Kunyoshi trotted away and consulted the tax register for the Tomonari family. "Yes," he muttered, "six years ago. The following year nothing. Tsuzuki District. Just a moment. I'll get you the last record before the property fell into the hands of the state."

They bent over the documents together. The Tomonari family belonged to old noble warrior stock, but most of the "mouths" listed for their twenty-three households were personal servants or peasants working Tomonari land. Some of the peasants owned their small parcels outright and were assessed separately, but most were counted into the Tomonari household and the senior Tomonari was assessed accordingly. At the time of this final assessment, his immediate family seemed to have consisted only of a wife and an adult son. The son also had a family. He was listed as having three wives and four children. It fit. The land consisted of rice paddies, millet fields, and a great deal of uncultivated forest. The assessment of rice taxes was significant enough to make it a desirable estate.

"Where would I find the names of the family?" Akitada asked the archivist.

Kunyoshi pursed his lips. "Household registers," he said, and dashed off. This time it took longer. Apparently they were kept in a separate building. But Kunyoshi returned, his face slightly flushed and smiling. "Here you are," he said and placed a fat scroll before Akitada. "It should be in there somewhere. These are all the households in Tsuzuki District."

Akitada sighed and began to unroll the pages covered with some of the smallest characters he had ever seen. They were glued together to make one long continuous document. So many households, so many names. He found what he wanted an hour later, somewhere near the middle of the scroll:

Household of Tomonari Nobutoshi, 60, local chieftain, rank 8:

Wife: Nihoko, 55.

Son: Haseo, 35.

Son's wives: Sakyo, 30; Sachi, 25; Hiroko, 20.

Minor children: two boys; four girls.

The other names belonged to servants and slaves. Someone had drawn a thick line after the entry and scribbled in a different hand: "Household broken up by deaths and confiscation of land." A date matched Haseo's sentencing date.

So Haseo was finally found. But what had become of the wives and children? No family names were listed for his wives.

Which one was the wealthy one who was supposed to have taken in the others? How was Akitada to find them? He rolled up the scroll and went to find Kunyoshi, who had returned to his other duties. "What happens to the family who used to live on a confiscated estate?" he asked the old man, handing back the scroll.

Kunyoshi was not helpful. "The peasants stay, I suppose," he said. "But the families of the condemned move elsewhere."

"It's the wives and children I'm concerned about."

"Such women may choose to consider themselves divorced. They return to their own family or remarry, I believe. Some enter a convent."

"What happened to the Tomonari land?"

"Ah!" Kunyoshi brightened. "I remembered something about that. I think I may have mentioned a certain important nobleman who was quite unreasonable in his demands that he should not have to pay a rice tax?"

Akitada did not remember but nodded.

"He's the one who rents the confiscated estate. He claims that it had fallen into disuse and that he spent his money and used the labor of his slaves to put it back into production; therefore he should be immune from taxation. But the tax office held that he was liable for the same amount as the previous owner because he could not prove that new acreage had been created." Kunyoshi rubbed his hands. "And quite right, too." It was clear that he had not liked the irate nobleman.

"What's his name?"

"Yasugi. As if he weren't rich enough already in his own right. Pshaw!"

"Yasugi?" Akitada stared at the old man, his mind awhirl. Could it be that this detestable man now controlled the Tomonari estate? "How . . ." he began and stopped. He snatched the household register back. When he found the entry again, he saw what he had missed before. Haseo's youngest wife was Hiroko. The name was common, but Akitada did not believe in coincidences. The beautiful Hiroko, the woman he had come to desire with every fiber of his being, was Haseo's widow. Had she been eager to exchange the shameful existence as wife of a condemned man for the luxurious life with the wealthy Yasugi? Or had Yasugi somehow coerced her into marrying him? Akitada wanted to believe the latter. True, she had lied to him, but she had been terrified of her husband.

Giddy with excitement and hope, Akitada thanked Kunyoshi so profusely that the old man looked stunned.

At home, Akitada went straight to Tora. He found him looking a great deal better and eager to talk about his adventures.

"Wait," said Akitada, "I have news." He told him what he had discovered that morning.

"What a strange thing! So the sword was Haseo's all along," said Tora. He shook his head in wonder. "To think that we wasted all that time just because you got the name wrong."

Akitada frowned. "You're missing the point. The case is not solved. Haseo was charged with killing his parents, possibly with this." He took the sword off and placed it on the floor between them.

"Never," said Tora. "Somebody else did and you'll find the bastard. And then you'll find his family and make that greedy Yasugi give back their property to them."

And set Hiroko free. Akitada sighed. It was not that simple. Even if he found the real killer and located Haseo's family, the government would thwart the return of name and land to his heirs by instantly wrapping the case in bureaucratic red tape and innumerable codicils. But he had always known that.

Tora's priorities were different, and he now reminded Akitada of them. "I would help you, but I'd better go back to the market to ask more questions about Tomoe's murder."

Tomoe. She was connected, too. Hiroko had lied about their relationship. Had Tomoe perhaps been a witness to the crime? And if she knew the real killer of Haseo's parents, might she have been killed to keep her from telling? But that could not be. Five years had passed. If she had been a threat to the killer, he would have got rid of her years ago, before the trial.

Tora was watching him. "Are you wondering how Matsue got hold of the sword?" he asked.

"No, I was thinking about your blind street singer. Matsue could have bought the sword. In five years anything might have happened. He took good care of it anyway."

"Why do you think he was watching Tomoe?"

"Perhaps he liked her performance and was interested. She sang martial ballads and he was a swordsman."

Tora snorted. "He hated her. I figured maybe she told him off when he got too bold. Some men hold a grudge about that sort of thing, and he had no respect for women."

"Well, you said yourself, he did not kill her, whatever he thought of her. By the way, what about the coroner's report?"

"What about it?"

"The coroner found evidence that she had been with a man."

"The swine raped her first and then killed her. He's a dead man if I get my hands on him!"

"Not so fast. Nobody has said anything about rape. She may have entertained a lover before the killer struck. Or she gave herself to the killer voluntarily."

"She would never do such a thing. She lived like a nun. I should know." Tora flushed and looked away.

So the rascal had tried. Akitada said dryly, "I see. I grant you it's truly impressive that she should have turned down even your advances, but the fact is that neither you nor I know anything about her. There may have been a man in her life. There may have been a husband even. The coroner said she had given birth."

"Amida. I never thought of that. She was so . . . alone. You just felt she needed someone in her life. What happened to her kids, do you think?"

"I have no idea."

Tora sighed. "I've never met anyone like her before, you know, so helpless and so . . . stubborn. She never complained. She was a fighter. And for what? To be slashed to pieces by some beast. I bet he did rape her. Tomoe had a pretty figure."

Akitada tried to remember the woman he had seen only once and then through the eyes of prejudice. "I should have listened to you," he said. "And she should have accepted your offer of help."

Tora said bitterly, "And I shouldn't have spoiled it all by try-ing to sweet-talk her. She probably thought I was just like all the rest." A brief silence fell as they weighed their culpability against the evil fate that had stalked Tomoe. Suddenly Tora said, "Wait a moment. The soothsayer in the market warned her to leave the city. She believed him but said she needed to earn a bit more money first. What for?"

"You shouldn't believe soothsayers. One of them just gave Tamako a terrible fright. Such people do more harm than good."

Tora's eyes widened. "What did he say?"

"Some silly talk about Yori. The trouble is that during an epidemic, such dire predictions have a chance of coming true."

Tora gulped and opened his mouth, but the door slid open, and they turned. Tamako peered in, her face strained. It seemed to Akitada that he had not seen her in a pleasant mood for weeks now. "Yes?" he asked, perhaps a little more irritably than he intended.

Her eyes flicked from his face to Tora's. "I'm sorry," she mur-mured. "I knew you had returned and wondered . . . but I did not mean to interrupt. Please continue your conversation." She bowed and withdrew, closing the door behind her.

Akitada felt relieved and a little guilty. No doubt she had another complaint of a domestic nature. The unwelcome guests had probably caused a disruption in the smooth running of the household. "How are your friends today?" he asked.

"Fine. I'm to say thanks for the hospitality. Kinjiro mostly sleeps, but Mr. Chikamura has hobbled off to police headquarters to lay a complaint against his nephew's friends." Tora added morosely, "If they take the trouble to check the house, they'll find the Scarecrow and Genzo."

Akitada jumped up. "Heavens, I forgot about that. Kobe was out this morning, so I left a message about your adventure. He may be trying to see to me. I only came home to change. Soga has died of smallpox, and two senior officials found fault with me when they came to see who was running the ministry."

"Soga has died?" Tora clapped his hands in glee. "That's great news. Congratulations, sir. What a piece of luck!"

"You'd better keep those sentiments to yourself. I'm in enough trouble without having my retainers start to celebrate."

Tamako apparently had taken care of her problem, so Akitada went to the small bathhouse, where he stripped off his dirty clothes, leaving them in an untidy pile on the floor. The wooden tub was covered with a lid, and the water inside was still warm. He sluiced himself off, and then immersed his body, feeling gradually refreshed after a sleepless and bruising night and the troubles of the morning.

He considered how best to investigate the Haseo case without losing his position in the ministry. Soga's illness and death had given him a brief respite, but instead of being free from hostile oversight, he was once again under scrutiny for dereliction of duty.

He needed to visit the village where the crime had taken place. He must find and talk to witnesses, especially that nurse. What could have made the woman tell such a vicious and tragic lie?

Akitada saw no possibility of getting official leave, however brief, at a time when all the government offices were short of staff. But he could speak to Judge Masakane. He might even be able to read the trial transcript, learn precisely what the nurse claimed to have seen and heard, and find out what corroborating evidence there was, for surely there must have been something besides her word against Haseo's.

He had no time for long deliberation and got out of the bath after only a few minutes, slipping on a light cotton house robe. On the way back, he thought to look in on Yori, but when he stopped outside his son's room, he heard Tamako's voice reading to him. Akitada frowned. The boy should be reading himself. More pampering. He was afraid he would just lose his temper again if he went in, so he went instead to change into a good robe, comb and retie his hair, and put on the prescribed headgear. On the way to the ministry, he stopped to have himself shaved by a barber who made a good living by offering his services to those who worked inside the Greater Palace.

His appearance met with Nakatoshi's silent approval, but Sakae said rather cheekily, "A vast improvement, sir. My compliments."

Akitada met this with a grunt and fled into Soga's office, where he spent the subsequent hours dealing with routine paperwork. He had debated briefly whether he should move back to his own room—now occupied by Sakae. The two visitors had so obviously disapproved of his having assumed honors that did not belong to him. But he decided that efficiency would suffer and remained.

The afternoon passed much too slowly. There were no more surprise visits or "inspections" and no urgent problems to be solved, but it was not until sunset that Akitada could pay his visit to Judge Masakane.

Masakane lived in a modest villa south of the Greater Palace and received Akitada with cool courtesy. They were seated in the judge's study overlooking a small garden rather similar to Akitada's. The judge said bluntly, "I assume you've come about your retainer's case. What was his name again?"

"Tora. But since his case has been postponed because of the epidemic, I came about something else. I trust you and your family have been spared?"

"I'm an old man and alone in this world. Death holds no fears for me. It is life that concerns me. There's too little time for a man to leave a good name behind."

Akitada said warmly, "No need to worry about that, Your Honor. You are praised by all as a fair and wise judge."

He had meant the compliment, but Masakane drew back stiffly. "Don't flatter me, young man, or I shall think you plan to damage that reputation."

Akitada flushed. Young man—and that superior tone? How dare Masakane think he had come to influence his judgment! He bit his lip. No sense in showing his anger. He needed help, though not in the way Masakane expected. This would not be an easy interview after all.

"As I said, I'm not here about Tora," he began and saw that Masakane relaxed slightly. "My visit concerns another case, one you tried five years ago. The accused was a man called Tomonari Haseo. Do you recall it?"

"Certainly. I am not senile yet. It was a sensational double murder. Are you going to question my verdict?"

The judge's belligerence told Akitada that he still disliked and distrusted him. Anger stirred again. The old man was insufferably rude, and Akitada was fed up with the disrespect he had been shown by all and sundry lately. If the judge was already hostile, he had nothing to lose. He raised his chin and said rather sharply, "I was taught that justice requires us to question the truth. The man you condemned to exile is dead, but he was my friend and I'm alive to keep a promise. That is why I am here. Tomonari Haseo was falsely accused and the real murderer is free."

Masakane's eyes narrowed to slits. "You talk nonsense. At best you are carried away by false sentiment. At worst . . ."

Akitada interrupted, "I trust my record speaks for my integrity, sir. I must ask you to think before making rash accusations."

The judge looked startled. He bent forward a little, as if he distrusted his hearing. "Are you correcting my manners?"

"I'm only pointing out that we are not going to get anywhere unless we both attempt to observe minimal courtesies, regardless of our private opinions."

Masakane smiled thinly. "How foolish you are. I don't want to get anywhere, as you put it. It is you who wants something from me."

Akitada sighed in defeat. He rose and bowed. "In that case, forgive me for having troubled you."

Masakane waved a thin, spotted hand. "Sit down. Sit down. I have nothing better to do. What do you want to know?"

Akitada sat. "I would really like to read the trial transcripts."

"Impossible. They have been sealed, and you would need an order from the chancellor himself to unseal them."

"Then I must rely on what you remember." Akitada saw Masakane's frown, and added quickly, "It was more than five years ago, and no doubt many witnesses appeared in so heinous a case. I know that the main witness was the accused man's own nurse."

"And what a witness! Distraught, of course. She suckled him and raised him through his childhood and now had to condemn him. But she served in his father's house and she saw it all happen. This was a much stronger case than the one against your retainer. There was no doubt in anyone's mind that the accused was guilty."

"She claimed to have seen both murders done?"

"Yes."

"But were there other witnesses?"

"Why worry about them? It is the nurse who is your problem."

"I believe she lied."

Masakane stared at Akitada. After a moment, he said, "I have heard that you pursue even the most far-fetched notions with incredible determination. Sometimes successfully. But this time you're quite, quite wrong."

"What about the other witnesses?"

Masakane pursed his lips. "Let me see. A maid testified that father and son had quarreled before. And a monk saw the murderer run toward the house with a terrible look on his face. Ah, yes. A local overlord offered your friend employment when he heard that he wished for independence, but he was turned down quite rudely. I think the young man said he knew of a better way to get what he wanted."

"The local overlord would not by any chance be Yasugi?"

"Very clever. Yes, it was Yasugi. Of course he is the only man of influence in the area. The Tomonaris came down in the world as the Yasugi family rose. There was no love lost between them. All in all, Yasugi behaved rather well, I thought."

"He may have had his reasons."

Masakane frowned. "It doesn't matter. His testimony was not needed. Anybody in the village could have told you that father and son did not get along."

"What happened to Haseo's wives and children?"

"I expect they went with the condemned. It's customary."

Akitada almost jumped up. "No, they did not. He was alone in Sadoshima. He left his three wives and six children behind."

Masakane raised thin brows. "In that case the women may have remarried or returned to their families. Was there anything else?"

Akitada rose and bowed. "No, Your Honor. Thank you for your time. I hope you will forgive the rude intrusion."

"Hmmph," said Masakane.

◆

Akitada was frustrated. He had exhausted the sources of information in the capital. Haseo's hometown was the only place where he could learn about everybody's movements on the day of the double murder and find out what had become of Haseo's family. He firmly put aside the notion that he also wanted to see Lady Yasugi again.

When he got home, the gate opened to let out an elderly man accompanied by a young boy carrying a wooden case. The older man's dark robe and the case identified him as a doctor. Seimei, his face tense with worry, was seeing them out.

Akitada wondered if Tora or one of his friends had taken a turn for the worse. Looking after the two figures, he asked, "Who needs a doctor?"

"Yori, sir." Seimei's voice was as bleak as his face.

"What? Yori? What's the matter with him?"

Seimei hung his head without answering. With a sudden sense of dread, Akitada took him by the shoulders and shook him. "Speak, old man. What's wrong?"

Seimei winced. "It could be smallpox, sir. Of course it is still early . . . and besides he is such a strong, healthy boy . . ."

But Akitada was already running toward the house.

CHAPTER TWENTY-ONE

SMOKE OVER TORIBENO

*J*t was twilight in Yori's room even though the sun had not set yet. Reed curtains had been lowered across the openings to the veranda and garden, and Yori was surrounded by low screens and blanket stands. Inside this cocoon the little patient lay under piles of silken quilts, ministered to by his mother and Seimei. The air was stagnant, warm, and heavy with the smell of pungent herbs.

Akitada pushed aside one of the blanket stands so roughly that it toppled and spilled the quilts and robes across the floor. Tamako jerked around and stared up at him with red-rimmed eyes.

"How is he?" Akitada asked harshly.

She shook her head and turned back to the child.

Akitada knelt beside his son. Yori was so smothered by bedding that only his eyes peered out at his father. The eyes were dull and feverish. Akitada pushed aside the quilt to touch the boy's forehead. The child was burning with fever, yet his skin was dry as paper.

"Father, I'm so hot," Yori whispered hoarsely. "I'm on fire."

Akitada flung back the bedding. The little body looked small and forlorn among all the quilts. Someone had wrapped a thick layer of floss silk around the hips and lower abdomen. Yori started to shiver violently.

"Don't uncover him." Tamako's voice was sharp. "The doctor said he must be kept warm at all times." She tucked the blankets back around Yori.

"He is uncomfortable," protested Akitada. "He needs air. And something cool to drink." Yori whimpered and nodded.

"No. He mustn't," Tamako cried. "We must do as the doctor said. Nothing to drink. It's our only hope." And she pushed her husband aside and leaned protectively over the child.

Akitada felt helpless and frightened. Instinct made him shift the burden of responsibility. "Why was I not told?" he demanded.

"I tried to tell you twice, both yesterday and today. You were too busy." Tamako's voice was matter-of-fact, but he knew from her averted face and stiffly held back how deep her anger against him was.

"You certainly did not make yourself very plain in that case," Akitada snapped. "You should have known that I expect to be informed of the illness of my only son."

Tamako rose. She was white-faced and looked exhausted. It occurred to Akitada that she had probably sat up day and night with Yori. He recalled now that he had heard her reading to him earlier and was ashamed that he had blamed her for pampering the boy. Rising also, he extended a conciliatory hand, but she pushed it away. "You care nothing for your son or me," she cried fiercely. "You only care for your work, and for solving your cursed crimes, and for other men's women. Time and again I've begged you to protect us from the illness, and each time you've mocked my fears and reproved me. Now see what you have done!" She burst into tears and ran from the enclosure.

"Tamako!" Akitada started after her, but Yori began to cry and he went back to his son, knelt, and took him into his arms. "It isn't true, Yori," he murmured. "I do care very much for you. Are you feeling very bad?"

"Yes," whispered Yori, putting his arms around his neck. "I love you."

Akitada could not speak for a moment. Then he said, "Thank you. I love you, too. I'm sorry I've been so busy lately, but I'm here now. What do you want me to do?"

"Take the covers off again."

"But the doctor said . . ."

"I don't like the doctor," wailed Yori. "I'm hot. And thirsty."

So Akitada laid him back down and peeled back the quilts and the boy's robe, and the silk floss wrapping until he lay quite naked. Yori closed his eyes then, but he held on to his father's hand. Akitada gazed fearfully at the small body, so beautifully made, so sturdy and smooth, as yet unmarked by the red spots and pustules of the disease. He allowed himself to hope.

Seimei touched his shoulder and whispered, "Sir? He must be covered up. The doctor was quite specific about that."

Akitada whispered back, "Oh, Seimei, he's terribly hot. What's wrong with giving him a little relief? And how about some cool tea or water? He's thirsty."

"The idea is to make him hot to raise a sweat and break the fever. And he must not have any liquids. They will cause dysentery."

Yori started to shiver and cry again.

"But he'll burn up or die from thirst," Akitada protested. Yori's crying turned into a wail.

"Sir, you're not being very helpful," said Seimei sharply. "He must be kept quiet. Perhaps you had better come back a little later."

Tamako reappeared and fell to her knees beside the sobbing

child. She covered him and held him, rocking him in her arms like an infant until he stopped crying.

Akitada left quietly.

For the next ten days life stood still for Akitada. Very little intruded on his self-absorption, or rather, his total absorption in events over which he had no control. He sent a note to Naka-toshi to tell him that smallpox had struck his family and that he would not be able to come in. He did not contact Kobe and abandoned all thought of Haseo's past and the murder of the blind woman. He stayed at home but did not exchange more than the barest civilities with those around him.

There was nothing for him to say or do. Decisions about Yori's care were in the hands of others. Tamako was white-faced and determined, her comments to Akitada brief and cold. Sei-mei worked silently. Neither seemed to need any sleep. They re-mained with Yori day and night, while Akitada roamed the house and the garden, periodically passing through the sick-room to gaze helplessly at his writhing child. He kept hoping for a private moment when he might touch and hold Yori, per-haps to make him more comfortable, or to ease his misery by telling him stories, but Tamako's hostile back seemed forever to interpose itself between him and his son.

Later, much later, he would blame himself for not ordering everyone out of the room, for not easing the boy's fever and his agonizing thirst, but at the time he was so torn with guilt and uncertainty that his will had become paralyzed. Mostly he kept fear at bay with restless and pointless activities. He rearranged his books. He inspected the storehouse. He got out some tools and trimmed overgrown shrubs in the garden.

The telltale spots appeared and spread. Akitada reminded himself that many people survived, and that Yori had always been a strong and healthy boy, but the ice-cold lump in his stomach did not melt. That day he did an extraordinary thing and knelt in front of the household altar to pray to the small

Buddha figurine. Since he did not believe, this effort came particularly hard, but by then his fear had grown too great, and he
prostrated himself before the Buddha with the fervor of an as-
cetic. He offered his own for Yori's life. The next morning Yori
seemed better. The fever subsided and he rested more quietly
for the first time in many days. But the rash festered and spread,
from his face to his arms and chest, and then over his whole
body. The child was in agony, unable to speak or swallow because the blisters and sores had invaded his mouth and throat.
Akitada's beautiful son became a swollen, suppurating mon-
strosity, and Akitada took the small Buddha statue from the altar and smashed it.

During this period, Akitada felt a great need to be with his
son, yet could not bear to look at him. And so he would come,
cast furtive glances in hopes of improvement, then sit miserably
by for a few minutes as Seimei and Tamako, and sometimes the
doctor, tended to the moaning child, only to leave again when
his stomach twisted at the suffering. He was afraid now to touch
his son, for even the small hands were grotesquely swollen and
disfigured. The slightest contact caused him pain. He looked at
Tamako and was ashamed. Her face was a weary mask, her
lower lip swollen and bloodied from biting it whenever she had
to handle the screaming Yori, yet she persisted. He marveled at
her strength and his own weakness.

His inadequacy made him very humble. He asked Tamako
if he might read to Yori. She nodded without looking at him.
They had exchanged so few words since Yori's illness began that
they were like ill-met strangers. Akitada read to Yori without
comprehending the stories and without response from the child.
When Yori was awake, he stared with glazed eyes at the ceiling
and whimpered a little now and then, but most of the time he
seemed asleep or semicomatose. Akitada would pause and gaze
at him, wondering if he was seeing death, and drop the book to
rush from the room. Later it occurred to him that music might

be more soothing. He brought his flute and sat, playing tune after tune, always ending with a lullaby Yori used to love as an infant, convincing himself that the sound eased the pain and put him to sleep.

The moments of hope were particularly dreadful: If the child had a more restful night, or took a few sips of rice gruel, or if the doctor did not express any unease, Akitada was filled with irrational joy. In fact, the doctor was a ceaselessly optimistic fellow whose many visits Akitada gladly paid for because they made him think—however briefly—that Yori was improving. But each hope was crushed, and each time death was closer and more certain, until even the most credulous father must abandon false expectations—and Akitada was not a credulous man.

Yori died quietly. He stopped crying, moaning, even whimpering, and became very still. Akitada and Tamako were in the room but did not know when he stopped breathing, having convinced themselves that he was only asleep. When Seimei told them, Akitada felt the pain slice through him so sharply that he gasped. He looked at Tamako and extended his hand— to comfort her or to be comforted, he did not know which. But Tamako flung herself across the small corpse and burst into a long wail. "Oh, oh, oh . . ."—just that, without cease—"oh, oh, oh . . ." Akitada lifted her from the dead child. He held her tightly, hoping that by holding on to each other they might find relief, but she fought free and ran from the room, still wailing in her grief.

◆

Akitada neither wailed nor wept. He knew what must be done. He had arranged funerals before. Because of the epidemic, he could get only two elderly monks for the sutra readings and chants. The temple was apologetic: They had too many funerals to attend, and a number of their younger members had succumbed to the disease themselves. The yin-yang master designated the proper day, and casket, bearers, and materials for the pyre were purchased at enormous expense.

The family accompanied the small casket to Toribeno. The cremation ground lay on a wide plain southeast of the capital at the foot of the eastern mountains. They left the Sugawara residence at dawn and walked into the rising sun. Only Tamako rode in a sedan chair, borne by two villainous-looking men who had demanded a ransom in silver for the service. When they reached the outskirts of the city, the sun dimmed behind a heavy haze of grayish-white smoke which rose above Mount Toribe and spread like a blanket over the plain.

They crossed the river, and turned southward along its banks. The riverbed was partially exposed by the long drought; abandoned corpses lay there, and the remnants of small funeral pyres, some with only half-consumed corpses amongst the ashes. Most people could not afford funerals like Yori's, especially not if they had lost several family members to the disease. Unpleasantly well-nourished dogs roamed about, baring their teeth at them as they passed, and a sickly smell drifted on the morning breeze.

Theirs was a very small cortege: just Yori's parents, Seimei, and Tora. The others had stayed behind to guard the house in these uncertain times. The cook had taken to her heels days before, the moment she realized that the young master had smallpox.

They soon joined other funeral processions, some more elaborate, some even smaller than theirs. They passed several temples, all crowded and conducting services. Ahead stretched the thousands of stone grave markers of the capital's cemetery.

Akitada saw all this with mindless detachment. Someone directed them to their site; someone else relieved them of their precious burden. It was placed on the pyre—a generous one, since Akitada had paid a huge bribe to the superintendent of the cemetery. The same two aged monks quavered their chants, while a heavily veiled Tamako placed Yori's small possessions on the pyre: the lacquered sword Akitada had bought him for his New Year's birthday, the book from which Tamako had read his favorite stories of legendary heroes, Seimei's copy book full of strange Chinese characters, and some filled rice cakes Tora had searched the city for.

And then Akitada lit the wood with a burning pine torch.

They watched the flames catch, rise into the morning sky, watched the new white smoke ascend to join the drifting haze above—the smoke many believed to be the soul of the dead bound for the Western Paradise.

But Yori was too young to know what road to take. The heaviest burden for a parent is to know his small child is alone and helpless. His failure as a father gnawed at Akitada and he felt as hollow as a dead tree.

The wood crackled and hissed. The monks chanted. And gradually the smoky air assumed another, more choking smell.

Akitada thought of the fire, the heat of it, grieved that the small body which had suffered the burning fever should now be given to the flames. He closed his eyes and took shallow breaths.

◆

That night Tamako came to Akitada's room. He was awake when his door slid open, staring into a darkness so heavy that it burned his eyes as if it were the sun or a raging fire.

Her footsteps told him that she was barefoot, and he wondered what she wanted. He knew soon enough. She lifted his cover and slipped in beside him. Without uttering a word, she reached for him with hot, eager hands, peeling back his robe and pressing her body against him. She wore only a thin silk robe that parted in front.

He did not know what to do. A great pity for her seized him, and then he was disgusted with himself for responding to her lovemaking on this night of all nights. Tamako had never been

this demanding, had never behaved with the wild abandonment of a public courtesan before. In all the years of their marriage, she had been a gentle and modest woman who took quiet
pleasure in their physical encounters but never initiated them.
Now she was clutching at him, seeking his mouth with hungry
lips, and when he was ready, she pulled him onto her, grasping
him with arms and thighs as if he might get away, meeting him
almost violently, until she cried out her own fulfillment and
slackened into abrupt lethargy.

Akitada finished, and rolled aside. He felt sick and was
afraid because she lay so very still. "Tamako?" he asked, touching her temple through sweat-drenched hair.

She gave a single hoarse sob and was gone.

The sound of the door closing lingered in the darkness. The
sharp scent of their lovemaking mingled with the smoky stench
of Toribeno, which still clung to the funeral robe he had draped
over a stand.

After weeks of coldness, his wife had come to him on the
night of their son's funeral. Why? Because she wished to replace
the dead child with another as quickly as possible?

Akitada's stomach heaved. He gagged on hot vomit and staggered into the garden.

◆

The next morning, before sunrise and with most of the household still asleep, Akitada saddled his horse and left. Only Genba
knew where he was headed, but he would pass the information
on to the others.

Akitada wore traveling clothes and had Haseo's sword slung
over his shoulder. It seemed appropriate that he should take up
Haseo's battle with it. His own sword was lost, probably forever,
but family tradition paled when you had just lost your only son.
Of course, there might be other sons some day. Tamako's fren-
zied use of him during the night could result in pregnancy, but

Akitada's flight—and he knew that was what it was—told him that he feared the prospect. He did not want another child to take Yori's place. He never wanted to lose another child so horribly.

He passed through the capital quickly, riding straight down Suzaku Avenue toward Rashomon. The streets were almost deserted, though red-coated constables were in evidence near the markets. Another distribution of grain? As long as the markets remained closed, the threat of famine was added to the grim specter of smallpox.

The official scavengers were busy at the Great Gate, a customary place to leave your unburied dead. Beyond stretched the *Saikaido*, highway to the western ocean, toward a green and mountainous countryside. In the far distance, hidden in a blue haze, was Haseo's home and the sacred Hachiman Shrine. Akitada left death behind, hoping to find a way back to life.

Along the highway was more evidence of the epidemic. He passed two rotting corpses. In their haste to flee the city, a man and a woman had succumbed to the disease, proving, like Soga, the foolishness of trying to escape fate.

Akitada considered fear and found he had none. It seemed to him that this was so because he no longer valued his life. Only those who found happiness and contentment in their existence feared losing it. It was a cruel twist of fate that death had snatched Yori, so young and full of joy and laughter, and left behind his father.

But dwelling on Yori's death caused unbearable pain, and so Akitada fled—leaving behind an empty house, agonizing memories, and constant reminders of guilt. He followed the trail of an old murder and betrayal, hoping to drive his demons back into the shadows of his mind.

By the time he reached Toba, he had reviewed the facts of Haseo's case and felt hungry. He could not recall his last meal, or any meal he had felt an appetite for. Now that he had left the nauseating smoke of Toribeno behind and the air was sweeter,

his body clamored for sustenance even when life seemed unbearable. Unfortunately, all the doors of the small town were
closed to him. People feared travelers from the capital.

He rode on with a painfully empty belly. The highway soon
crossed the Kamo River. There was boat traffic here, and a few
miles farther he found a temple and stopped.

The monk who greeted him at the gate said they were low on
provisions, having fed so many fugitives from the capital that
they had only beans and millet left. The beans and millet had
been boiled into a thick, pasty stew, but Akitada ate hungrily.
He had taken only a few bites, when a small family arrived, a
man with two women and two children. One of the children was
a boy Yori's age, and Akitada choked on his food. Leaving most
of it behind, along with a donation, he fled back to the road.

Soon the Katsura River joined the Kamo, and more boats
plied their trade on the water. He passed the vast Ogura swamp,
through which the Uji River flowed to join the Kamo and the
Katsura, and within another mile the Kii joined also, forming a
wide river delta of swamps and sandbanks before becoming the
fast and treacherous Yodo, which carried all the heavy shipping
to the Inland Sea and Korea and China beyond. At the river
confluence, the highway crossed a long timber bridge and turned
west. All around Akitada was a flat landscape of watery rice
paddies, with occasional farms shaded by trees rising like islands from a green and billowing sea. Here the peasants worked
their land as they always had.

The mountains rose to the south, blue against a paler sky.
Some inner need drove Akitada to visit the shrine first. To reach
Mount Otoko he passed the barrier into Settsu Province and
then crossed the river by ferry.

Before ascending the sacred mountain, Akitada bathed in
the river and changed his clothes to cleanse himself of the pol-
lution of the past days. It was getting dark before he reached the
shrine on top of the sacred mountain and stabled his horse.

Perhaps he was foolish to come here, but something drew him to this place, a spiritual bond with the ancient gods of heaven and earth. As soon as he had passed under the red-lacquered *torii* and entered the forest path, he felt that he was in the presence of the gods. Large trees—camphor trees, he thought, but it was too dark here to be certain—enclosed him like sheltering wings. He felt calmer than he had in many months. His grief did not entirely disappear—he was convinced it never would—but it felt more natural, not like some foreign object which had been thrust deep into his belly and lay there festering. He felt a part of the mountain, the trees, the night, and when the tears finally spilled from his eyes, he let them fall unchecked.

Near the shrine was a small Buddhist temple where he asked for and received a place to sleep. And here he found his first rest after many sleepless nights.

He awoke well after sunrise to the cooing of hundreds of doves, and rose to pay his respects to the gods. There was no one about as he walked to the shrine building in the cool mountain air, rinsed his mouth and his hands with the clear water in a stone trough, and then prayed humbly to the gods of the mountain, and to Hachiman, protector of warriors and immanent spirit of this sacred place. He found no answering enlightenment for his troubles or Haseo's, but he felt a sense of peace, and when he stepped from the shrine, the morning air seemed purer, the scent of camphor and pine fresher, and flocks of doves rose to circle the shrine hall.

He could see for miles from this mountaintop, across a green and fertile land, across the web of rivers, rice paddies, lakes, and villages, all the way to the distant hazy shimmer that was the capital. This land of the rising sun would endure. All else was immaterial, transitory, and of no importance. Men, like the doves of this sacred mountain, were individually short-lived and insignificant, but they too would endure like the mountain itself. And during their fleeting lives, they could soar.

◆

The priest was a member of the Ki family, hereditary head priests of the Hachiman Shrine. He was past middle age, very dignified in his white garments and black court hat, and he received Akitada with smiling courtesy in his private apartments. Another priest, perhaps Ki's secretary, was bent over some paperwork.

Shinto priests could marry and, apart from their training in ritual and their devotion to the gods, were not much different from ordinary men of rank and education. But this was the shrine of the guardian deity of the Imperial Family, and Ki was accustomed to receiving emperors, chancellors, and nobles of the highest rank. After a few polite preliminaries and fielding a question or two about conditions in the capital, Akitada asked him about Haseo.

The priest's smile did not fade. He nodded. "I knew him and his family well. They were faithful supporters of this shrine. A dreadful affair. What is it that you wish to know?"

"Did you think him capable of the crime?"

Ki hesitated. "All men are capable of extraordinary acts—both good and evil—if it is fated and their nature demands it. Let me explain. Haseo wanted to take up the life of a warrior, but his father refused his permission. The elder Tomonari wished his only son to manage the family estate and provide him with heirs. Haseo married and fathered two sons, but he held on to his dream of becoming an officer in the Imperial Guard. On the day of the murder, he came to me to take his leave. He was about to tell his father of his decision." The priest sighed deeply. "They say there was a violent quarrel."

Akitada found Ki's continued smile irritating. He could accept Haseo's anger with his father, but not what the priest suggested. He asked, "What became of his family?"

Ki hedged. "Surely it cannot matter, since they were not witnesses to the murders?"

Akitada said harshly, "When Haseo died in my arms in Sadoshima, his last thoughts were for his family."

Ki, still smiling, shook his head. "It does you great credit to be concerned on your friend's behalf, but I assure you that they are well. Consider please that great harm might come to them if the past were stirred up again."

There it was again: the warning to leave matters alone. Akitada persisted. "There was a nurse who witnessed the crime. Can you at least tell me where she lives?"

"She is dead. Of the people who were in the house that day, no one is left now. They have all died or gone away."

As if they had never existed, thought Akitada. Had they fled because of shame or due to coercion? "Who lives on the Tomonari Estate now?"

"No one. The manor and the land belong to the emperor. Lord Yasugi is the administrator and sees to the cultivation of the fields."

Strange the way the lines crossed and recrossed: Yasugi held Haseo's lands; Yasugi's unhappy wife was Hiroko, who knew Tomoe, the blind singer of ancient warrior ballads, who was also known to Matsue, who had had Haseo's sword.

Akitada found neither answers nor encouragement here. Perhaps he should not have expected it. As head priest of the emperor's tutelary deity, Ki would certainly do nothing to interfere with present arrangements. Before leaving, Akitada asked one more question.

"Did Haseo have any close male relatives his own age? Perhaps a first cousin?"

Ki raised his brows. "None at all. That is what caused the

quarrel between father and son in the first place. There was no one else to carry on the family name."

The priest's secretary rose and left the room on silent feet, and Ki cleared his throat impatiently. Akitada asked, "May I take it that you know of no one else who might have done the killings?"

"Believe me, if I did, I would have said so at the time," Ki said in a slightly reproving tone.

Akitada had no reason to doubt him and made his farewells to the still smiling Ki.

Outside the elderly secretary awaited him. "I beg your pardon," he said urgently, "but I couldn't help overhearing your question."

"Yes?"

"I grew up in Tsuzuki District. People gossip among themselves about things they don't mention to outsiders."

"I understand. What is it that you know?"

The old man fidgeted. "*Know* is perhaps too strong a word. As I said, it's mere gossip. The old lord was said to have fathered a child with a servant. People saw a resemblance when the boy grew up. When Lord Tomonari gave a farmstead to the mother of this boy, it confirmed people's suspicions. Mind you, there may be nothing to it. Except for an outward resemblance, Sangoro had nothing at all in common with the young master."

"Where does this Sangoro live?"

"His farm is just over the hill from the Tomonari place. His mother used to walk to work every day."

Akitada thanked the priest and walked down the mountain, trying to recall where he had heard the name Sangoro before.

◆

The Tomonari Estate was substantial, and peasants worked its fields, treading waterwheels, pulling weeds, and building dams between paddies. They did not raise their heads to stare at the lone horseman, and Akitada soon saw why. An overseer stood on a small hill, a whip tucked under his arm.

The gate to the manor stood open, and Akitada rode in to look around and perhaps to ask directions to Sangoro's farm, but there was no one about except a scattering of chickens. He dismounted and led his horse to the water trough. The manor resembled many such across the land, a cluster of simple halls with thickly thatched roofs, their wooden walls blackened by age and the elements. The main residence lacked the amenities of noble houses in the capital, but this was a rural household; the men who had built it had maintained a simple lifestyle close to the land around them. Now it looked neglected. The doors were shuttered, grass grew on the roof, and swallows nested under the deep eaves.

The silence and emptiness reminded him of houses in the capital where everyone had died. It opened again the door to memory, shattering the peace so fleetingly won on the mountain. Overcome by his loss, he sank down on the rim of the trough and put his head in his hands.

After a time, he became aware of an odd sound among the clucking of chickens, chirping of birds, and occasional snorting from his horse. Someone was thrumming a zither. Abruptly his memory leapt backward and he was standing again outside the wall of the Yasugi mansion.

His heart beating faster, he tied up his horse.

CHAPTER TWENTY-TWO

HIROKO

ℬehind the main house was a small overgrown garden, and beyond that an area of shrubs and trees from which rose another, smaller pitched roof. The music was louder here. The zither player plucked the strings tentatively, halfheartedly, putting long pauses between clusters of notes so that the cheerful folk song struck his ear like a lament.

Someone had made a rudimentary path through the small wilderness, and Akitada took it, skirting thorny vines and dusting his boots and the skirts of his traveling robe with yellow pollen from wildflowers. Bush clover bloomed here among buzzing bees, and saffron flowers, and small pink carnations almost suffocated by ferns. Many years ago, as a small boy, Haseo must have played in this garden.

Like Yori.

She was sitting on the wooden porch of a vine-covered garden pavilion, her attention on the zither before her. He almost did not recognize her in a peasant woman's gray cotton robe and trousers, and with her long hair braided into a single plait. Her face was bare of cosmetics, but her beauty made his heart contract at the futility of his desire.

Reminding himself of her lies, he strode up to the stone step of the porch and demanded, "Are you alone?"

She started and the melody splintered. Then her eyes widened and her face softened into joy. "How did you find me?" she asked.

He said coldly, "By accident. I had planned to call on you at your husband's house, but this will do very well. How do you come to be here, and where are your people?"

The joy faded. "I have been banished. Yasugi sent me here."

"You mean you are a prisoner?"

"Something like that." She studied his face anxiously. "You have changed, Akitada. You look . . . ill."

He brushed that away. "I'm well enough." He glanced into the building behind her. It was empty except for a straw mat and the sort of bundle people make of a change of clothes when they travel. "You stay here? Why didn't they at least open the main house for you?"

"They say it's haunted. Someone was murdered there."

"Yes," he said harshly. "I know, and so do you. This used to be your home. You lied to me."

She opened her mouth to protest.

"No, don't deny it. Your first husband was the Tomonari heir. He died in exile for crimes he didn't commit. Tell me, did you believe him guilty? Is that why you accepted so eagerly the rich man's offer? Did you at least wait until the authorities confirmed your first husband's death before you leapt into Yasugi's bed?"

She had turned very white. The ivory plectrum in her right hand jerked across the zither, and a string tore with a loud, dissonant twang. She dropped the plectrum and bent her head, hunching her shoulders as if she expected him to strike her. "Please don't."

He was unmoved. Life was full of horrors, and he had no time for pity; he wanted answers. He said fiercely, "Your husband was my friend and died in my arms. His last thoughts were of you and the others, of the children. He believed you would stay together, and I promised I would find you. But I found only you, married to a rich man and living in luxury. Where are the others? Where are his children?"

She shuddered but did not answer, and that angered him. He went to her, seized her shoulder, and shook her until she raised her head and met his eyes. "Damn you, woman! You will speak and you will not lie to me this time, for I shall have the truth somehow. Your personal feelings no longer matter to me."

She flinched as if he had struck her, but her eyes remained dry. "No," she said softly, "I see that now. I think I knew it when I first saw your face. You're changed. But I have never lied to you, whatever you may think. You never asked about my first husband."

"You lied about your relationship with the murdered street singer," he thundered. "I checked your family records. You are an only child, yet you claimed she was your sister and told me a string of lies about your parents abandoning her for making an unsuitable marriage. You even embroidered the tale by making out that her husband was an unfeeling brute who divorced her when she got smallpox. Who was Tomoe really?"

"I did not lie. One may call one's husband's wives 'sisters.'"

That stopped him. "Tomoe was Haseo's wife?"

"She changed her name because she had to earn her living on the streets." Hiroko looked at him reproachfully, and he wondered if she was feeding him another elaborate lie.

"Even if this is true, the rest was a pack of lies."

"It was all true. The Atsumis rejected her when she decided to accept the offer of a common gate guard. She and the children lived with him for a year, but when she became ill and blind, he threw them out. She was too proud to ask her parents for help after that."

Akitada felt as if the ground were shifting beneath him. If this was indeed finally the truth, it was monstrous. He sat down abruptly on the stone step. She rose to fetch a cushion for him, inviting him to sit beside her.

"Please tell me about Haseo," she begged.

He obeyed. When he was done, there was a long silence. Then she nodded. "Yes, that was like him. He could be very kind. And it's good to know that he did not forget us in the end." She sighed. "I have been angry with him for too many years."

It was hard to know how women felt about their husbands. Apparently she had blamed Haseo for their abandonment. Akitada changed the subject. "How long have you been here?"

"Since we returned from the capital. Don't look so shocked. I much prefer it to the company of my present husband."

"You have your maid with you?"

"No."

"Surely you're not alone?"

"Someone brings me food once a day."

He felt outrage at Yasugi's treatment of her. At least two of Haseo's wives had been abandoned to fates worse than exile. Uncomfortably aware of the offer of marriage he had made her, he said awkwardly, "You cannot stay here. Do you have relatives?"

She bowed her head. "Only a great-uncle in the capital. He doesn't want me."

Akitada felt wretched, but he simply could not bring this beautiful creature into his household now. In truth, he no longer wanted her there.

She guessed his thoughts and twitched a shoulder impatiently. "Don't worry. I'm not your responsibility."

"I wish I could offer you my home—" He broke off helplessly.

"I know. Once the cherry blossoms have fallen, not even Buddha can reattach them. We are not the same people any longer."

He felt constrained to explain. "My little son has died."

She raised her eyes in dismay. "When?"

"Four days ago. I left the morning after the funeral." As he said it, he felt as if the suffocating pall of smoke from the pyre once again darkened the sun, and his tongue tasted the acrid stench.

She was still staring at him. "You left? But what about your wife? Your other children?"

"There are no other children. And Tamako is quite strong."

She moved away a fraction. "Oh, yes. She will need her strength. Left all alone to grieve the death of her only child."

Akitada detected a note of reproof. "You don't understand," he snapped.

She gave a small bitter laugh. "Oh, I understand only too well. You wanted to get away, to turn your back on an empty house, to immerse yourself in your work in order to blot out the pain. All men please themselves. Haseo did, too. I suppose that's what makes women strong."

He eyed her resentfully. "You think I'm pleased? You cannot possibly know what it feels like to lose your only son. Besides, my behavior is not for you to judge."

She rose, her pale face flushed with anger. "I know your grief only too well, my lord. I lost my son. And you have judged me all along."

He stumbled to his feet. "You lost a son?"

"Yes. He was my only son also, though I still have a daughter. He was barely two years old."

"Yasugi's child?"

"I have no children by my present husband." She twisted her hands, and for the first time her eyes filled with tears. "My daughter is no longer with me. Yasugi keeps her from me. She's almost eight, and he threatens to sell her into prostitution unless I submit to him."

"Dear heaven!"

"I no longer have any choice," she said bitterly. "You do."

Akitada was dumfounded. "You mean you have refused Yasugi all these years? But why did he marry you if you had no intention of living with him as his wife?"

She leaned against the wall and hid her face in her hands. "He hoped to break down my resistance. I agreed to accept his protection for myself and my children if I could live undisturbed in separate quarters. He was eager to help and very solicitous in those early days, and I was young and afraid, and foolish enough to think that he would be like a father to me." She shuddered. "Once he tried to rape me. I screamed and servants came. After that he only beat me. When that didn't change my mind, he took my children away." She drew a deep shuddering breath. "I think he killed my son. He said it was an accident. That he fell and broke his neck."

Akitada sat down abruptly and muttered again, "Dear heaven."

She fell to her knees beside him. "What am I to do? I've tried to protect my children and failed. I tried to help Tomoe and she was murdered. I have no strength left. He has won."

Their eyes met—hers swimming with tears, his shocked. "Do you suspect Yasugi of murdering Tomoe?"

She cried, "I don't know. Tomoe wanted me to leave him. Only what could I do to support myself and my daughter? There is only prostitution. Tomoe said prostitution was better than having our children killed one by one. And the next day she was found dead. I think my maid told Yasugi what she said."

Akitada felt a great surge of love and pity for her. He wanted to touch her, console her, but knew he must not. "You've been wronged, Hiroko," he said. "All of you were cruelly wronged. Haseo first, and then his family. None of it is your fault. We shall get your daughter back and find the others. When I return to the capital, I shall file a suit on your behalf. Haseo was innocent and the Tomonari land belongs rightfully to Haseo's oldest son."

She dabbed her eyes with her sleeves. "His name is Nobunari. He must be twelve. I don't know where he is or if he is alive. Tomoe wouldn't tell me. She was afraid Yasugi would force it from me."

Akitada remembered the silver coins in Tomoe's box and the two names written on the slip of paper. Nobunari and Nobuko were her son and daughter, and they were both alive, or had been when she died. If only Hiroko had not accepted Yasugi's protection! But Akitada had offered the same not too long ago. Alone in the world, a beautiful woman was subject to the selfish whims and desires of men. "What happened to the third wife, Sakyo?"

"She returned to her family and took her little girls with her."

Akitada thought of those three abandoned wives and their children. One married a rich man, one fled to her family, and the third ended in the gutter. "Haseo thought all of you would stay with Sakyo."

Hiroko said bitterly, "The Katsuragis didn't want their name tainted by the scandal. They took only Sakyo and were thankful she had no sons who would have borne their father's name. Sachi—Tomoe—married quickly. I took my children and went to my great-uncle, who convinced me to accept Yasugi's offer because he didn't want to be burdened with us."

"Do you know where your daughter is?"

She nodded. "With one of Yasugi's managers, not far from here."

"Then we shall get her. Is there anywhere you both can stay for a few weeks?"

"Perhaps we could stay with the shrine maidens at the Hachiman Shrine."

Akitada thought of the smiling priest Ki and shook his head. "It wouldn't be safe."

"There's a temple that has quarters for a few nuns. One of them is an elderly cousin of mine."

"Yes. You should be safe there until you can return to your own home." He glanced toward the roofs of the mansion behind him.

She nodded and gave him a tremulous smile. "Yes. Now that we have someone to remember us. Thank you, Akitada."

His heart twisted. He did not want to pursue that dangerous path but could not help himself. "Tell me about you and Haseo."

She flushed and looked down at her hands. "I was very young when the matchmaker came. She asked if I was healthy and felt my hips and belly through my gown. I knew I was chosen to give children to this strange man. I hated Haseo then, but I fell in love with him later. Haseo was always gentle. And he was very handsome." She sighed. "We were all in love with him, but he loved fighting more. He left us for long months to live in the capital. At first I thought he was visiting the courtesans, but he went to study sword fighting and to keep company with soldiers. I soon learned that I was nothing to him."

Akitada heard the bitterness, but he had learned that wives expected a great deal more than their husbands could give them. He asked, "What about his parents?"

"His father was very stern. Haseo avoided him. I think that angered his father. They both had tempers. Haseo's mother was kind and timid. She tried to make peace. Haseo loved his mother."

"Do you remember the day of the murders?"

She looked at him doubtfully. "That day, we—the wives—were not in the main house. We didn't see or hear the quarrel, but I knew Haseo was planning to do something . . . he looked angry when he left."

"You saw him just before the murder?"

"He left me in the morning." She blushed.

"The crime happened at midday. Haseo was arrested at the scene. What was he doing until then?"

"I don't know."

"Did he take his sword? This sword?" He showed it to her.

She looked and recoiled slightly. She answered so softly that he almost did not hear, "Yes, he had his sword."

Akitada began to suspect that Hiroko had believed her husband guilty. "How did you find out about the murders?"

She looked away and let the words pour out. "They brought us the news. First a servant, weeping. Then the steward to tell us that Haseo had killed his father and his mother. We didn't believe it, but Yasura had been with Haseo's mother and she saw it all. Yasura used to be Haseo's nurse. They said she was like a madwoman, crying, 'He did it. I saw it. He killed them both.' Later the constables led Haseo away. I ran after him. I saw blood on his clothes, and the look on his face was terrible. They took me away then, and I never saw him again." She sighed and wiped away tears. "So long ago and still so terrible."

He waited a moment, then asked, "You did not attend the trial?"

"No. There was a hearing at the Yasugi mansion. Yasugi is the senior district official. A judge asked all of us questions and made us put our names to our testimony." She paused. "Yasugi was very kind to me that day."

So Yasugi had been involved in Haseo's trial and had been solicitous of his beautiful young wife. That the biggest landowner should hold the top administrative position in his district was common practice, but it raised more suspicions in Akitada's mind that Yasugi had hatched a plot to incriminate Haseo. He had had a double motive: Haseo's beautiful third wife and the Tomonari Estate. But it did not explain how the murder happened, and Hiroko was no help there.

She was calmer now that she had poured out her story, and

he said, "Your husband . . . Haseo was innocent. A man called Sangoro may help us prove it. Do you know him?"

She frowned. "Sangoro? He grew up with Haseo and tried to be like him. Haseo's father was amused and let him strut about when the boys were young, but later he could see that it put ideas in his head and that Sangoro was becoming disrespectful, so he put a stop to it. But Sangoro left for the capital and only came to visit his mother sometimes. There's a distant cousin living at the farm. I think Sangoro works for Yasugi now."

"Does he indeed?" Akitada wondered just what sort of work he did. He was no farmer. He glanced past her at the bundle inside her room. "Could you leave now? We could stop at Sangoro's farm on our way to get your daughter."

"Now?" Apparently she had not thought what her next step would have to be and how quickly it must be taken, but she was still the same Hiroko who had disguised herself to attend Tora's trial. She went inside to pick up her bundle and rejoined him. "I'm ready," she said.

He helped her onto his horse, tied her bundle to his own saddlebag, and mounted behind her. There was no sign of Yasugi's people, and they left the Tomonari manor unchallenged.

A narrow footpath led from the manor over the crest of a low wooded hill into the next valley. Intensely aware of Hiroko, Akitada made himself think of Matsue instead. He hoped he would finally learn what role he had played in Haseo's tragedy.

Sangoro's farm consisted of a wooden house and two sheds, the whole surrounded by a low stone wall. Its fields were poorly cultivated, some having gone to weeds, and others showing only thin crops. Near the house, a few vegetables struggled in a small plot. But there were many chickens and, surprisingly, a horse tied up beside one of the sheds.

When Akitada saw the horse, he stopped in the shelter of the trees. "You'd better wait here. Can you ride?"

She nodded and let him help her down. "What are you afraid of?"

"I have a notion that Sangoro has come home." He led her to a grassy spot where she could sit and wait. "If there is trouble, take my horse and flee. Get your daughter and head for refuge."

Her eyes went to Haseo's sword at his side. "Please be careful."

When Akitada reached the farmhouse, he saw that the area inside the stone wall was littered with a number of dead chickens. He had no time to investigate, because the live ones began to cluck noisily, and the door swung open. The man on the threshold shaded his eyes against the sun, but Akitada knew him instantly. They had met. On three separate occasions.

In the broad sunlight the resemblance was not pronounced. Matsue's features were coarser and fleshier, the eyes colder and more calculating. Akitada saw that his right hand was no longer bandaged; the stumps of the missing fingers had scabbed over by now, but he held the hand awkwardly as if it still pained him.

Akitada approached until only the length of two swords separated them. Matsue's expression was unwelcoming. "Yes?" he asked, frowning.

"Are you Sangoro?"

"I am." The frown deepened. "You look familiar. Have we met?"

"Not precisely, though I know who you are. In the capital you pass under the name Matsue. I'm Sugawara."

Matsue's eyebrows rose. "What do you want with me?"

Akitada put his hand on the sword. "During a recent raid of a robber's den in the capital, the police found this sword in a room you used to occupy. It belongs to the Tomonari family. How did you get it?"

Matsue took a step forward and extended his left hand. "That's mine. Hand it over!"

Akitada stood his ground. "By what right do you claim it?"

"More right than you have." Recognition finally dawned and Matsue flushed with anger. "It's you again."

Akitada kept his eye on Matsue's good left hand, but it was the other, the wounded right hand, which suddenly lashed out. The blow landed on Akitada's temple and would have knocked him out, if it had not been injured. Still, Akitada lost his balance, stumbled, and fell to one knee. His sight darkened long enough for the sword to be snatched from its scabbard. He heard the soft hiss of the blade and scrambled to his feet and out of striking range, realizing that he had fallen for a child's trick that was about to cost him his life.

But Matsue stepped back, the sword in his left hand and a lazy smile on his face. Akitada realized that he was trapped against the stone wall. He waited for Matsue's attack. Akitada had hoped for death. Now he was about to have his wish.

"Don't try to run," Matsue drawled, strolling into striking distance. "You'd lose your head in an instant. I find I'm getting almost as good with my left hand as with my right." He lashed out and neatly decapitated a chicken that had strayed within his reach. The headless fowl walked about drunkenly before falling on its side, twitching a couple of times, and lying still. "You see? Now what's all this business about the sword? Why are you following me? The Tomonaris are dead and gone."

"Except for you."

Matsue's eyes flickered. Akitada watched him, wondering vaguely if there was a chance he could get the sword back by keeping him talking.

Matsue looked at Haseo's sword and smiled unpleasantly. "Nowadays I'm my mother's son, not my father's. It appears the Tomonari name has fallen into disrepute. Still, this sword is mine by rights. It should've been mine from the start. I'm the older, even if the spoiled brat got the teachers, the money, and the attention."

Akitada began to inch along the wall. "Your mother was a peasant. At best you were a bastard."

Matsue's eyes flashed. He cried, "My mother came of good stock and was serving his first wife when my father took her as concubine. I was born three months before my pampered half-brother."

Akitada shifted his position a little more. "So? Dalliance with maids is common. The resulting children have no claims unless their father legitimizes them. Tomonari did not recognize you."

"You lie." Matsue swept up the point of the sword until it touched Akitada's throat. "He acknowledged me. Ask anyone around here." He made a sweeping gesture with the sword. "He gave my mother this farm. Why else would he do that?" The sword point returned to Akitada's throat.

So Tora had been right about the document. Akitada did not doubt that Matsue was Tomonari's son, but a man who was so determined to protect the succession that he had forced a re-bellious Haseo to accept his family duties would hardly legiti-mize a bastard child. Still, such casual relationships could leave deep emotional scars. Akitada would have felt some sympathy, had he not been convinced by now that Matsue was the killer. Dodging the sword point by stepping aside, he said, "If it is as you say, why did Tomonari not keep you and your mother in his household instead of sending both of you away when you started making claims on him?"

Matsue glared. "Maybe my mother didn't want to stay. Maybe she wanted her own place. This place. But we were wel-come in the great house anytime. My mother nursed my half-brother along with me and we grew up together. It was our home as much as theirs."

"Ah. The nurse Yasura was your mother." Ki's secretary had mentioned that she lived close enough to walk to work every day. And if Matsue was the murderer, she had the strongest reason of all to lie. "She lied to protect you," Akitada said. "Because it was you who killed them."

Matsue's face hardened. "You made a mistake hounding me," he said softly. "What you guess won't matter, because you won't live to tell it. Yes, I killed them. And then I hid and I watched as my brother found their bodies. Sometimes the gods *do* right a wrong."

Akitada said angrily, "You let him go to trial for something he had not done."

Matsue laughed and raised the sword a little to caress Akitada's jaw. "My honored brother wasn't a bit grateful that I rid him of our father and made him Lord Tomonari. He wept like a child; he clutched his mother's corpse; and he pulled his sword—this sword in my hand—from our father's chest. My mother was wailing her head off until he shook her and asked her who'd done the deed. For a moment I was afraid she'd tell, but she didn't, and that's when I knew I was safe. All I had to do was disappear and let things take their course."

Akitada was sickened. "Why did you kill them?"

Matsue's face darkened. "They pushed me too far. I'd come home to ask my father for a little money to pay some debts, but he laughed at me. I reminded him that I was his son and that he'd given a hundred times as much to my half-brother. He got angry and called me names. Our shouting brought his wife and my mother. When they turned on my mother, blaming her, it was too much. I saw my precious brother's fine new sword lying there, and I killed them both." Matsue raised the sword into the sun and squinted along the blade. "I could never afford a fine weapon like this. Not a nick in it, and it sliced through her neck bones without a sound." He lowered the blade and chuckled. "Can you imagine, her head stayed on. You should have seen her face. But she put her hand to her throat and it looked like she pushed it off herself. It was the funniest thing I've ever seen." He gave a high-pitched laugh.

He was a madman, Akitada thought, one of those demonic creatures who take pleasure in killing. He discovered, with mild surprise, that he did not want to die, especially not here, not like this. He would not wait to be cut down, perhaps after a desperate cat-and-mouse game of dodging Matsue's blade. He would attack and get the sword back. He would almost certainly take a sword wound, perhaps be killed, but if he was quick, he would be inside Matsue's reach before the other man could execute a fatal strike.

He gathered himself, set his eyes on the hand which grasped the sword hilt, and charged.

But Matsue did not react the way he had hoped. Instead of striking out, he sidestepped and tripped Akitada, who ended up prone. Putting a foot on Akitada's back, Matsue placed the sword's point just where the jawbone joins the neck and laughed.

"That was stupid," he drawled. "Of course I can't let you live."

With his face pressed into fresh chicken droppings, Akitada prepared to die. Death was never pretty, but better in chicken dung and by the sword than the way poor Yori had died. Better in a fight like a man, not like a blind woman running from a maniac's knife. He thought of Tamako and braced himself.

But Matsue did not strike. Somewhere in the distance Akitada heard the sound of a galloping horse. He twisted aside, felt Matsue's foot slipping, and grabbed for his legs. Matsue came down on top of him and knocked the breath out of his lungs. Akitada had only one thought, to get the sword back. A violent struggle ensued, but this time it was Akitada who rose with the sword in his hand.

The rider came to a halt in a cloud of dust and squawking, fluttering chickens. The slender figure in gray straddled the horse, controlling the animal with expert ease. Hiroko was certainly no obedient female.

"Is he the murderer?" she demanded.

Wiping the dung off his face, Akitada thought she looked as

magnificent as those ancient warrior goddesses who rode and fought like men. "Yes," he said wearily.

Matsue got up and stared at the fierce woman on the horse.

She looked back at him and her face contorted into a mask of fury. "Then what are you waiting for?" she cried. "You've got the sword back. Use it."

Matsue exploded into action and flung himself at Akitada with a howl. Again they struggled for the sword, again the chickens scattered and cackled. Hiroko shouted. The horse snorted and danced just feet away. Matsue was desperate, but this time Akitada hung on to the sword and managed to free his arm. He started to back off, when Matsue delivered a vicious kick to his stomach that sent him staggering backward to the ground.

Hiroko screamed shrilly, and Akitada scrambled to his feet.

The horse burst past him, tossing him aside, its hooves barely missing him. He heard a shout, the sound of a thudding impact, and a howl of pain. Matsue was down. He lay moaning and twitching, as Hiroko spun the horse around in a spray of gravel and rode over him a second time. This time, Matsue lay still.

CHAPTER TWENTY-THREE

KOBE

*M*atsue was motionless, but he was alive. Blood trickled from a head wound, and he had a broken leg and probably other injuries.

"Is he dead?" Hiroko slipped from Akitada's horse and came to look. "No? I meant to kill him."

"Why?"

"I've dreamed for years of murdering the man who destroyed us." She handed Akitada the reins. "I'll take the other horse and go on by myself."

Akitada was aware of a sense of shame. Twice he had let Matsue get the upper hand and once he had been disarmed. And Hiroko had watched the whole ignominious affair. "No," he said without looking at her. "I'm coming with you. You may run into your husband or his people."

She said nothing and walked to the shed to get Matsue's horse. Akitada looked after her, trying to think how to thank her for coming to his rescue. When she rejoined him, he said awkwardly, "You probably saved my life."

"It was nothing. I'm only sorry he still lives."

Her manner rankled. "Matsue must live to confess to his crime in court. Help me get him inside. He's not going anywhere with that broken leg, and I'll get back as quickly as I can."

They had dragged the large Matsue almost to the threshold, when a small, bandy-legged peasant arrived and watched them in astonishment. He pointed at the unconscious Matsue. "What happened to my cousin?"

Akitada straightened up, wondering if this was a new complication. "An accident," he said. "You must be the one who manages his property."

The man thought the question over carefully, then nodded. "I work here." He thought some more, letting his eyes move over them. "What kind of accident?"

"His horse threw him."

The peasant looked at the horse and at the dead chickens and spat. "Horses aren't for peasants. I told him so, but he got angry and hit me." Shaking his head, he helped Akitada carry Matsue inside the house, where they dropped him on the floor.

Apparently the cousin had little love for Matsue and was not particularly bright. Akitada said, "He has a broken leg and got a knock on the head, so he may be babbling nonsense when he wakes up. Don't pay any attention. Just put a splint on his leg, keep him still, and give him a bit of water now and then. We'll borrow his horse for a little, but I shall bring it back by tonight."

Matsue's cousin nodded, and Akitada went back outside, where he helped Hiroko to mount and swung himself in the saddle.

They were both lost in unpleasant thoughts. Akitada ruminated about his pathetic performance with Matsue and assumed she did the same. No doubt she thought him completely inept. More to break the long, awkward silence than out of curiosity, he asked, "Where did you learn to ride like that?"

"Haseo taught all of us. It's the warrior's way."

After another silence, Akitada said, "I should not have let so much time pass before righting this wrong."

"It was good of you to think of us at all."

He gave up. She had become indifferent, possibly even hostile. It served him right for desiring what could not be his. For a while they rode in silence through a land of green rice paddies, while he mulled over his long list of poor judgments and the human losses his inadequacy had caused. And always, in the back of his mind, the heaviest guilt of all. But that wound to his conscience was much too deep to dwell on, and he resolutely bent his mind to his purpose.

Breaking the second, longer silence, he asked, "Can you tell me anything that might help me find Tomoe's children? I take it they are not with family or friends?"

"No. I've been thinking about it for weeks. What must be going through their minds now that their mother does not visit anymore."

He did not mince his words. "They may be homeless. Or worse. The money their mother earned was for them. She lived on millet and water." Hiroko turned a stricken face to him. He knew he burdened her with guilt also, but hiding the facts had brought nothing but tragedy to all of them. "I think they're in someone's care, and if that person depends on payment, he or she might be tempted to sell the children. Did she visit them often?"

"Dear heaven. I didn't know. Yes. Every few weeks, I think. She would spend a day with them. She told me about Nobunari's studies, and Nobuko's pretty singing voice."

"She was blind. How did she make the journey? Did someone take her?"

"No. She trusted no one, but she could make out shapes and managed to walk familiar streets."

Akitada frowned. "She could have been followed without knowing it."

Hiroko suddenly looked frightened. "Do you think Yasugi is behind this?"

"I don't know who killed her. At the moment I'm worried about the children. You say the boy was being taught by someone. Did she mention a school or a tutor?"

"No. I should have asked. It seems now that I was always talking about my own troubles." She hung her head.

A common failing, he thought, and more guilt to spread around.

But at least Hiroko was reunited with her daughter without further incident. When they reached the farm, the little girl was sitting under a tree.

"Suriko," called Lady Yasugi. The little girl jumped up, shaded her eyes against the sun, and then ran toward them. Two women came from the house. Akitada looked for the men, but apparently they were working the fields.

Hiroko slid from the saddle to scoop up the little girl, and Akitada's heart contracted. Just so he used to catch Yori into his arms. He would never again feel his son's arms around his neck. A child—boy or girl, it mattered not—was a gift from the gods.

Holding her daughter, Lady Yasugi lifted a face shining with joy. When she saw his expression, she sobered. "Thank you," she said. "I shall never forget this."

He nodded, then turned to speak to the women who had come to join them. It was surprisingly easy to tell them that Lady Yasugi had come to take her daughter with her for a short visit. They smiled and bowed, and in minutes the little girl and her bundle were on Hiroko's horse with her, and they galloped off.

The small temple where they proposed to seek refuge looked

safe enough, but Akitada disliked leaving them. When they parted, he took some gold from his saddlebags and handed it to her. She refused.

"Don't be silly," he said harshly. "You'll be expected to make some sort of donation and you need the goodwill of the nuns. Pay me back later."

She accepted then, and he swung himself into the saddle. To his surprise, she came close and put her hand on his. Looking up at him, she said, "Don't forget your wife, Akitada. Go back to her. Go now."

Akitada took her words for a final rejection and was seized by such desolation that he could not speak. Wherever he looked in his life, he saw only failure and loss. Yes, he would go home to Tamako, though he knew what he would find. There was such a distance between them, so great a separation of mind and body, that nothing could bridge it. Only his sense of duty made him face it, for the alternative—to divorce his wife—filled him with more shame than he could bear. And this extraordinary woman, this woman who had rushed to save him from Matsue with the skill and courage of a warrior, seemed more beautiful and desirable to him than ever before, and that also filled him with shame. Without another word, he turned his horse and left her.

◆

He found Matsue-Sangoro conscious and cursing. Apparently his demands that his cousin send for Lord Yasugi had been ignored. Akitada warmed to the foolish relative and, after checking the splint on the broken leg, he secured his prisoner and bedded down nearby for a restless night.

At the first sign of dawn he had the cousin help him tie Matsue onto his horse. The man showed no interest in their destination and asked no questions. The process of tying Matsue's wrists and legs was painful to him; Matsue gnashed his teeth, cursed them both, and glowered at Akitada from blood-shot eyes. Akitada, whose belly still ached from Matsue's kick, ignored him. When he gave the cousin some silver for his trouble, Matsue spat at both of them. Akitada picked up a piece of the rope they had used and lashed Matsue across the face with it. The cousin grinned foolishly.

Mistreating a bound and wounded man was cowardly, but Matsue's actions, past and present, filled Akitada with such rage that the man was lucky he was still alive. Since Yori's death, something seemed to have hardened at his core. He had no empathy left. During the journey, he ignored his prisoner's complaints about a swollen wrist, as well as his curses. They stopped only once to water the horses and to allow Matsue to relieve himself.

At midday they reached the capital. Smoke still hung thickly over Toribeno, but both markets were open, and people had crept from their houses to buy food. There was an air of new hope in the city.

Akitada took Matsue to police headquarters and turned him over to an officer. Then he went to Kobe, who looked drawn and tired but was willing to listen in spite of their recent quarrel. Kobe even offered wine, which Akitada accepted gladly. It had been a long journey, and he had eaten nothing since the previous day.

Kobe watched him and nodded. "Good. You're starting to get some color back." He refilled the cup. "What in the name of Amida happened?"

"I brought in the man who killed Tomonari Nobutoshi and his wife. The crime happened five years ago in the Tsuzuki District. Tomonari's son Haseo was found guilty and exiled to Sadoshima."

Kobe sat up. His eyes sharpened with interest. "I remember the case. The son was supposed to have slaughtered his aged parents in front of his old nurse. The nurse's testimony was damning."

Akitada downed another cup of wine and held it out for a refill. If he kept this up, he might become sufficiently numb to face his wife. "The nurse was the real killer's mother," he said. "She blamed the murder on Haseo to save her son. Apparently this Sangoro was Haseo's half-brother."

Kobe snorted. "They certainly kept their quarrels in the family. Do I take it that the nurse has confessed now?"

"No, she's dead. Sangoro has confessed."

"Ah. But will he repeat his confession in court?"

"Probably. If he does not, Lady Yasugi will testify against him and against her husband."

Kobe's eyes widened. "Yasugi is involved?"

"I believe he stirred up the trouble between the father and both sons. He may have suggested the murder to Sangoro, but in any case he took advantage of the situation afterward. Apparently he manipulated witnesses, especially the nurse, to testify against Haseo. Yasugi lusted after Haseo's wife and the leases on the Tomonari Estate."

Kobe murmured, "Hmm." Then he shook his head. "I don't give you much hope there." Seeing Akitada's anger flare up, he said quickly, "Oh, I believe you, but Yasugi is beyond the law in this instance. It will be the word of others against his, and Yasugi will certainly prevail. You can, of course, cause him some unpleasantness, but on the whole I wouldn't recommend it."

Akitada said hotly, "Not even if we can prove that he killed one of the Tomonari children? Not even if we link him to Tomoe's murder?"

Kobe stared. "You can link him to the murder of the blind street singer?"

"Lady Yasugi and Tomoe were both married to Haseo. At the moment Tomoe's children have disappeared. The boy is the heir."

Kobe thought about it for a few moments. Then he poured himself and his guest more wine. They drank. "You have proof?" he finally asked in a weak voice.

"No. I've pieced a plot together. I was hoping that you could get Matsue to implicate Yasugi. Matsue has a broken leg. Surely that will help during the interrogation."

Kobe shook his head in wonder. "Now I know you've lost your mind. You want me to torture a confession out of this Matsue and also have him testify against Yasugi?"

"I know they're both guilty," Akitada said stubbornly. "As for the torture, they've done worse than that to innocent people. Let them find out what it feels like." Akitada gulped down another cup of wine—he was not sure if it was his fourth or fifth—and decided it was time to go home. He stood up and immediately lost his balance. "I've got to go," he said, slurring his words a little. "My wife's home alone. Mourning our son."

Kobe stood also and came around the desk. "Your son died? So that's what's wrong."

Akitada nodded. To his shame, his eyes filled with tears. "S-smallpox," he muttered and lurched from the room.

He was not sure how he got home. He let his horse find the way. Kobe's wine had raised a thick haze between himself and his surroundings, but in his heart he was terrified of walking into a house which no longer held his son.

Genba opened the gate and shouted the news across the courtyard. Tora and Seimei came running. Akitada let himself slide from the saddle and stood unsteadily, peering at each in turn. Their faces and voices were filled with pity. He muttered, "Thank you. Is all well?"

He meant Tamako, but Tora answered, "All are well except Kinjiro."

He had to think for a moment before he remembered the scrawny boy Tora had brought. "Kinjiro?"

"Smallpox. Just like Yori. He survived, thank the Buddha, but just barely."

Struck by this news, Akitada looked toward the house. "Tamako's taking care of him?"

"No," said Seimei. "The boy left before we knew. Tora searched for him and found him days later in the hospital. He said he didn't want to cause more trouble."

Wine was supposed to desensitize a man, but when Akitada thought of the half-starved street urchin dragging his feverish body to a public hospital rather than add to the turmoil in the Sugawara household, he started to weep. His three retainers waited helplessly.

"See that he has what he needs and bring him back as soon as he's better," Akitada said thickly. Handing his reins to Genba, he rinsed his hands and face at the well and then went in to greet his wife.

Seimei helped him off with his boots and traveling clothes. Dressed in an old house robe, Akitada went to Tamako's door and announced himself. For a moment there was silence, then he heard the rustling of her clothes, and she slid the door back.

They looked at each other. Tamako was pale but composed.

"I'm back," he said unnecessarily.

She nodded and stepped aside to let him in. "I'm happy to welcome you home, my lord." She spoke tonelessly, making him a formal bow.

After six years of marriage and the loss of a child, she should have shown some emotion, he thought, but too much had happened between them. Not knowing what words might be appropriate, he finally said, "I went to Tsuzuki ... to arrest the killer of Haseo's parents."

"I see." She invited him to sit and sat down herself. Her room was in semidarkness, the shutters to the outside closed. "Shall I send for some tea or food?" she asked.

Such propriety. He shook his head. "No. Kobe has filled me with wine. How are you?"

"Well." She paused. "And you?"

He nodded. "They tell me Kinjiro is in the hospital."

She made an apologetic gesture. "I didn't know he was ill until he was gone, but he is better. Not everyone dies, it seems."

Unspoken, her reproach for Yori's death rose between them and sent an icy shiver through his body. He shied away from the subject and began an account of his trip. Her eyes went to his face when he spoke of Hiroko, but she did not interrupt. When he was finished, she said only, "How terrible! Poor women. I'm glad you could help Lady Yasugi."

"I still have to find Tomoe's children." He got to his feet and bowed. "Thank you for taking care of things in my absence."

She rose also and bowed back. "It was my duty. I'm sorry I did not perform it better."

"Not at all. You do everything very well."

But he knew that her efficiency as the mistress of his household mattered little when they no longer shared each other's lives.

Seimei had food and tea waiting for him in his room, and Tora was waiting also.

"What happened to Mr. Chikamatsu?" Akitada asked.

Tora gave a snort. "He's back home, supervising the building of a higher wall between him and his nosy neighbor. And he wants Kinjiro to come live with him when he gets better."

Akitada nodded and, finding that he was very hungry after all, ate and drank while he filled them in on what had happened in Tsuzuki. When he was done, Tora said, "So she did it for her children. And you think Yasugi was behind all of it, don't you? You think he's going to kill Tomoe's children too."

Akitada hesitated. He hated Yasugi, wanted to believe the worst of him, but he really had no proof. "I don't know," he admitted. "Perhaps."

"Tomoe was afraid of him," persisted Tora, "and Yasugi's own wife thinks he had her son killed. I'm going to find those children." He got to his feet.

Seimei murmured, "A hasty hand bungles."

Akitada was nearly sober, but his head had started to ache. He should have been exhausted, but the same nervous energy that had pushed him since Yori's death was still with him. He frowned at the tangle of problems and wished he had not drunk so much of Kobe's wine. "We have no proof that Yasugi is killing Haseo's sons to prevent future claims on the estate," he said, "but there are other reasons for finding the children quickly. The trouble is, unless we know where to look, it could take weeks. Tomoe was too protective to mention their whereabouts to anyone. She trusted no one." He rubbed his temples and thought about it. "We know that she paid for their keep and went to visit them regularly. The boy, who is the heir, was probably getting some sort of schooling. It isn't much, but it's suggestive. I think the children are staying with a peasant family just outside the city. It won't be far because she walked there. If her son receives instruction, it may be near a temple or district school. She certainly did not earn enough money for a private tutor."

Tora said eagerly, "I'll scour the countryside around the capital."

"A blind woman would stay on well-traveled roads in case she got lost. I think you must look south of the city," Akitada said. "I wonder if her parents owned property there. She would choose a place she knew from her childhood." He stood up abruptly. "Seimei, my good robe and hat. We're going to see Kunyoshi again, and then I'll report at the ministry."

◆

Kunyoshi was well and seemed to have grown even more efficient. The disease had spared the old and struck the young.

When Akitada asked his question, he plunged eagerly into his dusty documents and reported that the Atsumis owned two farms. One was too far away, but the other lay just south of the capital and near a minor temple.

"That must be it," said Akitada with a sigh of satisfaction.

Tora said, "I can be there in less than an hour. Are you sure she wouldn't have gone farther away?"

"Remember, she was blind. Go home and saddle a horse. No, two. The boy is twelve and will have learned to ride. Get the children and put them in my wife's care. She will know what to do."

With Tora dispatched, Akitada walked to the ministry. To his amazement, all seemed business as usual. The anteroom held a modest number of petitioners, and Sakae bustled about with papers under his arm. When he saw Akitada, his complacent manner gave way to dismay. "Oh, you're back," he cried.

Akitada raised his brows at this rudeness. "I trust you and Nakatoshi have managed in my absence?"

Sakae averted his eyes. "Yes . . . er . . . perhaps you should report to His Excellency. The, er, provisional minister." He nodded toward Soga's office.

"The provisional . . . someone has been appointed already?" Such efficiency during a state of emergency was nothing short of stunning. Akitada was still staring at Sakae, his mind in turmoil, when the door opened and the cheerful face of a short and chubby individual peered out.

"Hah! Thought I recognized your voice, Akitada," he cried warmly. "Come in, come in."

Akitada barely managed to hide his astonishment. In a reasonably steady voice he said, "Kosehira. What a very pleasant surprise!"

Fujiwara Kosehira embraced him, then pulled him into the office and closed the door on Sakae's avid interest. He immediately became serious. "My poor fellow! I heard the news about your little son. I am so sorry for you. You look terrible and shouldn't have hurried back to work so soon."

"Thank you, but work is a distraction." Akitada did not want to dwell on the black abyss of his grief. "Is all well with you and yours?"

Kosehira nodded. "I sent them away after all. Now I'm the only one staying in my big house, except for one servant. It's an eerie feeling, being all alone. I keep hearing ghosts. Perhaps you will come to keep me company some evening?"

Akitada looked at his friend gratefully. "Of course. I shall need your cheerful and practical advice. But is it true? You're taking Soga's position?"

Kosehira flushed. "A temporary appointment. I rely on you totally. Know nothing of this stuff. You were gone and I was available, and well, it's always a matter of rank, isn't it? I know very well that you should be running the ministry. I hope you don't mind."

He looked so nervous that Akitada smiled. The smile felt strange after so many days of sadness. "Nonsense," he said, "I could not be more pleased. Frankly, Soga hated me. I fully expected to be dismissed with a bad report." He glanced around the office. "But where is Nakatoshi?"

Kosehira's face had lit up at Akitada's first words. Now it fell. "Under arrest."

"In jail? Why? What happened?"

"I found a treasonable letter written by him. Yesterday. I walked into the office and saw him slipping some paper away before leaving the room. He looked so guilty that I decided to take a look. And there it was, right on top of one of the document boxes. I was deeply shocked, my dear Akitada. The letter was addressed to Ito Mitsutaka, that notorious renegade in Mutsu Province. Nakatoshi suggested to Ito that this would be a very good time for an uprising, the capital and surrounding countryside being decimated by smallpox, and the government no longer functional with so many officials dead. Dreadful. I had him placed under arrest immediately."

Akitada stared at his friend. "I don't believe it," he said flatly. "Are you sure that poisonous snake Sakae wasn't behind this?"

Kosehira frowned. "Sakae? Why should he do such a shocking thing?"

Akitada sighed. "Because he's Sakae and he hates Nakatoshi. Who has the letter now?"

"I do. The court is not in session, so I kept all the evidence."

"What evidence? The letter is all you have, isn't it?"

"Just about. Except for Sakae's signed statement that he heard Nakatoshi make critical remarks about the government."

Akitada gave a snort. "Of course. Let me see the letter, please."

Kosehira got a locked box, fished a key from his sash and opened it. "You don't think Nakatoshi wrote this?" he asked uneasily, extending a folded piece of the kind of paper used for government documents. "I tell you, I saw him hide it with my own eyes. He got very red in the face when he saw me looking at him."

Akitada scanned the fairly long document and studied the signature at the end. "I don't doubt that you saw him hide something," he said. "But this is not in Nakatoshi's handwriting."

"What? Are you sure?"

"Absolutely. Nakatoshi writes an excellent hand. This looks strained, too careful. As if someone had been trying very hard to be neat. An interesting allusion to the Chinese rebel Chang Lu—not many people know his story—but otherwise this is not particularly well written. Nakatoshi expresses himself much better. Has he seen this?"

"No. I thought it best to get rid of him quickly. I must say, he looked upset."

"I can imagine." Akitada rose. "I'd better go see him now, if I may. He must be frantic."

◆

Akitada did not know whether to be furious at Sakae for his vicious plot to oust Nakatoshi or to be glad that he finally had a way to rid the ministry of the troublemaker. He had enough other problems, but in his present state he welcomed anything that would take his mind off the black misery which lay in wait and pounced the moment he allowed himself to think.

Kobe greeted Akitada with a jocular, "Back already? You look more yourself with that frown on your face."

Akitada still felt guilty about the memorial and returned the smile uncertainly. "Yes, I'm troubling you again. This time it's about my clerk, that is, a clerk at the ministry. His name is Nakatoshi. I just heard that he was arrested."

Kobe nodded. "On a charge of treason."

"I believe he was framed by a colleague."

"Oh come! Surely not again."

The similarity to Haseo's case had not struck Akitada, who instantly felt stupid for not having realized it. He said, "I cannot help it. It's a different case and a different motive."

Kobe raised his brows. "Right after solving one case, you've already solved another?" He still smiled.

Akitada flushed. "This was not very hard, a mere malicious child's trick. I've been expecting something of the sort all along. I thought I would come and reassure Nakatoshi."

As they walked toward the cells, Kobe said, "You didn't ask, but your prisoner in the other case has made a full confession. It didn't take any persuasion. We had him looked at by our physician, who found a badly broken wrist in addition to the broken leg. He will probably lose the hand and was so demoralized that he talked. His hatred for his half-brother was something to hear."

Akitada grimaced. "I can well imagine. What about Yasugi? Did he implicate him?"

"No. He pretended not to understand our questions. Sorry. At least you have the satisfaction that Yasugi didn't profit in the end. He lost his wife and will lose the land."

Akitada nodded. "What is likely to happen to Matsue?"

Kobe gestured to a guard to unlock a cell door. "Oh, exile and hard labor, I should think. Like his brother."

"Good!"

Nakatoshi started up when they walked in. He looked terrified. When he saw Akitada, he burst into tears. "I didn't write it, sir. I swear. I'm innocent." To Akitada's embarrassment, he fell to his knees and knocked his head on the dirt floor.

"I know, Nakatoshi. Get up. I'll have you out of here shortly."

Nakatoshi staggered to his feet and wiped his eyes, leaving smudges on his face and sleeves.

"Tell me," Akitada asked, "how was it that Lord Fujiwara saw you hiding the letter?"

Nakatoshi sighed. "I found it among my papers. When I saw Lord Fujiwara watching me, I panicked."

"Ah. And how did it get among your papers?"

"I don't know. I'd never seen it before. I thought maybe it had fallen out of another batch of documents. But then I saw my signature."

"Could Sakae have put it among your papers?"

Nakatoshi looked embarrassed. "I wondered about that. He doesn't like me."

"Yes." Akitada put his hand on Nakatoshi's shoulder. "Don't worry. We'll clear up the matter and have you out of here shortly."

In the corridor outside, Kobe asked, "This Sakae is the real culprit?"

"Oh, yes. Proving it is another matter. I cannot very well resort to torture."

Kobe glowered. "I don't particularly enjoy that part of my work, you know."

Akitada stopped. He had to try to mend matters between them. "Forgive me. To my deep regret, I always manage to do or say things to offend you. Believe me, I have the greatest respect for you and your work. During this time of crisis, I could do nothing but complain while you've saved hundreds, perhaps thousands, from death by riot and starvation. I'm very sorry I've offended you." He touched Kobe's arm. "I hope you can forgive me and we can be friends again."

Kobe cleared his throat. He said gruffly. "Yes, of course. I shouldn't have got so angry. And you're making too much of me. When there's a need, we both do what we can, even if it's thankless. But that reminds me." He dashed off, leaving Akitada standing in the courtyard, wondering if he had embarrassed Kobe into flight. But the superintendent returned in a moment, carrying a sword.

"You found my sword," said Akitada, taking the Sugawara blade from Kobe's hands. "That was very good of you."

"It belongs to your family." Kobe looked embarrassed. "I wish I knew what to say about your son. I lost two little ones myself a few years ago. One doesn't forget, but perhaps there will be more sons for you, and daughters, too. Someone to live for. To save the sword for."

"Yes," said Akitada bleakly, and pushed the sword into his sash. "No doubt, you're right. But for now I'd better see about catching Sakae."

CHAPTER TWENTY-FOUR

EVENING BELLS

Tora tied up both horses at the temple gate. The young monk gatekeeper greeted him eagerly; visitors were rare in this small temple. When Tora asked if the temple conducted a school, the young monk brightened even more. "Indeed we do, sir. Perhaps you would like to see for yourself? Our learned Master Genku is instructing the boys in the lecture hall."

Tora followed his directions to a small wooden building. Its sliding doors had been thrown open on this warm summer day. From within came the sound of young voices chanting in unison. Tora stepped up to the narrow veranda and sat down, instantly attracting the attention of the pupils inside. The elderly monk who presided over the small class ignored the visitor.

Tora easily picked out Haseo's son. The boy was the only one the right age, and he had a certain bearing. In a way he reminded Tora of Kinjiro. Kinjiro was two years older but was smaller-boned than this boy, and both had the same fierce look in their faces—as if they were engaged in a battle against the world. This boy had tensed under Tora's scrutiny. When Tora tried a reassuring smile and nod, the youngster scrambled to his feet in a panic.

"Sit down, Nobunari," the schoolmaster called out sharply.

Tora stood up and bowed. "Forgive the interruption, Master Genku. My name is Tora. I have a message for Master Nobunari about his mother."

The boy still stood, eyeing him nervously.

Genku said irritably, "Why do you interrupt the lesson? And why do you call Nobunari 'master'?"

"Because," said Tora, "he's the oldest son of Tomonari Haseo."

The boy made a decision. "I'm Nobunari. What is the message?"

"Ah," said Tora, making the boy a bow, "I was right. The message is from my master, Lord Sugawara, senior secretary in the Ministry of Justice."

The boy frowned. "About my mother?"

Tora cleared his throat and looked at the other boys who had been following the conversation with avid interest.

The monk rose with a sigh. "Perhaps we had better go elsewhere." He set the class an exercise, and led Tora and Nobunari to an adjoining room.

"Now, young man," he said sternly to Tora, "what's all this? It had better be important."

"It is." Tora turned to the boy. "I've come for you and your sister. My master offers you his protection. You'll be safe with him."

Nobunari bit his lip. "Is anything wrong with Mother?"

Tora had worried over this part all the way here. Now that the moment had come, he did not know what to say. So he did not say anything and watched helplessly as the color slowly drained from the boy's face.

"What happened?" the boy whispered. "I suppose she's dead. That's what you came to tell me. I want to know what happened." He choked on the words, but his voice was fierce even as tears began to fill his eyes.

"I'm sorry," said Tora. "I just didn't know how to tell you. Someone killed your mother two weeks ago."

The monk muttered, "Amida!"

The boy clenched his fists. "Who?"

"I don't know. I found her. She'd been stabbed. At first the police thought I'd done it."

The boy stared at Tora. "Mother told me about you. She called you a friend. Besides, you don't look like one of them."

Tora asked quickly, "She told you who was after her?"

But Nobunari frowned and became distant. "This Lord Sugawara. Why is he sending for us?"

"That's another story. You see, we met your father. In Sadoshima."

Nobunari jumped up, his face shining with excitement. "My father is alive? When did you see him? My sister and I shall go to him right away."

Tora gulped. He was not doing this very well. "I'm afraid you can't. You see, your father died also. I guess you're his heir now. We didn't know how to find you. I'm sorry we were too late to help your mother."

Nobunari sank back down. He looked grim. "My father did not murder my grandparents, but they sent him into exile and he died. And my mother got sick and went blind. She had to work like a beggar for our food, and now she's dead, too. What good is life?"

Master Genku said piously, "We must obey the will of Heaven."

The boy glared at him. "Why?"

"We must find the Way during our lifetime. If we find it, we go to an abode of happiness after death. If not, our souls suffer eternal misfortune."

Nobunari's anger flared, "My father died for another man's

evil, and my mother died because she had to support us. To pay for my lessons. You took her money, though you taught me nothing. Did my parents follow the Way? Or are you following it? What is the Way, Master?"

The old monk started to bluster. Tora interrupted, "It's time Lord Tomonari and I left." He gestured to the boy to precede him. The youngster stalked away, his back rigid with anger and grief.

When they reached the gate, Nobunari saw the spare horse and his fury abated a little. He swung himself in the saddle and set off down the road. When Tora caught up, the boy asked, "Were you serious about that 'Lord Tomonari' business?"

"Yes."

"Who killed my grandparents?"

"His name is Sangoro, but he goes by Matsue now. He's in jail."

The boy gave him a look. "Why did he do it?"

"He says he's your grandfather's son and that your grandparents insulted his mother. Your father was blamed because Matsue's mother lied to the judge to protect him."

The boy was silent for a long time. Then he said, "I see. Maybe I would've done the same thing in his place. I used to want to kill him for what he did to all of us, but it's better this way. I shall kill my mother's murderer instead."

He was only twelve, but Tora did not doubt him. He thought of Haseo's sword and wondered if his son would put it to the test the moment they found the killer. He asked, "Do you know how to use a sword?"

"No, but I shall learn." Nobunari pointed to a small farmhouse some distance from the main road. "That's where we live. Mother paid them to keep us."

It was a poor sort of farm. When they dismounted, a young girl came flying out of the door. "Nobunari," she yelled, "what's happened?"

This time Tora let the boy do the talking.

◆

Akitada found Sakae in his own office. The clerk was clearing his personal papers and books from Akitada's shelves.

"I see you have settled in," Akitada remarked.

"I was just getting the office ready for you, sir." Sakae gave him an ingratiating smirk. "Allow me to express my condolences."

"Thank you." Akitada was idly picking up Sakae's books. "I expect you heard what happened to Nakatoshi."

Sakae made a face. "Yes. It was a shock. I would never have believed it of him."

"Hmm." Akitada had found what he had been looking for. He slowly turned the pages, skimming the text. "I agree," he said. "Though perhaps it was not altogether surprising for you."

Sakae stared at the book in Akitada's hands. His ears were turning red. "I b-beg your pardon?"

"It was you who framed Nakatoshi, wasn't it?"

"Me? Certainly not."

"I wonder, Sakae, can you have any idea what will happen to him because of the letter?"

"He shouldn't have written it. I suppose he'll be dismissed."

"He's in prison now, awaiting trial for treason. Treason is a capital offense. I expect he will be executed."

Sakae gaped at him. "For writing a *letter*?"

Akitada nodded and watched beads of sweat pop up on Sakae's brow. "Really, Sakae," he said mildly, "for a law clerk you're dismally uninformed. I think you must go and confess to the trick you played on your rival. You weren't very clever about it. I could see that the letter was not in Nakatoshi's hand. Furthermore, you miswrote the recipient's name."

Sakae flushed deeply. His eyes gave away his panic. "It wasn't me. You can't prove it was me. Maybe somebody else . . ."

"No. I recall that you're very proud of an essay you once wrote on the subject of Chang Lu's rebellion. In fact, you couldn't resist quoting a line from the Chinese source in your letter. And I see you marked the passage." Akitada held up the book. "Not much point in denying it. I have already informed Lord Fujiwara and Police Superintendent Kobe of your trick."

Sakae wilted. He shrank into himself and wiped the perspiration from his face. "What will happen to me?"

"Oh, no charge of treason. If you admit it, you'll be dismissed . . . which is what you had planned for Nakatoshi. I suppose when your hopes of taking my place were dashed by Soga's death, you decided to take Nakatoshi's. It was as foolish as it was dangerous. I doubt that you can hope for future government service. Of course, if you insist on your innocence, we have no choice but to have you arrested."

Akitada left the sagging figure of Sakae to contemplate his punishment and went to Kosehira's office. Kosehira was reading his correspondence and muttering under his breath.

"What's the matter?" Akitada asked.

"Sakae can't write. I won't put my name and seal to this." He tossed an official letter toward Akitada, who glanced at it and put it down.

"I told you. Tomorrow Nakatoshi will be back. He writes the best hand in the city."

Kosehira raised his brows. "You mean that treasonable letter really was Sakae's work? Why, the sly toad! Wait till I prepare my report. He will certainly never work for the government again."

"That's what I told him. But I need your help with a more important matter. It concerns the heirs of a man who was also falsely accused and died in exile. Shall I tell you about it?"

Kosehira listened to Haseo's story with shock and pity. His suffering and that of his family brought tears to his eyes.

"We cannot charge Yasugi," Akitada ended, "but I think the nation owes it to Haseo to return his family name and property to his children."

"Yes, yes," cried Kosehira. "I shall put it to His Majesty myself. No, better. You shall come and tell him what you just told me. He's a very softhearted young man, even if he's the emperor. And that reminds me. Do you remember his uncle? That priestly fellow who watched us pray for His Majesty?"

Akitada did and made a face. "I hope he doesn't remember *me*!"

Kosehira laughed. "On the contrary! He hasn't forgotten. He thinks you saved His Majesty's life when you made the Buddha nod and has proposed a very nice reward for you."

"That is kind of him," said Akitada weakly. The irony that he should be rewarded for an act of impudence and blasphemy struck him as a perfect example of the futility of all human hopes.

◆

The children had been quiet on the journey to the capital, and Tora was both thankful and worried. He kept glancing at them. Each had wept briefly and then accepted the inevitable without questions. Nobunari sat his horse well and held his sister's slight figure with protective care.

When they passed the market, it occurred to Tora that they might be hungry. "Shall we stop for some noodle soup?" he asked. "The restaurant just inside the market gate makes a very tasty broth with buckwheat noodles."

Nobunari glanced toward the market tower. "I would like to see where my mother worked, but we have no money."

"My treat." Tora paid an urchin to watch their horses and took the children to the drum tower. The market was still thin of shoppers and vendors, but people looked hopeful again. The fortune-teller sat in his old spot on the platform and greeted them. Tora introduced the children.

The fortune-teller looked at them and smiled. He said, "You must be very proud of her. She was a good person and strong for a woman, but candles are consumed as they give light."

Nobunari looked around the market and announced in a fierce, loud voice, "I'm going to find her killer and cut off his head."

People stopped to stare. Tora asked quickly, "Any news of Kata?"

The fortune-teller nodded. "The police raided his school and found a body. People say it was the beggar who used to hang around here. Nobody liked him, but to dismember a person while he's still alive is the work of demons." He shuddered.

Tora thought of his escape from the hut. Apparently Kata's gang had taken their fury out on the beggar. He suddenly felt sick.

Nobunari had listened. "That must be the beggar my mother mentioned. I'm glad he's dead."

Seized by a sudden suspicion, Tora asked, "What did your mother say about him?"

"That he was always hanging around, making rude suggestions, and scooping up her coppers because she couldn't see. Mother could see a little, though. She could tell it was him bending down and she could hear the coppers clinking and his nails scraping the floor."

Tora thought about this and something else. Tomoe had mentioned her stalker's stench. Tora's nose was not as fine as hers, but he remembered that the beggar had been filthy and foul-smelling. Then he remembered the day he had stumbled over the beggar and the half-healed scratches on the man's face and neck. And a piece of silver Kata had given Tomoe the day she died. When the gang had searched Tora and the beggar and found Matsue's document on Tora, they had also had found a silver coin on the beggar. Coins were not always uniform. It seemed to Tora now that Kata had looked strangely at that coin and the beggar. What if the slimy creature had seen Kata pass the coin to Tomoe and had followed her home to rob her? And to rape her in the bargain. Tora growled under his breath.

A small voice demanded, "What's the matter, Tora?"

Tora gulped and managed a smile for Tomoe's daughter. "I'm hungry. What about you? Shall we go sample the noodles?"

"Oh yes. Please."

They parted from the fortune-teller and walked across to the restaurant where Tora had last entertained their mother's killer. The thought sickened him, but he ordered three bowls of the special noodles and felt better when he saw the children eat hungrily. No point in troubling them with the story of their mother's murder, but he could not wait to lay his discovery before his master.

◆

Akitada was anxious about the children and went home early. To his relief, Tora had just returned with them. Akitada's lack of confidence made him doubt such luck, and he looked them over, touched them, and asked them questions before speaking to anyone else. He found them subdued, but they were such nice children, so handsome and well-spoken, that their composure in the face of their own loss was a lesson to him.

Tamako hovered nearby, and Seimei also. Their eyes were moist with emotion. There were children in the house again.

Tora, a fierce and exultant look on his face, pulled Akitada out into the corridor and closed the door. "I know who did it," he said, "but I don't think we should tell them."

"What are you talking about?"

"I know who killed Tomoe. I figured it out. Remember the beggar in the market? Remember how filthy he was? Well, Nobunari says his mother complained about some stinking beggar pestering her and stealing her money. I think the bastard saw Kata give her a piece of silver and followed her home that evening."

Akitada thought about it. He did remember the beggar who had felt his robe and called Tomoe a whore. It made sense: not revenge by Matsue, nor a plot by Yasugi against the Tomonari family, but a common everyday crime among the poor. "I think you're right," he said. "I should have seen it myself. You were certainly more observant. Only how are we to prove his guilt after all this time?"

Tora blushed at the compliment. "No need to prove it. The filthy bastard's dead. Kata took care of him when he found out that the beggar had killed his good luck." Tora sighed. "I should've walked her home that night."

"It was more my fault than yours, because I would not let you. But I think you must let the police know. I want your name cleared once and for all, and they have the means to round up Kata and his men to get proof that the beggar killed Tomoe. We don't even know his name."

Tora's face fell comically, but then he grinned. "Good. That'll give me the chance to tell that patronizing bastard Ihara that I've solved his miserable case for him."

Akitada spent the rest of the day with his family and young guests. He watched his wife fuss over the children as if she were their mother. She saw to it that they were bathed, measured them for new clothes, brushed Nobuko's hair and tied it with one of her ribbons, and asked them what their favorite foods were.

He wondered if she, too, needed to fill the emptiness in their home and in her heart. Perhaps her coldness had been a matter of preserving a hard-won outer calm. When Haseo's little daughter made an amusing comment, he found himself smiling at Tamako and was foolishly glad to see her smile back.

They had not begun to grieve, and there were still many un-resolved matters between them, but time and effort might change that. Perhaps some day there might be another child, and they could build a new life together. Akitada accepted that the fault had been his more than Tamako's. He did not know if he could change his nature, but at that moment he made a silent promise that he would try to be a better husband.

There was one more task to be done. After the evening rice, Akitada went to get Haseo's sword and, with a formal bow, he placed it into Nobunari's hands. "This was your father's," he said, deeply moved by the moment. "It's yours now, along with his title. And his lands will shortly be yours also. Make sure that you honor your father's memory. He was a good and brave man. And watch over your father's family so that none will ever go hungry or homeless again."

The boy bowed. "Thank you, my lord. I promise. They are my family now."

As Nobunari examined his father's sword, Akitada thought how proud his parents would have been and felt a deep sadness for Haseo, who had died in a distant land and for Tomoe, who had sacrificed everything for her children. Nothing was certain in life but death. And yet, though brief and fleeting, life was full of possibilities.

Later he went to his room to be alone. Exhaustion after the past weeks had finally caught up with him, and he felt empty. Outside the open shutters, the sun was setting, casting a golden light over the garden. Somewhere, in a great distance, the evening bells began to ring. Another day had passed and darkness lay in wait. The nights ahead seemed endless, and desolation overwhelmed him.

Akitada walked onto the veranda. There was an extraordinary stillness in the air—almost a breathless waiting. He listened and then he understood. Yori's spirit remained, here in this house, close to them for the forty-nine days after his death. After a moment of wonder, he went back inside for his flute.

In the slanting rays of the setting sun, Yori's father stood in the garden and played the lullaby which had soothed his son's suffering. And when the last note faded with the light, he told him of his pride and love.

HISTORICAL NOTE

𝒯he preceding novel takes place in eleventh-century Japan, toward the end of the Heian Age (794–1185 AD). The setting is the capital city Heian-kyo, which was founded in 794 and gave its name to the classical period in Japanese history and civilization. It was from here, from the Imperial Court and a centralized government by nobles, that the affairs of the nation were governed for three centuries of peace and tranquility.

Ancient Japan patterned its government and institutions after T'ang China, and the capital was laid out in the Chinese style as a perfect rectangle with a grid pattern of streets running due north, south, east, and west. As in the Chinese capital Ch'ang-an, the Imperial Palace with the government buildings (the *Daidairi,* or Greater Palace Enclosure) occupied its own city in the northernmost center and, along with the surrounding mansions of the nobles, took up almost a third of the whole area. The capital stretched over 6000 acres and is said to have had as many as 200,000 inhabitants at times. It was not fortified, but earthen ramparts and moats surrounded it, and gates stood at major entrances. Of these, Rashomon, the southernmost gate, was the most important and famous in Japanese literature. Suzaku Avenue divided the city into a Right Capital and a Left Capital, each half with its own administration, market, prison, and temple. The original layout was intended to impress foreign visitors, and the city must have been quite beautiful with its wide, willow-lined avenues, its many rivers and canals, parks and gardens, and great gates and palaces. But the Right Capital never fully developed. It soon fell into disrepair and became a haven for criminals. Furthermore, traditional building practices and materials, while they allowed for quick construction and deconstruction (whole palace buildings were moved from previous capitals to Heian-kyo), meant that the capital periodically suffered severe damage from fires, storms, and earthquakes.

Ancient Japan also took most of its culture from China. Ultimately, the Chinese system of government failed in Japan, but in the Heian age it still prevailed and produced a period of unparalleled peace and cultural achievement. The country was governed by a hierarchy of bureaucrats who ruled by Chinese precepts and used the Chinese language. However, the system was never a meritocracy as in China. In Japan only the sons of the "good people" attended the imperial university, entered the government service, and achieved the ranks which assured them of wealth and power. The highest ranks fell mostly to members of one family, the Fujiwaras. They supplied wives and concubines to the ruling monarchs and crown princes and thus were not only closely related to the emperors, but served as regents (and de facto rulers) to the many minor children who ascended the throne. The chancellor, assisted by the three great ministers of the right, left, and center, supervised the Great Council of State, two controlling boards, eight ministries, and assorted bureaus and offices. From the Greater Palace Enclosure of Heian-kyo, this central government ruled the rest of the country through governors appointed in the capital and sent to their provinces for four-year terms.

The Greater Palace Enclosure was protected by several armed divisions of the military guard, but crime was rampant in the capital. In 816 AD the government placed law enforcement for the capital (and eventually the provinces) into the hands of the *kebiishicho,* the police department. The police, a semi-military force, wore red coats and carried bows and arrows. They kept order, investigated crimes, arrested criminals, brought them to trial before judges, and enforced punishment. In addition, each ward of the capital was also supervised by a warden who reported to the police. The most serious crimes, as defined by the Taiho Code (701 AD), were in order of severity: rebellion against the emperor; damage to the Imperial Palace or royal tombs; treason; murder of one's kin; murder of one's wife or of more than three members of a family; theft or damage of imperial or religious property; unfilial acts toward parents or senior relatives; and murder of a superior or teacher. As in China, confessions were necessary for conviction, but flogging was common during interrogation. Buddhist prohibitions against the taking of life meant that the punishment was flogging, prison, or for severe crimes, exile to remote and unhealthy areas of the country. There, forced labor, exposure, or lack of food often resulted in the deaths of the condemned, though exile could be lifted. There were two prisons in the capital, but imperial pardons were common and sweeping. As a result, crime and criminals were numerous and widespread by the mid-eleventh century.

One of the many disasters that visited Heian-kyo and most of the country repeatedly was smallpox. This disease was introduced into the islands of Japan through merchant trading with China and Korea and ravaged the population, particularly in densely populated areas. It was early recognized as infectious, but people tended to seek supernatural intervention, or to accept the danger fatalistically. In 737 AD, the Great Secretary of

the Right issued a detailed order about the treatment of smallpox. This involved wrapping the victim, keeping him warm,
and withholding water completely. Warm rice gruel, seaweed,
and salt were prescribed, even when "mouth and tongue fester."
There is no evidence that medical knowledge had progressed
much by the eleventh century, but by then the disease was becoming endemic; that is, people developed resistance and only
the young and those who had never been exposed contracted it.
In 1020 AD, the young emperor, who was twelve at the time, fell
ill but recovered. Those who survived the fever and festering
sores were permanently disfigured and often blinded.

There is little contemporary information about the common people, but the lives of the nobles are well documented in
diaries, novels, and biographies. Men led public lives, usually in
the service of the emperor; they engaged in sports, hunting, and
literary pursuits, or entertained their male friends at lavish par-
ties. Women lived secluded in their own quarters of the mansion, where they supervised the household and their children,
and spent time reading romances, painting, or making music.
Customarily, a nobleman had more than one wife and might
additionally keep concubines. Women were slightly better off
in the Heian Age than they were in later periods, for they could
own property and were protected by the continued influence of
their own families. Marriages were arranged between the groom
and the bride's family, and matters such as her status in the husband's household and her control over her private money were
negotiated beforehand. Often a young couple resided with the
wife's parents. But a husband could divorce his wife simply by
informing her of this decision. He was also free to take other
wives. Women rarely left the home, except for family emergen-
cies, service at court, or pilgrimages to temples or shrines. Women
of the lower classes, while often poor and forced to labor alongside the men, enjoyed greater freedom of movement and rarely
had to compete with other wives.

The Japanese practiced both Shinto and Buddhism, with Buddhism somewhat more popular among the nobility and Shinto the ancient native faith of the imperial family and the peasants. The two religions coexisted peaceably, sometimes even in the same temple or shrine complex and during the same festival. Shinto involves the veneration of *kami*, representations of ancestral spirits and of nature, and the practice of ritual purification. It is responsible for many taboos, among them those involving death. Buddhism came to Japan from China via Korea and teaches concepts of personal salvation. Funerals were handled by the Buddhist clergy and normally involved cremation. The cemetery and cremation ground for the capital lay outside the city, and funerals were generally conducted after dark, but in times of catastrophe corpses might be abandoned in the streets and on the banks of the Kamo River. It was believed that the soul of the deceased remained near its home for forty-nine days after death.

For readers familiar with Samurai literature, it should be pointed out that daily customs of the Heian Age differ in some respects from those of later periods. Tea was known, but expensive, and consumed primarily for medicinal purposes. Rice wine was the preferred drink. Foods were simple, consisting of rice, other grains, beans, vegetables, fish and—as hunting was not yet forbidden—fowl and venison. Men did not shave their heads unless they were monks, and women of the upper classes let their hair grow very long and wore many-layered gowns of colored silks or brocade. Although there are references to cotton clothing, cotton was not known at the time, and the material used instead was hemp.

In the eleventh century, the martial arts were more at home among the provincial nobility, who maintained small armies to defend their lands; however, the court nobles also practiced with swords and bows and arrows. Swordsmiths performed a specially honored craft, working both in government service and independently. It was during the Heian period that sword construction first reached the level of perfection for which Japanese swords are admired. Swords were thought to be imbued with a divine spirit and Shinto rituals accompanied the work of the smith.

I have generally followed R.A.B. Ponsonby-Fane's description of Heian-kyo (*Kyoto: The Old Capital of Japan, 794–1869*). It is old, but still the most complete account available. In the absence of proof to the contrary and because of the habit and ease of rapid reconstruction after disasters, the general plan of the city and most of the important buildings described by Ponsonby-Fane are assumed to have existed in the early eleventh century. The information about smallpox is taken from *Population, Disease, and Land in Early Japan, 645–900* by Wayne Farris.